QUARTET

THE MARCH

A small boy is watching a ... the man purses his lips, ...ou.n with his tongue and, raising his cupped hand, spits out a live, wriggling worm.

The place is Norrland, the barren coastland of northern Sweden; the time is 1903. Johan Sanfrid Elmblad is a socialist agitator who has been sent to preach trade unionism to the conservative, god-fearing workers in the local timber mills. The mission is a humiliating failure, but the meeting between Elmblad and the small boy, Nicanor Markstrom, will have profound consequences for them both.

The March of the Musicians is a superbly crafted documentary novel about how the workers in one small area of Northern Sweden gradually awaken from an entrenched apathy – political, spiritual, emotional – and begin to fight against their appalling conditions. Such, however, is Per Olov Enquist's ability to understand the motivation of these people who patiently allow themselves to be exploited by the sawmill owners and tormented every Sunday by hellfire preachers, that he transforms what is no more than a footnote in the history of the Swedish labour movement into a story with universal meaning. And such is his empathy with his characters that in the end these flawed human beings achieve almost heroic stature.

PER OLOV ENQUIST

Per Olov Enquist was born in 1934 and is one of Sweden's leading novelists and playwrights. Literary and theatre critic, he is a well-respected political commentator and has played a significant part in Sweden's cultural life. He was awarded the Nordic Prize for Literature in 1969. His novels *Downfall, The Magnetist's Fifth Winter* and *Captain Nemo's Library* are all published by Quartet Books.

PER OLOV ENQUIST

The March of the Musicians

Translated from the Swedish by
JOAN TATE
With an Introduction by KATHRYN MEAD

QUARTET ENCOUNTERS

Quartet Books

Published in Great Britain
by Quartet Books Limited 1993
A member of the Namara Group
27/29 Goodge Street, London W1P 1FD

Originally published in Swedish under the title
Musikanternas uttåg

Copyright © by Per Olov Enquist 1978
English translation copyright © by Joan Tate 1985
Introduction copyright © by Kathryn Mead 1993

A catalogue record for this book is available from the
British Library

ISBN 0 7043 0190 3

Printed and bound in Great Britain by
BPCC Hazell Books Ltd
Member of BPCC Ltd ·

INTRODUCTION

In over thirty years of writing Per Olov Enquist has relished many different literary forms, but all his work ultimately grapples with what the Russians call the 'damned questions', that buzzing, querulous, insistent chatter about the fundamentals of human existence that may occupy the philosopher but of necessity haunts the novelist. His reflections, centring upon a search for truth and meaning, and exemplified by ceaseless explorations into the nature of being, would seem to mark him as a prototypical twentieth-century existentialist; but Enquist, although at times an unflinchingly dark writer, is wholly devoid of the restrictive pessimism that can inform the classical existentialists.

In his early work, as might befit a recent graduate of Uppsala University with a dissertation under his belt, Enquist's search for truth was largely externalized, as if rationalism and exhaustive research could in themselves yield up the Grail. This approach led to two searching novels, *The Magnetist's Fifth Winter* (1964) and *The Legionnaires* (1968), the latter a finely honed analysis of the limitations of historical enquiry which was to win him two of Sweden's highest literary awards.

Stung by the accusation that the Swedes were itinerant 'professional moralists', ignorant of their own ethical insufficiencies, Enquist took it upon himself to discover exactly what underlay the forced extradition of 146 Baltic prisoners of war from Sweden to the Soviet Union at the end of the Second World War. In 1945 the anticipated fate of the Balts had stirred the nation to a frenzy of self-reproach, which had ironically served ever since to reassure the Swedes that they possessed an innate humanitarian sensibility quite alien to the jostling militarism of the Cold War superpowers. Enquist revealed that their position was considerably more compromised; that paradoxically, by occupying the moral high ground, the Swedes could be said to have contributed to the very betrayal they deplored. Moreover, historical 'truth' was almost unavoidably an inflated amalgam of rumour, ignorance and whimsy, no matter how cautiously the historian might shake the kaleidoscope.

Central to his unease was the perception that any attempt to order human experience must have at its heart the instinctive bias of the investigator; the very concept of 'objective truth' was illusory. In this way, all enquiry ultimately becomes an act of self-definition radiating from a central core of insight. Until I know myself, I cannot know you. If I cannot know you, I am in no position to make pronouncements on the world that surrounds you.

All of Enquist's most recent writing, however, by exploring this personal psychological labyrinth, takes the huge ontological step of perceiving that what we dismiss as 'bias', seeing through a glass darkly, may be a creative form of handicap; artistic and personal authenticity can only be defined by a stumbling and brave-hearted examination of what is inauthentic. *Downfall* (1985), *The Hour of the Lynx* (1988) and Enquist's most recent novel, *Captain Nemo's Library* (1991), all sound a passionate note of authorial self-reproach in the face of such scrutiny. His vision of the true self is subjected to repeated re-examination, shifting with extraordinary dexterity from novel to play to the ravishing austerity of the prose-poetry of *Downfall*. This very deliberate change of focus from the body politic to the soul has been attributed to the fact that Enquist no longer lives in Sweden and so, by implication, can no longer draw so readily upon social and political material. More plausibly, perhaps, it turns upon the truth that as a writer matures, wherever he lives, if he is to remain in touch with the wellspring of his art he must somehow come to realize Keats' magnificent observation, that 'the genius of Poetry must work out its own salvation in a man; it cannot be matured by law and precept but by sensation and watchfulness in itself. That which is creative must create itself.' Enquist would perhaps add a further, more mystical note: that central to the process of self-realization is the presence of love, which alone can truly generate the work of social redemption, so often attempted by the mechanistic interventions of politics.

Love in the individual is invoked by an evolutionary journey from alienation to solitude to abandonment that is best described by three pivotal characters in his work, the freedom marcher of *The Legionnaires*; Elmblad, the socialist agitator in *The March of the Musicians*; and the nameless child narrator of *Captain Nemo's Library*. Their stories describe a process of growing moral enlightenment, presented as the inevitable consequence of suffering. For the freedom marcher the challenge is one of perception, to acknowledge the schism between thought and feeling that accounts for the bloodless character of his solidarity. It falls to Elmblad to inhabit the pain of absolute isolation and the child to transcend it, by allowing his eyes to be opened to the fractured anguish of the very perpetrators of his own abuse. So it is that the journey comes full circle and that by the acknowledgement of our individual isolation Enquist is able to describe a universality of experience, rooted in the suffering of childhood, that alone enables us to see the Other's face.

This is achieved, especially in recent years as Enquist's experience as a playwright has deepened, by an artless quality in his writing that, of course, masks great craft. His most resonating sentences are frequently deadpan pronouncements of studied understatement that fall two beats after the main body of the text and roll like muffled thunder across the heart: 'There, in Västerbotten's coastlands, she was to spend her youth.' He is talking to Eva-Liisa, who appears in slightly differing forms in both *The March of the Musicians* and *Captain Nemo's Library*, and who, as many of his characters, is a fictional representation of a member of his own family, his foster sister. Like Sara Lidman, his near contemporary, and Vilhelm Moberg of an earlier generation of Swedish writers, Enquist has drawn increasingly upon his own provincial roots to substantiate and enrich the metaphysical probings of his work. The Västerbotten communities of rural northern Sweden that he describes, like some hardy and atavistic form of cellular life, subsist by making a triumph of deprivation. Their pietist stoicism, at once admirable and horrifying, is rooted in the dubious heroism of endurance. *The March of the Musicians* is, as a narrative, an account of the tragi-comical attempts by early trade unionists to fertilize this barren stock. They fail, not so much because of the Hobbesian principle that the collective can never be more than the sum of its parts, but because here was a people whose unconscious consent had already been given over to a form of living death. Death has many faces in the book: the father who cannot stop smiling because inwardly he rages; the mother whose religiosity is a howl of displaced mourning; Elmblad, who walks a daily Calvary, 'a sandbag in his heart'; Uncle Aron, whose rape of a child is famished perversion of his own unanswered plea for love; Eva-Liisa, aged eleven, who in a moment of stellar anguish kneels to be told that the seeds of sin lie in her heart.

This is the stuff of desecration, the mutilation of innocence that Dostoevsky once famously argued disproved the existence of God. Enquist works in a more dappled light. In *The March of the Musicians* it is the very abuse of her son and daughter that wakens Josephina to a harrowing epiphany. Her long drive through the Västerbotten night, bearing, like Mary, her injured son upon her lap ('This was the land of her childhood. Why should she not find her way?') restructures the ordering of her universe. Like Nicanor and the spontaneous strikers at the sawmill she realizes that worldly injustice cannot be answered with religious pap – and the first vitalizing drops of rebellion begin to flow in her veins. From here it is a short step to her emigration to Brazil, prompted by the novel's assertive refrain, 'there is always something better than death'.

Of late Enquist assumes a starker position. There may indeed always be something better than death, and that is the work of love, but there may be a sense in which a human being has to die, either literally or metaphorically, in order to reach it. This is an insight which mystical writers cautiously divulge, not only because it is open to misinterpretation but because if it is not already understood it cannot easily be grasped. It is a matter of 'apprehension' – for Shakespeare – a mark of the divine in man. So it is with Enquist, whose prose becomes increasingly destructured and self-referential as he pieces out the symbolically coded narratives of *Downfall* and *Captain Nemo's Library*. Of the many themes shared by these searing novels, there are perhaps three that predominate: the redemptive power of love, the need to embrace what is Fallen in man and the need to give voice to the voiceless. *Downfall* opens with a sentence of extraordinary grace and complexity: 'Express my face in breaths.' It is a command to the writer to communicate from a child murderer, himself a tortured child, who dies in an attempt to escape the menacing air that surrounds him. Here is one who has never been able to draw breath, the primal act of being, without which no sound can rise in the human throat. He forms a symbolic link with the seven 'stillborn' children of *Captain Nemo's Library*: the three who are actually stillborn, the three who undergo the soul murder of annihilated childhoods and the last child whose implied presence and restoration makes the novel such a tender account of the work of psychological integration.

Other writers (notably Maya Angelou) have explored the deep-veined network that binds language and silence and suffering, but Enquist's greatest distinction is a visionary understanding of how this is intertwined with the mystery of resurrection. The mouth-multilated figures of Nicanor and Maria (or in real life, Enquist's actual father, whose secret notebook of unread poetry was burnt at his death) embody an extraordinary linguistic insight: that the word 'mystery' derives from the Greek verb used to describe the closing of lips and eyes. 'Tha'll nowt be much of a man for words,' mock Nicanor's tormentors, severing his tongue and stamping down topsoil on the hidden growth of new life. By such torture vision is driven inwards and finds in the dark roaring unsighted-ness of utter abandonment the oblique presence of God, at once manifested and self-manifesting, as a cat, a hero from childhood fiction, a dying child – wherever that which is inwardly broken can focus the regenerating beauty of numinous and abiding love.

The American poet Robert Bly once chided American haiku poets for their failure to grasp that in such poetry it was not metrical precision that animated the verse but the poet's vision of light as defined by the dark. Enquist is a European master of this kind of work; he writes of the unwatchable with depth and resonant compassion. In so doing, he enables us at the last to lift our gaze and look into the human face with confidence, delight and a dawning recognition. It is no minor homecoming.

Kathryn Mead

The March of the Musicians

PROLOGUE

1903

THE MAN WITH THE
WORM TIN

1

THE WIND WAS BRISK and had swung round to almost due east, so was now blowing straight off the Gulf of Bothnia and Finland, forming white horses on Bure Water, the sea covered with small white lines, the wind holding and remaining steady. The boy was barefoot, his legs scratched, dark brown and rough, though the sores had healed well and his legs looked light and strong, his feet quite white. He was walking swiftly and purposefully along the shore, not stopping, keeping above the wet stones on the water's edge, his eyes fixed all the time, stubbornly and watchfully, on the figure out there on the far tip of the point.

It was a fine clear day. The boy had to screw up his eyes against the slanting rays of the sun; the man out there on the point was only a few hundred metres away now, his contours becoming clearer and clearer. He seemed to be fishing. He was holding a fishing-rod in his hand, standing a little way out in the water, perhaps on a stone. Yes, it was a stone.

He grew clearer and clearer.

Now the boy could see everything very distinctly. The man had taken off his shoes and placed them on a stone, and he had rolled up his trousers. He was quite large and fat. He was wearing a black jacket with something like a white shirt underneath. No tie. The boy walked out towards the far tip of the point, cautiously, and when he was only ten metres away, the man at last turned his head and looked at him.

No Bure man, then, thought the boy immediately, and stopped. Him's a stranger. What if him's a Stockholmer?

5

The fishing-rod was a thin switch of birch. He had fastened a line of black cotton thread to it and had a wooden peg as a float, now bobbing wildly about in the waves. The boy stood quite still on the shore only five metres away from the man, watching him with a tense absorbed grimace. No Bure man, he thought, convinced now. No one from Bure. Not from here. The man's legs were quite white below the rolled-up trouser-legs, the tips of his moustache determinedly turned upwards, his fat belly swelling out over his belt. There he was, standing in a place everyone knew was impossible if you wanted to catch anything. A stranger, he was.

He kept fidgeting, never really standing still, jerking at the rod, apparently cheerful and content, smiling with his whole square head turned to the great stretch of water and then back towards the boy, shaking his head in troubled way, looking solemnly up, blinking at the float, nodding affirmatively but aimlessly at the houses on the north side, then suddenly shaking his head again and smiling thoughtfully.

But he said nothing.

'Tha gittin' anythin'?' the boy said at last.

The waves washed over the stone and the man's feet at regular intervals. After a while, the boy's question seemed to penetrate through to him. He drew up his float and hook and looked anxiously at the remains of the worm. Then with a melancholy smile, he shook his square head, carefully held the hook between thumb and forefinger, and with small digging, chewing, mouthing movements, started shifting his mouth and jaws. He seemed to be trying to get something out, either words or saliva, or quite simply some object such as a plug of tobacco inside his mouth, which now had to be coaxed into the daylight. He pursed his lips, cocked his head to one side, his cheek ballooning out and then flattening, something rotating round inside as if he were trying to get something out with the aid of his tongue: then, with the greatest caution, he raised one palm and pursed his lips into something like a kiss. The boy stared at him watchfully, his eyes wide with astonishment. Then he saw something sticking out of the man's pursed lips, something pointed and wriggling.

Something long. Alive. A worm.

He took the worm between forefinger and thumb and pulled it out of his mouth; very wet, glisteningly soft and wriggling, the worm was hauled out of the cavity of the mouth, for a moment dangling softly in the clear sunlight. Then with astonishing speed and deftness he placed it on the hook, looked thoughtfully for a moment at the boy, again moving his jaws for a few moments with a chewing, settling movement, as if the worm's companions in there had for a moment been gripped by alarm or melancholy, but could now settle down in peace again; then he threw out the line once more.

The boy was now gazing at the man with an expression of extreme watchfulness and great sympathy.

He stared intently at the man's cheeks, the actual cheeks, as if with his gaze he could penetrate through the skin and make out what was there. The cheek seemed to bulge, perhaps well filled, but he couldn't be sure. He took a few eager slippery steps out into the water, gazing at the part of the cheek behind which he thought he could make out wriggling, crawling movements, shading his eyes with his hand and smiling slightly.

'Tha's got worms in tha mouth?' he said in a high shrill voice.

The man looked at him with a blank expression, apparently brooding on something, frowning, then cupping his hand behind his ear as if he hadn't heard, or not really understood. Taking another step forward, the boy cried out in an even thinner and shriller voice:

'Tha's got worms in tha mouth?'

An expression of thoughtful solemnity came over the man's face. He frowned heavily, his eyes fixed for a moment on the horizon, then suddenly his face broke into a friendly smile, as if at last he understood. He nodded calmly, almost knowingly, then turned carefully and laboriously round on the stone so that he was facing the stretch of water, ground his jaw once or twice, then leant over and opened his mouth.

He held his tongue flat, like a floor of the mouth's cave, and there were the worms.

The boy stood right up close to the man and looked straight down into his throat. There was a brisk fine wind, the water white, the sky prodigiously high and pale blue, and from very close, the boy could see the two worms lying on the man's tongue, slowly and sluggishly, perhaps despondently now, writhing round each other.

'Ay,' said the boy, nodding violently, his head jerking back and forth for a long time, as if wishing to indicate very clearly that he had seen and understood. Oh, yes.

He suddenly felt it was an incredibly good day. He smiled eagerly and encouragingly at the fat man bending over in front of him. Then the man carefully closed his mouth, straightened laboriously and, with a resigned expression, looked at the float, now helplessly washed up right against the stone. He smiled reassuringly across the water, looked down at his feet and shook his head, then pulled up the bait, turned carefully on the stone, stepped down into the water and slowly and unsteadily started wading towards the shore.

After hesitating for a moment, the boy followed him.

Not until then did he see the case, brown, with white metal clasps, apparently very well filled, propped up against a stone. The man sat down on the stone, held his hand up like a bowl, and with a swift movement of his mouth, spat the two worms into his cupped hand, gazing at them with an expression of loss, then placing them carefully in the damp dark place between two stones.

'That tha durst,' said the boy bluntly. 'I wouldna.'

The wind was blowing strongly and the water glittered. The man peered cheerfully and candidly at the boy, then opened his brown case and placed it on his knees. The boy could now see the contents quite clearly, mostly papers, printed papers that looked like posters. The man took out a small bundle, the paper yellow and the print black. He looked thoughtfully at the boy and said:

'But you'd dare help me with these, wouldn't you?'

Him's a Stockholmer, the boy thought immediately, stiffening with fear. So it was certain. He turned quite cold and took a careful step back, but then stopped.

Him's a Stockholmer.

The water was like grey glass, rustling and soughing lightly as he floated up to the surface with his eyes wide open: he loved diving deeply and then slowly floating up towards the light and air. The water was dark glass, then grew lighter and lighter as he rose like a bubble and suddenly he was up and all the sounds back again.

The stones were slippery. He got out. It was probably time to go now. He had to go up there.

He was thin and always froze when he went swimming, his lips turning blue and his teeth chattering: he stood quite still, shivering as he waited for the warmth to come back. The yellow posters lay on a stone in front of him, about ten of them. He had promised.

8

The man with worms in his mouth had made him promise. The papers were yellow with a bright red border round them. Black text. It said: *The Vote, Social Democracy and the Future of the Workers' Movement.* Beneath that, in black handwriting, was *Public Meeting in Bure, Crossroads, Thursday 6.30.*

At the bottom, in print, was *Come in Force!*

Drops of water had fallen on to the top poster, then dried, so the paper was rather wrinkled. He was cold and his teeth chattered as he thought: I promised.

I promised. I'm to put them up.

On his way up through the forest, he stopped only once, by the prayer-stone as usual, a flat boulder, about six feet in diameter. Last summer, the first summer he had stayed with Uncle John, he had suddenly promised the Saviour that he would one day be a preacher. He was only seven at the time. He had decided quickly, falling to his knees, praising God and promising to be a preacher. He did not really know why this had come to him, but only knew that in some way he was impatient and wanted an end to it. Afterwards, he had been worried for quite a long time and he wanted his promise confirmed more definitely, with a sacrifice, for instance. But he had not known how, in which way, until he thought of that frog business. He had sought out a frog and then he had had his evangelical promise confirmed. Like Abraham and his son.

But it was rather unpleasant. The frog had seemed to divide itself, gushing out when he had cut into it.

He picked up the posters and for safety's sake prayed for a while over them as well. Then he left. He was no longer cold.

He put the first one up on a stack of timber, the second one on the wall of the drier, just by the entrance. The third he put on the link-track, low down. The fourth he put on a pole almost in the middle of the timber yard. He put the fifth on a pine tree on the Skerry road and the sixth on a pine further in in the forest. He started putting up the seventh, but then found he had run out of drawing-pins.

He didn't put the last three up at all, but that did not lie on his conscience for long. He had hardly met a single person all the time; at least, no one who had asked him what he was up to. Nevertheless, he felt peculiar and ill-at-ease. It would have been better if he had understood what was on the posters, but he didn't.

As he could make neither head nor tail of it all, he went all the way back later on to check that everything was in order. Everything was in order, the pieces of yellow paper where he had put them, but nevertheless he suddenly felt very frightened and started whistling.

Three left. One ought to, he thought. To be sure, it wouldn't be a bad idea. To . . .

He stood just by the entrance of the timber yard office, thinking. People were going in and out. He had never been there before, but perhaps he ought to.

At first he stood unnoticed and silent inside the office, ignored until the manager asked from his place in the inner room what the hell that young devil was hanging about there for. Then they all looked at him. He held out the three remaining posters. Gradually, complete silence fell.

They all read carefully through the lines of print, one after another.

The fly settled on the lamp and crept slowly upwards. Black on white. When the overseer's face came closer, he could see the veins in his eyelids, like blue spider's webs. Some people said, the boy thought as things started being difficult and peculiar, that he was a drinker. The wall was brown and he knew now for certain as he stood there staring at that brown wall while the manager's face and eyelids moved in and out of his field of vision, that he had done a stupid thing going into the office with those posters.

It was horrible when they questioned him. He was frightened. Nor was it any better when they said nothing. It would have been better if they had teased him.

He had put himself in a bad position.

The overseer said again, straight down into his stiffly anxious face:

'Where is he? Is he here at the sawmill, or in Örviken, or where the hell is the bastard?'

The boy was still barefoot. His hair was very dark, cut short, hacked at with what must have been a very blunt pair of sheep-shears and not very professionally done, either, the wisps of hair uneven, and in one place where the shears had gone in too far, his scalp shone through painfully white. The boy was standing in the middle of the floor, keenly regretting everything, which was clearly discernible from his feet and knees. How unnecessary, all

10

this, ran on and on through his head. I could've buried them posters. Now them's bloody angry with me an' maybe them'll tell Mother and . . .

Suddenly a warning signal went click in his head. He had gone and thought that bad word again, which was as sinful as saying it. He decided to think the thought again without the bad word: now them'll sure to be *angry* with me.

They probably would.

Suddenly, to his own astonishment, he heard his own voice. It came out quite involuntarily as he opened his mouth and asked a question.

'What's it mean, what's on them?' he said, his voice squeaking and far too shrill. 'What's them social whatsit an' all?'

But no one seemed to hear him any longer. They were talking to each other in low, urgent voices about how and where they would be able to find a man who seemed to be in the district, and the boy and his question were not worth bothering about. The boy glared miserably down at his bare feet; the white parts looked silly and peculiar and he deeply regretted leaving his boots at home that morning. It was hot in the room, the voices eager and excited, so he didn't understand very much. They were going to have a scout around. Search, the overseer kept saying. Something ungodly was going on, that was now quite clear, and he felt with a leaden certainty in his chest that he had been running errands on behalf of the ungodly, though unwittingly. Perhaps it hadn't been so foolish to go into the office after all?

He suddenly felt safer, though still oppressed. He felt he wanted to contribute something, that there was more to say.

'Him's a Stockholmer,' he said suddenly, loudly and informatively. 'Him's that. Him's got worms in t'mouth.'

They all looked at him, everyone in the room, and fell silent with questioning looks, the only sound that of flies buzzing quietly against the window.

'Him's a Stockholmer,' the boy repeated by way of explanation, his voice firmer now. ''Cos him's got fishing-worms inside t'mouth.'

11

2

THEY CAUGHT Johan Sanfrid Elmblad at about three o'clock on 7 August, 1903, only three hundred metres from the actual Bure sawmill, and he made no attempt to deny his identity or excuse himself or escape.

An unknown man had been seen strolling about or snooping on the bridge across the river; the reports varied. Anyhow, he had looked like an outsider, maybe even from the south. It was not difficult to put two and two together and make him a socialist. Five men were immediately sent out from the office, and they found him at once. He had got as far as the sawmill and was clearly up to certain activities that were later explained. Anyway he was snooping around or hiding between two stacks of timber. Not surprisingly, he had a small bundle of those yellow and red posters on him. Then they caught him. One of the five men called out in quite a sharp, firm voice and he had at once stopped with an almost timid, or at least guilty gesture, and then they grabbed him. Two stackers had at once got a hold on him to ensure he understood the seriousness of their intentions, and had then carefully forced him down to the ground. The fat man, later revealed to be Ombudsman Johan Sanfrid Elmblad, had remained almost silent, except for a few grunts and groans, though there was little point in him struggling.

They sat him down with his back to the timber store. More and more men arrived, and it could be said that there was quite a commotion. The man in question was wearing a respectable if rather shabby black suit. He had dropped the case of pamphlets and posters in the scuffle, but someone fetched it and put it on his lap. He was sweating profusely, giving them all the impression he was frightened, his fat square face twitching as he kept wiping his forehead, his eyes flickering in the manner typical of Stockholmers of his kind. He didn't dare look any of the men in the eye. The manager arrived a minute or two later and then they were able to begin the interrogation.

First of all they asked him what the hell he was doing on company land. Then the fat man started asking in an indignant, rather panicky tone of voice whether he did not have the same rights as others, and was told by the overseer that he definitely did not. The man was trembling all over, clearly finding it difficult to speak, managing only a few incoherent and incomprehensible phrases about wanting to 'discuss the question of the vote' and 'the aim of the workers' movement being to unite them all'. He was unable to collect himself sufficiently to make a more coherent speech. One of the bystanders, Karl Erik Lindquist from Old Fahlmark, the foreman, asked him whether he did not think the Swedish workers now standing round him, the honest and united workers of Skellefte district who had caught him, were not a good enough workers' association and whether he did not now understand that they were firmly resolved to deal with a louse like him. This took him aback so completely he had nothing to say in reply. The manager then asked the men surrounding him what they should do with this socialist bastard. Several men suggested with laughter that they should give him the once-over and then throw him into the water. The overseer then asked Elmblad if he had properly understood what the men thought of him, but he received no reply. After a few light kicks in the fat stomach to emphasize his words, the overseer again asked whether he realized how slim the chances were of the socialist message striking root among these workers. The man nodded and replied that he did.

A shout of loud laughter rose from the men.

'What's tha name then?' one of the stackers finally asked.

The fat man was now sweating profusely, his face quivering and his lower jaw trembling as if he were on the verge of tears. He seemed quite incapable of replying and kept swallowing repeatedly, as if making great efforts to form a reply which would not or could not emerge.

'What's your name?' repeated the overseer.

It was August, the sun shining low between the timber stacks, the air soft and pleasant.

The boy stood amongst the men, gazing curiously at the man lying there. He looked quite different now from earlier that morning. Then finally it came, in a low voice, as if he were ashamed of his name.

'Elmblad,' he said. 'Johan Sanfrid Elmblad.'

Afterwards, stories about what this Elmblad had been up to were collected up and the fact that he had come from Örviken in the first place was confirmed.

He had been there the day before. He had hung around the timber yard in Örviken without attempting to conceal on whose behalf he was acting. Naturally it had gone round the men that a socialist agitator had come to spread alarm, and between them they had decided what ought to be done about it. Elmblad, it was said later, had gone around talking in a particular way, and the workers had been disturbed that no one had tackled him so that they could work in peace, but they had been unwilling to say anything. Finally he had gone down to the loading wharf and from the quay had started making a speech on organizational matters.

They had smiled 'yes' to everything he had said, which had seemed to encourage him, as he had thought they had liked his 'preaching'. In the end, he had opened his case and pulled out a bundle of newspapers, editions of the notorious *Folkbladet*. Then he took out a piece of string, deftly tied it round the bundle of papers, and asked those out on the barge to catch the papers and share them round. They caught the bundle he threw out to them and passed it from man to man. When the bundle finally arrived at the man farthest out in the prow of the barge, he grabbed it with both hands and swung it with all his might straight out into the water, laughing as he did so.

'That's what we does with socialist papers here!' he had shouted, and the whole team of forty men had then agreed with loud laughter and shouts.

Elmblad had appeared not only astonished but totally dejected by this. He had stood there on the quay for a long time, staring at them in dismay, clearly unable to find anything to say in reply to their shouts. Crestfallen, he had stood there witnessing the failure of his efforts. Then he had trudged off, leaving the men on the quay and the barge.

That had happened in Örviken at about eleven o'clock the day before. Twenty-four hours later he was caught in Bureå.

They found a rope and wound it several times round the plump body, then four determined men carried him down to the harbour on their shoulders, Elmblad whimpering all the way and asking to be released, but the men were determined and strong and took no notice of his protests.

'That's the last time you set foot on company land, you socialist bastard,' said the manager, who was walking ahead of the little procession. Elmblad had been very agitated to find himeslf bound and snivelled loudly for all and sundry to hear, but now he was quite silent and apathetic, apparently resigned to his fate. The manager, a short man, much disliked by many true believers for his constant unpleasant swearing, appeared to be in a very good mood, patting Elmblad now and again on the head, often with good-humoured comments about how things would be all right, he would see. When the procession reached the quay, they put Elmblad down on the ground for a few moments, then told him that he was going to be given a free ride in a boat to Ursviken, after which their ways would part for ever, and that the meeting the next day would no doubt be very thinly attended. When Elmblad realized they were about to put him into a boat, he started looking worried again and, stammering, exclaimed that the wind was too high and he was afraid of boats and did not wish to go out on the water.

This suddenly seemed to make the men hesitate. The wind was undoubtedly high and the waves rough: neither did any of them wish to act as oarsmen, and for a moment there was a great deal of irresolution and confusion. Elmblad was sitting on the ground, released from the rope, his case on his lap. One of the stackers suggested that they should use the company tug; it would take far too long to row that far and it was in everyone's interest that the socialist should be removed as soon as possible. After a brief discussion, this was agreed.

It was almost five by the time he was taken on board the tug. The ropes were cast off and the group that had been present throughout now thinned out considerably, leaving behind only three men, the manager and a few children. Elmblad sat down on deck; a small group waved from the quay as the boat put out, but Elmblad remained on deck without turning round.

3

THE INN was a two-storey building.

Many years ago someone had painted it a pinkish red that was probably meant to resemble cranberries-and-milk, but the jaws of time had gnawed away at the colour and many winters had washed it out, so that all that was left was a peeling, pale pink remnant, indescribably dreary, like regurgitated meat.

After a trying day ending in a quiet sea trip, Elmblad checked in at the inn in Ursviken at about seven in the evening and at once went to bed.

His room was on the first floor.

He took off his jacket and placed his trousers on the floor, trying to keep the creases in by putting his suitcase on top to press the wrinkles out. Then he lay still in bed, fixing his eyes intently on the knotholes in the ceiling boards, Slowly, very slowly, his fear or agitation began to fade: soon it was once again possible to think clearly.

The bastards, he thought with monotonous obstinacy, over and over again. Bloody Christian worker bastards and their cowardly ignorant repulsive bloody godliness.

But I was lucky, all the same, he thought.

After a while, his eyelids started trembling; very slowly, he closed his eyes, breathing more and more calmly and evenly, his mouth slowly opening and his lips slipping apart; five minutes later he was asleep. His hand fell off his chest, and a stream of dark snuff-brown saliva started trickling slowly out of the left-hand corner of his mouth across his cheek. Just as it was about to disappear behind the tip of his ear, he suddenly woke up, and sitting straight up in bed with a jerk, he said out loud: 'Bastards!'

A second later, he remembered where he was.

Outside, pale thin dusk was beginning to fall, like a soft tulle curtain slowly being drawn, blurring the contours of the houses and birches and the water. The aspens were trembling imperceptibly, whispering out in the yard, and a dog was barking steadily far away on the other side of Ursvik Bay. He sat quite still in bed, everything at the same time quiet and very disturbing. It could have been worse, he thought. Much worse, in fact. Those cursed, stupid, bastard Norrlanders, he thought, though thinking like that did not improve matters. But it must be wrong that things should be like this.

In other parts of the country, company lackeys, or the police, or all kinds of people chased him and harassed him. But here it was the workers themselves. That was the bitterest pill of all. These bloody pious sheep didn't understand what was best for them; yes, that was the bitterest pill. His own people, and they laughed at him and fought like hell, too.

Seskar Island, for instance.

He had gone there by boat, which was to tie up and take on a load of timber, and he was to go ashore to make preparations for

16

the meeting. He had seen the small crowd of people and heard the shouting from a long way away. The shouts were in fact at him. They had brayed like donkeys, asking the captain if the socialist bastard was on board. The captain had said he was. Then the men had yelled back that he bloody couldn't tie up because he couldn't come ashore there. The captain had stood there looking confused, an irresolute smile on his face, assuring them that the socialist bastard was thinking of stopping off at Luleå and wasn't coming ashore. So he had been allowed to pull in to the quay and start loading. But the crowd had stayed on the quay making sarcastic comments about Elmblad's plump appearance.

Not the police. Not capitalists or the bourgeoisie. The crowd on the quay were workers. Not the others. Not the enemy. The enemies up here in this bloody desolate Norrland were his own people. That was the bitterest pill.

But there were others, he remembered, trying to cheer himself up. In Båtskärsnäs he had gone all round the sawmill district searching for someone who should have met him but had never appeared. He had suddenly run into a whole crowd who were not against him and wanted to listen. Strangely enough, some of them had been involved in the Sundsvall lockout. When they realized Elmblad was the ombudsman, they were pleased and insisted he should stay on until the next day, which he had promised to do.

Which I promised to do, he said solemnly in a loud voice at the unpainted, knot-holed ceiling. He waited for a moment for silence to fall again in the room: which I promised those who were there.

Who were there.

The silence and the solemnity seemed right in some way; and when the prickly ache in his loins suddenly returned, he was horribly disappointed, or perhaps irritated, or simply miserable: not again, just when I had managed to calm down. Not at this moment. He lay for a while trying to forget the gnawing, pressing little pain, but it grew worse and worse, and in the end he gave up.

The chamber-pot was under the bed.

He pulled it out, then cautiously slid his long pants down and tried to urinate, without hope, but at the same time not giving up beforehand.

He stayed like that for a long, long time, kneeling on the wooden floor, with no success. Nothing came, but the pain continued and did not abate. Nothing came. It was torment. Everything was torment.

Everything is torment, he thought. That's how it is. Torment. He ought to do something. He was homesick. He could not pee. What was he doing here? According to the plan, tomorrow he should be holding a large public meeting in Bure parish for a congregation of pious tormentors who would almost certainly do everything short of murdering him; everything was torment; he could not pee; nothing came. What was he doing here? So pointless, so excruciating, kneeling on this clean scrubbed floor with his pants down and the pot in front of him, feebly shaking his wrinkled little member. But not a drop came and the pain and pointlessness and misery were utterly complete, refusing to go away. His torment was grey; suddenly he was overwhelmed by immense self-pity and started weeping. Poor me, he thought, sobbing, poor me, what's the point, what is the point of all this?

He fell slowly towards the bed, leaning his forehead against the mattress and pressing his face against the grey material. He was still on his knees, the pot between them. He closed his eyes and waited. The mattress smelt of camphor.

That night his wife came to him in his dreams and, as always when he dreamt about her, she was holding the little imbecile by the hand. She was wearing her grey working blouse, the yellow hat on her head, but her loins were naked and starkly white. She was wearing canvas shoes. She was holding the boy's hand and he was dribbling slightly and looking content. They were staring at him distrustfully or accusingly, but they said nothing. Then very slowly they started to fade away, giving him no opportunity to tell them what it was he felt he had to say; they grew whiter and whiter and finally the dream was as white as her white thighs and stomach and he was wide awake.

He dressed. He stood for a long time in front of the mirror, staring blankly at his face, which was just the same as before. Then he went down to the dining-room.

The girl served him with *finka*.

It was the third time that week he had had *finka*, hard crisp-bread broken up into small pieces, then cooked in a frying-pan with milk. They served this hot doughy white mess in a heap on the plate with a knob of butter on the top. It was not untasty, the girl informed him as she served him, in fact really nourishing, as long as it was made properly. It was like *blöta*, which he had also learnt to like, though perhaps mustier, and cheaper too.

18

The girl put a cup of cranberry juice down in front of him.

He was in the middle of the dish when they came. There were four of them, and none of them weaklings. They came in through the dining-room door in a rush as if the door had been thrown open by a raging force outside, and after first looking with embarrassment down at their feet, they stepped across the bare floor, hestitating over whether they dared walk on the newly scrubbed surface. Then the first of them boldly tiptoed across and the others followed cautiously behind. Before he really realized what was happening, they were standing all around him.

He recognized one of them, the one-eyed landlord of the inn, now glaring at him rigidly with his white fish-eye. Beside him was a squat old man wearing a master-tugman's traditional cap and proudly refusing to remove it. He had never seen the other two before, but one thing was quite clear: they were workers, large men, and they were very angry.

Slowly, he put the fork down on the plate.

He took his hand off the table and put it on his knee.

One of the men leant forward and after a brief pause said in a matter-of-fact voice:

'Will tha not offer us'n a beer?'

A faint clucking sound came from the other men, almost a snigger. They were all looking down at Elmblad with barely restrained laughter, their eyes wide with expectation, or was it rage? Elmblad shook his head in silence and continued to stare down at his plate.

'This'un's hard t'please,' he heard the voice say again, diagonally behind him. Now things had taken an unpleasant turn; he did not move a muscle, but waited tensely. Suddenly everything gave way in front of him, his chair was jerked away and hurled aside with a kick and there was a crash as he sat down on the floor. The men were no longer smiling; on the contrary, they seemed to be very serious or disturbed by what had happened.

'That,' said Elmblad in a voice which he could hear was shaky and not at all convincing, 'That was rather unnecessary, wasn't it?'

He got up. When they started speaking to him, it was in the Skellefte dialect tinged with Swedish, and as always he found it difficult to understand what they were saying. After a while, they started speaking to him in such loud excited voices that he understood the situation perfectly well without understanding the words, so he abandoned his attempts to reply and fell silent, waiting despondently for them to finish.

They did not sound directly unfriendly.

The landlord was the noisiest. He was raging and swore several times, again and again reiterating that Elmblad was a serpent of Satan and should be exterminated.

Elmblad was sweating profusely. He could feel it dripping all over his body, perspiration running in rivulets down his face, over his moustache, down his neck, and he was ashamed but could do nothing about it. It was all a nightmare, the men standing round him with their solemn, excited, angry red faces, their mouths moving, and on the table the plate of *finka* and a half-empty cup of cranberry juice.

Elmblad, he thought silently, it's time you left.

Afterwards he did not really know how it happened. He just left them, without a word, and they did not follow him. He walked through a door, then through a hallway. He was quite alone. He walked down some wooden steps. They creaked. It was quite quiet now. He came out on to the outside porch. It was sunny, and windy; his face was still bathed in sweat and he was breathing heavily. Sun in his face, wind; that felt good.

Elmblad stood on the steps, trying to think. Would this never come to an end?

Then something whipped quietly past his head and splashed softly down in front of his feet. He turned round and looked upwards. Up there on the first floor of the inn was a veranda just above the entrance, surrounded by delicate, decorative fretwork, once painted white. They were up there now, four men from Ursviken, of whom one was the landlord, another a master-tugman, and they were all spitting down at him, like children. They were all very cheerful now and there was no savagery in their spitting. They were showering him with plugs of tobacco and streams of brown saliva and they were doing so with good humour and laughter, a boyish joke.

For a few moments Elmblad was at a loss. Then he took a few steps to one side, easily evading the gobs of spit. Their gaiety and exhilaration suddenly confused him completely, as if something didn't quite fit. Nothing made sense. Then he started walking across the yard and with increasing determination continued down towards the harbour and the water.

Later, in his journal, he wrote: 'After this occurrence, I wondered whether I should not simply leave everything. But then I was seized with a desire for revenge. Leave! No, I'll fight the wretches, even if I fall! After making this decision, I went down to the blacksmith who owned a sailing-boat, and I made him promise to sail me over to Bure, where the meeting was fixed for 6.30 that evening. We agreed he should take me there for two kronor and wait for an hour while I spoke, then bring me back.

4

WHEN ELMBLAD STEPPED ASHORE in Bureå, one jacket sleeve was torn, his shirt was filthy and the back of his black jacket was streaked with dirt.

He looked a mess.

He kept on repeating it to himself. Johan Sanfrid Elmblad, you look a mess, he thought. You can't stand up and make a speech in this state. You look like a tramp.

Though circumstances had been against him to the last.

He had waited down on the shore, seated on the ground. It was three o'clock and he was still on the Ursviken side. It was still quite windy and he could see the barges on their way south towards Bjuröklubb and Umeå, bobbing wildly in the rough seas further out. It was really interesting to watch, as the waves were clearly causing the tugboat considerable difficulties. But because of the wind and the sound of the waves breaking, he had not heard them coming. He had only felt the first sudden blow from a stick and in his surprise had almost fallen over. Then the next blow came. And the next.

The stevedore foreman, he was said to be. Elmblad found that out later. Anyhow, he was large and strong, and he was laughing as he wielded the stick. A man in police uniform standing further away was also laughing loudly, simply watching the thrashing and laughing. That's how it was. But then the policeman had evidently lost some of his good humour, probably because Elmblad had started calling for the police, and he had started blustering and swearing. Elmblad had had to put up with it, as they say. The two of them had thrashed him soundly. It had been difficult not to lose his temper.

Though necessary, of course. So he had put up with it.

So after a boat trip that had been far too rough to be pleasant, he was still looking a mess as he stepped ashore in Bure country, the sleeve of his jacket ripped, damage that had unfortunately been his own fault because he had tried to wrench himself free much too roughly from the powerful grasp the policeman had had on his arm. During the whole trip across, he had sat in silence, perhaps dispirited too, but the fresh wind and spray had helped to calm him down. It had been a rather difficult situation, anyhow. As he later described in his report, he had not been pleased.

He gave the blacksmith an extra krona to accompany him to the meeting. It was better to have this man, by no means a weakling, walking beside him.

He walked up along the Skerry road, feeling the people's eyes on the back of his neck, staring through the windows.

The children joined him first. They came in increasingly larger groups, gazing at him with curiosity and terror, refusing to answer when spoken to and following close at his heels. They were like a pack of scared dogs, in amongst them the boy he had met the previous day, the boy who had helped him put up the posters. The boy was wearing shoes now, but he refused to open his mouth or even let on that they had met before. Nevertheless, he seemed intensely interested, and he kept himself to the forefront of the children. Elmblad was troubled by the children's presence, but he pretended not to be. When he got to the crossroads, he sat down and waited by the churn-stand.

After the children came the women. Then the first men, then a few more. At about five minutes before the time announced, there were fifteen children round him, slightly fewer women, and six adult men, all regarding him in a silence that he did not sense as hostile, only guarded. Together they amounted to maybe thirty people. Under the circumstances, that was not at all bad.

Just before half-past six, four policemen arrived, appearing from nowhere with three large dogs. They split up into two groups and stationed themselves on each side of him.

They did nothing, but they kept their eyes riveted on him.

The presence of the policemen seemed to instil a fervour into them all, or perhaps it was uncertainty. Quite suddenly, his task appeared to be immensely difficult. He hesitated, not knowing quite what to do. The churn-stand was about three feet high, steps up one side, and nearby were a meeting-house, a shoemaker's and an unused open space. It was now past the announced time, and they were all looking at him intently, as if at heart they did not believe he would dare to start, yet were hoping something would happen.

The policemen had sat down on the verge.

The women looked worried, but two of them were tittering. The situation, thought Elmblad, is tricky. It certainly is.

The boy who had helped him with the posters was standing at the front, and Elmblad suddenly saw to his astonishment that the boy was nodding at him with excitement and delight, as if he had just thought of something encouraging and wished to share it.

These people are incomprehensible, thought Elmblad. Missions in Westerbotten are like wandering in the darkness. I don't understand them.

He climbed slowly up the three steps and looked over the crowd. This was it. Now he would begin. He picked up his case, opened it, took out the papers, and when he looked up again, he saw one man suddenly leaving the crowd. It was his friend the blacksmith from Ursviken. He was walking away with rapid steps, as if he had to leave as quickly as possible, so that no words or cries would tempt him back: he had soon vanished in the direction of the harbour. Elmblad was at once certain he would not be sailing back that evening.

Now, thought Elmblad with a sinking feeling of desolation in his stomach, now I'm stuck. Now there's nothing else for me to do but make my speech about attempts at organization by the workers' movement to the working classes of Bureå. And so he started his speech.

Afterwards he went round those who had stayed the course, offering his pamphlets for sale.

They stared at him, in a not unfriendly way, and one of them, a man in his fifties who seemed better educated than the others, explained that for his part he would have liked to buy one if he had had any money, and if he could be sure the book, or the pamphlet, whatever it was called, would not immediately be confiscated by the waiting policemen. Elmblad said he understood his viewpoint and did not insist.

The policemen had got to their feet.

There was not much he could do, but he realized the little that he could do should be done now. Three of the older men walked away in a group towards the wooden bridge across the river: he suddenly felt they represented his only chance of rescue, and he ran after them with ungainly waddling steps. They turned round and when he panted up to them, they did not seem surprised. With some embarrassment, he asked whether he might join them; the eldest of them glanced quickly behind him at the policemen, who had still not started to come after them, then nodded and went on without a word.

'Where are we going?' said Elmblad after a while.

They were outside the village now, walking through the forest along a path up a slope. It was almost eight o'clock, and dusk was descending. The older man walked in front, then the other two, then Elmblad, and then, some way behind, another group consisting of the four policemen, the dogs, and a couple of men who had clearly joined in out of pure curiosity. Last of all came a boy. Elmblad kept turning round to see if they were any nearer, and he had no difficulty recognizing the boy from the day before.

The dogs were pulling hard.

'Where are we going?' he said again.

The dogs yelped. The forest grew thicker, running into dense spruce, and dusk was falling. Elmblad knew suddenly and surely and finally that he had to do something then, soon, at once, if he were to have a chance of any kind.

'You can go on,' he said to the silent back in front of him. 'Thanks for the company.'

Then he ran off the path and blundered blindly straight into the forest. Almost at once he heard shouts and dogs barking.

5

HE FELL several times, details blurring in the twilight, and as he was not used to running in the forest, he hurt himself quite badly several times. The ground was rising continuously, and when he looked back, he appeared to be on his way up a mountainside, or anyhow up a slope. His pursuers were invisible, but he could hear them all the time. He was very tired and tried desperately to remember where the points of the compass were.

I should have headed for the sea, he thought.

The case of pamphlets was still in his hand. He was gasping for breath, unable to run any longer, just walking mechanically straight ahead. Suddenly he found himself in a grass-covered glade, spruce forest thick all round him. He must have scratched himself, as his face was bleeding. He was very tired. Driven by a sudden impulse, he crawled in under the thickest spruce and lay down on the ground, his case under his head. He buttoned his jacket up as tightly and as high as he could, then lay still.

The ground was damp, but he ignored that.

He could hear the dogs. They seemed to be searching in a circle, close to and far away, and as he had no wish to hear them, he tried to pull his jacket up so that it covered his head and ears. The material of the jacket shut out some of the sounds, making them blurred and vague, as if filtered through a dream, and that was better. He had been sweating violently as he ran; now he had stopped sweating and it had turned unpleasantly cold and damp, but he did not move or open his eyes or change his position one single inch.

They must have come closer, and in the end he felt a kind of indifferent relief when he realized one of the dogs had found him. The dog was panting right beside him, nosing eagerly and silently, not barking. Then there were a couple of short loud barks, and he heard a boy's voice apparently admonishing the dog and restraining it.

The dog had found him. But the boy was with it, not a policeman, and when Elmblad opened his eyes, he saw the faint outline of the thin boyish figure silhouetted outside the tent-like shelter of the spruce. The shadow came and went, and he could just make out the dog roaming uneasily in and out like a restlessly hunting shadow. The boy had it on a cord.

The boy. He was there.

No one else.

This was what he had always imagined in his nightmares, but so far his nightmare had not been like this. What he had expected had always been much worse and more tormenting, a southern lynching in the moonlight with dogs tearing and ripping at his legs, and knives, and hanging: Uncle Tom fleeing in the forest, just as the plantation owner's men had caught up with him, but before the whip. But it was not like that here. This was the coastland of Västerbotten in the summer of 1903.

The dog sniffed at his back, panting and moving excitedly close to him, but not biting, not snapping, not doing anything. Elmblad could hear now because his jacket had come down, leaving his head free again, and he could hear that the forest was no longer silent. Out of the darkness came whispers, cries and barks, from a distance and quite close, giving the whole situation an atmosphere of strangely secretive unease. The boy and the dog were now both underneath the spruce where Elmblad had curled up. The boy had crawled in on all fours, like a dog, and his face was very close to Elmblad's, a white spot with no visible dark features.

'Is it you again?' Elmblad whispered quietly. 'Don't say anything and keep the dog quiet.'

The boy nodded eagerly.

'Just keep quiet,' said Elmblad.

The boy sat quite still, the dog panting behind him, but quietly. Then he saw the boy's face coming even closer: then his eye-sockets became visible, and the half-open mouth.

'What dost tha ate dun in Stockholm?' said the boy's breathless whispering voice right in his ear: the boy was now very close, his eyes deep hollows in the white face. Elmblad did not understand what he meant, so did not reply, just waited.

'Ist tha really a Stockholmer?' the boy said again, in the same tone of voice.

Elmblad nodded silently in the dark.

'Dunt tha come from Pite? Ain't tha a Pite man, then?'

They could hear barking much closer now. The boy was still staring intently at him from very close: but suddenly Elmblad saw him retreating, jerking at the dog's string, sliding out behind the branches and vanishing out of sight together with the dog.

Then Elmblad heard the boy shouting in his shrill elated voice, now utterly unreal:

'C'm on! Him's here! Ah've found him! C'm on! Hurry an' come!'

As he shouted, the other men's shouts suddenly came closer and all the dogs started barking. Elmblad lay very still under the spruce, his eyes tight shut.

6

QUITE A TIME must have gone by. Suddenly he could see every-thing very much more clearly. The moon had risen and was three-quarters full just above the treetops, the glade now bathed in moonlight.

They had tied him to a pine tree.

They had tied him up with a fairly thin rope. Without hurting him they had conscientiously wound the rope round his legs, his pelvis, his waist, finishing off with a couple of turns around his chest. There had been no brutality. The men had worked with carefully restrained movements, neither shoving nor striking him. Nor had that been necessary. He neither wished nor was able to do anything else but resign himself.

Their calm and consideration had also reduced the terror he had felt at first. He noted with special interest how closely and thoroughly they wound the rope round his body, including his pelvis. The rope seemed to cover him, as if protecting him. He remembered very clearly what had been churning round and round in his head all afternoon, from the moment he had got into the blacksmith's boat, then during his speech and the chase through the forest, then rising more and more until the thought became a painful hysterical burning spot that filled his whole mind as he had lain pressed down under the spruce, up until the moment when the first man stretched out his hand and took hold of him. He was afraid they would *cut* him. That they would have this idea of cutting. Not that they would kill him, or anything like that. He didn't mind that. He was not afraid to die. But he was hell-ishly, horribly frightened of someone starting to *cut* or *clip* or . . .

That was it . . . that they would cut. That was what kept flaring in insane flashes of lightning through his head over and over again, visions of horror about how they would catch him and hold down his arms and legs and then pull his trousers down and then . . . He always stopped thinking then, as it was too terrible. That was really the only thing he was afraid of, that someone should come on the jolly idea and . . . He had heard what the Lapps did, anyhow. They flung their reindeer down and *bit it off with their teeth*.

They were terrible people living up here in northern Norrland. Terrible people, a terrible country. A bunch of pious faithful company lackeys and castrators, Christian castrators, horrible, impossible to understand them. And when they wound the rope so tightly round his pelvis, when they made such a tight cocoon of his rather plump body, for a moment he felt great relief, something almost like security.

They were seven men, three dogs and a boy.

The moon was shining very brightly now, giving the forest precise contours, the shadows from the tallest pines falling sharply and clearly across the glade. The pine tree stood apart, a little way out into the open space, and there they tied him. After they had finally got him properly anchored to the pine, a certain hesitancy seemed to afflict them all; they were clearly unable to decide what to do next. One of them lit his pipe, the others sat down on the ground and started talking in subdued voices. There were only two of the policemen there now, the other men, as far as he could make out, ordinary working men. Elmblad strained to hear what they were saying, but it was difficult, for they were speaking quietly and in that incomprehensible dialect he had never been able to learn.

But what was clear to him was that they were not discussing him. It had something to do with the sawmill. It sounded as if they were discussing piece rates for the stackers, whether they had gone up or down, but he could not make out exactly which.

Anyhow, it was all beyond his comprehension.

The boy kept moving about, as if not really at home with the men, or as if looking for something. Sometimes he patted the dogs, then he would vanish into the darkness. The mild August night was unusually still, the wind had dropped, the moon almost completely circular above the treetops, and apart from the whispering or mumbling voices of the men, the silence was complete. Elmblad felt strangely ridiculous. They had hunted him down and found him, tied him to a pine tree, but now that he was securely lashed in the forest in the coastlands of Westerbotten, the men seemed to have forgotten him, or lost interest in him.

As if to crown everything, signals from his cursed bladder started recurring. That damned cursed prostrate. He needed to urinate and couldn't when he wanted to. But he would certainly be able to if he ought not to or did not want to. It would take time anyhow, and be painful. What should he do? He tried crossing his legs, but the rope prevented him. And as he started thinking about it, his need to pee became hopelessly insistent and he didn't know what to do about it.

Ask them to loosen the rope so that he could take it out himself and pee? They certainly wouldn't allow that. Besides, he would probably not be able to, if he were allowed to, and that would be so painful he didn't even want to think about it. Or ask them to help him, which seemed even more impossible? Anyway, he thought, and the thought turned his stomach ice cold, that would probably turn their thoughts to . . . to . . . Perhaps someone would pull down his trousers for a joke and one joke would lead to the next. Then their attention would be focused on . . . And then someone would . . .

And then the knife.

And then.

His breathing grew faster, and suddenly he was sweating again. It was unbearable. He needed to pee. What should he do? Should he let it come in his trousers without saying anything? It would be pleasantly warm at first, then cold and sticky and horrible. They would be sure to notice, sooner or later, and start laughing, thinking he had wet himself because he was frightened.

But he was, wasn't he? The problem was also that he had no other trousers with him. Sawmill agitators did not take large stocks of trousers with them on their travels. The organization's budget did not stretch to that. So?

The boy was now only a few strides away, staring attentively at Elmblad. Still no reaction from the men. The burning pain in his bladder grew worse and worse; he closed his eyes and tried to think about something else. But when he closed his eyes, nothing appeared but the dream he had had the night before, his wife with her burning white loins and grey blouse, holding the little imbecile by the hand, and both of them looking at him, seeing right through him. The pain and discomfort went on, so it was better to open his eyes. The moon was yellow and gentle and consoling, looking right into Johan Sanfrid Elmblad and seeing his condition, and the moon, as yellow as a meadow flower, smiled kindly and whispered: it is night, it is dark, no one can see you. And so Ombudsman Johan Sanfrid Elmblad pushed his back hard against the trunk of the tree, holding his breath and pressing and pressing, waiting, trying again, the moon continuing to look gently and kindly straight into him, and a few minutes later he felt the first slow warm drops trickling out.

*

The first interrogation was very short and blunt.

One of the men, whom the others called Aron, was the first to put a question. He appeared to be some relation of the boy's, maybe his father, or elder brother, or uncle; they kept together and spoke to each other occasionally, and he never saw the boy speaking to any of the other men. So he was asked why he was in Bureå, but when Elmblad tried to describe why agitation was necessary and why the organization's efforts were meant to be for the workers' best, they became impatient, and the questioner, whose name was perhaps Aron, in language that sounded biblical but was Swedish mixed with dialect, asked him instead to tell them where he had been. The way he had come, they meant. He had to tell them all the places; from Gefle by boat to Luleå, then Kalix, the meetings in Karlsborg and Nyborg, omitting his maltreatment in Karlsborg, where he had been thrashed. Then Haparanda, the unsuccessful landing at Båtskärsnäs, then back to Luleå.

Piteå. Three days later, he had taken the steamer to Skellefteå archipelago.

There was nothing else to tell.

The man called Aron had a squint and kept on asking whom he knew in Piteå, and whether he had not been sent by Black Josef, or any other adherents of Freedom to Work. Elmblad thought they were joking, or insulting him, so said nothing at first, but the questions were repeated until he told them rather roughly that of course he had nothing to do with blacklegs or traitors. The man they called Aron looked crestfallen and surprised at him, shaking his head in dismay.

'Tha's nowt a Pite man, then?' he said again, as if to make absolutely sure. When Elmblad shook his head, their stock of questions seemed to have petered out. They were all looking at him in confusion and dismay now.

The questions had come to an end.

On Elmblad's part, the whole situation was quite incomprehensible. Neither did the two policemen appear to have anything to say, nor any suggestions as to what they should do with him. Elmblad had thought that at least the usual suggestion to 'give the scum a good thrashing' would be brought up, but no.

Elmblad closed his eyes and waited. His back was aching, the rope now more uncomfortable, and his trousers were wet through.

If I start blubbing now, he thought, I'll never get over this.

*

The boy was the first to say anything.

Sounds came out of the boy's mouth, that shrill uncertain voice he now knew so well, but which still always surprised him. The voice had a triumphant undertone, as if he had long been keeping an important secret to himself and had now finally decided to reveal it.

'Him's a Stockholmer,' the thin boyish voice was heard to say. 'An' him kin ate worms.'

Then he added:

'Him had worms in him's mouth. Ah seed 'em.'

The information seemed to enliven the assembled company. The five men received the information first with scepticism, then with amused disbelief, curiosity, dismay, bewilderment and a touch of well-concealed enthusiasm. Mumbling and grunting, they all looked at their prisoner with renewed interest. In the moonlight, Elmblad could see their faces very close to him, the light sharpening the contours but at the same time eliminating all colour, so their faces became inhumanly milk-white, almost blueish-white in the fragile moonlight, so they no longer looked menacingly dark or superior in strength. No, their faces looked like skimmed milk, milk thinned out with water, the cream removed, the fat gone. Skimmed milk for red workers' children, that was it. But the pale hollow faces of the men he now saw in front of him seemed to have a problem to chew over that interested them far more than his message about socialism and union organization. They were standing very close to him, and one of the men with a cunning, hopeful and devout look on his face, asked him:

'Tis true? Kin tha ate worms?'

Elmblad thought for a moment. This was something that appeared to interest them. Ever since that day almost forty years ago when as a small boy he had first learnt the trick of making his mouth into a worm-tin, he had never regarded it as unusual or disgusting to have a worm in his mouth. But neither had he ever eaten a worm, swallowed one, that is. Now this pale man from this strange Norrland coastland was asking whether he ate worms. What could you answer to that, he thought, in this situation? What was it that interested him? If he said no, what would happen?

At first, Elmblad said nothing, but finally he shook his head, though carefully, almost imperceptibly.

31

The boy seemed upset.

'Ah's seed him!' he cried, shrilly excited. 'Ah's seed him wi' worms in him's mouth. 'Tis true!'

There were a few moments of confused silence. Evidently no one knew what the conversation was really about, and the moon was shining very brightly now, lighting up the glade more and more with its clear gentle light. The fat man was drooping in the ropes round the tree, looking bewilderedly from one man to the next, not really knowing what they expected of him.

' 'Tis true?' repeated the man called Aron. ' 'Tis true?'

At the same time he raised his hand and thoughtfully poked his finger straight into Elmblad's stomach. Immediately, the captive fat body convulsed, the mouth trembling, cheeks shaking, the jaws clamped shut, as if by chance the finger had happened to touch on the button that had released a long dammed-up but rigidly controlled terror. Now it gushed out, free and uninhibited.

Elmblad nodded.

He nodded more and more eagerly, as if he had decided to fall in with them and make up for previous errors. Now that he seemed to be being co-operative and positive, they were all interested. The crooked-shouldered, squint-eyed man called Aron turned to the boy with an expression of renewed respect and esteem, and said in a firm voice:

'See if tha kin git a worm.'

They all nodded in confirmation and the boy set off into the darkness to look for a worm for Johan Sanfrid Elmblad.

'Skellefteå', he wrote later in his report to the union, the report that was then bundled together with all his other reports and pushed into a cupboard in the Workers' Movement archives, 'is at present one of the darkest and most backward places in Norrland. All attempts to find a meeting place in the actual town came to nothing. The Good Templars dared not because of the Pastor, and the chairman of the Mission Society gave the same reply, as did all individuals who were approached. The Pastor alone ruled the community, and opinions the Pastor considered false doctrines and anti-Christian were to be kept at a distance. That the hierarchy within the community is powerful is evident in that not even the Free Thinkers have been able to make converts there. The Salvation Army has made some attempts but failed. The people all look up to the Pastor with admiration, in some cases with fear,

32

and they all wish to remain in his favour. There is also a large contingent in town of those who have appropriated the small-holders' lands – the sawmill owners have settled here and are contentedly in agreement with the activities of the Pastor. The number of workers is not particularly large, and those who exist are nearly all natives of the district. There are a few incomers, people who have not wished to accept responsibilities within the organization in other areas, and have been able to find sanctuary here for the time being.

'In Löfånger parish there was only one parish meeting-place, but that was not for me. Could do nothing. This was the darkest of all the villages, and the fear of socialism appalling. However, the villages should preferably be visited in the summer, when roads can be used as meeting places. Nothing can be done here in the winter. But they must not be dropped, because it is from such villages that the strike-breakers come. I had hoped for a good meeting at Bure sawmill. But that was not be be! The hall was owned by the company and had a special watch committee, whose first task was to make sure no socialists were allowed into the hall. The committee had carried out its duties conscientiously.

'Nothing, however, is more painful than the events connected with my visit which I must now describe.'

7

THEY LIT a small steady fire from dry pine twigs and bits of a tar-stub, then sat around the fire waiting for the boy's return.

He came in the end.

He appeared quite soundlessly from the darkness, then walked swiftly across the open space, two large fat earthworms in his hand.

They were still muddy.

'Here's tha worms,' he said.

Elmblad was still drooping, shapelessly fat and crumpled against his pine tree. The rope had stretched a little round the upper part of his body, which was now leaning slightly forward, but the men had tied an extra turn of the rope round his wrists to eliminate the risk of his wriggling free. Elmblad was keeping his eyes obstinately closed, as if he were very tired or had given up, his head hanging forward quite needlessly.

One of the men went up to him and, poking him cautiously in the stomach, said:

'Elmblad.'

There was no reply, but Elmblad's eyes slowly opened.

'Elmblad,' the man repeated, now somewhat impatient but still not unfriendly. 'Us'ns got t'worm now.'

The boy was standing very close, the two worms dangling between the thumb and forefinger of each hand. They all stared at Elmblad.

'Seein' . . .' the man went on, clearing his throat as if unused to making speeches. 'Seein' tha's said tha kin ate worms, we thinks tha shud show us'n what kinda man tha is, sort of.'

The boy started carefully cleaning the mud off one of the worms. At last it was really clean, glistening and wriggling strongly, apparently very lively as it wriggled round the palm of the boy's hand. Elmblad stretched his head forward slightly and looked down into the hand.

'Could you free my hands first?' he said in a polite voice, with no sign of distaste.

They looked hesitantly at each other, the light from the flames flickering across their faces, and as the light from the fire was softer and warmer, their faces acquired quite a different character, no longer ghostly pale blue, but warmer, friendlier, more human. The whole situation with the worms also seemed to have enlivened them, because it was amusing and within their comprehension; several of the men smiled or laughed covertly. But before any of them could decide, the boy had stretched out his hand, holding the wriggling worm between his thumb and forefinger right up against Elmblad's mouth. He was smiling excitedly, as if at last he was going to have the opportunity of showing the assembled company the promised trick his trained dog was supposed to be able to perform.

And the dog could. Elmblad opened his mouth carefully, thrust his head forward as far as he could and, with a swift, almost reptile-like movement, snapped the worm out of the boy's hand. It slipped in, then his mouth closed.

In the faint flickering light from the almost extinguished fire where the tar-stub was still glowing, all of them saw Elmblad's cheeks moving. His moustache twitched, the fat cheeks shifted

34

and moved, the cheek on the left bulging and falling in again. Then the whole of his face was still.

'Him's gotten it in t'mouth!' said the boy triumphantly, but with a touch of disapproval in his voice.

They all leant forward and inspected Elmblad's cheeks.

'Ate't oop,' said one of the men.

No movement.

'Ate t'worm oop.'

No movement.

'Ate't oop!'

A scared, childishly frightened, almost foolish smile flitted across Elmblad's face. His cheeks trembled, bulged, twitching and sliding up and down as his gaze slid uncertainly across the men's faces: he realized then that they meant it, and the half-smile that was trying to appeal to them, hesitantly and ingratiatingly, died away. He closed his eyes, apparently drawing a deep breath, and then suddenly his Adam's apple moved convulsively up and down, and he swallowed. As the worm slid down his throat, it must have offered some resistance, or with its violent wriggles indicated it did not find this pleasant, because Elmblad suddenly stiffened, as if all his concentration had turned inwards, towards something that was being enacted totally internally.

It was a remarkable sight.

They were all carefully studying his face, on which the eyes were now fixed on a point apparently a long way away and at the same time within him. Then his whole body began to become involved, swaying as if trying to free itself from the rope, his head poking helplessly forward, his fat neck stretching to its full extent, his mouth opening, his face scarlet, his eyes squeezed to slits, his tongue out; then he vomited.

The vomit shot to the ground and landed in a neat pool. They all leant over and stared at the pool. Most of its was white, but they could also see quite clearly that Elmblad had eaten *finka*. And there, right in the middle of it all, a worm, very much alive, was wriggling about.

They looked gloomily at each other, then at Elmblad. He was licking his lips and, from either embarrassment or shame, was trying to look unmoved. A thin thread of saliva still hung from his moustache.

'Him couldna ate't up!' said one of the men in an offended and dismissive voice. 'Him's a liar.'

The boy shook his head excitedly, almost insulted. It was just back luck! Something had gone wrong, but that was a coincidence. He was sure!

'Why are you doing this to me?' said Elmblad.

He had not said anything for so long, they were very surprised when he eventually opened his mouth, and they could find nothing to say. The thread of saliva was still hanging glistening from his moustache; the red colour of his face had faded, and he looked as he had before. As they had nothing to say, and it wasn't easy for them to answer his question, because it was a difficult question to answer, they all turned and gazed at the worm, now becoming more and more listless and docile, wriggling in the pool of vomit.

'You're workers, aren't you?' said Elmblad again, his voice slightly more eager and appealing. 'What the hell's this about? What the hell are you doing this to me for?'

The boy had now poked the worm out of the vomit with a small stick. It was hanging over the stick, fat and apathetic, hardly moving. Either it was in a bad way, or actually dying. The fire was giving less and less light, the moon beginning to vanish, and soon it would be impossible to see anything. The air felt colder.

The boy held the stick with the worm on it towards Elmblad's mouth and said in an appealing voice:

'Ate it oop now, so's them kin see tha kin!'

The silence went on so long it felt like a night. The boy's hand was trembling slightly, the worm hanging almost completely immobile, and Elmblad realized it would have to be. It was inevitable. There was no turning back.

So he stretched out his head again, extending his fat neck, and in the same reptile-like way as before, he snapped up the worm; then he tried again.

8

WHEN IT WAS OVER, only Elmblad and the boy were left.

They had loosened the rope slightly to enable Elmblad to sit on the ground with his back to the tree-trunk, but he was still tied. Before they left (and they had said very little) one of them had implied that he should be pleased. Things could have been worse. He would have to sit out the night here. Then he would have to arrange to get himself out of reach of the righteous anger of the workers. They had not treated him badly, had they? And they also had less patience with Stockholmers and socialists up here than elsewhere in the country.

That was roughly how they put it, though in another language which he only partly understood, a soft language, expressing consideration, superiority or menace, gliding gently over the vowels and extending into capricious floating hills and vales, a frightening and incomprehensible language spoken by the working men of this frightening land of darkness to which he had been prepared to come quite voluntarily and with his eyes open, and to which he hoped he would never have to come again.

Never again to this land of darkness.

Never again to the river valley of Skellefteå.

The boy was there; they had left him behind, on guard. One of the dogs had also been left, presumably as protection for the boy, protection against the socialist and socialism. Dogs were needed for that. The boy's task was to loosen, at dawn, as many ropes necessary for the socialist to free himself after a while, and then the boy was to run off.

That was the boy's task.

It was August 1903. That was when Johan Sanfrid Elmblad had gone to the river valley of Skellefteå for the first time, his first agitator's trip through Lövånger and Bureå and Ursviken and Sävenäs, that was the route. He tells it all in his report, except the minor detail of the worms he had vomited up. He saved that for his diary, as if ashamed of it. He says about the boy that 'for several hours I was forced to sit tied to a tree-trunk with a boy from the district as guard-dog'. He says he 'talked to him on several topics, but only come up against an impenetrable lack of knowledge of everything I said.'

He probably means lack of understanding.

He also mentions the dog.

When dawn came, they were still sitting there. Elmblad had collapsed over the ropes and for a while had been very cold and severely shaken, but now it would soon be over. On two occasions he had relaxed and urinated in his trousers, but he had long since given up and his apathy was finally a help as he stopped thinking about the unpleasantness of it all. He just sat there, not even attempting to talk any more. He had asked two questions during the whole time he and the boy had been alone.

The first was:

'What's your name, boy?'

And the boy had answered:

'Frans Nicanor Markström.'

And then, soon afterwards, he had asked:

'Won't you let me go now?'

But *nay*, the boy's silence had echoed back from the dawn.

The boy was sitting with his back to a tree-trunk, his arms round his drawn-up knees, and he was happy.

Dawn came slowly trickling between the trees, thin spider-grey veils slowly and imperceptibly lifting off the forest, one by one, until only the last soft grey light remained and thin sunlight spattered the treetops. The sounds from the forest were much clearer now, bird-song echoing as if the trees were columns in a gigantic temple, but not of marble. No, it was not stone one thought of, but green moss and clear echoing bird-song. Green moss, birds. The boy was sitting quite still and he seemed to be floating in a sea of stillness and movement. He looked up at the tops of the pines and watched the matt yellow colour of the trunks appearing and becoming clearer and more alive. That was the colour he loved most of all, the yellow colour he loved to drown in during the hours he spent lying on his back in the forest, his gaze turned upwards. Only here is the yellow so beautiful in the forest, he always thought. They haven't got that colour further south. They haven't got any pines, not this soft yellow. He had been down south, far down south, once, right down to Lövånger, and when he had come home, he had said: 'Down south, down Lövånger way, them's not got no forest worth speakin' of.'

Nor down south towards Holmsvattnet, either.

He had not felt lonely or frightened for a single second that night. It had been exciting, and he had had Uncle Aron to talk to if anything had happened. Our Aron was nice. But everything had been peculiar, all the same. At first when Elmblad had stood there fishing with worms in his mouth. Then the posters. Then the search, and he had been the one to find Elmblad first. On Sunday when there were prayers in the prayer-house, maybe the preacher would thank God in his mercy for having turned away the tempter, and then he would be sitting on the wooden bench at the back, but everyone would know who had done most on God's behalf. He would take no notice, although he was the one to expose the Stockholmer.

Elmblad was asleep, his head drooping forward, his moustache sticky, the front of his suit soiled, one sleeve of his jacket torn, and he had urinated in his trousers several times, which was also apparent. Now he was asleep. He was a lamentable sight; the boy inspected him with a sense of surprise, resignation and reluctant admiration. He had been given his deserts, Elmblad had, though no one had struck him. A Västerbotten Christian did not strike a fellow-creature, everyone knew that, but he maybe teaches him a lesson.

Elmblad would certainly never come back, so something had been gained. For sure.

The dog shifted uneasily at the boy's side: it was lying curled up, but now and again raised its head uncertainly and sniffed, then lowered it again. It was morning and the start of a lovely August day; the light morning mist had lifted and every detail was very distinct, the colours clear. It's beautiful, the boy thought. It's best in the morning. Yet somewhere inside the question gnawed at him like a mysteriously irritating stab of pain – *what did this Elmblad really want*? What did he mean? Why had they set up the search? Why was he so dangerous?

And inextricably bound up with that: *fancy him havin' worms in his mouth*.

Elmblad was sleeping heavily, his mouth wide open, hoarse rattling breathing coming from it. Soon he would be free, the ropes would be loosened, his hands released, his case put in front of him. Everything in order. No injustice committed, no damage done. Then the boy would run off, inaccessible. But the time had not yet come.

The boy was sitting curled up with the dog at his side, watching the light come. Soon it would happen, and then he would see no more of this fat man. Elmblad was asleep, drooping in the ropes. The boy kept his eyes riveted on him. It was such a fine morning, like the start of an adventure, as if he had caught a glimpse through the door of life and seen a piece of the puzzle outlined. He felt completely happy.

PART ONE

1

THE CELESTIAL HARP

'The work. The sawmill was eight-framed and also included
the timber yard for checking and loading. In the timber yard
were also lath-stacking and bundling and the loading of
these goods. There was a charcoal yard where charcoal was
made from scrap timber and waste from the mill, largely
during the winter. In summer this waste was made into
firewood. Status. Top group: machinists, saw-setters, manager, agent, office staff. Then electricians, stokers, greasers,
sawyers, edgers, sorters, stackers. Otherwise no status.
Work took place at the mill for 7 months in the year (timber
yard) plus extra winter sawing for two months.'

1

THE END OF THE STORY came almost exactly seven years later.

It was September, the air very clear, one of the most beautiful
autumn days of the year of 1910. What Nicanor was to remember
most of all was his mother, Josefina Markström, her closed,
concentrated, stony face dissolved by an emotion she could not
control, suddenly trying to get the railway carriage window open:
the train was still stationary, the newly built station in Bastuträsk
beautifully painted red, and all the birches littered with those
fantastic yellow and red colours. Quite out of control, she had
started banging desperately on the carriage windows, shouting
that they had to be opened, she wanted to *smell* Bastuträsk. She
was wild. They both tore at all the windows, but could not budge
them. She stared helplessly through the rather dirty windows out
at Bastuträsk station, as if wishing to imprint on her mind what it
looked like, longing for the smell of it.

The whistle blew and the train jerked to a start. Then it was all over; they had left a part of their lives, and something new had started.

Nicanor had wiped her eyes and let her blow her nose in the blue handkerchief, and after a while she had calmed down. But the same sentence had revolved round and round in his head, and sixty years later, he could still quote it exactly. *There's always something better than death.*

That was so. *There's always something better than death.*

It was said to be taken from a well-known story, but he had forgotten which. It wasn't hard to find out which now; the famous 'Town Musicians of Bremen'.

The beginning of the story, the part about the march of the musicians, goes roughly like this.

There was a man who owned a donkey and the donkey had grown old and useless, so the man wished to put an end to her life, because she could no longer haul his sacks to the mill. The donkey escaped and set off down the road to Bremen. After a while she met a hunting dog. The hound was toothless and useless to his master, so was to be shot. But the donkey said to the hound: '*There's always something better than death.* Come with me!' Then they met a cat and the cat was mangy and old, no longer able to catch rats, so the cat's mistress wanted to drown her as the cat was useless. 'Come with us,' said the donkey and the hound. 'We can always be the town musicians of Bremen.' Then they met a cock. The cock crowed hoarsely and miserably, telling them that company was coming the next day, and he was going to be made into soup. 'Listen, old redcomb,' the donkey said. 'You crow yourself hoarse for the people who're going to wring your neck, but you can put your voice to better uses. If we all make music together, it'll be fine. There's always something better than death.'

So they all went on towards Bremen, the old donkey, the useless hunting dog, the mangy cat and the hoarse cock. They had nothing to lose but their lives, so they set off on the long journey to Bremen.

Nicanor would always remember that: the words *there's always something better than death*, Josefina's despair when she was not allowed to find out what Bastuträsk smelt like, the windows that were stuck, and then finally the train whistle.

2

THE BOY'S NAME was Frans Nicanor Markström, and he was called Nicanor. It was an ordinary name. He was found dead one March day in 1973, when he was almost seventy-eight.

I knew him well. This book is not only about him, but it is also about him.

He had curled up naked in bed. That was how they found him. He must have been dead for several days. He was lying on his side, his arms pressed together, and he had stiffened in that foetal position. They straightened him out, putting his stiff joints to rights and closing his mouth. He was very thin and dessicated, like a dead leaf, no, more like a dead withered bat, his arms like shrunken wings, as if on his way into his final sleep he had parried the thought of flying. And then his mouth. In death it had at last opened, that jaw he had nearly always kept closed out of fear of strangers discovering his secret. In death his lips had parted, opened, as if in the end he wanted to let his deformed tongue out of the cage of his mouth.

The diagnosis was pneumonia, or something like that, which was simplest. Three days before he was found, he had appeared for the last time. He had lived for the last five years in a small modernized two-roomer in what had once been a barrack block just north of Selet, downstream, where the E4 crosses Bure River; then late one evening a young girl had gone through the ice, just below the Nyström girls. She had taken her scooter-sled late one evening, gone along the river bank and had suddenly gone through the ice and drowned. She was twelve years old and deaf-and-dumb. They had not even found the body in the darkness, but had been forced to drive the ambulance and some cars down to the river's edge, pointing the headlights outwards and switching them on. All those vehicles had stood there like mysteriously staring creatures from another planet, their gigantic yellow eyes throwing paths of light far out over the river. The firemen were out on the ice, and an inquisitive crowd was standing behind the vehicles.

The boy called Nicanor Markström, now seventy-eight years old, had seen it all from his window and had gone out. He lived only a short distance away. He had been inadequately clad and it was bitterly cold, but he seemed keen to help (though what could he do) and had slithered out on to the ice and gone on down, cautiously, very cautiously, a shrunken black figure wandering into the paths of light from above.

They had yelled at him to go away, quickly; it was dangerous.

And endlessly slowly, Nicanor Markström had slithered back to the shore and up on the river bank.

Thinly clad as he was.

He had stood there far too long, staring out across the ice. They found the scooter-sled, but not the girl: they presumed the body had been dragged under by the current and was now drifting about down there somewhere. That same night there was a sharp frost and the ice groaned and roared for another week before it broke, and when the girl was found, Nicanor was dead.

I was living in Los Angeles that spring. They wrote and told me. Nicanor dead.

That was the end of all our conversations. I would have to fill in the rest myself.

I like to think the drowned deaf-and-dumb girl filled his last feverish dreams. That would be logical. I think I know how it was. She pursued him right through his seventy-eight years, that unknown drowned girl appearing in his dreams, as if she had always been there at the bottom of his life, and had now been raised by the currents and the waves rising through all those years. She was given Eva-Liisa's face, and Uncle Aron's hands, and then at last the puzzle was complete.

That night the ice sang. In his dream, it was like grey transparent glass: the girl rose and sank in the dream, wandering through the grey glass, closer and closer to him. The ice roared, a deep, swaying, echo-filled roar that came and went, the girl rising and sinking in the floating grey glass, and he saw that she had Eva-Liisa's face.

He also recognized the song of the ice. It was all horribly familiar and clear, as when he was a child. There were always white January nights (when the moon was almost white) and it was cold cold cold; the telephone-wires were fixed to the wall of the house, the house that was like a sounding-box, and the wires sang. The song had come the winter after the Bell apparatus had been installed. It was an unprecedented song that seemed to come from the stars, and it came night after night: always when it was cold, roaring as if the wooden house had been a cello and someone out there in the sparkling ice-cold darkness was drawing a gigantic bow across the strings; a thousand years of Västerbotten loneliness singing, wordless and sorrowful, all through the nights.

He lay like that for the last hours of his seventy-eight-year-old life, his limbs trembling and his spindly legs drawn up to his chest, as if to keep in the warmth, lying still and listening to the roar of the ice. It was like at home. One end of the wire was attached to a wooden house in a village in Västerbotten, the other out in space, the wires suspended from dead stars, whining and roaring, the song from space which was wordless and about the wordless.

It was the celestial harp.

In his dream, he saw the deaf-and-dumb girl's body very clearly before him. That night, she drifted deeply, very deeply, rising and sinking against the billowing underside of the ice, carried by the slow current in towards the bay, rising and sinking, her arms raised as if in an embrace. More and more clearly in his dream, he saw that she had Eva-Liisa's features: she came from a mute foster-sister, riding through the water towards him, rocking, dumb and blind and deaf, but full of the lure-calls and prayers and whisperings of the story.

Remember me. Remember me. Never forget me. Do not make my death worthless and useless, I am not mute, we are not mute. Make use of my muteness if you do not hear my words. Tongueless and maimed, like you, make use of me all the same. Mouth open, filled with water, like Uncle Aron's last mute triumphant roar, make use of me. We exist here. We meet now. The water grey as glass, but sounds are heard, and we are many who can cry out our mute cries together.

In the darkness of the night and of his dream, he saw her face very clearly, her body thrust up against the ice, her eyes open and very friendly, dark and slanting like Eva-Liisa's, her face open and friendly and defenceless, and she smiled at him. There was no doubt about it, it was Eva-Liisa's face, the great wound on one cheek was there, just as in the last time he had seen her in Guarany, half her cheek gone. But in the dream it was no longer horrible and frightening, but quite natural. Her eyes were still there, dark and slanting and warm, telling him she liked him, and Uncle Aron, too, and she no longer minded about what had happened. They told him what he wanted to know: that they were all siblings again. The hands rose towards him in a gentle, clumsy, embracing gesture, Uncle Aron's hands, and that was also right and natural.

Everything was right in the end.

Remember us. Remember us, we who had all the opportunities, like you. Don't forget us. Here we are. Mutilated and mute but on our way.

We are on our way.

And he could hear her voice through the water-grey glass, so clearly, and every word she whispered reached him and he could understand. And the sounds from the ice grew and were clearer: the celestial harp was singing again and at last he understood. The wires were attached to the wooden house, stretching out into black space where they fastened themselves, the song very clear, the gigantic bow moving across the strings, the song perfectly comprehensible. He realized he was back in the Westerbotten coastlands. And at last he understood.

3

DURING THOSE LAST FIVE YEARS, I met Nicanor very seldom. This book is not about him, but about the others. I mean that what he told me will have to be included, but not Nicanor himself so much.

I presume that is what he would have liked.

Three years after his death, he acquired a posthumous and at the same time quite anonymous fame that would have filled him with astonishment, delight and anxiety. One of the last times we met was in the spring of 1972, after the closure of the sawmill, in March, clear sun, clean fresh air, and the newspapers had not yet started writing about the pollution from Rönnskär. We went for a short walk across the ice and up by the stacked timber. They were dismantling the frames, and Nicanor, in passing and in a slightly bitter but essentially humourous tone of voice, remarked that people who buy up sawmills just to close them down and earn bloody millions should not be allowed to be involved with our fine young athletes. A youth leader should be looked up to. He screwed up his face into genial creases and smiled at the fantastic sun and the snow stretching endlessly out towards the Bay of Bothnia, and I laughed, but then Nicanor's little sermon happened to end up in a play and, to general astonishment, there was a terrible fuss about it all.

Though Nicanor had been dead for three years then, so he escaped all those strange arguments.

Just as well, too. Nicanor would never have coped with the media. They would never have grasped what he was saying. And if they had grasped it, they would not have understood. The story is too long, whether he had started with the celestial harp, or Uncle Aron's sack of stones, or the rats in Guarany.

So things went as they went.

Nicanor was fifteen when they found Uncle Aron. That was in April 1910.

To the very end of his life, he would remember that sow Anna-Lena Wikström, running all the way from Bommen to Oppstoppet and into the kitchen without even having the wit to stop in the doorway and wait, and how she had cried out in a loud, triumphant, excited voice: *'Them's finded our Aron an' him's swollen right oop! Him's dead!'* And how Josefina had straightened up, turning rigid, her face at once acquiring the disapproving, stiff, troubled expression that always appeared in situations that upset her. She turned abruptly, went across to the wall-clock, opened it, took out the key, would up the clock, stopped the pendulum, put back the key and closed the clock door, all with a grinding, almost ritualistic precision (and it was a ritual – someone was dead) that made both Nicanor and the girl stare at her dumbly. Then she turned round and said to Nicanor in a thick, hostile voice, as if only the two of them were in the kitchen and on principle she refused to speak to their visitor: *Give her a slice of bun-loaf and a bit and tell 'er t'go!*

Josefina had liked her brother Aron quite a lot. Nicanor realized that, suddenly.

So he gave the now slightly less triumphant Anna-Lena Wikström a slice of bun-loaf and a bit, which meant a lump off the sugar-loaf, and nodded silently at her to go. And she went. But while he was pulling on his lumber-jacket and putting on his shoes, he watched his mother, noting the closed, almost savage expression on her face, as if with a huge effort she was trying to stop the skin from splitting.

No emotions or tears. That fitted. She was strong.

He went down to the boom, by which time the corpse had been hauled out and laid down. Despite the cold, the body had not been especially well preserved; it was swollen and balloon-like and the hands were simply grotesque. Especially the fingers. The skin had poured out over the quicks of the nails, and the nails were nothing but small blueish-white hardened pieces of gristle sunk into a pig-like swelling, white superfluous fat and flesh, shredded by water. The flesh on the palms of the hands had been torn to shreds. It was like being hit in the stomach with a sledgehammer. When Nicanor arrived, the circle round Uncle Aron opened respectfully, for now there was to be grief. He seemed to glide towards the body, unresisting, unable to do anything else except stand there staring down, feeling everything like a blow in the stomach from a sledgehammer, and round and round in his head revolved one thought only: *His hands. His hands. His hands.*

It was 24 April, 1910. That was when they found Uncle Aron. He had done away with himself.

Suddenly there was only one single thought in Nicanor's head: Eva-Liisa mustn't be allowed to see. Not this. Not like this. He turned round and ran away from the body and the circle of respectfully grieving people and ran and ran. Up by Lundström's on the Skerry road, he met her. She was swaying along with her green coat swinging round her legs, no gloves, her hands red. She had heard, and wanted to see.

He grabbed hold of her and they fell over. Then they got up. After a while, she tore herself free again, but he caught her. A few minutes later, they started walking back uphill, he holding on to her carefully, very carefully, and she weeping. That's what happened when Uncle Aron was found.

The thing about Uncle Aron was that he did not find women very easy.

He was a short man, born with a crooked body (as if as early as in the act of creation God had assumed he would carry planks in the timber yard and become crooked anyway) and he had a squint in one eye. That eye turned in towards his nose, while the other stubbornly stared straight ahead, giving his face an irresolute expression and actually making him look slightly comical. He had moved from Hjoggböle to the village, and lived in the bachelor barracks on the Skerry road.

He was, as they say, quite a well-known figure.

Nicanor liked him, but nevertheless was always a little ashamed of being related to him. Aron was not stupid, but he did look terribly foolish. No, not terribly, but rather. He never got drunk, or fought, he was always friendly and it was not his fault that he squinted; snuff hardly ever ran out of the corner of his mouth, and he was neither notorious nor ungodly. And yet to Nicanor it was incomprehensible that this crooked, squint-eyed and slighty comical bachelor from the dismal barracks on the Skerry road could have been born from the same womb as his own stylish, dignified and deeply Christian mother, Josefina. True, there were some likenesses (when she was tired, one of her eyes also turned in towards her nose) – but the lack of *dignity* in Uncle Aron seemed to disqualify him from being a genuine member of the family.

There was dignity in the Markströms. But in our Aron – no. When Nicanor saw him after his death, dragged out like a rotting walrus and stinking white and swollen, it was just that lack of dignity he would remember to the very end. Painfully and with delayed intensity, it gave him a feeling of guilt. The rigidly squinting eyes staring blindly up at a totally indifferent sky made Uncle Aron an undignified corpse right into death; it was desperately logical.

His hands like toads'. Hands which most people presumed had never touched a loving woman.

Yet Nicanor knew, yes, he knew that was not so. His uncle lying there like a toad (he had floated up and drifted in amongst the timber and fastened on a boat-hook and the iron had torn the clothes across his stomach, ripping open the flesh) – Uncle Aron had made love. His hands had touched skin, the skin of a woman. Hands against skin.

But first the story of Uncle Aron's hands and Elsa who had an accident and was given a wooden leg.

There were industries along the coast. Industries require people, and there were people in the inland villages. Many of them came, because they needed the money and their holdings could not support them all. So they came walking from Forsen and Sjöbotten and Hjoggböle and Gamla Fahlmark, carrying food-packs and bottles of yoghurt, walking the long way across Bure Heath and down to the sawmill. A few of them managed the walk morning and evening, those from the nearest villages. Others stayed during the week, often lodging with a family for a small but noticeable sum. Every weekend, they went home again. At six o'clock on a Saturday evening they finished work and started walking. At six o'clock on Monday morning they had to go back.

They were nearly all men, the young unmarried men (Uncle Aron was one of them, since he had moved into the village: then he was willy-nilly defined as a young unmarried man and placed in Prästjärnet) living in the barracks.

Some of them were women.

They worked as stevedores, probably the very first female stevedores in Sweden. They stowed poles and pit-props into small cargo boats: the work was considered slightly lighter and therefore more suitable for women and paid about two kronor a day. They were called the pit-prop girls and came from the villages, numbering at the most about twenty.

Most of them were in the thirty-to-forty age range, and they were like anyone else. But a special and probably fundamentally false mythology very quickly grew up round them. They were considered to be up to things. Minor dramas were said to occur in the boats and their morals were considered to be maybe questionable.

Perhaps the seaman's special reputation of being loose-living had been infectious. Anyhow, it was soon said of the pit-prop girls that they obliged the crewmen. Stories were related and the standard tale ran something like this: a captain on a timber boat would come down into the hold waving some money and walking among the women asking if it would be possible to take a little turn in among the stacks. And then how this one or that one (most of them had secret obscene nicknames) would demurely plod after him and the couple would disappear into some sufficiently dark corner, and the old girl then lifted her skirts, leant forward and let the captain drive his gleaming, pulsating, seaman's rod between her willing buttocks.

On this level, the story was enacted purely linguistically. A juicy rod, willing buttocks, and all the usual. The language was full of a somewhat strained, formal and at the same time tittering stiffness, with word-constructions which bore the imprint of having been refined in some of the murkiest corners of the company barracks. A special song about the pit-prop girls also saw the light of day, and was to be perpetuated. It is incredibly long and is sung to the tune of *Amanda Lundbom*, describing in loving detail the meeting between a randy seaman and a willing pit-prop girl. ('But two weeks after the loving/ It started itching a bit down there/ It grew lovely and purple/ From the cunt-rage that it'd been through.') What a word – 'cunt-rage'!

The song was not only long but also moralistic. There were some verses at the end, triumphant verses, one might say, about

50

how the covetous captain 'was sent on a cure' and 'his long prick operated on'; the moral was that he had received the wages of sin. The song had nothing to say about what kind of cure the pit-prop girls were sent on. If one relied on it alone, the impression could easily be one of the courageous female stevedore in Bureå harbour being a kind of Skellefte parish Robin Hood, cunningly greasing her proletarian pussy with gonorrhoea bacteria, temptingly holding up her skirts for the repulsive enemy from southern Sweden, in other words the *Stockholmer*, poisoning his lecherous rod and then, carried along by the enthusiasm of the working masses, triumphantly watching his sorrowful departure to the hospital and the operating table.

It was a legend in several senses, a legend not entirely easy to interpret, but it was certainly not simply an expression of popular vulgarity, and it was also based on the incontestable fact that the women had to work for twelve hours a day, excluding their journeys to and from work, for two kronor. This not entirely meaningless financial reality created a kind of background to the pit-prop song and all those phenomenal words about cunt-rage and purple pricks.

The story of Uncle Aron and Elsa and her wooden leg must be placed against this simple background.

She was from Gamla Fahlmark, thirty years old and a widow with one child (her husband had drowned one July day in Sjöbosand) and she earned her living on the timber boats. She rented a room in Bureå during the week, having left the child with an aunt, and trudged home at weekends. Sometime during the summer of 1902 (it may have been the following year) a stack collapsed on her down in one of the holds. Damned nuisance, as someone said afterwards, the old sows are so careless. Anyway, the good Lord intervened on Elsa's behalf and punished her for her carelessness. She survived, but her right leg was crushed to the bone-marrow and they did not even try to save it, as any idiot could see that that mishmash could not be saved. Medical aid was summoned in the form of a helmsman with some knowledge of first-aid, and realizing an immediate operation was necessary, he chopped off the scraps on the spot (Elsa had fallen into a merciful slumber and was given no opportunity to make a different decision). She was taken to Skellefteå, where she rapidly recovered, then was given an artificial leg and discharged.

51

Her wooden leg was to make her famous. The aunt undertook to look after the child for good.

Pegleg Elsa rapidly became a legend. No matter what her moral standing had been before the accident, after it a landslide in her social reputation seemed to take place. Perhaps because of the wooden leg. Perhaps mostly due to the fact that as opposed to most of the others, she was pious neither on the surface nor beneath it. She kept herself at a noticeable frosty distance from all pastors and preachers, she was always ill when there was to be a parish catechism meeting and was often scolded by the Pastor for this, to which she said nothing, never answering back, but her eyes black and blazing.

She lived off 'going out' as it was called, that is baking, washing and scrubbing for the better-off. Stories very soon began to circulate about her. Nicanor heard several of them.

The one he remembered best and most clearly was one he heard on a summer's afternoon in 1907 while sitting on the boom outside the timber yard. A gang of about ten lads was there, with a large red-haired twenty-year-old from Hjoggböle called Levi Hägglund in the middle. He told them what it was like with Elsa, a fascinating lecture, and they all sat there not daring to breathe in case the narrator should stop. They were sitting on the boom with their feet in the water, Levi Hägglund standing up like an apostle, telling them what he had done with Pegleg Elsa. It was an insufferably long story, full of the fixed stereotypes of erotic fables, 'trembling breasts' and 'wonderful thighs' (though in dialect and with the characteristic shifts between preacher's Swedish and Skellefteå tongue that always appeared when at root it was a fine old familiar dirty story), and then the prick was erect and wham and sweating and panting panting and the culmination.

They listened, full of envy and disbelief and astonishment.

What Nicanor remembered best was Levi Hägglund's magnificent ending. He remained standing all the time, as if addressing a great crowd, gazing out over the sea, his podgy red face shining with devout enthusiasm and triumph, and he kept shaking his clenched fist at his congregation as if trying to thump his incredible knowledge into their heads. He was almost shouting. '*Yuhsee, lads,*' he bellowed with great gravity and a strong desire to convince any possible doubters, '*yep, her was a wimmen, her was!*' He drew a deep breath, seeking for inspiration, seeking for a metaphor so that, like any good preacher, he would convince his disbelieving parishioners, and at last found a good comparison.

'Lads,' he said with great solemnity. 'Ya see, lads, *her wuz so wantin' it t'sap wuz running' in her pegleg!*'

Then they understood.

Later on, Nicanor thought: how dreadful, and how dreadfully unfair. That she should need to. But that was after he had realized Uncle Aron had been there, and had for the first time been allowed to feel the skin of a woman against his hand.

Aron, Aron.

Everything I know about him I have from Nicanor, and sometimes I find it hard to see him clearly. I realize that what happened later was important, that Uncle Aron was never simply a slightly crazy minor figure to Nicanor; that he *expressed* something; and what happened later to Aron and Eva-Liisa was the painful central point from which so much else radiated. What was constantly reiterated in the stories around Uncle Aron was the vague, indistinct sense of his being an unusable person: someone who had been used and had never had a chance.

In Aron's case, the string he played on the celestial harp was fastened to a black spot of anti-matter, far out there. A kind of attachment, but an uncertain one. Sounds came, the song was heard, but was unsingable. Had he lived fifty years later, I am sure he would have been able to grasp my hand and physically show me he had a *place* in life, a touchpoint, a living point of pain. He could, for instance, have been manager of Bure Athletic Club's B-team, every Saturday fixing the jerseys (black-and-white stripes) and buying exactly six bottles of lemonade (in the B-team they had to share drinks between two; the manager and the goalkeeper always drank together), and who he was would have been known and no one would have bothered about his squint and clumsy hands and half-crooked back; or that he had no luck with women.

His existence would have been *worth while*.

That midsummer, Nicanor had gone to a youth festival in Sjöbotten; according to him it was the summer of 1906. Preacher Stenlund was to be the main speaker. He arrived in a trap from nearby Skellefteå and was regarded with the respect and solemnity always shown towards preachers, townspeople and superiors. One should be able to look up to a youth leader, as Nicanor always used to say later. The festival (organized to stop young

53

people drifting off to dances during the midsummer holiday) started at six o'clock in the evening. It started with singing in unison, after which Preacher Stenlund led the prayers. The sermon came next and was over by a few minutes past nine.

Then there was an interval and they had prayer-house coffee with buns.

Some of them decided they would dance round the maypole. That was after coffee had been drunk and before marching into the pastures of Jesus and Pastor Stenlund. It was a bit daring to take to folk-dancing, though the repertoire was respectable: *Maiden Maiden Fair*, *Let Us Dance on the Dew*, and *My Lass, My Lass* and so on. For about ten minutes they swung round in a ring dance with a delighted, embarrassed and exhilarated giggling, and there were several true believers among the dancers.

And they danced.

But at about ten, Pastor Stenlund came out on to the steps (he had a side parting and a heavy, slightly wooden face) – and without a word stood watching the dancers, then raised his hands to the skies and asked the dancers to be still, crying out:

'Listen, young people! Listen, young people!'

The dancing and singing ceased. They all stared intently at Pastor Stenlund, who was frowning in distress. He gazed up at the sky, allowing the silence to deepen, then, nodding in confirmation over the crowd, he made a short speech.

'Listen, young people!' he said in his deepest and most heartfelt tones. 'Ask yourselves something. *How would you feel* (here he paused dramatically, allowing his gaze to glide over the slightly embarrassed faces, young and old, now turned intently towards his own) – *how would you feel if the Saviour returned to this earth at this moment and found you* – (here yet another layer of solemnity and shattered illusions) – AND FOUND YOU DANCING?'

He slowly lowered his head, thoughtfully, then nodded, repeating as if to himself in a quiet but, in the paralysing silence, penetratingly audible voice '*And found you dancing . . .*'

Nicanor was to walk home afterwards. After the interval, Pastor Stenlund had led the singing in unison, then the prayers, preaching again, and then it ended. It was all over now. The youth festival was over. They had not gone on dancing.

It was a long way across the Harrsjö marsh; you had to go round across Bure Heath and Gammelställe, then go down round towards Strömsholm, and the road across the pine-heath was sandy and yellow and terribly dusty. But on this summer night, everything was very still. Nicanor loved this great wide pine-covered plain. It was clean, covered with yellow tree-trunks forming a sea of yellow walls that could be broken through in all directions. It was light. He walked the long way down to the village and when he was half-way there, he heard someone coming behind him.

It was a cyclist. Nicanor saw him from far away, a figure crouching over the handlebars, trying to keep up speed as much as possible, at the same time balancing on the narrower and firmer cycle-path that wound its way alongside the road.

He was riding fast. Even at a distance, Nicanor saw at once who it was.

Uncle Aron.

As Aron was obviously intent on setting up a record of some kind, and his speed was so great, it took him some time to come to a halt. He slowed down with some dignity and managed to stop about thirty metres ahead of Nicanor, then with great care propped his bicycle against a pine tree. He had had his cap on the carrier, and now quickly put it on, as if receiving someone.

Thus clad, he stood waiting for his nephew.

There was something odd and alien about Uncle Aron, visible from far away: in his stance, for instance. He seemed exaggeratedly relaxed, leaning with exaggerated modesty against the tree: but he was no longer shy, only tensely and excitedly subdued, everything indicating that something unusual had happened. Yes, his relaxed stance simply screamed that something unusual had happened. A son of our district, apart from his hard work in the service of the community and the company, had succeeded in the unusual pursuit of . . . succeeded in . . .

Yes, he had *succeeded* in something.

It was something. The nearer Nicanor came, the clearer Uncle Aron's face became, restrained, dignified, quite calm, and it had acquired a quite new and almost *religious* touch. It glowed with modesty and manliness, and as he approached, Nicanor began to have some inkling of what had happened, though deep down he refused to believe it. He *knew* Aron, didn't he! He *knew* him so well. Why should miracles and marvels happen to Uncle Aron whom he *knew* so well?

Aron was still standing in the same easy position. Nicanor

looked questioningly at him, but Aron remained silent, contentedly and stubbornly, and finally a question became necessary.

'What is it?' said Nicanor, breathlessly.

No reply. But a ghost of a smile flitted across Uncle Aron's face,
a sorrowful, understanding, affectionate smile for Nicanor, still
so young and innocent. The smile flitted across his face, his eye
stubbornly and doggedly turned in towards the narrow craggy
bridge of his nose, then swept across the hollow veined cheeks,
with their convoluted network of red and purple tracery, brought
to the surface by the winds and snow of many winters, and then
widened so that the not entirely faultless teeth shone out in a
buttercup yellow grin, for a moment both warm and forgiving.
The smile spread further, culminated and vanished.

Then he answered.

He spoke one single, but expressive word. Looking straight at
Nicanor as one man to another, then slowly raising his right hand
and holding it under Nicanor's nose with the sausage-like middle
finger slightly above the others, staring solemnly and challengingly at Nicanor, like a command between friends, he spoke this one
expressive word:

'SMELL!'

Nicanor bent down, close to the hand, and sniffed.

Everything vanishes with the years. Emotions thin out, experiences are washed away and words no longer exist where they had
been before. But certain smells always remain. For decades,
Nicanor was to remember the smells of that summer's night on
Bure Heath, how they merged into a special and puzzling unity:
the scent of pines and the smell of sand, the prodigiously light
fragrance of the magpie's cry and of heather, the smell of night
and of light, and right in the middle of it all, the slight but
incomprehensibly heavy, plump fragrance of woman, the
puzzling and pungent smell that came from Uncle Aron's
finger.

Yes, woman it was. He understood later it must have been the
smell of a very lonely woman called Elsa Burman, who had been
through some bad times, but who had never got used to loneliness
and had once agreed to share it with another rather unusable
person. The smell of woman it was. It was still there on Uncle
Aron's hand and although Nicanor was too young at the time to
recognize the smell, he knew it. No words were necessary. Aron
knew that no words were necessary. He lowered his hand, the

same expression of proud but modest simplicity still on his face, then he cleared his throat shyly, spat irresolutely, seized his bicycle with his left hand and, without a word, started walking.

Nicanor moved up alongside him and after taking the cycle from him, walked on with it. Something was going round and round inside him; he had to say something about what had happened, but what? Suddenly it came to him, quite self-evidently.

'But what'd tha've said,' he asked, 'if t'Saviour'd returned jist as tha'd put in tha'finger?'

There was no reply. Uncle Aron was walking with his knees slightly bent, his crooked stance making it look as if he were pushing his body sideways ahead of him. He had not heard, or had not understood, or else the words had not sunk in. He was murmuring quietly, singing a song, presumably a spiritual song of lasting value, though he was singing it just because he was pleased.

He's probably pleased I'm here, too, thought Nicanor. I won't say anything else.

Uncle Aron's arms hung straight down, swinging heavily and methodically back and forth as he almost ambled along, apparently adjusting the swinging of his arms so that his right hand would never rub against his body, as if by holding it so far out it would never touch anything, thus never lose the heavy mysterious scent of life and women that Uncle Aron had let Nicanor, as the very first, share.

4

It was Anna-Lena Wikström who had come running and shrieking, *Them's finded Aron! Them's finded our Aron!* There was a certain malice, almost menace in her voice, Nicanor thought. The bitch. Perhaps that was why his mother had asked her to leave with a slice of bun-loaf and a bit of sugar.

He floated up two months later.

He had taken his backpack and filled it with stones. Then he had gone down to the sea, out between Storgrundet and Yxgrundet, his ice-spit in his hand and the sack of stones on his back. And as it says in the gospels that a millstone shall be laid round the neck of the sinner who has seduced one of God's children, so had Uncle

Aron quite voluntarily placed this sack of stones on his crooked back, gone out into the darkness late one evening and, with hideous determination, had made tracks down towards eternal damnation.

They had found the place. The snow had drifted and obliterated almost everything, but they had found eighteen potatoes scattered round the hole. It had taken some time to solve that mystery, but they had solved it in the end.

The day before, they had found out that Eva-Liisa was with child, and as the child had come about in the way it had, so what happened happened. Uncle Aron and Josefina had had a conversation, and that evening he had filled his backpack with stones and left.

It must have been a lonely walk he had undertaken that night. So quiet, it must have been. Not that there was any lack of sounds: it had been blowing in hard from the Bay of Bothnia and the snow was full of sounds. But it was probably rather quiet, all the same. There is no silence like that within the eternally damned in the coastlands of Westerbotten as he walks into damnation. Uncle Aron probably heard no sounds: no celestial harp or pious hymn; smelt no smells, either. He probably did not even recall the night on Bure Heath when he had allowed Nicanor to share the fragrance of woman.

Other things had come between. Now he was walking with the millstone round his own neck and a hideous determination to complete something for once in his life, to do it as it should be done.

When Nicanor saw him two months later, dragged up and stranded like a swollen white toad, torn asunder, a knife seemed to go right through him. He had not taken *responsibility* for Uncle Aron. And while the corpse-watchers stood there with their foolish, inquisitive, greedy faces, Nicanor felt his task ought to have been to *defend* Uncle Aron: and now it was too late.

Suddenly he remembered: Eva-Liisa. She must not see.

So that was why he had run up to the Skerry road and was in time to meet her as she came down in her green coat, her swelling belly before her. He held on to her and they fell. And they got up. She tore herself free, but he caught her again, saying that, for Uncle Aron's sake, she must not do the child any harm.

Only a few minutes later, they were walking home, and she said to him: 'They've cut you to pieces. This has happened to me. Uncle

Aron is dead. People who want to work aren't allowed to. I don't want to stay here any longer.'

Nicanor held her hand, and they walked. That was what happened when Uncle Aron was found.

2

SO THAT THE SIN
SHALL NOT SPREAD

'Whatever torment Jesus suffers,
Tears aflowing, lamenting great,
He our debt of sin doth bear,
The pain that Jesus always bore,
No mortal man hath e'er borne more.'

1

NICANOR'S MOTHER directed the ceremony with great vigour. She fetched the Bible and psalm-book from the bedroom, placed the holy scriptures on the kitchen sofa, showed those of her sons present their places in front of the chairs set out, where they were ordered to kneel: then Eva-Liisa was directed to her correct place, which was in front of the sofa, on her knees, between Father and Mother.

Then all was ready, gathered as they were now for devotions and prayer. In other words, exorcism of the Devil could now begin. There were all to pray together for Eva-Liisa (who was then eleven years old), to pray the Devil did not entangle her in his mesh and that the infection of sin should not spread to the others, the innocent children, to Nicanor and his three brothers. That was what must happen, and it did happen, too.

Eva-Liisa Backman.

She was an alien bird to Nicanor from the very first moment: a strange alien bird with dark hair and brown-black eyes. If he had known what 'love' meant, he would have said: 'I love her.' But he didn't know. And yet she became his beloved big sister. She came from Karelia one June day in 1904, and he would never forget it.

She had a birthmark on her cheek as large as a ha'penny, brown and clotted. Her eyes were slanting and brownish-black, her nails chewed to the quick, the cuticle bitten to the flesh. Her fingertips were often bleeding, her hair black and cut short. She wore a metal chain round her neck, with a locket hanging from it.

In it was a picture of her mother.

No one knew whether it was true or not. The picture of this strange mother was to Nicanor and his brothers a source of constant astonishment, mixed with a secret suppressed respect. They often asked to see the picture, and at first Eva-Liisa willingly agreed. Then she became more and more reluctant. The woman in the little oval locket was middle-aged, seated at a piano against an alpine landscape with a palm tree beside her, and she had, as Nicanor's mother expressed it, a *gypsy look*. That meant she was a trifle exotic, as if a foreigner, or at best a Stockholmer. She seemed to be playing a piece of music, but was staring, almost with hostility, straight into the camera. Her clothes were a trifle showy.

It did not look at all good.

They could imagine what kind of person she was.

'Her's a gypsy,' said Josefina categorically, once and for all. And so it was decided.

In May 1904, Eva-Liisa arrived in Ursviken on a timber boat and that same evening was taken to the cottage hospital in Skellefteå for an appendix operation. She had been delirious, and her mother, who worked on the boat as 'ship's hostess' (it's true; that is what it says in the only existing records) – that is, cook? captain's mistress? female first mate? – had gone with her to the hospital, then visited her once after the operation, returning to the ship, which sailed for Hudiksvall two days later on its way to England. Behind her she left Eva-Liisa, together with a written authorization assuring those caring for Eva-Liisa that they would be fully compensated by the girl's father, said to be a famous scholar by the name of Thesleff, and that he would contact them; to put it briefly, an extraordinary muddle of fairly unbelievable statements. Eva-Liisa recovered, the boat had sailed, as had her none too faithful mother, and a column in the local paper reported her wretched case as she sat chewing her nails, the locket still round her neck; what was to be done?

Nicanor Markström's father, K. V. Markström, brought her home in a trap one June day in 1904. She was to be their foster-child for the time being, and no one knows of any financial agreement. She spoke sing-song Finn-Swedish, was carrying an

61

incredible frilly lace blouse from Karelia in a parcel on a string round her neck, and she said nothing for the first few weeks. Then she was swiftly put to work by Mother Josefina, who with irritation watched her sons ogling her. Then suddenly she was one of them.

One of them. Though not really.

That was when they lived in Hjoggböle: she had to move up into the attic, a large unfurnished attic that was used until October. Then she was given the left-hand alcove. The attic had its charm: the roof-lining nails penetrated through the weather-boarding, forming a mat of nails, and in the summer the attic was almost the best room in the house: airy, solitary, full of silent everything and nothing. As no one really thought she would be staying for more than a month, she was allowed to start there. Then she stayed: the left-hand alcove was not really winter-proofed, but it sufficed and her fur cover was warm. For the first few weeks, she sat up late at night by the attic window, staring out over the sea, the aspen trees trembling cautiously in a quiet whisper, and at three o'clock dawn came rolling in over the sea, the mist lifting and everything becoming sharp and clear.

No birds, a long time until winter. There, in Västerbotten's coastlands, she was to spend her youth.

She often sat there by the window on long summer evenings when the mosquito windows were in and the wind cool and clean. She had been born in Karelia, and Nicanor always imagined she was thinking about Karelia as she sat there. He did not really know where 'Karelia' was, and in his imagination, 'Karelia' was always a kind of mythical landscape, with the features of old engravings or Doré illustrations in the Bible: as if this remarkable 'Karelia' had been a mountain landscape in the Orient, with picturesque waterfalls and singing shepherds driving their herds through the glades.

Eva-Liisa sat there, enclosed in her silence by the attic window in Hjoggböle, thinking about Karelia. She was indeed an alien bird.

And the daughter of a pianist.

Pianist-daughter: Nicanor's mother liked reverting to that description in her more aggressive moments. To be honest, not a single one of the brothers had the slightest idea what a 'pianist' really was, or exactly what a piano sounded like. But the word alone sounded dangerous, exciting and sinful. It was sinfully foreign in the same way that the word *socialist* had both attracted and frightened Nicanor when he had met that fantastic fat man who used his mouth as a worm-tin, the night Elmblad the agitator was captured and taught a lesson, the night Nicanor had sat on guard and suddenly felt so happy, as if he had seen the door of life slightly ajar. 'Pianist'. They knew intuitively that 'pianist' meant someone striking the sinful keys of an instrument which had no place in Christian homes; the ringing tones that arose must be of the Devil, in comparison with the heavenly pious sound that arose from treadle-organs from Petterson & Hammarstedt found in several parlours of the faithful here on the coast.

To have a mother who played a piano was not a good thing. Certain instruments were of the Devil, others of God. Only through certain ceremonies could any of the Devil's instruments be made fit for the service of Christ. Guitars were instruments of God, in most cases.

Saws were, too, undoubtedly.

Handsaw performers were well regarded and respected. They trotted up on to the prayer-house platform, clamped the handle of the handsaw between their knees, bent the blade into a curve and attacked the back of the handsaw with a bow, giving rise to a long and unendurable wailing, a dismal and in every way devout and faithful note. From the point of view of the history of music, social and religious circumstances combined in a unique manner when it came to playing handsaws. Most of the men worked in the forests (in the winter) and knew the instrument well.

But the notes from the vibrating saw-blade declared that the world was a vale of tears, dismal, slow, climbing from one note to the next with supreme effort, quite without intervals; the music *confirmed* that changes in this vale of tears must happen with supreme effort and preferably so slowly as to be unnoticeable. That the vibrato in its trembling violence contained undertones expressing sentimentality, suppressed with great effort, longing for the Bridegroom, as well as longing for Hawaii (the latter was a dream, never accounted for and somewhat sinful), reinforced the total effect. Respectable sentimentality, pain, a drop of Moravian blood-mysticism as well as gloom: yes, handsaw music was of God.

The problem was the strings.

To the strings belonged the violin, and, from experience, the violin was undoubtedly potentially ungodly. By chance, Nicanor once witnessed what happened when Oskar Nyberg's eldest son, to everyone's dismay, was given leave to buy a violin by his father. Oskar Nyberg himself was like most people, a true believer, a pillar of the parish, one of those people on whom God built, if not his temple, at least his prayer-house: he was born in Holmsvatt-net, a smallholder, and had only seven children, of whom five, however, were boys. All of them were devout true believers, except the eldest, who one midsummer had once been seen swearing and playing cards out on Bure Island. However, what happened now was that one of the middle boys, Petrus, baptized after the apostle with the same name, was interested in music and had long wished for a violin. After five years' industrious labour at extra jobs, he had managed to collect up enough money to buy one himself.

The question was: should he be allowed to buy one? Oskar Nyberg finally yielded, but not without conditions.

The promise was given in ceremonial form. The ceremony was performed in Oskar Nyberg's kitchen, witnessed by all the Nyberg children except the eldest (ungodly), by old man Nyberg himself, by Nicanor (sheer chance) and by the preacher Amandus Eriksson from Innervik, who was to lead the prayers that evening and was now functioning as an additional witness or a representa-tive of God, or whatever.

Briefly, this was what happened. Oskar Nyberg first fell to his knees by the stove and led the prayers; he was brief. Then he rose, went across to his son Petrus, who was standing pale and dignified in the middle of the floor and staring in embarrassment down at his feet. Oskar had the Bible in one hand. 'Petrus!' He began his speech in such a powerful voice that his son started unhappily, his eyes flickering round the room, searching for a fixed point. 'Petrus, ah now gives tha leave t'buy a violin. And tha kin play on t'violin, but on one condition. Tha has to promise . . .' – and here his father's voice deepened and the tension in the kitchen rose – 'that must promise *tha'll nivver play at a dance!*'

After the word 'dance', a silence so full of frosty loathing descended that everyone in the kitchen drew breath; but son Petrus nevertheless managed to control himself. He placed his fingers on the outstretched Bible and said in a thick voice (was he moved or nervous?): 'Aye, ah swear . . .', at which Preacher Eriksson from Innervik spontaneously started praying and then concluded the ceremony by taking up the last verses of

Lina Sandell's 'Live for Jesus! Nothing else is worth calling life!'

Petrus was to keep his promise never to play at a dance. Unfortunately he kept his promise to such an extent that he never even learnt to play the violin: whether God's watchful eye or his own lack of musical ability had paralysed him, no one knows, but he scraped away for a few months with increasing hopelessness, and then ceased. About a year later, when he began to realize with some anxiety that his capital was lying unused, he went back to the old man and asked whether, despite his promise to God, it would not be possible to be allowed to *lend* the violin to an acquaintance who eventually might wish to play at a dance (or perhaps the not ungifted Petrus had thought of hiring out the instrument, who knows). Oskar Nyberg would never have thought up such a thing himself and had not considered this alternative sin, so he quickly shuffled out again, fetched the Bible, ordered everyone to their knees, and then made his now gloomily resigned son swear a complementary additional oath before God and everyone present that he would not *lend* this instrument of the Devil for sinful performances.

All this is naturally by the way; but in this environment it was not exactly a *recommendation* to have a mother who had once been a pianist; that is the point. Nicanor's mother, the spiritual and economic head of the family, so to speak, who really decided everything, did not comment much on Eva-Liisa's peculiar family background. But deep down at heart she must have been convinced quite early on that Eva-Liisa's mother, as portrayed in the locket, was so tremendously sinful, whore-like, Stockholm-like, not to mention pianist-like, that perhaps, perhaps remnants of this original sin remained in Eva-Liisa.

Why, she must have asked herself, why why should this sinful infection afflict our house? Neither did it improve matters when poor, innocent Eva-Liisa, in a desperate attempt to explain that this pianist of a mother really existed, declared that the piano business was not really ungodly, adding that her mother had once, as she put it, 'given concerts in Helsinki'.

'Given concerts in Helsinki.' They had never heard the like before. To a smallholder and forestry worker couple, whose forefathers had lived for four hundred years within an area stretching from Byske in the north to Lövånger in the south, these were revealing words. In amongst it all, Nicanor's parents possessed a core of great warmth and generosity, but also an aggressive guardedness against anything remotely like *arrogance*. One should be meek. This did not sound meek.

'Given concerts in Helsinki!'

A sceptical, meek, but critical smile flitted across the faces of the Markström family. At first nothing was said, then the words 'given concerts' started appearing in different circumstances, mostly wrong ones. It started with Nicanor's father, certainly not exactly given to humour usually, testingly pressing his stomach after dinner, humming and hawing, then looking round and saying quietly, almost apologetically:

'Ah, well . . . now ah thinks ah'll jist goo aht to t'privy and gi' a concert!'

His remark was to be industriously quoted and was followed by innumerable similar humorous remarks on the same theme, if in other variants. Eva-Liisa said nothing. Perhaps she realized that what she had said had fallen on the wrong soil, but it all must have seemed very strange to her, this remarkable Västerbotten mixture of piety and sentimentality, sternness and vulgarity, warmth and chill, growth and death.

Puritanism and impropriety.

The customs of this dark land were not easy to understand.

Slowly, very slowly, they took her into their world.

The first time she was to be taken to the prayer-house, both parents were clearly nervous. It was a Sunday towards the end of August and gentle Gabriel Annerscha, so easily moved to tears, was to preach. In his lifetime he became a living legend, and everyone knew he would not be brief. In his gentle farmer's voice he would say '*Lissen now, agin, me friends*' over and over again, as if brightening the grey porridge of preaching with cheerful little berries, and it would all probably take at least three enduring hours.

Would Eva-Liisa know how to behave?

Nicanor's father, K.V., was obviously nervous. The prayer-house was the natural place to produce the much-discussed new addition to the Markström family: the girl from Karelia who had been abandoned, the foster-child said to have a mother who played the piano. The prayer-house was the place for the introduction and the nearest Hjoggböle could get to tribal initiation rites for young girls in the interior of the Congo.

K.V. was nervous. He rubbed his hands together as if he were cold, went out to the water-bucket and drank a scoop of water, glanced covertly at Eva-Liisa as if checking whether her clothing had the correct anonymity, so there would be no impression of vanity, then finally said with utterly artificial naturalness:

'Listen t'me, our Nicanor. Tha kin sit on t'wood-bench and tek our Eva-Liisa with tha.'

There was no need for further orders. Nicanor understood exactly. He was to occupy the wood-bench at the back of the prayer-house as quickly as possible, the bench by the stove, taking Eva-Liisa with him and pressing her up into the corner. Then she would not have to sit with the family the first time. In case anything should happen. Until people got used to it.

In any case, she was placed on the wood-box. And there, in some way, she was to remain.

Isolated, but close to Nicanor's side.

2

UP TO THE VERY END, he dreamt about her.

She rose up through his old man's dreams and she was both a girl and an old woman. They were not nightmares, just very matter-of-fact and natural, Eva-Liisa's face as it had been when she had come to them, and the wounds he had seen when he had last laid eyes on her. Both at the same time. And with her eyes wide open, not accusing but questioning. In his dream he knew with absolute certainty what the answer was, but the question, what was that?

Something to do with the rats in the pit, too.

That was something from their early years. Nicanor and she had dug a pit behind the shippon to catch the rats. They had dug a hole and lined it with boards, nailed properly, with metal at the top. The rats were flung into it, very much alive and kicking, for a while. It was both fun and rather terrible at the same time. Sometimes they threw down potatoes and waste to prolong the fun and so that they could watch them fighting. The worst and best of it was their civil war, while they still had the strength. Nicanor and Eva-Liisa just sat there very quietly watching it happen.

There was nothing malicious or nasty in their expressions. They just sat there, on those pale yellow summer evenings in the coastlands of Westerbotten, watching curiously, thoughtfully and innocently the rats fighting their meaningless civil war below. They presumably thought: *we aren't rats*, and the hungry rats went on fighting their meaningless civil war, their own struggle against their own, cannibalism and hatred and desperation, under the interested and curious gaze of children, registering and observing it all.

In his dream, her eyes seemed to ask: why didn't we learn from what we saw?

Or perhaps: what should we have done?

3

No one really knew how it first started. But suddenly it was there. Suddenly she started stealing.

Not much. No more than a tiny indication.

Perhaps it is wrong to say a 'tiny' indication. There is a difference between theft and theft. Two öre is not always two öre, one krona not always one krona. The first and only remaining account-book kept in the Markström household stems from 1908, when they had moved to Oppstoppet; it is painstakingly kept, in pencil, and if the income for the year is added up (it is done! and correct!), it turns out that Karl Valfrid Markström, never a reluctant worker, earned 864 kronor during that year. That was all, the rest breaking down into part-time work: received from D. A. Markstedt in Kåge, 12 days at 4.20. (Excellent! Did he go home for the weekend?) Sorting at the timber yard, 103 hours at 32 öre. Less good, though nearby, so he could sleep at home. January, altogether fifteen guard duties at the sawmill at 2.94 per duty – lucky! Lucky! Who else had income from December to February, when the mill was often closed? Expenditure is noted down equally precisely.

And so on, and so on. 864 kronor in one year. Theft was nothing to joke about (not theft at that level).

Theft was the glimpse of the snake in the grass. Sudden cold in the air, and fear.

At first it was a two-öre bit when she was to go shopping. It was not discovered to start with, but then Karl Valfrid counted through it all with his usual Lutheran conscientiousness and came to the astounding conclusion that two öre were missing. There must have been an accident, but to make sure, he asked Eva-Liisa where the two-öre bit had gone. She denied all knowledge of the whole matter, but so violently, so angrily and so quickly, it was obvious to everyone that she must have taken the coin. They asked her before God to tell the truth. And then, suddenly, without really being pressed, she ripped off her left shoe, took out the two öre she had hidden there, flung it on to the table with a bang and ran out.

They all looked at one another, dumbfounded. Not only stealing, but also showing anger.

Stealing was a mortal sin, as was showing anger. It was quite clear that this would cause a sensation in the family. This poor soul had been taken in by the Markströms, a goat among the sheep, and even then she didn't hesitate to steal. There must be a bad streak in the girl.

Only eleven years old and stealing.

The tone of the celestial harp became more muffled, moaning sorrowfully and desolately over their confusion like a cow far from home. What should they do? Her father was said to be some kind of grand gentleman who wrote books about gypsies. But her mother was a pianist. Perhaps her father wasn't up to much, either, for that matter.

Eva-Liisa said nothing. For a time they said nothing, and only a furtive tear in Josefina's eye betrayed that she was suffering agonies over the icy breeze from the burning fiery furnace of eternal damnation (that was how they all thought, much too hot, much too cold) which had touched them.

Eva-Liisa said nothing. She often looked at Nicanor with her dark unfathomable eyes, but when he asked, she had nothing to say. She sat looking out of the attic window, as if through everything she had suddenly observed the blossoming countryside of Karelia, the waterfalls, the shimmering alps, the shepherds with their flocks of sheep and the grass, so fresh and green.

A week later she was caught at it again.

Josefina Markström fetched the Bible and psalm-book from the bedroom, placed them on the kitchen sofa, and thus they were all gathered together that Sunday afternoon for devotions and mutual penance.

69

There was a genuine master-of-ceremonies built into Josefina Markström's tall, strong, gangling body. She was especially skilful at this type of small domestic mass. She planned it thoroughly, knowing exactly where the chairs should be placed, who should kneel where, which psalms were to be sung, how the atmosphere was to be made to rise and fall into the sinful consciousness. At first a few heavy sighs on the Sunday morning, while they were eating *blöta*, a small trembling crease round her mouth, preferably a tear (furtively wiped away), yet another tear in the middle of the day, an atmosphere of growing oppression and melancholy. Best and most correct was not to have dinner at all (hungry stomach, shrieking and rumbling, a feeling of physical penance!) – and, of course, firm control so that the atmosphere should not be disturbed by inappropriate jokes or comments or songs of worldly origin.

It was a remarkable sight. They were all kneeling, the floor as usual feverishly scrubbed clean, bearing witness that this was a family which did indeed live in great poverty, but was by God both pious and (to the same extent) not in the least mucky.

There they knelt. There was nothing ecstatic or Seventh Day Adventist (an insult!) or anything in the slightest bit frivolous about Nicanor and his family. They were perfectly matter-of-fact, fairly emotional, but with no trace of ecstasy: they knelt there, austere, collected, refusing to break out into hallelujahs or any other such Stockholm worldliness and superstition. They were composed and concentrated, and as Mother Josefina, seconded by her husband, read prayers and discourses in antiphon, the solemnity and sorrow deepened.

Eva-Liisa in the middle of them all.

They sang hymns from *Songs of Zion*. This was the Free Church's own hymn-book, based on communion, and they used it because it had a very special touch of unpretentiousness about it. It was simple, piously proletarian, with undertones of Moravian blood-and-tears mysticism; with its mixture of popular appeal, objectivity, mystical suffering and unpretentiousness, it was advantageously different from the more stuck-up, rigid and somewhat *Stockholmish* psalm-book. '*Songs of Simon*', as it was commonly called, *didn't pretend* to be anything special, wandering with small unpretentious and unaffected steps along the narrow path to Heaven, with no boasting.

Songs of Zion belonged in their world; the haughty *Book of Psalms* did not

So on this remarkable Sunday afternoon, they broke into a hymn from *Songs of Zion*. *'When I look on me, I must be fearful, For I am but, a poor lost sheep,'* they sang, Josefina's shrill, lamenting voice leading her kneeling flock of sheep. Her voice was distinguishable in quite large congregations, famous locally for its penetrating shrillness, and also for the candour with which she used it. Her voice rose shrilly, sorrowful and plantive between the notes with that gliding relentlessness common in the Västerbotten vale of tears, audible right through everything, dismally penetrating. *'When I look on thee, then hope awakens. To seek the lost, dost thou go,'* she sang in a hopeless, accusing voice, with Father K.V.'s voice droning behind, like a rowing-boat chained to the stern of a tramp steamer and bobbing about helplessly in its wake. Their sons mumbled discreetly along with them, none of them having sung this hymn very often. It had presumably been sought out and chosen especially for the qualities of its text, the mistress-of-ceremonies feeling deeply that the hymn was speaking directly to the thieving little pianist-daughter from Karelia. But the tune was difficult and unfamiliar. Josefina's devoutly shrill voice ploughed on ahead while the others tried to listen and form a sentence out of the notes.

'When I look on me, I do but tremble, For I with sin and guilt am laden.'

Leaning right over the chair, apparently devotedly pious, Nicanor was looking tensely and watchfully at Eva-Liisa out of the corner of his eye. She was leaning forward, her eyes closed, her face closed, as if contracted, her lips moving faintly as if making a genuine attempt to follow the hymn, although deep down she neither wished to, nor was capable of it. *'When I look on thee,'* they sang in a choir as harmonious as a flock of birds, *'Thou canst shed all fear, For thou, Lamb of God, all my sins dost bear . . .'*

Then Josefina Markström led the prayer.

'Dear Jesus,' she said in very *Swedish* language, and in the very *Swedish* voice she sometimes used on formal occasions, which in the children's eyes always gave what she was saying a more serious and sacred character. *'Dear Jesus, thou canst see that our Eva-Liisa hast sinned. Turn to her in thy mercy and wash away her sins in the blood of the Lamb. She has stole and tooked money*

71

and not told t'truth and thrown a two-öre bit on to t'table (and almost at once her language started to careen, as if Skellefteå dialect were a refractory horse reluctantly allowing itself to be curbed by the sacred Swedish and only to start with allowing the formality of the situation to decide the level of language) *and now we pray to you dear Jesus in your mercy take pity on this child who is such a sinner and who scarcely understands what she has done this unhappy Sunday* – here there was a pause while Josefina wiped away the first tears and at the same time clearly took the opportunity to adjust, so to speak, her prayer language so that it should be more in keeping with the formal speech commonly called 'Schwedisch'. *'Dear Jesus,'* she went on with the same tremendous solemnity and righteousness, *'thou seest us poor things here in our need, and tha probably knows 'tis hard to get t'bread to go round all thems mouths, but us works from morn to night and sweats and labours and is wretched, but dear Lord Jesus, thou knows we doesna steal here! Nay, Lord Jesus, us hasn't never stole, ever, never has we stole!'*

Then Nicanor heard through the paralysing stillness of the kitchen how Father K.V.'s thick cheerful voice ingratiatingly seconded her: *'Nay, 'tis true, never has us stole!'*

And from his place by the chair slightly farther back, Nicanor saw that Josefina Markström was weeping. Yes, really weeping, no false crocodile tears, but genuine tears of grief or anxiety or agitation. He had seen his mother cry many a time, but this time her tears disturbed him in a special way. He felt a desire to console her in her grief and at the same time to scream out his opposition to the tears and prayers and hymn-singing and the *stillness* in the room. But with tears pouring down her cheeks, she continued praying more and more fervently, apparently trying to assure Almighty God that the Markströms had never never been thieving people or laid hands on other people's private property or stolen money. *'Dear Lord Jesus,'* she went on after a brief pause for breath, *'thou cares for us all in thy goodness, thou looks on them who languish in this sinful world and are evil, take this girl Eva-Liisa in hand and lead her right so she does not be like those what goes away and takes others with them and lives in sin. Thou knows Dear Jesus the seeds of sin are down inside her heart and do not let the sin from our Eva-Liisa infect the innocent children.'*

At this point remorse and anxiety seemed to afflict Nicanor's parents right in their very hearts. Mother Josefina started sobbing

72

loudly, and in the silence of the Markström kitchen her sobs were like thunder in their ears. A moment of bewilderment followed, then Karl Valfrid Markström joined in, rather hesitantly, in a more mumbling and grunting way, so it was hard to tell if he was crying or praying for the damned. They were both weeping, partly from grief over Eva-Liisa and her thieving, partly from anxiety that the seeds of sin would blow from this young but already depraved seedcorn to their own children and implant evil in them. So she finally concluded with *'and so Lord Jesus thou Saviour of the world, thou will surely help us so the infection of sin doth not spread to our Axel and our Daniel and our Nicanor, dear Jesus, tha's so good see to it that them doesn't be like Eva-Liisa. For the sake of our blood, Amen.'*

'For the sake of our blood, Amen!' echoed her husband with triumph and relief from down by her right side. 'Amen, amen, amen, amen,' scattered but loyal, came from the boys. Then there was a brief silence, and Mother Josefina looked urgently at Eva-Liisa.

'Amen,' at last came from her, too.

'Now us'll sing "I Am a Guest and Stranger" in unison,' announced the head of the household in a slightly tardy attempt to appear as the real leader of the ceremony. He launched into the hymn slightly too high, and the others followed him in somewhat strained voices.

They sang, and Eva-Liisa sang. 'For here on this earth,' they sang, 'sin is everywhere. Giving to all that's beautiful a strange and alien air. Though it cannot condemn, then self-condemned it is, it can still torment me. But it shall not be there.'

That is what they sang. 'Home, Home, My Beloved Home' they sang. All five verses. And then it was all over.

They were all strangely silent that evening.

Nicanor did nothing much but look at the others, as if wishing to know something but not daring to ask. What he saw was nothing extraordinary. His father was working laboriously at his account-book, noting down the week's income and expenditure; the account-book was an exercise book with lined pages and a blue cover, and he was to keep it all his life. Josefina was silent and sitting as if she had a stiff neck, which she usually did when she was tired or upset or angry or sad, though it was not usually possible to find out which. They were given supper, heated-up rye-porridge and cranberries, and they were all given equal portions. Josefina's face as she served out the food was stern and dismissive. She moved awkwardly, apparently wishing to observe the most meticulous fairness in sharing out the food. Nicanor suddenly wished that she would pat them on the head when they went to bed, pat them all, Eva-Liisa as well, but he knew that never touching one another was part of their morality.

So it was food and justice and goodnight and a rigid face and that was that.

He could not sleep that night. He got up and fetched a drink of water from the bucket. His mother and father were asleep on the extending sofa in the little bedroom; through the kitchen door he could see Josefina's averted face, soft in her sleep, childish as she slept with her mouth half-open in what looked almost like a confused, happy smile. He stood still, breathing carefully so as not to wake anyone. She was sleeping, like a child.

He stood there for a long long time, trying to understand something. Then he decided, and cautiously climbed the attic stairs, opened the door, and looked in at Eva-Liisa's bed. The light from the summer night shone softly across the floor and he saw she was sitting up in bed, the cover drawn up to her throat, the pillow behind her. When she heard him, for a moment she looked frightened, then she turned her head slowly back towards the window.

She's remembering Karelia, he thought. Those alpine valleys and grazing sheep.

'Eva-Liisa,' he whispered.

She did not reply. As he sat down cautiously on the edge of the bed, he saw that her face was quite swollen, and then he understood. Her head was leaning against the bedpost, but her eyes were turned to the window. She was no longer crying.

He had no idea what to do.

He had nothing to say, and anyhow she would not reply. The window was fly-spotted, the aspens outside trembling imperceptibly, and her gaze seemed to have fastened on something out there, never to turn back towards him. 'Eva-Liisa,' he whispered, and the silence persisted.

He looked round.

There was a food-cupboard on the other side of the room; suddenly he slid down from the bed and slipped quietly across the floor. Just inside the door was the sugar loaf. No one was allowed to touch it, but he picked up the tongs, clipped off a piece, then closed the door.

When he was back on her bed, she looked at him.

Her eyes dark, fixed on him steadily. By fixing her eyes on him, she seemed to be wanting to force out an answer, or to ask for something, but her eyes, watchful and swollen, did not surrender, and he no longer believed they were in Karelia looking at alpine flowers shimmering against the snow. Hair short, nails bitten, Lord in thy mercy see to it that the sin does not spread so that the boys do not become like her. For our blood's sake.

She scarcely seemed to be breathing, as if asleep, but her eyes were open.

He stretched out his hand, holding the lump of sugar towards her. She did not move. She did not take it. He waited for a long time. Outside, the aspen leaves moved softly, trembling gently, but all he saw was Eva-Liisa's eyes, very dark, watching him. He held the piece of sugar closer to her, right up against her mouth. Lips dry, slightly bitten; she was breathing. Close, close to her lips, he held it. And then, at last, he saw her lips part almost imperceptibly: and with the very tip of her tongue, she carefully touched the rough white surface of the sugar-lump.

3

A SMILING MAN

'At the same time we testify to
our gratitude
for the extremely humane treatment
we have received as always
on your part,
signed with true esteem.'

1

NICANOR'S FATHER often said during those years that the vote was
not worth much. God gives a voice to the poor.

He thought it was complicated, retaining the right to vote,
because if he couldn't pay the tax, he had no vote. K.V. reckoned
things were simpler with God. He remembered, for instance,
when he had been summoned to a meeting in Skellefteå. He had
had a vote then, because it had been a good year, and it was an
important matter they had to get through. He went. The Bure
Company then sent an agent who voted away the whole of
Skellefte rural district. So K.V. went home and would have
nothing to do with it all; he had been out-voted. It was all quite
clear, wasn't it? It was difficult keeping the vote, and if one had it,
it was worthless. That was tough. He had struggled hard to get
that money together. He had hauled coarse timber home and
hewn it down to small square blocks, and they wanted a
tremendously fine surface on those squares. They couldn't be cut
on the cross; the edges all had to be straight. They had a board that
was at the correct angles and they used that as a pattern. They
called one kind *bålingar* 9"9; if he kept to the thumb-measure of
the top-end and the foot-end of it, then he got well paid. A krona
or so. He had to haul it a long way, too. He had owned a horse
then and drove all the way to East Fahlmark, where he rested with
the horse, and then on to Bureå. Then down to the building in

Bureå where the measuring was done. They had thumb-measurers and first measured the foot-end and then it was checked that no edge was crooked or narrow; everything had to be absolutely perfect. And so pernickety – if there was the slightest bit wrong with a square it was thumbs down. But if the whole square was crooked it was just chucked aside, and he wasn't even allowed to take it home. It was thumbed away. Outworkers like him were treated like dirt.

The socialists, then? He knew what they were like; they ranted and raved, but they didn't understand what things were really like.

He would give his vote to God. Every poor soul had forty thousand votes with God. You couldn't be out-voted there, and neither were crooked timber squares thrown aside as useless waste. That was what he thought. God is just and before his judgement seat you weren't thumbed-down.

They were always being told that God had given them the land, and they also saw that the land was growing.

They could all see that. The coast was rising. Västerbotten's coastland was growing slightly larger year by year. They knew it was not the same for everyone. It was not so for the heathens in the Congo, nor for people who had to live down south. But Västerbotten was constantly growing bigger. Another century came and the rising went on, despite the fact that some people had prophesied that the year 1900 would see a turn, and the land and the coast would again sink into the sea, as if Westerbotten were a giant sleeping on the edge of the sea, slowly breathing in so the water had retreated, then breathing out so the water returned. But the waterline obstinately persisted in creeping back. A centimetre each year. Step by step, step by step, the land grew. And if God took all those endless pains, if he showed such endless patience, why shouldn't they themselves do the same, and show the same patience?

Was it the water decreasing, or the land rising? They did not know. But God pointed the way. Infinitely slowly, the land was rising. That was how it had to happen. Changes happen slowly. One centimetre per year.

Here in the coastland of Västerbotten, they grew up.

*

There were few workers, but more peasants.

The word 'smallholder' sometimes seemed to be far too grandiose and anything as magnificent as 'farmer' or 'freeholder' was almost unheard of. They had two, three, sometimes four cows, never any more. They could hardly live on that, so there had to be something else. In spring, summer and autumn, there was Bure sawmill, and stevedore jobs in the harbour. The stevedore teams usually came from the villages and kept together in gangs. The sawmill closed in winter and the workers were sent home, the harbour froze over and there were no more stevedore jobs, leaving nothing but timber-work in the forests. That was a way out, as long as the snow was not so bad that the horses gave up or froze to death.

So most of them went from place to place. Small peasants and part-time sawmill workers or stevedores or timber workers. The villages lay within a five, ten or fifteen kilometre radius of the sawmill, and they mostly walked, then cycled; it all became a technical matter of transport. It was important to transport yourself, if you reckoned on survival.

Were they workers? Many of them thought of themselves as peasant farmers. Many of them didn't really know. They worked, that was all.

His name was Karl Valfrid Markström, born in East Hjoggböle, and he had four children, of whom Nicanor was one.

Nicanor's first memory of his father was in connection with the pearl-owl, Tengmalm's Owl, to use its proper name. She was on the roof, and K.V. took down the shotgun with its blue-painted stock and brass fittings to shoot the owl. Then he fired. The owl fell. But when they went to fetch the owl, Nicanor could find no pearls in it at all. He started crying, but his father told him there were no pearls in it and that was only the name of the owl.

Otherwise, his father was often away. He might come cycling home from Bureå late in the evenings, fifteen kilometres across Bure Heath, sweating profusely, and he always started by saying, '*Lissen, our Muther, gi' me half o'juice.*' Then he would drink it all, slowly, straight down. But he never asked for a whole glass of juice. One always asked for less than one needed, for blessed are the meek for they shall not *inherit* the earth, no things wouldn't go that far, but the meek and humble are not uppish and know what's what.

The villages were always very small, making discreet little gaps in the forest cover.

Otherwise the forest covered everything, floating like a smooth, light green coverlet over everything, running down to the coast and drowning in the sea. Then right through the forest ran faint little ribbons, cycle tracks or roads, between the villages.

The villages were always small, and poor, but they seemed to have a permanent attraction for their inhabitants. Once the people had settled there, built houses and become domiciled, they stayed. They and their children lived on, generation after generation, through the centuries. They remained small peasants and timber workers, they married within their class and within their village, or within one of the neighbouring villages; families stayed put, the pattern never breaking. It would be possible to place the point of gigantic pair of compasses in the middle of the village and draw a circle of eighteen miles' radius and if one then went back three hundred years, the whole family and all its branches would still be within that circle.

They lived there. There they would stay, until the moment the Saviour returned and raised them up to his kingdom. Thus was it prescribed.

'*Tha'll be a real man!*' he often used to say approvingly to Nicanor. '*A real man!*'

In the villages, the women decided everything.

It was simple to see why. Man and wife had a common place of work, the smallholding. There they worked together from morning to night, from early-morning milking to the last bedding-down of the cows. But during the periods of the year when the husband had to leave home, when there was work in the forest, or in industry, or on the boats, then the wife was left alone at home.

She was the only authority to hand.

There were some advantages. It was wretchedly hard work, but it also meant power. The husband left at five o'clock in the morning, did his day's work, came home dog-tired in the evening, just able perhaps to help muck out for half an hour, then eat and fall into bed. When he worked in the forest, he might be away for long spells. One winter, K.V. worked at hewing timber in Malåt-räsk for three months at a stretch, and they saw him twice during that time. But the women stayed behind. They decided everything,

79

about cows and children, milk and churning, mucking out and evening prayers, patching clothes and ensuring the cows went to the bull, buying food and administering the household finances, handing out chastisement and praise, being the highest religious authority and in the lead at family missions to the prayer-house.

Sometimes, at regular intervals, the husband came home from work. He was dead tired and what had he got to say, what was his view: he was a wage slave and brought money to the household. The periods he spent at home and worked on the land were the best. Then the children could observe two professional working people who were equal, although the wife's word actually carried the most weight.

Sometimes, at regular intervals, a rumour reached them from the great outside world that there were said to be societies in which the woman stayed at home doing nothing at all, simply staying at home, dissatisfied at not having a say (amazing!) and wanting to be free and all that.

It sounded peculiar. It must be a country far, far away, a peculiar country where the women didn't make decisions, and where the women didn't work, and where they even allowed themselves to be oppressed and subdued. It must be in the Congo, or down Stockholm way, where the heathens were Swedish. Though within the parish there was actually an example of that kind, of what they called a flibbertigibbet. She was the Pastor's wife. She did nothing but idle about at home. She was regarded with a mixture of respect, astonishment, contempt and confusion. It was presumed she represented the modern woman.

The coastline rose. The sleeping giant was breathing.
Slowly.

In 1324, the regency of Magnus Eriksson issued a proclamation, according to which 'those who believed in Christ or wished to be converted to the Christian faith' were invited to settle between the Skellefte and Ume rivers. They were to be allowed to take what land they wanted, and enjoy temporary exemption from taxes.

They poured in from Hälsingland.

In 1413, the population of Västerbotten was reckoned to have risen to about nineteen hundred people. In the middle of the 1500s, this domiciled population had grown to about fifteen thousand. In 1413 Skellefteå's population was only four hundred and fifty. There were a hundred and fifty people in the parish of Lövånger. In 1543, there were fifty-four villages in Skellefteå, three hundred and fifty households and altogether two thousand six hundred and thirty-two people. In the town of Skellefteå there were nine hundred and forty-five people, four hundred and fifty in Bureå.

In 1700, Skellefteå parish had three thousand inhabitants in fifty-seven villages. In 1900, Skellefteå had a population of nineteen thousand nine hundred and fifty-two domiciled.

Small ploughed patches of cultivated soil in the carpet of forest. Small villages along the coast, patches concentrated along the river mouths. Patches of ground, marshes, a few mountains by the coast.

That was what Elmblad called the dark lands.

But it was rising.

It was alive, rising very slowly out of the sea.

2

K. V. Markström had a small highly unspiritual streak in him. He sang songs, not hymns or psalms, but songs. Totally worldly songs. Josefina disapproved officially, but nevertheless found a certain pleasure in listening to them. Then she sharply reproved her husband with a bright, elated expression, so that he would know he would be allowed to do it again.

'*A piteous song for you I'll sing,*' he sang in a shrill, jolly voice. '*Tears to eyes old and young it'll bring. I canna help it if my song's a poor thing, 'cos it's about Klemensnäs sawmill men.*'

The song was well known and K.V. often sang it. Nicanor knew it off by heart. It was the song about what was called the Klemensnäs letter.

Sometimes it is easy to forget that the situation earlier on was different.

The opposition was different; the tendency to start up conflicts or avoid conflicts had rational foundations; the schisms had grown up so naturally and had existed there for so long; the opposition was so much better organized and had different methods of punishment and reward; respect for authority was based on painful and concrete experiences. One did not capitulate, because capitulation was pleasurable.

The famous betrayal had its roots, but those roots did not really turn out as one expected.

Nicanor's father included the Klemensnäs song in his repertoire.

The song stemmed from a small incident, in its way illuminating both the spiritual and union development of the Skellefte district. It occurred in 1894, and the song was written the same year. The situation had its origins in a crisis and was the result of long, patiently-borne suffering. Year after year, incomes had gone down, dismissals occurring capriciously and dictatorially. Everyone was living at subsistence level, and the situation north of the river was even worse, as unlike the workers on the south side, the people there had no hope of help from relatives with smallholdings in times of need.

It was a wretched situation. It was the norm. The norm had finally become unendurable.

They decided to take action. One May evening in 1894 a meeting was called in the forest. About a hundred workers went to the meeting, gathering in a glade, all of them indignant. After half an hour of the usual grousing, a plank and two stones were procured, a small platform constructed, and the first speaker called for silence. They were all perfectly well aware of what he told them, but on that chilly May evening they nevertheless listened with great attention. It was all about semi-starvation and misery and the very real threat of a reduction in wages.

It was, witnesses related later, an exciting evening. Many of the men had stood up and said there was no longer any point in working. A man called Bengt Lindkvist had said that if a man can't live off his work, then he might as well stop working. We'll starve to death anyhow.

After about an hour, they were agreed. A resolution was to be drawn up. Their rage was great. A half-hour break was taken and three men were detailed off to compose a letter to the company. It became the famous Klemensnäs letter, and the protest meeting of those hundred angry Västerbotten workers resulted in the following remarkable, and later on, almost classic document.

The Manager.
Mr O. V. Wahlberg.
Skellefteå.

As the new sawing instructions have to some extent increased the square-sawing over and above the old instructions, and our earnings have thereby been reduced proportionately in comparison with those of the previous year, we respectfully request whether a levelling could not be made to anticipate this reduction? We would be very grateful for any accommodation in this case in ways that you yourself may decide upon.

At the same time we testify to our gratitude for the extremely humane treatment we have received as always on your part, signed with true esteem.

Klemensnäs, May 1894.

Then came a long list of names. A worker called P. G. Sjölund was the first to sign. So far, all was well. The letter was written, read out, signed, and the list of signatures was very long.

After that, the real difficulties had arisen.

They were all agreed that the letter was very good, the formulation successful, the tone just right. There was nothing jarring in it. But when it was asked whether anyone in the crowd would be willing to hand over the document, difficulties arose.

At first there was a long, oppressive silence. Standing on the plank between the two stones was the man who had written the document, waiting with the paper held up in the air. There was a long, oppressive silence. A man from Yttervik had then asked to speak and was of the opinion that the most natural thing would be for the first signatory, Sjölund, to take it up to the gentlemen. Sjölund was utterly dismayed and vehemently rejected the suggestion. He had a wife and family, and if the company started thinking he had initiated this 'union' action, he would certainly be dismissed.

Then the kids would starve to death like kittens. He said no, and it was clear that he also meant no.

The man on the plank, the one holding up the paper, changed hands.

Other names were suggested. Oscar Henriksson. Per Lindgren. E. A. Fällman. A. Degerstedt. N. H. Markström. Wiktor Sjölund. A. Renberg. A. Lundström. N. Nygren. They all refused.

The man on the plank lowered his arm.

It was now very late in the evening and several of the workers had already left. They had to get up early the next morning.

The man on the plank sat down.

The Klemensnäs letter is written in ink in firm, careful handwriting, then folded into three. It still exists. The wording of it does not seem to be exactly revolutionary, but no one dared hand over the letter.

It has to be remembered that the situation earlier on had been different.

'*At the same time, we testify to our gratitude for the extremely humane treatment we have received as always on your part, signed with true esteem . . .*' Was it worse in Klemensnäs than anywhere else? Not at all. On the contrary, really. The company was run on a rather less authoritarian lines than many other similar companies. However, the fear was real. The situation was different.

Two hours later, they had still not found anyone to deliver the document. In this way, the action ran out into the sand. The letter was never delivered. Nevertheless, the letter became known and discussed, because a song was written about the event, and often sung: '*Talking of this and that, that is easily done, but doing something about it, that is not such fun. For unity's rare and far from well among Klemensnäs mill personnel.*' The moral of the song was simple: the song ridiculed the cowards who had first started shouting their protests against starvation wages, and then had not dared deliver their protest.

Agreement had been unanimous on all matters: the normal situation of exploitation and semi-starvation was unendurable, the document should be courteous, the letter was correctly formulated, and no one dared deliver it. Complete agreement had reigned over it all.

The coast was breathing. It was rising; it was alive. Opposition takes many forms.

K. V. Markström had, as has been mentioned, an unspiritual side to him: he sang songs. He also used to sing the Klemensnäs song, in the uncertain assurance (not malice, but almost) that the honoured workforce of Klemensnäs mill had acted *wrongly*,

84

uncertain whether it was the original action or the breakdown of it that had been wrong. Had the cowards come to their senses? Or the foolhardy become wise? Or the courageous cowardly?

K. V. Markström probably did not know. He just sang, *'If seven should meet a raven, the eighth finds nowt but a crow. If nine go ahead, the tenth'll go back. That's a definite and positive fact.'*

That is what he sang. For unity was rare and not very well. Not only among the honoured Klemensnäs personnel.

3

A PHOTOGRAPH of K.V. and Nicanor still exists.

It was taken some time in the twenties, after his cerebral haemorrhage. Nicanor kept it faithfully, for he remembered so well when it was taken; as already mentioned, *after* his father's cerebral haemorrhage. First they put K.V. on the pot to get him to squeeze out as much as possible (wise after previous occasions), then they stuffed paper into his underpants, hauled on his Sunday trousers (rather tight as he had put on weight during his illness), washed him properly, combed his hair with water in a vague attempt to make him look like a handsome pensioner, then they had dragged him off to town. In the photo, Nicanor is standing at his side, dead solemn, pop-eyed, as if holding his breath. He was.

The sleeves of Mr Markström's jacket are rather short and he is sitting on a chair with his son's hand resting on his shoulder in a fatherly way, he himself with his hands in his lap (his own lap, that is) in a pose meant to indicate calm and confidence (maybe safety in God?) but which to the more critical eye of posterity looks more like an obscene gesture, as if he were up to some kind of two-handed masturbation and had discovered too late that his member had gone. But he is sitting on a chair, his backside firmly seated on several issues of the Skellefte newspaper, Nicanor at his side.

The background is the correct one, an alpine landscape.

Much later, Nicanor was often to return to this photograph: he could sit staring at it for hours, as if beneath its yellowed surface there was a secret which would finally be revealed. The mystery was his father's face. The grotesque thing about that face was how closely it resembled the face of a living human being. The eyes, after his stroke, were indeed empty, as if they had been torn out and replaced with china knobs, and the face was indeed slightly crooked. But underneath that crooked, dead, porcelain-like, rigid face, a smile is emerging, a faint echo of life: as if the surface had died, but deep down underneath life still existed, as if he had stubbornly refused to give up this life completely, a life that for a decade or so had been dead and destroyed. Nicanor seemed to think he could distinguish a sign of life in his father's almost extinguished face. They had dressed up a living corpse, propped him up with newspaper in his backside and a poker up his spine, placed the alpine landscape in the right place and clicked, but this living corpse, far away from the kingdom of the dead, was still trying to send a message to him, a message evident in the almost dead face that was supposed to be that of Karl Valfrid Markström.

The frightening thing was that this dead person was trying so hard to resemble a living one. Nevertheless, he hadn't been successful.

K. V. Markström was scarcely five foot tall, and in 1924 he had a stroke and died three years later in the faith of his Saviour. It could be said of him that for only a few short minutes of his life, and then quite unconsciously, he had acted as a bridge between the Saviour and Socialism.

Quite unconsciously. But all the same.

The only newspaper he ever read was the conservative *Skelleftebladet*.

No battle-cries encouraging revolution ever reached him through that organ. The fact that workers at sawmills in Dal and Sandö had gone into battle for the right to form a union and had gone on strike, at which the sawmill owners, Kempe, called in strike-breakers armed with revolvers, was carefully not even mentioned, like the Sandö riots in May 1907, after which the three 'Sandö men' were sentenced to eight years' imprisonment each for assaulting a policeman with a stick. No, that world was not his, nor was it *Skelleftebladet*'s. Vague echoes of a workers' movement growing in the Skellefte area had indeed reached him, but these echoes had muffled and threatening undertones, as with card-playing and swearing, and the gate was shut, the outer door closed, to keep the sinful infection at bay.

86

Yet Nicanor's father took a lively interest in the world about him, only partly satisfied by the columns of the Skellefte paper. He loved reading out aloud the absurd little reports from the outside world that filled the paper's columns. He liked sitting on the kitchen sofa, just below the ticking wall-clock, reading in a loud, plaintive voice, while the family observed an attentive silence.

He especially loved the short little reports from Stockholm the editor of the paper for some reason considered suitable for the little people of Skellefte valley. '*Major-General Baron Ernst von Vegesack*,' he would read out in that plaintive voice that ought to have been reserved for Lutheran sermons for this vale of tears, '*celebrated his eighty-second birthday on Wednesday. For almost a year he has been unable to leave his apartment, but despite severe rheumatism and other afflictions, he still spends most of the day fully clad in his rooms.*'

That was all. The whole report. Nicanor's father fell silent and lowered the paper. The wall-clock ticked and he glared challengingly at his listeners, but what could they really say?

Yes, what?

Whenever he looked at the photograph of his father, Nicanor always seemed to hear an echo of that voice. The living corpse in the photo had a message for him, pathetic and frightening, echoing down through the years. Was the message of great importance, or meaningless? He almost expected the figure in the photo to move, put his hand inside his trousers, take out the newspaper that filled his underpants, pulling out the only slightly crumpled *Skelleftebladet*, unfolding it, and then, while the smiling alps and the faithful family watched him encouragingly, he would read in a steady, warm voice: '*For almost a year he has been unable to leave his apartment, but despite severe rheumatism and other afflictions, he still spends most of the day fully clad in his rooms.*' And then Josefina would at once be at his side, as usual, nodding with her most appreciative, positive and imposing expression and muttering, prompting him: '*Goodness . . . oh, my . . . just think of that . . . fully clad in his rooms . . . goodness . . .*'

What respect! And that hitherto never kindled fury, that understanding. That hitherto never kindled fury.

There he sits in that photograph and is dead, and yet is not.

*

Many people probably regarded Nicanor's father as an oppressed and rather weak man, even in the days before his stroke. That was partly true, too: he was certainly no ranting domestic tyrant. His build was against him, and his small sinewy body placed against his wife's tall, craggy, not to say muscular figure, sometimes made a comical impression. But it would be quite wrong to dismiss him as a hen-pecked and anonymous grey wage-slave.

Nicanor never ceased to be surprised by his father. True, his whole character was faithful, devout and adaptable, but he did not lack elements of bizarre humour, which occasionally, by being so precisely placed in totally wrong situations, could produce utterly insane results. Nicanor would never forget the Good Friday afternoon when the family was at home in the kitchen, waiting for that day of suffering to draw to a close. Subdued by the atmosphere, they were talking together in quiet voices about the frivolity of the world and the coming pleasures of the heavenly kingdom, at which his father, saying that there were some good sides to the vale of tears, with a somewhat dreamy and absent-minded look, remarked quite inconsequently: 'Well, t'best o'worldly pleaures is t'sit in t'privy!'

Worldly pleasures! Incredible! If only he had at least meant it as a joke – but it was his unfathomable gravity that would sometimes shatter those around him. Nicanor could not regain the expected degree of grief until Easter was over. K.V.'s way of suddenly and quite unblasphemously linking worldly troubles with heavenly jokes became almost famous: even in the 1970s there was still a story circulating round the Bure district that stemmed from Karl Valfrid Markström. It is not really all that funny, just typical. It came from the time when he was working in the timber yard, carrying planks. They were being stacked. The men were all extremely annoyed with the management, who, concerned about space, allowed each stack to get so high that the layers finally became horribly laborious to get up. The men had to place each plank up against the stack, like a pole, and reach right up so that the man on the top of the stack could catch hold of the end. Every time the foreman passed, they looked at him questioningly, but he gave no orders to start a new stack.

In the end, K.V. snapped. The next time the foreman came round, trembling with agitation and in an injured, indignantly moody voice, he said:

'Lissen, man, be us meant to tickle t'soles of t'Saviour's feet afore us'n gits to t'change stack?'

He was a serious Christian and a smiling man. This came to play a certain part. The smile on his face only appeared on certain social occasions, but then it came. He smiled, or 'grinnered', as they usually said in Bure language. Some people called him our Grinner-Markström. Anyone who had seen him at divine worship knew at once why, and it was also this eccentricity which caused him quite by mistake to act as a union-stimulating bridge between the Saviour and Socialism.

This is what happened.

The Markströms' place in the prayer-house was on the left. The family always floundered in with Josefina in the lead, then the boys in single file, their father in the rear. They sat down on the left-hand side, three benches from the front, next to the aisle.

Then Karl Valfrid sat there enjoying himself.

Perhaps that is expressing it too brutally. But the fact is, he smiled. He smiled slightly or looked radiantly joyful, and *all the time*, too. He sat down, placed his hand behind his right ear like an ear-trumpet, as if extremely anxious to snap up every syllable of the Christian message soon to be produced, then started listening.

He sat leaning forward, as if about to take off, fixing his eye intently on the preacher, smiling broadly.

Some preachers, especially guest-speakers unaware of local circumstances, had been shattered by the sight of this beaming man sitting so close to the front, and had ground to a halt or prematurely ceased preaching. Yet there was no evil intent behind his smile, nothing underhand or ironic or mocking. And first and foremost (which one could perhaps believe) there was absolutely nothing foolish about his smile.

It was just that he was *following* with such tremendous attention, putting his whole soul into demonstrating his loyalty. He hung on the lips of the preacher, syllable by syllable, taking every nuance, every statement, as an excuse to smile tremendously warmly, openly and *encouragingly*, as if every second counted to drive this preacher of the word on towards renewed peaks of joy, assuring him that he should continue, that they were all with him, that they were *united*.

It was just that his approval, the well-meaning nods and confirming smiles became, so to speak, confusing and sometimes directly absurd when the message was not made for joyful smiles. To be truthful, that was quite often, not to say mostly. '*And then the flames of eternal fire shall afflict those of you who are dead in spirit and do not obey the Saviour's admonition to fall to your knees and accept the commandments,*' Preacher Byggström thundered indefatigably from the pulpit. But should he glance in the direction of Karl Valfrid Markström, he would find nothing but a glowing and eagerly nodding face, appearing to lap up this manna from heaven like syrup. '*But say to yourselves you are the generation of vipers and shall be eternally damned to burn in the eternal fiery furnace,*' he added smartly, in that incomparable mixture of high Swedish biblical language and dialect so often served up from village pulpits. But that did not break K.V., who now appeared to be almost carried away by joy and delight. '*False prophets, liars and hypocrites all!*' the preacher attempted, now seriously disturbed, speaking straight down at the glowing face, only to be met by eager nods and intimate, understanding winks confirming one hundred per cent that things were indeed that bad and that this was really encouraging.

Day of Judgement sermons; some preachers devoted more time to evangelism than to the commandments, and then the effect was not quite so terrible. But his permanent beaming smile became directly offensive when the preachers were preaching the Passion Story.

It was generally considered that the Passion Story should be listened to in tears. Nicanor's father was of a different opinion.

'*They crucified him, and two more with him, two criminals, one on each side, with Jesus between them,*' the preacher began in his deepest, most sorrowing and subdued voice from up in the pulpit. But no. It seemed to be hopeless. They did not even have to raise their heads, bowed in grief as they were, or glance sideways at their father for the whole family to *know*. Yes, they knew beforehand, and the preacher knew, and everyone knew. Karl Valfrid Markström was inclining his head towards the ear-trumpet of his hand, smiling his indefatigable beaming smile, nodding hopefully and cheerfully, his whole sinewy body apparently taking an active interest in the bearer of these unhappy tidings, the preacher, who at the very sight of him appeared more and more inclined to retreat into himself and remain there. But he courageously continued: '*And the soldiers came and broke the legs of the first, then the second of the two being crucified with Him'* – excellent, nodded K.V.'s glowing face, on which no Passion message could dim the joy, or cause even a glimpse of melancholy to cast a shadow on his brow.

Some of the preachers had at last learnt their lesson. They knew they should never, never glance down to the right, for if they did, Karl Valfrid Markström's craggy smile would always be there, like a wild hambo dance at a funeral.

The remarkable thing was that the smile appeared only during sermons, quite unconsciously and mechanically linked with the melancholy or joyful tidings of the Bible, and as soon as the sermon was over, his joy came to an end. Briefly, it only needed the preacher to close the sermon with a resigned *Amen*, and K.V.'s smile would be extinguished, the flame of joy blown out. It would not flare up again until the next service. When the infinitely slow lament was taken up (Josefina in the lead, high, shrill and gliding! thus was the pain of Jesus, like none before on high) the father's face was quite ordinary again, closed and grey, as he mumbled in an embarrassed way through the song, always in the shadow of his wife, who like a tone-deaf Valkyrie was leading the singers on in a great shrilly lamenting surging wave, or however it could be described.

And to crown everything, he was not even aware he was smiling.

Not in the slightest.

Nicanor's mother evidently often heard snide little remarks about our K.V.'s 'grinnering', and at least once Nicanor heard her complain to her husband about his insane prayer-house face.

His father could make nothing whatsoever of it.

'Tha mustna sit thar a'grinnerin' at t'preacher,' she said, sharply reproachful. His father was deeply hurt and innocent.

'Tha's lyin',' he said, with unusual ferocity. 'Ah doesna sit thar a'grinnerin'! 'Tis a lie!'

'Tha dost!' she said categorically.

'Ah doesna!'

'Tha dost,' she snapped back with all her authority and refusal on principle to be contradicted. He glowered at her, reproachful but resigned, seeing an approaching storm and deciding not to persist further in the matter, but to beat a tactical retreat.

'Uhuh, tha sez so, does tha?' he said, in a moderate and

concilatory tone, moving towards the door. But out on the steps, he was again struck by the gravity of the accusation, and looking up at the sky to draw strength from it, he swivelled round and, thrusting his head inside the kitchen door, declared in his most obstinate and categorical voice:

'Ah doesna grinner!'

And so on. And so on. As far as Nicanor could remember, they stood there for about an hour, with intervals for his father's tactical retreats and strategic counter-attacks once she had had time to calm down, and they went on at each other (*Tha grinners! Ah doesna! Tha dost!*) without ever getting anywhere.

They were no doubt both acting in good faith.

Many people considered that this prayer-house smile was K. V. Markström's way of hiding that he was asleep and could hear nothing; that his smiling jaws were locked like the legs of a sleeping horse, and his eyes were closed although they appeared to be open. But that was not actually the case. There were other feelings involved.

A smiling man. It is a matter of interpreting the smile.

In October 1906, Johan Persson, a sawmill agitator, travelled up to northern Westerbotten.

Afterwards he wrote a report that is still to be found in the archives of the Workers' Movement, and it makes sad reading. He arrives at Skellefteå on the first of October and leaves the town five days later without having been able to achieve anything. It is the same old story. All attempts to find meeting places are in vain, everyone is frightened of the pastor, who runs everything, religiosity is strong, all attempts at organization useless. Black Josef's sewing-bees flourish here and there, worst in Sävenäs, the blacklegs working hand in glove with the company lackeys, and every attempt to organize unions within the Confederation of Trade Unions proving futile. Strike-breakers are innumerable, or rather men who would be willing to work in the event of a strike. The only struggle really being fought was the fierce struggle by the employers for the rights of strike-breakers to work during labour conflicts. In Byske and Piteå, local sections of the Swedish Workers' Association, supported by the employers. Blacklegs everywhere.

Hopeless.

Towards the end of the report, however, the tone becomes more optimistic. He describes a few more or less unsuccessful meetings he had had in the villages along the coast during those five days, then summarizes: 'However, it is certainly worthwhile working for the cause of socialism through powerful agitation even here. There is much to be gained for the future. There are workers in these backward areas who greatly encourage our speakers, and do not capitulate to the ministry. At a meeting in the *Bure* sawmill community I saw them smiling and nodding fiercely in support of our cause. So it is advisable to continue the work, and continue our agitation, if it is not to be a long time before even the workers and peasants of Westerbotten begin to come over to us and abandon their anxieties over the colour red.'

Johan Persson was right. His optimism, however, was based on a definitely, fundamentally, somewhat isolated case. He had held a meeting at the crossroads between the Skerry road and the coast road, where he had stood on a milking stool. It was evening, drizzling slightly, but otherwise pleasant and warm. Only about ten people had come, just counting the adults; about thirty children were there besides. He had spoken about his cause. His audience had not seemed very interested. They had gazed at him with their heavy stony faces and when he had addressed them directly and asked them questions, to try to spur them into action, they had responded with nothing but silence. He had gone on to speak of the equal value of human beings and had spontaneously quoted St Paul: 'Here is no Jew or Greek, no slave or freeman, no man or woman . . .'

From this point onwards in the speech a man in the crowd had suddenly shown considerable positive interest in the speaker. At the words of St Paul, he had cupped his right hand round his ear, as if to hear better. The man was rather small, but from his evident interest and generally positive attitude, Persson saw that here was a strong interest in the cause of socialism: all he had to do was to arouse it. The man had cupped his hand like an ear-trumpet behind his right ear, leaning forward as if about to take off, staring intently at the speaker, nodding encouragingly over and over again and smiling broadly, indicating that he had understood, and that he approved.

This was decisive for Johan Persson, and he based his report on this fundamentally positive incident. After the speech, the man had vanished before Persson had been able to contact him. But he had been there. It had been drizzling slightly, and not many had come, but if he looked down to his right, he could see one worker who supported his cause: a friendly, glowing, beaming man, quite clearly approving.

That was where to start.

4

A MATTER OF
VITAL AND PRIMARY
IMPORTANCE

'As our reputation as workers
is to us a matter of vital
and primary importance,
we are unable to sacrifice it
to someone else's discretion.'

1

IN MAY 1907, a tugboat called SS *Nya Trafik* came into the
harbour at Bureå. It was from Ursviken. A man called Seth
Lundmark was helmsman. There was also a man on board called
Zetterkvist: he let it be known that they were looking for willing,
responsible workers to work down south. Wages would be
good.

From Bureå, Ursviken and Frostkåge, they found altogether
eighty-four men who declared themselves willing to go. Among
them was Uncle Aron. They left in May 1907, and returned in
September the same year. Aron was taciturn about his experiences, but he did tell Nicanor that it had been for those willing to
work, to replace the work-shy. The work-shy were people who
didn't want to work, but went on strike. The boat had been bad,
too. They had had to stay on deck both ways, and it had been very
cold. They had had to find their own food and there was only a
bucket for toilet purposes. There was no life-saving equipment.
Many of the men had been seasick. On the journey home, a young
boy from Frostkåge, only fifteen years old, had been taken ill with
appendicitis. He had died. Earnings had been small. It had been a
miserable time, with people often shouting at them, although they
had done nothing but be willing to work. It had been unpleasant,

and then sheer misery on the way home. He had been very cold.

He had had very little to say and he was reluctant to go into detail. But one thing he did mention, and that was that people in the south saw things differently.

They had stood there shouting at them. Sometimes he'd felt almost ashamed. They'd yelled at them.

Who?

Uncle Aron never said. But it was clear that down south they saw things differently. He came back in September 1907, and in some way or other it was obvious something had happened.

Uncle Aron had once been given a butter-tub. He never used it, but from it rose a slightly sour, peculiarly pleasing smell.

The story of the butter-tub is connected with what happened later.

2

One late autumn evening in October 1907, the very first of a long series of meetings was held. It was held in Petrus Lundgren's kitchen in Oppstoppet.

That same summer, the summer of 1907, the whole Markström family had moved to Bureå. The meeting was to start at eight o'clock in the evening. It had been pouring with sleet and rain all day, leaving the ground in a very bad state because it had not frozen. Before the business of the meeting had begun, a number of comments on various subjects were made. Frans Lindström said that the Pastor should have been warned and asked to be present. Per Nyström spoke of the need for protection from rain in the timber yard. Amos Jonsson criticized the state of the roads in the village. Amandus Wikström recalled an event during drainage work in Holmsvattnet – at which the meeting began.

The kitchen was large, with plenty of room for fifteen people. They had not bothered to borrow extra chairs, but four men sat on the wooden sofa, two on the draining-board and three on chairs, while the remaining six sat on the floor. Petrus Lundgren's wife, as always, had her floor newly-scrubbed, which was why they had all taken their shoes off in the porch. To the left of the built-up fire was the water-pail and scoop. One after another, they arrived.

At a quarter past eight, they could begin.

Nicanor went with his father. A few minutes later Uncle Aron arrived.

It was not the first time Nicanor had been in Petrus Lundgren's kitchen in Oppstoppet; on the contrary. Since they had moved, he had been there several times. Petrus Lundgren was a cousin of Josefina's, and it was pleasant to have relatives. The Lundgrens were pleasant, and the especially pleasant thing about the Lundgrens' kitchen was that the mail was laid out there. This is what happened. The mail-bag came to Lundgren's at about six. They opened the sack and placed the mail in small heaps on the long bench, one for each household. It didn't matter if anyone came too early. If you came too early, this is what happened. When Nicanor went in without knocking, because you didn't knock, he went and stood just inside the kitchen door and waited. Then our Elsa Lundgren would say: '*Ah, there tha is, young Nicanor, sit thasel' dahn.*' Then he sat down on a chair by the door, or else on the sofa. There was a difference between paying a call and fetching the mail. If he were fetching the mail, no one took any notice of him. Then it was nothing special. If he were paying a call, then our Elsa or someone else would ask if he'd like some coffee. Then you weren't supposed to show too much enthusiasm and to refuse politely. Then she would persuade you a little and bring a cup of coffee. Then you had to say, '*Ah, tha shouldna've gun to t'trouble*'. Then you had to sit down by the door and drink the coffee: a cup of coffee and a bit of something. Quite alone. Meanwhile you had to chat a bit. If you were only fetching the mail, there was no coffee. Then you could sit and kind of look at the Lundgrens in general. It wasn't necessary to say anything then, either.

In that way, Nicanor knew the Petrus Lundgrens very well.

Sometimes, when he had gone there and they had wanted to show off a little to their newly-arrived cousins, quite well-meaningly, he had been offered food as well. Then he was a little more difficult to persuade. This was due to two things: partly you were supposed to have manners and be more reluctant when it came to porridge rather than coffee. It was food, after all. And partly because he didn't like the old man, our Anselm, the maternal grandfather in the family. He happened to have some

97

kind of sores or eczema in his hair, and was always scratching his head. It was probably eczema. He had white hair with a kind of brown cap underneath, and it was trying to sit at the same table when he was eating. First he would eat some porridge, then he would put his spoon down, thoughtfully look up at the ceiling and gloomily start scratching his scalp with his right middle fingernail. When he had collected up enough, he took down his hand and ate the proceeds up.

Nicanor was sensitive about that kind of thing and didn't like it. Neither did the others, most likely, but they had probably got used to it. Otherwise, Lundgren porridge was always good, rye-porridge, poured out on to a flat plate, where it stayed for a moment to set sufficiently. Then you took a little molasses (they couldn't afford syrup, but molasses was also good, although usually meant for the cows) and poured it into a hole you'd made in the middle of the porridge. Then you took a little porridge and a little molasses and a little milk and ate. Sometimes there was butter in the middle. He liked their food, though the old man's middle-finger exercises were difficult to become reconciled to. So he usually refused politely.

You could say you'd already eaten, or something like that. In that way, he knew the Petrus Lundgrens very well.

Uncle Aron was the last to come.

No one had ever seen so many people in the Lundgrens' kitchen before, and it might well have been a parish catechism meeting. But as the organ hadn't been dragged out of the little room there was clearly no question of that. Neither did the congregation look particularly pious, although that well-known true believer, Amandus Wikström, was there, though without his cows in tow.

Later on, it became known that he had taken the initiative over the meeting, which, to say the least of it, was surprising. Yet he had always had a' reputation of being a strangely unpredictable man. He was a true believer. He could break in cows. A rumour went round that he had helped Hjalmar Gustafsson, the agitator sent up from Umeå the previous year, by giving him a night's lodgings when he was having difficulties canvassing in the village and was being threatened by the agent's men. Our Amandus Wikström was small and sinewy, a clever man in a way, famous locally for his hand with cows. That arose from the days when he worked with his father in Ljusvattnet. He had then (this was in the eighties) practically succeeded in taming the cows so they obeyed all kinds of orders. He was spoken of as the cow-tamer in Ljusvattnet and distance and the years had exaggerated the legends about what he could do. According to the wildest legend, his cows could be made to stand up on their back legs, scrabbling about in the air with their forelegs, while they bellowed the theme of 'Our Lord is to us Almighty', all to order. Other sources, more in accordance with the truth, reckoned he had taught them to obey commands, so that his herd looked like a well-trained school class as it came along with our Amandus in the lead.

Then he had abandoned cows and dressage and farming, and become a worker. But the legends persisted. A number of classic sayings were also attached to his name. The best known came from the days when he had worked as a labourer in Fahlmark and had once by mistake put the manure tubs so near the shore that the spring flood had taken them. From that situation arose the saying: 'If tha lives t'nother year, *which tha no daht will*, then tha shouldna put t'shit-tubs neath t'waterline.'

Perhaps anyone who has not grown up in the coastlands of Västerbotten will find it hard to understand, but this was widely considered to be a drastic and controversial statement. The controversial part was the rather self-confident statement *which tha no daht will* – i.e. survive to the following year.

This was something fundamentally extremely presumptuous. This poor but brazen sinner presumed he would live until the following year, without at the same time calling on God's mercy and forgiveness to ensure He realized that one lived only by His grace: without that one could not reckon on a single night, at the most an hour. Talk about defying the Gods. Amandus Wikström became known from this utterance (which became legendary and thus reinforced) as a Västerbotten Prometheus, whose infinite pride was unmatched, and to crown it all, his prediction was fulfilled. He survived not only that first year after the catastrophe with the shit-tubs, but quite a few more. To many people's mortification, he turned out to be a tough bastard who never received his punishment, at least not on earth in this life. Josefina Markström always acquired lines of tight discerning piety around her mouth whenever she spoke of him. 'If tha lives t'nother year, *which tha no daht will*, tha shouldna put the shit-tubs neath t'waterline.' No doubt the Good Lord was good, the lines round her mouth said. But for some people it was especially fortunate

His goodness was so boundless. Otherwise he could have taken his shit-tubs with him directly down to a particularly hot place. Which she did not say.

Yet it was right there, in Petrus Lundgren's kitchen, that this notorious Amandus Wikström got up, cleared his throat, asked for silence, and made the tensely awaited introductory statement. Here we has, he said matter-of-factly, some of the workers of Bureå gathered together to discuss the present situation. There was no intention, he hurried on to say, to forestall any protests, to form a trade union or any other affiliation with the Confederation of Trade Unions. But, on the other hand, it was within the bounds of possibility to form a workers' association. The annual subscription would be reasonable and nothing ungodly would occur.

This was what was now to be discussed. The reason why the question had arisen was that the Company appeared to be inclining towards reducing wages. Yet again. And that the situation was very bad. They all realized that. So there wasn't all that much to discuss.

He spoke calmly, factually, almost impersonally, for ten minutes, and then handed over to the meeting.

At first it was rather quiet.

Once they got going, however, a great deal was said. The discussion was candid in every way. They talked about wages, and what you could earn. They also talked about what you got for what you earned, and the chances of survival. All this was thoroughly discussed. 'It was proposed,' they wrote in the minutes later, 'by Jöns Thoresson that the association should have a name, and the meeting agreed that the association should be called Bure Independent Workers' Association.'

It was almost eleven o'clock when the meeting ended and they all left for home.

It was done. They had decided. A Workers' Association had been formed. A minority headed by Frans Westermark had requested it should be stated in the rules that this workers' association was a workers' association and not a trade union, and that it was clearly stated that it was based on Christian foundations, but after two lots of voting, it was decided that this was unnecessary. That the Workers' Association was not a trade union was obvious, as it was not affiliated to the Confederation of Trade Unions, and neither had they any intention of affiliating to

100

the Confederation of Trade Unions as none of them was in the slightest bit interested in being affiliated to the Confederation of Trade Unions, and had anyone insinuated anything about the Confederation of Trade Unions, anyhow? No. As far as the Christian foundations were concerned, opinions varied. Some of the men considered the Christian foundations so obvious that it was unnecessary to commit that to paper, and anyhow there was nothing unchristian, bad or hostile to the faith in a workers' association. Others thought these Christian foundations more doubtful, as there were perhaps members who were either not true believers or who considered the question of faith nothing directly to do with the Company reducing wages at the sawmill.

They agreed to postpone the question until future meetings.

Nicanor, Aron and Nicanor's father walked up the road together on their way home. Aron seemed to be strangely upset; naturally, he had not said a word the whole evening, but now he carried on a long, surprisingly fluent and on the whole incomprehensible and confused monologue concerning his views on what he had seen and heard. 'So t'strife's coming here now,' he mumbled to himself as they trudged home in the dark. 'In Hudik 'twas bad and here in Bure 'tis on its way. There'll soon be strife all o'er the world. God's the worker's best friend, them says' ('Aye,' said K.V. routinely at his side. 'Aye, 'tis true, that it tis.'), but what difference did that make. He was speaking straight out into the rain and darkness and Nicanor and his father listened in bewilderment to his sudden outburst. 'Down south down Kramfors way them was fighting, and now 'tis comin' here.' An he'd bin up to Pite and bin beaten up there (that was surprising news to Nicanor, but his father seemed better informed and simply nodded in confirmation in the dark) and now they was comin' here. He'd bin called blackleg and strike-breaker and bin hit on the jaw although he'd only had – work.

Yes.

Yet he had said nothing at the meeting. He hadn't wanted to, as several of them knew he'd been up to Pite.

'Pite?' said Nicanor, straight out. 'Did tha go to Pite to work?'

There was no making out what Uncle Aron was saying, but he was anxious about what was coming, that was clear. He turned off down towards Skäret, but before the squat, crooked little figure was swallowed up by the mixture of driving snow and rain he concluded the longest and most confused monologue of his life

101

in a loud and heavily significant voice, saying to Nicanor and his father:

''Tis like what our Dad said, when Preacher Andersson held t'prayers from t'shippon roof, an' had fallen. Then him said an' it were true: *Them what gits oop on t'shippon roof, them may fall int't'muckheap!*'

They stared at Uncle Aron in astonishment. His face was frozen and rigid in the wet snow, his whole face distorted, his squint eye turned stiffly and dumbly inwards. He had said what he thought. Then he set of back home to the barracks and was swallowed up in the darkness.

3

THE NEXT WEEK, a man in the company office called Tiblad summoned Uncle Aron into the office.

Tiblad was the company manager. He was extremely friendly and asked Uncle Aron to sit down, then started on what became a long conversation. He indicated he was pleased to have sensible and reliable people to deal with, and that the workers of Bure were mostly reliable. He said Uncle Aron was one of the reliable core of workers. Finally he asked Uncle Aron how he liked working at the mill.

Uncle Aron had been sitting there meekly all the time, saying nothing, and at those last words he started, squinting at the manager and affirming that he liked working at the sawmill. The manager appeared calmed by these words, and smiled in a friendly way at Uncle Aron, who then, slightly uncertainly, but then more and more relieved, smiled one of his buttercup smiles back at the manager. The conversation continued, and a few minutes later the manager remarked that he knew about the meeting and had heard that an independent workers' association had been formed at it, hurriedly adding that this was none of his business, but he knew Uncle Aron was one of the workers behind the project. Before Uncle Aron had time to explain, the manager held out a pacifying hand and went on to declare his general attitude.

After having explained his general attitude, he asked Aron to explain his. As Uncle Aron started speaking, stumblingly and hesitantly, the manager took over again and asked Uncle Aron whether he would be willing to repeat this visit now and again, and tell him how the organization was getting on.

Aron eagerly accepted this invitation. The manager explained, however, that it might be just as well if no one else knew of these conversations, which were only to clear up any misunderstandings and to pass on impressions. After thanking Aron thus for his visit, he gave Aron a pack of butter.

The pack was wrapped in paper. Aron cautiously raised a corner and looked. It was butter. Quite a lot of butter, nearly two kilos. It glowed. He looked questioningly at Tiblad, who nodded in confirmation.

Butter.

That night Nicanor slipped into Eva-Liisa's room. She was sleeping lightly as usual, like a bird, and when he touched her hand she was already awake. They whispered together in the darkness for a long time, the wet snow driving against the window, and he could see her silhouette. They went on whispering for a long time.

He sat on the floor. He wasn't cold.

4

AT THE SECOND MEETING in Petrus Lundgren's kitchen, on the evening of 12 November, K. V. Markström was elected Vice-Secretary of Bure Independent Workers' Assocation. About twenty people were present, though only one of them with the Company's silent approval, but no one else knew about that except one person. That was Uncle Aron.

Afterwards, they all went quietly home through the still white snow. The upper regions were silent and white, with no celestial harp singing; everything was terribly still, as if waiting or expectant.

The minute-book was kept at the Markströms' house, and later on Nicanor preserved it. The minutes were written in a large red exercise book with blue lines, and the first page has gone, probably used as toilet paper or something similar. But otherwise everything remains.

All there is to do is to read it.

28 November. 'The question of what to do about rates in the Timber Yard arose, for the situation re increase in earnings is said to be bad. After a short discussion, the association decided to request a rise of 10% on piece-rates. One man, namely Oskar Bergman, was asked to calculate what that would be on the different rates.'

And from the same meeting: 'Suggestion from a member of the association that Walpurgis Night, the evening before May Day, should be work-free. The association decided to request this. The question of not working on Sunday evenings was brought up. This question was shelved indefinitely.'

There was some discussion on this point. The man to bring up the question of work-free Sunday evenings was from the villages; he knew what it meant. And anyhow, he added, they shouldn't have to work on Sundays at all. In principle, they were all in agreement. But when Elon Wikström had spoken later, he had many of them on his side. He said it was a bad and ominous sign that the association already seemed so *dogmatic*. From the outside, it would look as if they had become big-headed, self-important, and so on. To have aims was one thing, he said. To make demands in insistent tones was quite another matter. The truly watertight way was to show restraint. This had all then been sharply rejected by some of the others, who also considered that, faced with the coming winter sawing, they should demand a rise in the hourly rate from 27 to 30 öre.

The suggestion was in itself not considered unreasonable. But the word 'demand' was objected to. They agreed not to appear dogmatic, and that the resolution should be postponed.

Petrus Ehnmark asked that his dissent be recorded in the minutes.

The next paragraph, however, in this context, is puzzling. It says: 'The question was brought up about whether the association should continue its activities. After the matter had been discussed at length, it was decided to continue the activities of the association.'

This was the second meeting of the association. Then they went out into the immense white stillness of the night, the snow falling soundlessly, the fiery storm of revolution far, far away.

Yet that was how it started.

Or rather, the remarkable thing was that it started at all. In this white, chaste stillness.

104

'Whether the association should continue its activities.'

Did they doubt its purpose?

Probably. But they went on.

5 December. 'On the suggested payment for winter sawing, the representatives reported that the Manager had offered 27 öre per 100 for sawing. The association considered this rate too low. So the association therefore decided to demand 30 öre per 100 as minimum rate for sawing, for both timber workers and stackers. Kånrad Lundström's reservation not to hinder the employer should he wish to pay more for some work.'

Not to *hinder* the employer should he wish to pay more!

Then spring arrived again.

The meetings were held very irregularly, but nevertheless, Bure Independent Workers' Association seemed to go on living its discreet, volatile, but tenacious life.

16 April.

'Representatives reported that he could not meet the demands made by the association as laid down and 27 öre was the maximum in these bad times. And neither would he be particularly willing in May.'

Probably not – but who was this 'he' who seemed to speak with such a loud and authoritative voice? The manager? Or was it the *Company* taking on human form and in the minutes predicting bad times in May as well?

Paragraph 4 from the same meeting: 'The postponed resolution on work-free Sunday evenings was once again brought up, but after a long discussion, it was again postponed until the next meeting.'

There was something slightly peculiar about the fact that in this area alone profit and loss were being allowed to take first place over God's commandments, as prescribed in the Holy Scriptures. They constantly desecrated the day of rest with sinful work, and no one rose in protest. Perhaps generations of work with animals and shippons had blunted their sense of the sinfulness of Sunday work; on the other hand, a sawmill was no cow that simply had to be milked and pacified.

The question came up again and again, at closer and closer intervals. But no definite decision was made.

Yet another note from the same meeting: 'A question arose

105

about what could be done for the boys who work two shifts per day. After some discussion, a committee of three members was appointed to investigate the matter. G. V. Nyström, Nils Mattson and Frans Eriksson were appointed. Frans Eriksson reported his dissent.'

1 May.

'Due to the association's usual meeting place being unavailable owing to cleaning, the meeting was held at Viktor Holmström's house. Then the question of why there were such divided views on the celebration of May Day was discussed. The discussion constituted answers to the question.'

Later, further on in the minutes:

'Resolved to discuss the postponed question of work-free Sunday evenings at the sawmill. The question was postponed indefinitely. But Frans Eriksson suggested that the representatives should announce this matter to the employers so that it would not come unexpectedly should the association at some time in the future make a decision on the matter.'

Then once again a vein of despondency and uncertainty in the neat, if not yet practised, carefully written minutes:

'On the question of dissolving the association there was quite a long discussion. But it was decided to continue with the Association's activities.'

Then, two paragraphs later:

'A suggestion arose on thinking out what to do so as not to be worse off when a frame at the sawmill is under repair, but decided that things should stay as they are.'

In the same way, because things were as they were, or seeing that things were as they were:

'The suggestion arose that a back-hauler at the sawmill should have a man to help keep things clean in the frames. The suggestion was turned down.'

He thought he could *smell* the changes. First it was the smell of Petrus Lundgren's kitchen when they started: a heavy, gloomy, clean, rather cautiously respectable smell. Then the smell of the much smaller kitchen at Aron Häggblom's on the Skerry road: a warmer smell, of people sitting crowded together, warming each other and not disliking it. Then the meeting-house at the Good Templars' Hall. Chillier, cleaner, and also a little freer.

106

The changes smelt, and the men seemed slowly, slowly to lose their respect for something: not much, but like tiny imperceptible flakes peeling off a century-old layer of varnish.

They all began to like it, just a little.

Perhaps things weren't so bad after all.

It can be heard in the tone of the minutes, too. They had taken up the question of working on Sunday evenings innumerable times, and then suddenly, in the minutes of 16 May, 1908, there is the following abrupt and amazingly puzzling sentence:

'The postponed question of work-free Sunday evenings at the mill was brought up and it was decided that Sunday-evening work should be excluded from May 24th onwards.'

'It was decided!' That work would be 'excluded'! What a tone of voice, quite suddenly! If this were not what Elon Wikström called being *dogmatic*, and compared with the management and division of labour decided on by God, the community, the government and the shareholders, then nothing was dogmatic. Remarkably enough, not a single entry in the minutes of the next six months mentions the result of that decision; in actual fact, the points that follow in the same minutes already contain a new and more restrained tone, as if the men thought they had spoken too loudly and so, frightened and uncertain, they had listened to the echo and then started talking again but in lower voices, discreetly trying to remove the impression of a sudden outburst of rage.

It says:

'The question of rates for sawing was brought up for discussion and it was decided that the question should stay open for the time being and men should continue to work and see what daily rates they could achieve according to the piece-rate offered by the employer.'

But one decision was agreed on by all, and that was the question of financial assistance for the purchase of bibles for confirmation candidates. This decision can be interpreted in many ways, but, anyway, the whole resolution runs as follows: 'It was decided that the association should donate a sum of money to those boys who had left school this spring towards a New Testament for each of them; no definite amount was decided upon, but a third of the money that was allocated for this purpose.'

5

THE ELK MOVED like a grey, weightless shadow floating across the marsh; still too far away. Cool grey light, nearly six o'clock. Uncle Aron held his rifle quite still, fixed in position, his gaze following the grey shadow rustling across the sedge. The hide was old and held exactly two people. It was built on the edge of Harrsjö marsh, suspended over the edge of the ridge to the west, and they could still see patches of snow.

The shadow veered, stopped, then ran back in behind an island of pine trees floating in the middle of the brownish-grey surface of the marsh.

Aron grunted, shifted position and swung the barrel of the gun to the left. At that moment the elk-shadow came dashing over the marsh: the shot rang out and at once came rolling back on them in a faint, increasingly clear echo. The elk continued with no sign of hesitation, and a few seconds later had been swallowed up by the edge of the forest.

Aron quietly put his gun down, then rolled slowly over on to his back and looked thoughtfully up at the pale grey morning sky. His face was now quite normal, the excitement gone as he mechanically munched his jaws. Nicanor looked at him from the side.

'Could've dun wi' that,' Uncle Aron said finally. 'An' ah'll have tha know,' he went on in a tone of voice implying what he had to say was important, 'if 'tis goin' t'be a strike, then a man shouldna miss t'elk!'

Nicanor realized that Uncle Aron was in his own way trying to prepare him for the struggle he saw coming.

6

THE MORALITY had been there for as long as anyone could remember. It was complete, inherited, century after century. Someone must have created it once, but no one gave that a thought. It contained a number of commandments, never clearly formulated, moralistically Lutheran, and permitted people to work by the sweat of their brows and safeguard their honour.

It prescribed a great deal, too. The question of honour was the most interesting, for there was something in that, a possibility, a potential anchorage for the new ideas to come.

The whole thing was very complicated. On the other hand, the development of Swedish society had also been complicated. What had happened and was to happen, the treacheries committed and not committed – they did not become comprehensible until one dug down into these peculiar roots. Suddenly the points of attachment of the celestial harp seemed to exist in different and quite astonishing places. Some men adapted to a morality or ideology which had existed for centuries. Others used it for other ends.

It took time. It was terribly abstruse. The abstruseness, on the other hand, was perfectly natural.

No, not natural. But possible to comprehend.

On 23 September, 1908, the following was recorded in the minutes of the meeting of the Bure Independent Workers' Association:

'The chairman read out some suggestions that had been sent in to the association. And those interested [illegible] to contribute. The meeting went on to discuss the foundations of the rumour that a certain foreman had, through utterances to the employer, commented on such things as too high hourly rates being paid, and working hours not completely used. What ought the association to do in such cases? The question was discussed at some length, and it was decided that, together with those who had been affronted, the committee should investigate the question in the best way.'

That was the first omen.

The delegation was the first in the history of the association.

It consisted of Amandus Wikström, Egon Lundgren and K. V. Markström. Amandus Wikström acted as leader of the delegation and spokesman (his old image as cow-tamer had begun to fade). He spoke calmly and collectedly and was regarded in a new light, but all of them had been unanimously appointed by the association and assigned to investigate the Company's attitude. And they went. But once inside the office, they began to feel uncertain; Amandus Wikström did try to outline the main points of the question as clearly as possible, but it did not sound as convincing as they had hoped.

Tiblad did not understand, or did not wish to.

'So it's nothing to do with hourly rates, then?' he said, in a rather impatient tone of voice. 'No wage demands at all?'

'None,' said Egon Lundgren hastily. 'Nay, t'ain't.'

Tiblad suddenly looked sharply at K. V. Markström, as if he had just remembered something.

'You're Markström, aren't you?' he said in an almost friendly way.

'Aye, ah'm he.'

'You're related to Aron?'

'Aye.'

He looked straight at K.V. and his face took on an expression of amusement, or scorn, or contempt. No, not contempt: of guarded interest.

'No wage demands at all?' he said again.

'Nay,' said K. V. Markström, who felt in some indefinable way he was still being addressed, although that was not so. ''Tisn't nowt abaht money. But them's angry abaht t'men bin called bad workers.'

The silence in the room lasted a long time. Then the manager shook his head almost imperceptibly, smiled suddenly, and turning on his heel, he left the room, saying as he went:

'Uhuh. Then perhaps they are bad workers.'

They stayed where they were for a moment, but there was no point in that. Nothing, absolutely nothing, had happened. It had all been pointless. Our Amandus slowly replaced his winter fur-cap, which he always wore from quite early on in the autumn, quietly put a plug of snuff under his lip, sighed heavily, then looked at his friends as if he would have liked to have some comments from them. Naturally they did not oblige.

'So us'll have t'ave a meetin' then,' he said.

And a meeting they had.

The air was still, but the drizzle descended in small, tight, damp veils over all those gathered there. September had started fine that year, with bright colours and mild days, but then suddenly autumn had come to the coast like a long-planned assault, and within a week cold rain was hurtling down on to Bure parish in the province of Westerbotten, whipping in from the Bay of Bothnia. Standing on the top of Bur Mountain, the sea looked like heaving grey clay, before vanishing into a leaden grey fog in the direction of Finland. The poster on the notice-board by the Good Templars'

Hall had twice in two days been washed away by the rain, but it had been put up again by stubborn members of the association, who refused to give in just because of some rain. Then the rain stopped and became nothing but a light veil. The poster was still up, obstinately, if somewhat wet, still with the same provocative and sensational message. *Workers of Bure!* had been at the top of the first poster, unfortunately in ink, which had not withstood many minutes of rain, and so had run somewhat. WORKERS OF BURE! was an improvement on the next poster, this time with a more water-repellent pen, and underneath it:

'*Summons to Meeting about Employer's Affront to the Bure Worker.*'

And underneath that in very small handwriting: *Mass-meeting at 7 p.m. on Saturday.*

A great many came. In fact so many men came they looked at each other in some astonishment. So many, their looks seemed to say, what's going to happen now, with so many? Perhaps it had spread that the meeting had a very special purpose. First and foremost, it was not about anything frightening and technical, like proposals for forming a trade union, or supporting the cause of socialism, or producing dogmatic demands for fewer cuts in wages, no change in wages, or (in extreme cases) a rise in wages. No, the two hundred or so men there had resigned themselves to the ancient Swedish tradition of *knowing how to show restraint*. The drizzle fell lightly and persistently, and many men spoke (before the meeting even began) in calm factual voices, trembling slightly from suppressed agitation, about what had happened: about the charges that Bure workers had not worked hard enough, and had not been good and *honest* workers or industrious and responsible, or faithful and reliable; no, the charges had implied that the Bure worker was like one of them sloppy no-goods and slovenly nitwits wot nivver dost nothing right. The charges seemed to have struck home deeply and caused such wounded, furious, offended, mumbling rage that these men, who had all learnt for so long not to be dogmatic and not to add to things, were truly angry. And showed it. And were going to show it openly.

Amandus Wikström spoke first.

He was rather nervous. He was also indignant, so his voice shook from the start, rather like a child who had been unjustly beaten for something it had not done. His face was tense, and this was his first ever speech in public. But it went quite well, in the end. He said quite simply that the cup was now full to the brim. He said it was hard to support a family on the starvation wages paid by the company and that was one thing. There was actually nothing left for it now but to give the children pig-swill, 'cos them pigs has more flesh on 'em than t'Bure kids. But the wages were one thing. They had not come to jaw about that. They were not there to make demands. But if it was going to be implied that the worker wasn't worth that little wage, and when the company management started going on about the worker not doing his duty as a good and conscientious worker, then a man's patience ran out. 'Them that lives in t'barracks and freezes and ates blood-bread wot's old and unshaven and hairy, is them, and ates mould and stan's there in foul water, them doesna complain. But if them's questionin' t'honour of t'workers, then t'times cum t'talk. Us's gathered here t'tell t'truth, straight out.'

He fell silent for a moment, looking round challengingly, and out of the depths of the crowd in front of him came a voice, in the middle of that tense silence, shouting loudly: ' *'Tis raht. Gi' em a bash!*' This interjection caused a certain amount of uneasiness and was followed by some inappropriate tittering; for a moment this seemed to throw Amandus Wikström off balance; his eyes flickered and his jaws champed helplessly. But then he straightened up and went on: ' *'Tis gone far enough now! If this'n's how them sees us, then them kin git workers where t'hell them likes, but nowt here! An us's got t'tell 'em so!*'

He stepped down from the wooden steps of the Good Templars' Hall, his cheeks red despite the cold and increasingly persistent rain. There was some applause, subdued but heartfelt; most of them were clapping with wet gloves on. One single lamp was alight, throwing a pale blueish-white light down on to them, turning their faces ghostly pale. No one was smiling any longer. Amandus Wikström got down from the steps and there was a pause, then Egon Burström climbed up.

He was to read out the resolution.

It had been written beforehand; the wording of it has been preserved, as the first draft of the resolution was written in pencil on the last page of the Workers' Association minute-book. It was read out in a calm firm voice by Egon Burström from the steps of the Good Templars' Hall, and ran as follows:

112

'Meeting of Bure Workers numbering about 200 to discuss the question of the renewal of the Labour Agreement has unanimously decided to make the following statement:

As at present the greatest possible disorder exists in the management, it becomes singularly difficult for those present to come to any agreement on a change in terms that can be approved both by the Company on the one side and the Labour Force on the other. As it is particularly pointed out at every possible opportunity that the *idleness and apathy* of the Labour Force lie behind the poor results shown in reports from the months of June, July and August, not to mention future months when natural obstacles will no doubt contribute – to combat this constantly reiterated talk of the uselessness of the work-force that cannot be tolerated in future, we consider it necessary to contact the Shareholders and request that a factual investigation be made with assistance from the Government on our side. As our reputation as workers is to us a matter of vital primary importance, we are unable to sacrifice it to someone else's discretion.'

At the last passage, which he spoke with a sharpness that made the words stand out against the others, he stopped and looked out over the crowd. There was complete silence. They had listened throughout with great attention, a hum of surprise going through them at the bit about going to the Shareholders and the Government, but now they were silent. When he looked out over their faces, those reached by the bleak cold light from the lamp on the steps of the Good Templars' Hall, he saw that not one was smiling. The words Egon Burström had read out seemed to have touched them all in some peculiarly personal way. Their white faces were looking up at him, quite still and calm, and a response echoed back up to him. The words had been about the dignity of labour, the reputation of the work-force, and honour. Yes, it all echoed back at him in the stillness; there was good reason to listen. We're listening. This concerns us. It's important. We're with you, at last.

Egon Burström lowered his gaze to the papers in his hand, cleared his throat, turned the page and went on reading:

'As to the aforementioned unwarranted accusations, we take the liberty to draw attention to the singularly good relations existing here before between the Management and the

113

Labour Force. It was not uncommon for the Management to arrange social gatherings with Coffee, etc. The Labour Force has also demonstrated their understanding and appreciation of the Management by communally bestowing gifts as souvenirs from the work-force. To this is added that the majority of the work-force has been involved in working this business up from a Cottage Industry with a turnover of a few thousand to a million-kronor company. We have also been involved in testifying so that fifty or so Workers received the Patriotic Society's silver medal. That workers have become to some extent apathetic, idle and indifferent, and to some degree have lost interest in their work, is admitted, but how could this be otherwise when the sawmill mostly has to close for various reasons, largely due to foolhardy rebuilding, constantly done and re-done, to the Company's and workers' cost and loss of time for both the Company and the workers. It is open to doubt that there will be any sawing at all and we shall call upon [illegible]. When the situation is such that when we arrive at the sawmill one morning at 6 a.m. the timber to be sawn is still at Björkön, and at 1.29 it comes from there . . .'

The draft resolution ends there; a page has been torn out of the minute-book, so the ending is lost. It was read out. It was considered a proclamation. At nine o'clock that Saturday evening, it states, the meeting was closed. Or, in the exact words: 'Due to the cold and inclement weather, the meeting was dissolved at nine o'clock in the evening in full agreement.'

More and more frequently, he used to talk to her at night. He would come creeping in, touch her hand, and then sit curled up on the floor. They whispered. Eva-Liisa always had the cover pulled up to her chin, a warm cave, Nicanor below.

'What's happening?' she said.

'I don't know,' he whispered back. 'It started with the manager coming and making a great row,' he whispered up towards her head above the covers. 'No one knew what was wrong. But they'd been working badly, he said. And he came in and said the sawmill would have to close again. Then he sacked our Konrad Andersson. And everyone had to go home as a punishment. But they all know they do that because the Company loses nothing in the

114

winter when it's not working. But our Konrad was distressed and they say be cried.'

'Is that true?' she said quietly.

He had cried. 'There were some who thought the Workers' Association should take up the cause as theirs. They could try a strike until they got redress. And get him dismissed.'

'Konrad Andersson?'

'No, the manager.'

Then, after a long while, he heard her whisper:

'How awful that he cried.'

That was the first confrontation. The incident is first recorded through the representative's report, inserted on 6 October, 1908. It runs:

'The Director agreed to the workers' request to be paid for time when the sawmill was not working because of the investigation into the matter. At the workers' request that the manager should be dismissed for his repeatedly offensive manner, and that K. Andersson should be given back his job if he so wished, the Director replied that he would arrange that and all would no doubt be well. The Director declined any written communications from the association.'

7

THEN A WINTER CAME such as none of them had ever experienced before.

For two weeks, the first winter storm hurtled in from the east, forcing up walls of snow from Kvarken, filling all the roads with compact driving snow, smothering the sawmill in white swirling clouds, packing the ice up against the quay, closing the timber channels and turning the timber chains as thick as arms as the icy armour swelled. Naturally the sawmill was closed. It was closed from 12 December, all through January, and then came a hideously cold February, and the mill was closed, and then came a few warm days, and they worked for three days, the men working on the timber-rolling persuading themselves they were lucky, then the mill closed for two days, started up, closed for another day, like a capricious woman, they thought. It was hopeless; they went down to the mill and waited and were told there was nothing that day, and they went home, and then suddenly the mill was working.

The men received no pay for waiting. A man who didn't work got no pay, either. Waiting in the snowstorm didn't pay, either. So the winter was largely one of unemployment. And God decided the weather. It was pretty hopeless, and if the mill was working, it was almost equally hopeless.

One ought to, really.

Though. Nay.

Something had remained in the air since the previous autumn's famous meeting about the dignity of work. An emerging impatience, or insufficient patience: an emerging anger. Nicanor was to start work in the sawmill that spring. He was to work the same shifts as Uncle Aron, and he sensed that something was about to happen.

One *ought* to, really.

Then, only a week after the mill had started up again properly, the settlement came. On 18 February they were told that the rate per 100 timbers would – 'owing to the bad times' – be 32 öre. That was a reduction of exactly ten per cent. And the rest of the bloody pay lists looked exactly the same.

One ought to, really.

A man living in the barracks, whose name is not known, was the first. He took his lunch-tin and went home. He thought it no longer worth it.

Afterwards, no one really knew how it had happened. Afterwards, some historian would be sure to categorize the strike as one of those anonymous small labour conflicts which preceded the great strike, paving the way for it, presaging it: a limited conflict, a local struggle, caused by reduction of wages and misery and general arrogance on the part of the employers. But here, in the coastlands of Westerbotten, there was no soil for strikes, they all knew that. None at all. This was paradise for those willing to work.

And yet one man from the barracks picked up his tin and walked out. The others didn't follow him. No, it wasn't that one man started and the rest followed. One after the other, they thought it out carefully. Then they picked up their lunch-tins and went home. Perhaps it had something to do with the winter, or the storm that kept sweeping in so obstinately, tearing all work to shreds, or perhaps it was the piece rates and that eighty-five per cent, or perhaps it was the snow and the storm and the dignity of labour and semi-starvation and the unshaven ragged men and foul water and Konrad Andersson's tears, all combined.

What everyone could see was that men started to leave. Suddenly, they all went, left the sawmill. It was eleven o'clock one morning, a Monday. They took their lunch-boxes and left. Quite silently, very quietly. Not a procession, not really organized, not in ranks, not in a mob. But spread out, and slowly, they left the mill one by one, walking along the Skerry road with no drama whatsoever. That was what Nicanor was to remember most of all – how all of them found themselves on the move, not yet together, but one by one, in the same direction.

It was as if a storm from Kvarken had blown all the workers away from Bure Company.

He also remembered the silence. No one really bothered to say anything. That seemed unnecessary. But his chest felt warm and thick, and although none of the walking men said anything special, he was sure they all felt the same. They were walking quite alone, though at roughly the same time and in roughly the same direction, but he was sure they felt as he did, all those solitary men who had simultaneously taken a decision and almost together now were walking along the Skerry road, away from the sawmill.

And it was a strike.

The Workers' Association met at twelve o'clock the following day.

In their way, the minutes bear witness to the fact that the association was taken completely by surprise by the silent march from Skäret, and anyhow that they had not initiated the conflict. It was a strike, that was what it was. But what would happen now? And what was the association's attitude to be?

The complete minutes of this first meeting after the start of the conflict run as follows:

Para. 1.
The meeting was opened by the chairman at 12 a.m.

Para. 2.
The first question was whether, owing to the fact that those who had left work had not followed the regulations, the association

should take up the matter or not. It was decided that the association should take the matter up as its cause.

Para. 3.
Several suggestions were made on the form in which they should request increases to those who were on 85%. After a long discussion, it was decided by the association to request 37 öre per 100 timbers as minimum daily pay for the winter, and for timber for frames that might break.

Par. 4.
It was decided to request rates for boys per 100 in proportion to this 37 öre.

Para. 5.
Suggestions arose as to what attitude the association ought to take should their requests be refused. It was decided there should be a return to work on Monday morning until the results of negotiations were heard, should no agreement have been arrived at before.

Para. 6.
The meeting was closed for a while until the representatives could return from the Office, to which they had gone immediately with the association's requests.

Para. 7.
On their return from the Office, the representatives reported what Mr Tiblad, the manager, had said. From this it appeared that he would change the list and that they would get it back on Saturday, but that the rates would be the same. He had also stated that all men who wished to work in future should report to Master-Sawyer Gren before Monday midday, and that they would then hear when the mill would be working again.

Para. 8.
After a long discussion, the association decided that they would try to find out if there was anyone within the association who was thinking of reporting, and to this end, there would be a roll-call of members, and that those who were not going to report should reply yes, which constituted those who were present at the roll-call.

118

Para. 9.

It was decided that the meeting the following day should start at 3 o'clock.

Para. 10.

It was decided unanimously that any member of the association who during the Conflict was proven to have behaved deceitfully, or to have discussed the negotiations with unauthorized persons after or when the association considers agreement has been reached, would be boycotted.

The meeting was closed, date as above.

G. Bergman. Secretary.

5

ALFONS LINDBERG'S PRIVY

SOMETIMES QUESTIONS ARE ASKED – how did it happen? What were the conditions? What was the actual situation? Why didn't it turn out differently? Good questions. They can ultimately be answered more simply if the human beings actually, not theoretically, involved, are taken into consideration. When the movement came, the movement was already there. The former had to take the latter into consideration.

The men who formed the movement also formed its direction. That was not inevitable. It could have been the other way round. But human beings had to be taken into consideration, the fact that they looked as they did. Why did they look as they did?

Good question. One of many.

Were they going to be able to keep together?

The first small internal conflict within the Workers' Association soon arose. It concerned Alfons Lindberg. At that time, he was forty-five years old, and the question was whether the erection of the Office's new privy would be considered strike-breaking.

Alfons Lindberg was a good and industrious worker, a sufficiently true believer in his youth, later on somewhat more so under the pressure of a difficult marriage and other trials in his private life. He had joined the Workers' Association the previous autumn, partly because he had heard that the Workers' Association was handing out bibles for confirmation candidates (a rumour that was only a third true) and that reassured him, as clearly the Workers' Association was an offshoot of the Inner Mission, and partly because someone (not altogether correctly) had held out the prospect that the ultimate aim of the Workers' Association was that in future only members of the Association would count as established workers.

Apart from all that socialism stuff, he liked the thought of himself as established.

120

When this minor February conflict, which was suddenly not quite so minor, arose, he had just been given a special assignment. He was to build a new privy for the Company staff (that is actually true), a special little building to be nearer to the Office than the previous special one had been. The minutes are unanimous on this point. 'Another member, namely Alfons Lindberg, wished to know from the association what he was to do about work he had been asked to carry out shortly after Sunday, namely to lay the foundations and build a privy for the Office.'

That was paragraph ten. He was to receive three kronor a day, which was something, after all, and now there was this strike.

Alfons Lindberg was a native of Bure, a widower with four children. He had lived through a marriage beset with troubles. He himself was a peace-loving man, but in marriage he had been endowed with a wife who with her singular mixture of violence, concern and brutality had for many years cast a blight on his life. She fell into the category of human beings who easily become melancholy, and then she allowed her melancholy to take the form of unusually dramatic language.

She was not large, on the contrary, but her vocabulary when upset was terrifying. She was easily upset. Thus Alfons was often frightened, and he was considered to have exceptionally good nerves, but his straw-white hair revealed the truth. When our Alfons Lindberg had misbehaved, or when she felt low or melancholy about something, she used to threaten him, quietly and intensely. '*Tha listen ter me, if tha doesna behave thasel' I'll tear off tha arm and beat tha with t'bloody end so tha faints clean away!*' There was no trace of humour behind her words, and Alfons was genuinely frightened. He knew what immense resources of violence she could resort to, and what resources of concern as well. Sometimes the violence and concern melted together in a remarkable way. Famous is the occasion when in a fit of rage (she had suddenly felt melancholy and knew it was Alfons' fault) she had ill-treated our Alfons by striking him across the face with a pair of dirty old long underpants, underpants of coarse homespun cloth, as simultaneously she matter-of-factly and concernedly scolded him, again and again slashing the underpants across the face of her bewildered husband, saying: '*Cover tha's eyes, so them doesn't git hurt by t'buttons!*'

Then she got cancer; her melancholy turned inwards on her and she fell silent, often sitting weeping bitterly out in the privy, and first one breast was taken away, then the other, and she shrivelled and grew silent and yellow. Alfons sat holding her hand in the hospital once a week and then she was gone. He wept when he came home and told the children. Then, as was the custom, he went and stopped the wall-clock, weeping all the time. Perhaps he didn't mind all the beatings he had had. Anyhow, he had four children, and the neighbours had always wondered how he had managed to get through as many times as four, but they probably understood nothing about that marriage.

After his wife had gone home to God, he joined the Bure Independent Workers' Association, putting his trust more and more in God, poor and wretched, but remaining firm in spirit, even if the flesh shrivelled. He kept his head and his courage up. On his first visit to the Bure Independent Workers' Association, a month after the death of his wife, one of the members went up to him to offer his condolences. Ay, ay, well, well, they mumbled dismally to each other. It was rather quiet in the room and to fill the silence, the friendly soul had sympathetically added: '*Well, I s'pose tha's alone now?*'

Alfons Lindberg did indeed have a mild, good-natured face in which the eyes were rather too close together, but it wasn't exactly handsome, as his St Francis face was complemented with a lower jaw that protruded a trifle too far, and was usually moving with a rotating, shovel-like movement, as if he were always in the process of trying to catch drips from a cold in the nose. But his voice was powerful, emerging from that mild face like thunder on a clear summer's day. When this friendly soul asked Alfons whether he was alone now, the reaction was very unexpected. Alfons' eyes flashed and, obviously exhilarated as he arranged his features, the shovel of a lower jaw smoothly vibrating, and with his incongruously thunderous voice, he cried: '*Nay, alone, that I bain't!*'

A tremendous sensation. He was not alone! A tense respectful silence at once arose in the room where the Bure Independent Workers' Association was meeting, the proceedings about to start. You could have heard a grain of snuff drop. In this tense, expectant and curious silence, it was easy to hear the friendly soul's uncertain, fumbling and confused question: '*Well, well, yes, yes, did tha say tha weren't alone?*' At which the shovel vibrated and ground away in yet another enthusiastic spasm and thunderously trumpeted back: '*Nay, I bain't alone!*' At which the friendly soul, in the same confusion, but now seriously interested

122

in our Alfons Lindberg's new private life, said: '*Well, well, ay, has tha bin and foun' another woman, then, and moved in with'er?*' And the Workers' Association meeting, now listening in deathly silence (there must have been twenty people there, all equally paralysed) heard Alfons Lindberg thunder back in a powerful voice weighed down with implicit faith: '*Nay, I bain't alone, 'cos I has Our Saviour Jesus Christ!*'

At these words, the air seemed to go out of them all; they crumpled with embarrassment, mumbling, not really knowing what to say to this rock-like enthusiast. Now somewhat rebuffed and downcast, the condoling friend was the only one to stammer and mumble in an almost disappointed voice something like, '*Ay, ay, well, ay, him then . . .*'

So at the first strike meetings of the Bure Independent Workers' Association, when Alfons Lindberg asked to be allowed to speak, there were many who sat up in astonishment. He had not previously been much of a one for speaking, nor shown himself to be especially interested. He held up his hand. ' 'Tis a point of order,' he said, using a term he must have taken from previous meetings.

He was given leave to speak. The question was quite simply whether, despite the strike, he would be allowed to build the Company's new privy outside the Office, or not.

Did the others think this all a trifle embarrassing, or comical?

Some of them were clearly slightly embarrassed by the incomprehensible Alfons Lindberg: his contribution seemed to make the conflict, so vital to them all, futile, as if he had transformed it into a curiosity of rustic humour, instead of class-struggle (though everyone knew the former term very much better than the latter), and as if his contribution were in some way slightly shameful, like haggling at a funeral.

Bad comparison. The conflict was no funeral, and eventually Alfons Lindberg's problem was no haggle, either.

Anyhow, a dispute broke out like lightning.

This was the first dispute in the history of the association, and the first dispute in which hard words were brought into use. The rather dry references in the minutes to 'hard words' and 'fierce discussion' and the final line 'after they had calmed down, they decided' are only a pale reflection of the debate that started with Ebon Eriksson categorically declaring that the strike should be total, absolutely total, with no exceptions. Absolutely no exceptions. Neither for Alfons Lindberg, nor for the Company's privy. The Company gentlemen could hold back. They would just have to clamp up and hold back. That was what the strikers had to do, too.

This was very funny, and scattered laughter arose, as well as further suggestions on the theme of restraint. But for Alfons Lindberg, this view came like a bolt from the blue. He was not going to be allowed to. He had four kids at home who had to be fed.

He was not pleased.

''Tis nowt but a privy!' he pleaded desperately, standing up and measuring in the air with his arms to assure them that this extremely insignificant company privy would never be larger than the size of an embrace. *'I'se got t'kids an' wants t'build t'privy,'* he went on, straight into the hostile, impenetrable silence. His hands came closer to each other, beseechingly, the privy shrinking to two feet in his imagination. No. No. Scattered hostile objections arose from the others, for they had children themselves, but like solidarity, the strike was one and indivisible. *'Be them socialists goin' t'stop people shittin' now, too!'* he roared then, his voice even angrier, and he clearly found this angle of approach right and fruitful, as he immediately added the variant: *'I thinks shittin' has nowt t' do with t'strike.'* He then took a deep agitated breath and the argument culminated with a powerful: *'I thinks a man should be let shit in peace from strikers.'*

That struck rock bottom. A chorus of voices exploded in the cramped room. The agitated message was generally that Alfons Lindberg had brought the debate down to an unworthy level. *'Him canna understand nuthin',*' someone called out from the depths of the room. *'Him bain't worth talkin' to, he bain't.'* But in the centre of the storm, Alfons Lindberg stood there with his rotating shovel of a lower jaw, shouting: *'Tha canna forbids people t'shit,'* and then, *'What'll I feed t'kids on then?'*, and the quarrel rolled on, constantly on the theme that such unpolitical phenomena as shitting and privies should be exempted from the strike.

Then suddenly, Ruben Lindström spoke. As a seventeen year-old, he had been crushed under a falling tree and had lost his left leg, so he had become a shoemaker and spent his time losing heart in the soured air. When he was twenty-five, he had been charged with indecent behaviour for showing his dick to children. For this

124

he had been sent to prison for four months, had then returned and gone on making shoes, becoming more and more reserved. Watch out for our Ruben Lindström, Josefina always said to her boys. He shows his dick to little children.

All the small children thought this fantastically frightening and exciting, and they liked running errands to the shoemaker's workshop, but to their sorrow with no result, for Ruben Lindström never again showed his dick. He had been converted to Our Saviour Jesus Christ and then you no longer showed your dick. To crown it all, he had become well versed in the scriptures and was good at speaking, and then shoemaking had come to an end and he got work as a logger at the sawmill (he had a wooden leg by then and was said to float high and easily when he fell in, because the wood in his leg was good and dry), but he never again showed his dick. Quite inconsequently and abruptly, he now started telling them all about the toilers in the vineyards. For them it was like this (according to the Gospel of St Matthew): some went to work in the morning, others not until the middle of the day, and yet others just before evening came. But when all the workers were to be paid, it turned out they were all given the same wages. Full day-wages. So those who had slaved away all day were angry and said to their master that those who had worked all day should have more than those who had worked for only an hour. And it was wrong that they received a whole day's pay. But their master asked them whether they had not agreed together on their day-wages. And that was the case. And was their master not then right to give a full day's wage to those who had worked for only an hour?

The silence in the room was now complete, not to say confused. What was our Ruben with the dick getting at? But Ruben Lindström, looking solemn, gathered up his strength for a final summary and said: '*Now ask thasels, why'd them vineyard workers only worked for one hour? Was them lazy? Nay, them had no work. Them'd've liked to work all day, if them'd been let. So them gets a full day's wage.*'

And then, after a significant pause: '*T'Saviour thinks us should show solidarity!*'

A shocked sceptical buzz ran through the room. Hell, now it was being said that the Saviour also had views on the strike. Many of the men gathered there were singularly uninterested in what the Saviour thought about the matter, and anyhow, they considered our Ruben with the dick was not the right man to decide on the association's ideological course. There was some more quarrelling, now more restrained.

Finally total silence.

I think what happened was that they were all simultaneously struck by the same thought. This was unnecessary. One ought not to. Instead one should think carefully. Perhaps Ruben Lindström's little sermon had been of some significance, who knows? Opposition takes many forms. But suddenly they realized the situation was now such that they ought not, like starving rats in a trap, to devour each other.

They ought to show respect for one another.

Finally Ebon Eriksson said, in a perfectly calm and friendly voice, as if talking to a woman he respected and liked very much: *'Well, listen now, Alfons. Tha has ter do as tha pleases. Things canna be easy for tha now tha ole woman's gone.'*

And they all nodded.

After that, they all looked at Alfons Lindberg, at his jaws working, his lower jaw grinding round and round, like a ruminating horse, and they let him think it out to the end and ruminate to the end of what he was thinking about. He remained standing all the time. They waited without saying anything, friendly, expecting nothing, but no longer with anger and contempt. Then Alfons Lindberg had thought it through, and looking round, he finally said to them. *'Well, on thissen privy, the gaffer'll have t'build it hisself, then. Solidarity's fer me.'*

He nodded and sat down with a crash.

Most of them had probably thought he would leave the association, break the blockade and think about his kids. Who would have been able to think ill of that? This concerned a man called Alfons Lindberg with four children and no wife, and to cap it all his family was said to come from the Pite district. But Alfons Lindberg had plumped for solidarity. Just the word – where had he got that from? (Yes, of course, from our Ruben with the dick.)

In the silence after he had sat down, they at once knew, for the first time, that perhaps they had a chance of keeping together. If they had people like Alfons Lindberg with them, who then did they have against them? If these are with me, who will be against me? as the words of the Bible ran. Yes, they would be able to keep together. Against all odds.

Perhaps they would be able to win this first battle?

They tasted the words cautiously, looking round in the over-crowded little room.

This first battle.

When the movement came, the movement was already there. One has to take into consideration the human beings who were actually, not theoretically, there.

Sometimes there were surprises. Alfons Lindberg never did build a privy for the Company.

6

A PEACE OFFERING

'Thou makest us to turn back from the enemy:
and they which hate us spoil for themselves.
Thou hast given us like sheep appointed for meat:
and hast scattered us amongst the heathen.
Thou sellest thy people for nought:
and dost not increase thy wealth by their price.'

Psalm 44.

1

A VERY COLD FEBRUARY, felling in the forest almost at a standstill, the snow too deep, the horses having a bad time of it.

However, the conflict was not isolated.

It was a minor conflict, true, affecting only one little middling-sized sawmill, fourteen miles south of Skellefteå. In the light of history, it could never be compared with the huge conflict to break out six months later, which came to be called the Great Strike. It was never noticed outside the boundaries of the parish and the only surviving documentation is the minute-book which Gustav Bergman, the secretary, kept (mostly; one or two notes were made by others, but Bergman's handwriting is the most frequent) and which later on ended up in the possession of the Markström family. I read it at Nicanor's place. The conflict was minor, but not isolated, and not alone. It was one of innumerable minor conflicts that stretched in a constellation throughout the winter of 1908 to 1909, forming the background and preliminaries of the Great Strike. It was one ordinary minor dispute in the Swedish labour market: members of the Swedish Federation of Employers had initiated and won most of them.

It would have gone on winning them, if something had not happened to dramatize and unite all these minor conflicts. They were small pinpricks that were to weaken the labour movement in

128

its emergent stage, making those small insignificant and slowly bleeding sores which in the long run are fatal.

Hundreds of small sores were bleeding everywhere, external signs of the present mortal struggle.

In silence.

In Bureå, the external and concrete reason for the conflict was a fifteen per cent reduction in wages.

On 20 February, the Workers' Association received written confirmation from the Company that the new terms were final. 'The chairman read out the new rates which were lower rather than higher than the old rates, or 32.5 öre per 100 timbers instead of 37 öre. The association's unanimous decision was to refuse the new rates and stand by previous demands.'

At the very bottom of the page is a brief final note:

'It was suggested that approval be given to the strike by means of posters. The matter was postponed until the next meeting.'

22 February, 1909.

'At 7 o'clock the members of the association received yet another communication from the Office. There was nothing in it about a rise in rates, but the Committee asked whether the Manager would consider a percentage rise on the old rates. Which he rejected. The Committee informed the Manager that they had made enquiries and were going to call in the government conciliation officer. Which the manager could not object to.'

In the middle of all this was another note:

'It was decided that the association should pay the cost of scrubbing the premises on the 23rd inst.'

Then back to the conflict.

'As the wage dispute between B.C. and the association was not settled. Decided unanimously to call in government conciliation officer, and to that purpose, Konrad Bergman and Gustaf Nyberg were elected. The postponed matter of posters was once again brought up, but after a brief discussion was dismissed.'

26 February, 1909.

'3 bills were sent to the association and submitted by the chairman. For cleaning, 4.50, for 2 telephone calls, 1.05, and for wood, 1 krona. The bills were approved for payment.

'Discussion arose on how it is trade union members have the

right to work at a place where a non-organized workers' association has stopped working. The matter was postponed until further notice.'

Here the minutes change handwriting in the middle of a paragraph, and a rather less practised hand which is more difficult to read takes over: 'The representatives report: that they had thought the mill would be starting up on Monday morning, that the mill would [a short illegible piece here] shifts a week, i.e. starting on Sunday night at 10 o'clock and work finishing on Saturday night at 5 o'clock. Secondly that the regulations of the association should be changed in the following way: 1) no minor should have the right to vote in the association; 2) that disputes between sawmill and employees and the Company do not affect Timber Yard employees and vice versa; 3) that a strike may not be proclaimed until thorough negotiations have been carried out and not until two-thirds of the members with a right to vote have voted for it; 4) that on all occasions members quickly comply with orders [an arrow inserted here, and in another hand the word *rightful* written in before the word *orders*], corrections and instructions.'

The other hand takes up the pen again.

'It was decided to telephone the conciliation officer immediately to find out if he had received an official letter from us, and whether he had advised whoever represents the Company.'

'A roll-call of members was held and it was found that a majority was absent.'

'The report the representatives had received from the Company concerning work on Sunday evenings was discussed. It was decided unanimously by the association to protest vigorously against Sunday-evening work.'

The last comment of that day (which was perhaps felt to be very dramatic and must have been very long) is, however, a wholly uncontroversial note about a payment. In this context it appears to be a remnant from quieter days when the association had just started. Quite laconically, it runs:

'The payment of 10 kronor towards bibles for boy school-leavers was approved.'

27 February, 1909.

'It was decided that the representatives should go down to the Office with the Association's decision, i.e. refusal to work on

130

Sunday evenings and a request that the Employer and the association should jointly call in the government conciliation officer.'

'Representatives' report: 1) The Director agreed to call in the government conciliation officer. 2) regarding Sunday-evening work, it would be best to leave that until the conciliation officer arrives.'

They have almost stopped dividing the minutes into paragraphs; the impression is one of quick note-taking as reminders rather than minutes. The spelling is more consistent than before, although the handwriting varies.

'It was decided that Konrad Bergman and Gustaf Nyberg should go and telephone the conciliation officer and find out what arrangements he would like made for when he arrives. The association also decided to consider how to engage in work on Monday morning in expectation of the conciliation officer.'

In expectation of the officer; no doubt they were expectant.

So they were expectant. Why shouldn't they be expectant of the conciliation officer sent by the authorities?

Further on, the same day.

'On the question of whether there was any basis to the Company statement that auxiliary sawyers hindered primary sawyers so that day rates could not increase, the sawyers stated that this was definitely not the case, but the main reason was probably the 1st, to block-saw 8″ timber, and in addition in Frame 2 it was quite impossible to earn day rates just as to cut four-square 7″ timber in Frame 5 was equally impossible.'

'It was decided that the association should elect a Committee to represent the workers at the negotiations when the conciliation officer came, if required.'

2

THE EPISODE of the presentation of the vase comes in here.

The Markström family had partaken in and assimilated the conflict with astonishing calm. Perhaps the move from Hjoggböle to Bureå had done something to relieve the spiritual pressure in Mother Josefina's watchful eye, or however it might be put.

131

Whether out of consideration for her new neighbours or the old relatives at Petrus Lundgren's (where after all, the first meeting had taken place) – she did not drive her husband out to work. He was allowed to strike. Nevertheless, she followed the events with some anxiety. She was the originator of the peace-offering idea. She sowed the idea in her husband's head, he sowed it elsewhere, and that was how it happened.

No one knows exactly how the decision was made, but it was something to do with the coming of the government conciliation officer. As the idea grew, and several people simultaneously thought it a good idea, finally someone stood up and said it would somehow be good and right if they showed some goodwill in this difficult situation. If the conflict then moved on into negotiations, it would be good to have shown some.

Goodwill.

They tasted the word and found it the right one.

But the choice of K. V. Markström as leader of the delegation to present the damned gift was sheer accident. Albin Lindquist had spoken in favour of someone more non-political and neutral to present the gift, so that people who had already been involved in discord would not have to. He said the gift should appear to be a gesture of goodwill from the whole labour-force, not only from those who had initiated the conflict. As a result, someone not directly connected with the association should present it.

At these words, there was a long silence. Some tried to imagine who this outsider, this non-political man of goodwill might be. Some then looked at K. V. Markström, probably thinking of that permanent prayer-house smile of his that had crushed so many preachers' flinty hearts. Then the suggestion was made:

'Our Grinnery Markström kin, canna him?' came from somewhere at the back of the room.

So it was him. 'It was decided that on behalf of the Workers' Association K. V. Markström and Konrad Lundström should present a vase to the Director as a token of the Association's goodwill.'

And that is what happened.

Josefina received the news of her husband's exaltation with composure, and with her usual determination started arranging the more practical and organizational details of the expedition.

The vase was purchased at Lundgren's, the ironmonger's, and

132

cost eleven kronor forty. So far, so good. It was put into a shoe-box, embedded carefully in sawdust, then the box was wrapped in some left-over Christmas paper and tied up with strong string and a handsome knot.

Nicanor was sceptical about the whole arrangement. He said so, too: he didn't understand what Christmas paper had to do with it, as it wasn't Christmas, was it? He was silenced. The parcel had to look good, so they would not be put to shame. And surely they weren't going to present the parcel by hand just like that, were they? Josefina raised her increasingly enthusiastic eyes from the parcel and looked with dismay at her husband. He had been given the task on the basis of his famous smile, but she didn't know that. The way he looked at that moment would not do. So she dressed him up: Nicanor was given the special task of wetting and combing his father's hair, an assignment he carried out. Then K.V. was dressed in his Sunday suit, his hands washed (Nicanor quite clearly saw Josefina devoting special attention to the right hand, the one that was to touch the Director) and as a final touch, Josefina walked all round him, sniffing suspiciously.

No. He did not smell of anything at all. He was a whole, clean, sober and serious man, and she had no need to be ashamed.

Konrad Lundström was to come round at three o'clock. And at three o'clock he came. K. V. Markström put on his leather cap and they both left. The others were left behind, standing at the kitchen window, watching them go; Nicanor and his brothers and Eva-Liisa and Mother. They watched the two figures trudging off between the snowdrifts, one of them with a Christmas present under his arm. Josefina said:

'Now us'll say a prayer for our Dad when him's t'delegit the Director. Us'll pray t'God for him.'

She led the prayers for the Delegation.

They reported back afterwards, and after they had made their report, more and more complementing details began to emerge.

They had gone in the afternoon, shortly before dusk, walking along the Skerry road without saying much, Markström carrying the shoebox. Once at the office, Konrad Lundström, who did not have a reputation of being particularly timid, had knocked on the door. A female member of the office staff had opened the door. Then one of the clerks had appeared, looking confused and unaware of what was going on. Konrad Lundström was the first to speak.

'We wish to speak to the Director,' he said. Behind his back, his fellow-delegate fired a preparatory prayer-house smile in the direction of the clerk, not quite so wide and less certain than usual, but a start had to be made somewhere.

'Not here,' said the woman's voice from inside the room. The clerk seemed to start, but no doubt controlled his irritation.

'Then we'd like to speak to the Manager,' persisted Konrad Lundström, after a brief disappointed silence.

The clerk stared at him for a few seconds, than turned abruptly and went into an inner room. No had invited them in, but all the same Konrad Lundström stepped inside. He was buggered if he was going to stand outside like any old tinker when he was about to make a presentation.

After a moment's hesitation, Markström followed him.

He closed the door behind him. The room was tremendously hot, he thought, and he at once started sweating, but as his friend Lundström in front of him made no move to take off his outdoor clothes, neither did he dare do so.

But he held his cap in his hand.

They were standing in a handsome room containing both a tiled and an iron stove. There were two brown writing-desks on the floor and in the middle of the wall hung a monumental painting of pine trees, not felled. All the doors leading into the secret rooms were closed.

Markström was perspiring appallingly, the parcel under one arm, his cap in his hand. All they could do was to wait. The parcel suddenly felt very heavy. The Manager came in through the left of the two doors, jerking it open so determinedly that Markström jumped and almost dropped the parcel.

'Yes, yes, now what's this all about?' said the Manager, staring at them.

An undeniably straight clear question, but what should they do? The bearer of the parcel felt vaguely that, after all, he was the chosen one, the person to make the presentation; he blinked nervously, hoisting the gift up to almost face-level, and with a smile of clearly expressed understanding, he beamed at the Manager. As this provoked no response, K.V. raised the parcel a trifle higher and nodded in confirmation. Konrad Lundström glanced round uneasily to see what was happening behind his back, then swiftly decided to do this himself.

''Tis like this,' he said. 'Bure Independent Workers' Association (then he corrected himself sharply) Bure *Work-force*,' he said, 'in view of the coming negotiations, in which the Government Conciliation Officer is takin' part, they sort of thought they'd show their goodwill in the form of a gift to the Company and present this . . .'

K. V. Markström was still holding the shoe-box on high, like a character in the Bible proferring a sacrifice to the highest altar, his smile more confident now. Perspiring and silent, he was grinning broadly. Konrad Lundström hesitated for a moment, then glanced at his companion. The situation suddenly seemed to him to be utterly peculiar, on account of this strange man Markström, whom he had distrusted from the start. But he could not correct him in the middle of the ceremony. If only he wouldn't hold the shoe-box so high, and with both hands like that, such an odd sacrificial-lamb gesture. The whole matter was really rather painful. But K. V. Markström had really always been a rather peculiar man.

In the end he managed to get out the final words:

'And herewith the gift we wish to present to the Company as evidence of the Workers' Association's goodwill.'

He didn't even bother to correct himself this time, for at that moment K. V. Markström took a solemn and elk-like stride forward and held out the shoe-box, nodding and smiling eagerly.

The offering had been produced.

Obviously bewildered, the Manager took the parcel. As he did not really know what to do, he opened the parcel, first undoing the string, then unwrapping the Christmas paper, then taking off the lid. He took out the vase and a light shower of sawdust floated down to the floor. Instinctively, he looked at the bottom of the vase: the price ticket was still there.

'Oh, yes,' he said, apparently to himself, quite unable to stop himself. 'Eleven kronor fifty.'

They all gazed in silence at the vase. It was made of glass. There was a deer engraved on one side, its two hind legs on the ground, but its forelegs leaping upwards. All three of them gazed at it intently and with interest, for no one could find anything to say: they stared at the deer with its hooves fumbling up towards something that didn't exist.

THE LAST TIME I saw Nicanor, in March 1972, we spent a long time walking round the silent and empty sawmill area, the only people working there the men dismantling the frames. It was March, and we both sat for a long time listening to the stunning silence, the sun shining, a light wind blowing from Kvarken, an endless vista of white snow over towards Finland.

Silent, painless peace. Nicanor seemed to me to be sniffing for the smell of the mill, the smell of work, as if searching for a vanishing fragrance of sawn timber, now thinned out by the wind and becoming history, in the same way as he himself was shrinking and what had been his life was thinning out, soon not even to exist as the faint smell of dried-up abandoned old man's flesh.

But one could still smell timber. That was as before. The timber channels were as before. It was only the smell of work that had already been thinned out and had almost vanished. Four men were working on frame number two. By next week, the whole lot would have been dismantled; it was that simple to dismantle a sawmill. Someone had suddenly bought it up and decided to redistribute the supply of raw materials and make tax-beneficial redeployments, so suddenly the smell of human beings had faded very rapidly and painlessly. Something had died though.

Nicanor spoke quietly in that slightly guttural voice of his which I had at last learnt to understand, and he spoke of what we own. For a hundred years, men had worked here, but who owned the fragrance of sawn timber, or the fragrance of labour? Now they were ripping out the frames of the mill, and who owned the labour that had been done, who owned Uncle Aron's labour, or K.V.'s work, or his own? He had realized in the end, he said quietly and patiently, how things should be. A man's work should not disappear when it was done. A man's labour sort of went into what a man did. So two hundred years of sweat had gone into this sawmill; they had made it what it was, even to the scent of timber that couldn't be sold. That couldn't become tax-beneficial redeployment. The people who had worked here had become *one* with the mill. So a man's work was *still there*. That was as it should be. So you would know next time. So they would not be robbed again next time.

Now they were tearing the heart out of the sawmill and the scent of timber was being thinned out and becoming history. And yet, in actual fact, Aron and K.V. and Nicanor and Sanfred and Konrad Lundström owned it, they owned all this, including the fragrance of timber and people and work. What his father and grandfather and all the others had made, no one should be allowed to steal from them.

That evening I was allowed to borrow his old minute-book. I still have it. And he said: that was how we began. And we'll have to see how it will end. I haven't much longer left. But I remember, he said, that I thought everything had come to an end that time.

But that end was the beginning of everything.

The last minutes on the conflict, and the last notes of Bure Independent Workers' Association are dated 4 March, 1909. They run as follows:

'Para. 1.
The meeting was opened by the chairman at 7 p.m.

Para. 2.
The chairman reported the results of negotiations at the Office on 4th inst. The results were nil. The Director was definite that there should be no increase in present agreed rates. The Committee could not deviate from the decisions made by the association, particularly as no middle way had been discussed.

Para. 3.
It was discussed whether or not the association should continue its activities. Finally it was unanimously decided to dissolve the association immediately owing to the fact it considered it could no longer function in the interests of the workers.

Para. 4.
It was decided that Leon Jansson should be paid from the funds of the association for the day he was off work to fulfil his duty as chairman of the Committee negotiating at the Office.

Para. 5.
It was decided that the representatives should inform the Director of the association's decision.

Para. 6.
It was decided the association should have the premises cleaned and take payment for it from the association funds.

Para. 7.
It was discussed what should be done with the money remaining in the funds and after a brief discussion it was decided that after all bills had been paid, the association's funds should be donated to the sickness fund.

Para. 8.
The chairman finally thanked the members present at this last meeting and said that he did not know if their activities had been of the slightest use. On the suggestion of a member, it was decided that the membership list should be destroyed.'

They paid for the scrubbing of the premises, burnt the membership list, tried to forget the unsuccessful presentation to the Company, dissolved the association, and then it was all over.

They had carried on for two winters, and as the chairman had so rightly said, they did not know if their activities had been any use whatsoever. The government conciliator had come up and stayed for one night, then had departed to stay in a hotel in Skellefteå. On the first day he had listened for six hours to the statements of both parties, then he had politely bidden them farewell, shaken hands with the representatives of both sides, and gone back up to Skellefteå. When they had shaken hands, the Director had sent his regards to Mr Mehlberg, which had disheartened the workers' representatives somewhat, as they did not know who Mr Mehlberg was; suddenly it seemed to them that the knowledge of who this mysterious Mr Mehlberg was had placed the conciliator closer to the employer, so that he was no longer in the middle between them. After staying overnight in Skellefteå, he had telephoned the next day and said a few words in a conciliatory tone of voice, expressing the government's wish that in the interests of the community the parties should show moderation and come to some agreement.

Then he had left, and nothing had happened. He had gone and nothing had happened. The Director declared that the Company had finally decided not to deviate from their position.

That was the end of it.

A matter of vital importance.
When he had spoken those words about not knowing whether their activities 'had been of the slightest use', it had grown rather

138

quiet. Two years had gone by. Many of them quite clearly remembered that autumn evening when they had gathered outside the steps of the Good Templars' Hall and approved a resolution. It was about the dignity of labour, as it came to be called much later on and in another context, but it really was like that. That was where it began. *As our reputation as workers is to us a matter of vital and primary importance we cannot sacrifice it to someone else's discretion.* Not a bad beginning, really. Lutheran or not, puritanical or not, this was something important. Work was of value. They had suddenly realized it: their labour was of value, and at first they had limited the definition of this value to purely moral spheres. Reputation. Honour. Morality.

But if they had started like that, the next step would not be far off. It was a good first step, really. If they had decided that their labour was of *value*, then they could go on.

No, those two years of activity had been of a certain use. When they came to the point in the meeting when a decision was made to 'inform the Director of the association's decision', the association suddenly appeared to be divided in its reactions.

The decision was made without argument and they then had to choose the person to go to the Director and tell him that Bure Independent Workers' Association had died. Someone suggested Amandus Wikström.

Two years had gone by since he had spoken at the first meeting in Petrus Lundgren's kitchen, and something had happened to him. He was no longer the mysterious legendary cow-tamer from Ljusvattnet, able to make cows stand on their hind legs and bellow 'Our Lord is to us Almighty' in unison. The story about the washed-away manure tubs was in fact still told, but now seemed to have become detached from him. He was one of those who had formed the backbone of the association, and he had begun to think about a great many things. When someone proposed Amandus Wikström to take the message to the Director, he reacted extremely surprisingly.

He was overwhelmed by an unusual and quite inexplicable fit of rage.

He stood up without consulting the chair and spoke in a loud voice. He told them that he did indeed realize they had lost everything and that the association should be dissolved. But that was nothing to feel humiliated about. 'Ah willna stand there cap in hand scrapin' me feet and makin' a fool o' meself.' That was humiliating, and they should have learnt by now that no worker should humiliate himself. They were all good workers. They had nothing to apologize for. Their work was of value. The Director would soon find out anyway. They didn't have to go to their opponent and tell him. Anyhow, *he* wasn't going to.

He had said all this in such a loud voice they had all been surprised, and then he had gone out and many of them had been somewhat dismayed. After that, they chose Arvid Lindström to go and inform the Director instead.

Amandus Wikström had gone out and Nicanor had slipped out after him. Nicanor saw him standing out on the steps, looking around, no doubt thinking about that meeting about the dignity of labour, the time when he had spoken. That had been six months ago.

Nicanor glanced up at his face, and to his astonishment he saw that Amandus Wikström had tears in his eyes.

It was true. Amandus Wikström was standing on the steps, and Bure Independent Workers' Association had been dissolved, all in March 1909. They had questioned whether their activities had been of the slightest use. He had not wanted to go to the Director. It was finished. And he was not ashamed of being miserable about it.

The chosen Arvid Lindström took the information to the Director that same evening.

The Director had found time to receive him, and Arvid Lindström had told him Bure Independent Workers' Association had decided to dissolve itself. So there was nothing standing in the way of an agreement between the Company and the Work-force. The conflict was over. The Director had listened, than shaken Arvid Lindström's hand, a powerful handshake, Lindström had told them afterwards, a handshake totally without ill-will, firm and warm, as between friends. And no noticeable bitterness at all on the Director's side.

That was how it ended: in a handshake in which there was no noticeable bitterness.

7

THREE PATS OF BUTTER

'Food: everyday food was herring, potatoes, *bryta* (thin crispbread and milk), black pudding, pancakes, home-made bread, hard-baked, made of corn and rye. The black pudding also mostly consisted of corn. Pork and meat on holy days. Gruel of flour. In summer fresh Baltic herrings replaced pickled or salted herrings. Macaroni porridge: sweet. Rice pudding. 1916, hourly rates 30 öre at B.Co. Butter was 7 kronor 75 öre a kilo. Two kilos of butter was the equivalent of 51 working hours.'

1

BUT EVERYTHING STARTED with that ending.

Once upon a time there was a Workers' Association in Bureå. It existed for nearly two years, then collapsed. It was not affiliated to the Confederation of Trade Unions. In actual fact that was a very important dividing-line: Bure Independent Workers' Association was what the Confederation of Trade Unions called a sewing-bee. A non-affiliated association.

Sewing-bees were tolerated by the employers. It was affiliation to the Confederation of Trade Unions that made them dangerous. The struggle was over the question of organization. The struggle against the strong trade union was what was important. The struggle against the centrally organized and centrally governed trade union movement, the struggle which at the time and later on arrayed itself in such beautiful and libertarian rhetoric. With a thousand mouths, the enemy spoke of the free worker's right to do as he wished, the freedom to starve to death, freedom from his own dictatorial leaders, the right to work during shut-downs, freedom to be alone in the struggle, to escape centralization, to escape organizational ties.

All this would live on for a long time – ennobled and polished,

141

cultivated and exalted, but with discernible roots: the fear of the strong trade union.

Bure Independent Workers' Association died after two years. But everything started with that ending.

One evening, two days later, a message came for Nicanor. They wanted him to come, just him. The man who came with the message did not say much, but was persistent. It was important in some way.

The important matter was Uncle Aron.

In a roundabout way some of the men had found out that for eighteen months Uncle Aron had been going regularly to the manager and reporting on what had been happening in the Workers' Association. What Aron had told him no one knows. But he was not stupid. He could hear, observe, speak, and the fact that he had a squint and his body was twisted did not affect his mind.

So they had found out. How, no one knows. Perhaps someone had seen him and become suspicious. Perhaps someone in the company management had happened to let out the information when informers were no longer necessary and victory complete. That was most likely. It was reasonable and natural for them to want to show their power in this way. The wretched workers had thought that at least their inner defences were intact. But there were cracks there, too. There was no such thing as an impregnable wall. All walls crumble. All walls fall. Walls within the workers, too. The truly strong are on their own, they said persuasively. Or, in other words, there were always self-sufficient workers who thought nothing of thinking for themselves and not submitting to the masses and the orders of their dictatorial leaders.

Aron was one of those self-sufficient workers.

Anyhow, it became known that the slightly squint-eyed Aron had squinted more than they had thought. He had told them everything: whether there was really anything to tell was doubtful, but anyway he had worked on behalf of the employers. Late one afternoon, fate in the form of four disappointed and angry working men had caught up with Aron. They had dragged him into the privy behind the barracks, where they had questioned him, and when he had answered them and told them the truth, they had beaten him up.

He had admitted it at once, quite voluntarily. No threats had

142

been necessary. He had behaved contrary to the February agreement, paragraph 10, 'It was decided unanimously that any member of the association who during the conflict was proven to have behaved deceitfully, or to have discussed the negotiations with unauthorized persons after or when the association considers agreement has been reached, would be boycotted.' It was down there. As a member of the association, he had broken the rules, had informed the employers and betrayed their solidarity.

Aron had sat there quite calmly all the time, just nodding. 'Aye,' he had said, ' 'tis true. Ah's talked to t'Director.'

What had he been given for it?

'Ah got butter.'

'Butter?!'

'Ah got butter.'

They had then demanded that Aron should prove he was telling the truth. He had nodded and gone ahead of them into the barracks. Then he had quite calmly pointed at the hatch. There were six men in that room, three of them bachelors and three Hjoggböle men with families, but who lived here during the week. Those men always came back on Sunday evening with their rucksacks full of food that had to last out the week, mostly black pudding and pancakes. Black pudding and pancakes was their staple diet. They had to scrape the mould off first, then try to boil or fry it and eat it. That wasn't much to worry about. The problem was the barracks, which was cold and damp. And the milk, for instance, was always going sour. So they had sawn up the floor in the porch and made a hole there, so they could each let a carrier down into it. It acted as a cooler. But the disadvantage of that was that there was water there; and then that the water was bad and started to smell of dead fox. No one liked it. But there was no point in arguing about it.

Aron had gone straight to the hatch and pointed, and they had opened it up. Then he had pointed at his sack and said there was butter down there. And there, down in that foul hole, was a sack they had seen many times before, among the carriers. But now they hauled it up and opened it.

Believe it or not.

There were three large lumps, carefully wrapped in linen and tied together. They had opened one of the parcels and Aron had been quite correct in that it had once been butter. How long ago was the question. It looked peculiar, a colour none of them had

143

ever seen before, and for a moment they felt they were looking at a long since dead animal, covered with growth, slumbering in eternal sleep.

'There's tha butter,' said Aron quietly.

He had kept it all. There were three parcels, each one weighing two kilos. He had been given the first in the autumn of 1907, eighteen months earlier. Butter was expensive. Four weeks' labour lay in those lumps, growing. It was all utterly incomprehensible. The men had stood there for a long time looking from the butter to Aron, and finally they had very slowly been overcome with rage. Perhaps rage at Aron's treachery, perhaps something else: rage over him standing there so calmly and patiently, hands hanging down and eyes squinting, over his voluntary confession, over the fact that he had so obviously talked to the Director, over the butter lying there in three such meaninglessly stinking mouldering lumps, over everything being so utterly meaningless.

They took him out to the privy at the back of the barracks and beat him up.

They sat him down on the step where the little privy hole meant for children was situated. They sat him down so he wouldn't fall and hurt himself while they beat him up. They told him what he was to do and he nodded calmly and sat down. Then he was given what he could take. Once or twice he fell over to one side, but they hauled him up again. It was brutal treatment, but the perpetrators knew what they were doing and Aron knew what they were doing and he only whimpered slightly. But it was not amusing, thought the men beating him. Aron was an odd fish. He appeared quite calm, as if he thought they weren't doing anything to him. Or that it was meant.

Then they sent for Nicanor.

He was not a pretty sight. Although it was dark inside the privy and the moonlight coming through the open door made a poor torch, Nicanor could see Uncle Aron's face was in a bad way. His nose was still bleeding. He had been given what he could take. When Nicanor bent down and kept asking him how he was and what had happened, all he could hear was the heavy sobbing breathing of a person who is quite badly hurt and has certainly been given what he could take. Uncle Aron had blood down the front of his tunic, but not that bad and it would wash.

He had clasped his hands and was holding them quietly in his lap.

'Kin tha walk?' said Nicanor, hearing his own voice trembling. He had difficulty speaking because he was so upset or frightened or miserable, or whatever it was. But Aron did not reply. All he did was to blink rather laboriously and uncertainly up at his nephew leaning over him: then he slowly leant over to one side, carefully lifted the lid off the child's privy on the step he was sitting on and spat out something that might have been blood. Then he carefully replaced the lid.

'Him's tired,' said the man behind Nicanor, who had fetched him. 'If tha helps him home, him kin rest then.'

The moon outside threw a pale light across the privy floor; there was still some snow lying in thin patches. It had been warm during the day and cold at night, so the top was frozen, one of those nights when you could walk far across Bure Heath on the frozen surface and be quite free in the moonlight. You could walk where you liked, and the trees would be black, and the moon white, and it would be like daylight, and the surface would hold. You could run, slowly but far.

Suddenly Aron started weeping. He was still sitting on the privy step, the pain or the humiliation apparently not reaching him until now, or perhaps only now was he beginning to feel it. He looked wretched, blood round his mouth, weeping, unable to say anything.

Can't be easy to be Aron right now, thought Nicanor. Must be difficult for him. The man who had fetched him was standing staring behind him: he had told Nicanor a little and Nicanor could imagine the rest himself. It was unpleasant having him there. This was something that should be kept in the family. But then, all of a sudden, Nicanor thought: it doesn't matter. It doesn't matter if anyone sees. For Aron's sake, this was necessary.

For the sake of the whole thing.

So Nicanor quietly sat down next to Uncle Aron on the bottom step of the barracks privy, put his arm round his shoulders, not bothering about anything, and they both sobbed quietly together, and nothing was said and the pain slowly faded until it finally became almost tolerable and possible to bear.

He got him home.

He wrote the letter the next evening. He wrote it by hand, in pencil, and addressed it to the Social Democratic Party Office, Stockholm.

The letter ran as follows:

'Bure, March 21st, 1909.
For the attention of Mr Elmblad.

Honoured Mr Elmblad,
I am herewith writing to you to ask if you are making any more journeys along the coast this summer and if you are still doing canvassing work. I would like you to come via Bure parish in that case. You were up here once before, if you remember, though they were angry about socialism then. I was the boy who helped you put up the posters. There has been quite a lively independent workers' association in Bure for the last two years, but now it has been crushed by the employers. No one here dares to think such thoughts now, but many people do all the same. It would be a good thing if there was some canvassing here because otherwise the employers will reduce wages far too much. Many workers are also annoyed at the amount of slander about apathy and such things. With some canvassing it probably wouldn't be long before the Bure worker overcame his fear of the colour red.'

He wrote the letter late at night. When he had finished it, he thought for a long time, then added the following lines at the end: 'If Comrade Elmblad wishes to write, my address is Nicanor Markström, Oppstoppet, Bure, Westerbotten.

PART TWO

1

LISTEN NOW, REDCOMB

1

THE SITUATION with Comrade Elmblad was such that he was indeed still working at organizing the struggling and revolutionary masses in preparation for the coming struggle, in which, of historical necessity, they would be betrayed by their ambivalent and compromising leaders: or roughly that.

To be more truthful, in his more gloomy moments he was utterly convinced it was precisely the other way round. He was working at organizing; it was true up to that point. Otherwise it was mostly one long hopeless mess. Who in this hellish kingdom was really interested in the socialist cause, he kept thinking. Not many, anyhow not many from the working classes of the kingdom.

Sometimes he thought he hated them. He knew he hated them. Their utter indifference. Their inertia. Occasionally he felt a bloody great urge to stand up and say what he really thought. He would tell them, straight to their faces, that they were cursed cowardly idiots who didn't know what was best for them. He had sacrificed the whole of his life to change these cowardly, creeping, repugnant hypocrites who didn't know what was best for them, and to convert them to the cause of socialism. The working class could stuff it, particularly those nests of strike-breakers along the coasts of Upper Norrland, whom he wished in hell. May they all be exploited by the exploiters, tormented by all tormentors of workers, starved to death by capitalists, freeze to death in their prayer-houses and be thawed out in hell, they were welcome.

Strike-breaking rabble and fawners, that's what they were. Slug-gish, treacherous sanctimonious cattle.

He had felt like standing up and saying all that quite openly. Nevertheless, he knew better now. He had opened his heart to the executive in a report, not fully, but just a crack. And all hell had been let loose. He had immediately received a long, stony letter, by return, in which Comrade Elmblad was asked whether his view of the working classes was really as he had described. Such a presumptuous and elitist view of the working masses was quite unacceptable. They had demanded an explanation. So he had been forced to write an explanation: he had sweated over it for a whole week and only got away with it by the skin of his teeth.

So he still had the trust of the executive. But he realized the situation was bad.

In the spring of 1909, he was forty-eight years. old. Six years had gone by since the night he had been chased across Bure Heath, the night when the moon had shone and he had tried to eat a worm. And now, via the Party office, he had received a letter signed by Frans Nicanor Markström, Oppstoppet, Bure, Wester-botten.

He read it with surprise and heavy foreboding.

His reports were hell. He sweated blood over them, but they never seemed to have any style to them. He sensed that his epistles were notorious, laughed at and spat on by the Party executive, but he wrote and wrote and wrote.

'Report on canvassing in Nerike, 21–30 June, 1909,' he wrote in his large, clumsy, uneven hand, in which gloomy great capital letters were poised high above terrorized little downstrokes in irrational formations. 'Received letter of 12th with refusal of my request for payment for canvassing expenses. I must convey to the executive that it is incomprehensible how you let yourselves be hypnotized by the unsuccessful results of the most recent canvas-sing trip I shall now describe (?). If you had waited, perhaps the resulting judgement would have been different. Wednesday and Thursday, 23rd and 24th, I was in *Skyttberg* and *Kårbergsbruk*, where there is no organization whatsoever and the greatest dis-unity reigns among the workers. I could get *no* permission to hold a meeting for many reasons – 1st there is nothing but Company property – the Company owns all the land and – 2nd Rain! and

148

rain again. Further to that, many workers asked me not to arrange a meeting for the reason that their religious comrades would then only be given something to tell the Director – as well as whoever went to it, and finally there would be systematic dismissals. The Director told them he wants only workers who had the same interests *as him* or "who agree with whoever feeds them" – as he put it. 24th I was in *Rönneshyttan* with the same results as before in *Skyttberg* I dealt out leaflets got addresses and promised to return. There are many there who have been to other places and who have belonged to a union so it wasn't absolutely hopeless although there are several hundred who go round *boasting about medals* awarded for slavery. On 25th I was in *Nora* and *Gyttorp* but my God, what people! So apathetic I cannot describe how piteous. However, there is one union in *Nora*, the Tailors, but that is all. On 27th in *Björneborg* and *Christinehamn* to arrange meetings, but have had a reply from *Christinehamn* that they don't want anyone and that I would not get anyone to come *as they have heard me once before*. But they have the wrong person because I have *never* been there, and they . . .'

He often felt he wrote the wrong sort of reports. Their tone was wrong. Correct facts but the wrong tone.

He wrote his reports in wild, angry handwriting, full of underlining, exclamation marks, angry dashes and gloomy question marks. His disappointment seemed to be in his very hand, and when he had finished writing, he used to sit staring for a long time at what he had scraped together.

It was so aggressive.

What would they think? Perhaps they would only see that he was deeply embittered. Then they would think he had given up. Cantankerous. But he told them what it was like. They wanted to know what it was like. And if he told them precisely what it was like then he was slandering the working classes. And then some bloody letter came along, icy cold and well written, maintaining he had not seen the 'historical perspective' and that he had 'confused the present situation' with something. With the possible? No, that he drew general conclusions from private experiences.

What epistles! He wished he could write like that himself. What bloody good speeches they would be. The peasants would gape and shut up and go home and say a really scholarly fellow had been and as you could make neither head nor tail of anything he said, it must be right.

In Stockholm, they obviously believed he had become apathetic and thought nothing could be changed. That was not true. If there was any point in these damned reports, then it should be to say what it was like. To tell the truth. If some armchair strategist in Stockholm thought he was painting things black, then he should come up and look for himself. Because if it was true the working class of Sweden was starving, suffering, content with little, pious, and got the shivers at the very thought of socialisim, then all you could do was to say so. What the hell else could a man do?

When he thought a little more about it, at heart he did not like this part of the country and its bloody mentality in the very slightest. The working classes weren't the right ones. Wrong sort. Wrong sort.

He also had other problems with the Party, slightly more awkward ones, money problems. Of course, one was supposed to practise what one preached and indeed he didn't exactly live extravagantly, but he was in fact a tiny little bit easy-going or actually downright careless with money, and sometimes it was perhaps, you might say, troublesome to account *in detail* for *all* expenditure.

He was not very good with money.

Not especially, anyhow, and this had aroused a certain annoyance in Stockholm, not much, but slight annoyance, or perhaps slightly stronger than slight annoyance, maybe. Because he was so bad with money. He mostly had to borrow his way ahead, a month or so in advance. Well, several months in advance. And to crown everything, they had now written to him on this subject and reprimanded him.

One thing and another. He didn't remember all that well. But reprimanded he had been and that was unpleasant, and there had been quite a lot between the lines. In addition, they had asked him to stop what he was doing and instead go up to the coast of Norrland again. They had sent him a letter from this Nicanor Markström, and the accompanying letter had implied surprise that Elmblad had not made the most of previous trips to places where the ground was clearly as favourable as in Bure, for instance, where to judge from the letter a lively workers' association had clearly existed for a long time. A sewing-bee, of course, and not affiliated! But that ripe fruit could very easily have been plucked.

It was somewhat painful for Elmblad, and he wondered how he could explain to them. Nevertheless, it was true. He hadn't been to Bureå parish for several years. He had put it off. Why, he did not know. Or rather, he did know. It was something to do with that chase across Bure Heath, when the moon had been very large and shining and he had been tied to a tree for a very long time.

He read the Markström letter. 'I would like you to come via Bure parish in that case. You were up here once before if you remember, though they were angry about socialism then. I was the boy who helped you put up the posters.'

He remembered the boy perfectly well.

With absolute clarity.

He remembered those Westerbotten people, too. He had done quite a few canvassing trips along the coast, but it was true that, after the events in Bure, he had put off going to canvass there. No doubt about it. But he knew the problems.

Nevertheless he was not alone.

His reports are indeed badly written, often contradictory, often expressing an opinion of the Swedish working class which is either repugnant or at fault, or both. Nevertheless, he is not alone in this view. It may appear to be defeatist or negative, or simultaneously idealistic and cynical, but nevertheless, he was not alone. Other canvassers reported the same facts even if they did inflate the attendance figures at meetings a trifle and were more careful with their language. But there were problems along the coast of Norrland, great problems.

If you don't believe Elmblad, you can go to Janne Persson, Gustav Johansson or Johan Hallberg, who all described the same reality. In a report in 1908, Hallberg summarizes his experiences in Westerbotten and Norrbotten in the following manner (the spelling has been adjusted): 'May I allow myself a final word on the circumstances of the population in general. It is generally known nowadays that the branch of capitalist exploitation called the timber trade has wrought terrible destruction in the northern provinces of the country, not least in Westerbotten and Norrbotten, where the more severe climatic conditions contribute to the reduction of the standard of living of the poor. Along the coast, from Umeå northwards, which is generally fertile and less ravaged by the desctructive processes of forest-exploiters and where more or less usable communications in the form of roads make transport and disposal of existing products possible, there is less reason to talk of palpable poverty than in the forest communities, where conditions are usually so wretched as to defy description. Barely any negotiable roads, great distances between neighbours, the forests ravaged and the land in the hands of the companies – and these give just a slight idea of the people's discomfort and great difficulties in earning a living.

'Opportunities for work are usually extremely limited for the inhabitants of these forest areas. As long as the forests existed to be exploited, it was possible, by paying starvation wages, to maintain activity, but owing to severe competition from farmers in the coastal areas, who are able to take provisions from their homes to both men and beasts, then wages were as mentioned reduced to the lowest possible. I will not attempt to describe the wretched lot of company tenants. I simply wish to state the appalling fact that among this unfortunate category of human beings, blood-stained capitalism has sown the most terrible seeds which in many places have resulted in complete physical and moral degeneration, cancerous sores which will need many years of constant preaching – and educational work – to be cured. But first and foremost rapid and radical reforms are necessary here if a whole class of people is not to succumb completely to starvation and social deprivation.

'As the great majority thus consists of economically oppressed and spiritually crippled people, and added to that the destructive activities of religion that have produced the most profound mistrust and misunderstanding of the heartening ideas of socialism, it is possible to understand the difficulties confronting canvassing work. If one adds the fact that meeting-places are often impossible to acquire owing to fear of consequences from companies and their henchmen posted out in the villages, then it is possible to understand some of the more trying aspects of the work, and the reason why the desired results are very often absent. (— — —) From the end of March, activities are located in the dark and backward Piteå area, which is without doubt the blackest spot in Norrbotten. The often economically favoured farming population has over a long period of years constituted a veritable torment both to the area's poverty-stricken working population as well as to the inhabitants of the forest areas, in that their well-known avarice has enabled them to grab for themselves at appallingly low wages most of the work at the sawmills, as well as what is for the workers of the forest communities much-needed forestry and logging work, and this for reasons (?) indicated above. Several examples can also be produced from these areas of, for instance, during the stevedore's dispute in the summer, the farmers sending their servants as strike-breakers to the districts involved in disputes. Thanks to the destructive activities of religion, the central core of which in these areas is carried on methodically by ministers of the church and lay preachers in fraternal co-operation with those black offspring called Swedish People's Alliance and Swedish Workers' Alliance, they have managed to work up such fanatical bitterness against the workers' movement that in some villages it is scarcely possible to avoid coming to blows.'

Elmblad was certainly not alone.

2

ELMBLAD'S SITUATION WAS SUCH that he was always worrying. He worried about his family, about his job, about the workers' movement, and God knows what he didn't worry about.

He had sacrificed his whole life to the socialist cause – his family life, his finances and his health. Soon he would not be able to distinguish between what was boredom with his private life and boredom with the cursed working-classes and the indifference he met. But something else was wrong. His health was poor, too. He had already had bladder trouble in his forties. That came from being on the road. If you lived like a tinker, you got it like a tinker. It was hopeless trying to pee.

Once he had indeed dreamt of rescuing all those wretched people. He really had. But when he saw those wretched people and their wretched lives and their wretched toil and their wretched patience, and he saw their aggressive scorn for anyone who tried to help them out of their wretchedness, then he despaired and hardly knew what to do. He told himself it was fear he saw. They were all frightened. There was nothing wrong with that. There was absolutely nothing wrong about being afraid. But they constantly gave way to their fears. That was what was repugnant.

Some showed some opposition. But they were so few.

Perhaps it was different in the towns, but he did not work in the towns. How would they ever be able to win a battle in the labour market if those damned strike-breakers were not rooted out? Piteå. Westerbotten. Norrbotten. Those smallholders. That piety. That patience. The whole blasted mess.

Elmblad's wife was called Dagmar.

She was tall, with a birthmark on her cheek, and was of a nervous disposition. Elmblad liked her very much. Why that was so, he did not really understand. He did not see her all that often, but that made no difference. Some relationships improve by the parties not meeting, others deteriorate; things evened out. He wrote letters to her as often as possible, telling her about his experiences at work. Dagmar, his wife, was not interested in his work, not in the slightest, but she accepted his letters as a sign of friendliness and read them over and over again, until she practically knew them by heart. Then she burnt them and when he came home complained that she never got any letters. As evidence of his shabby treatment of her, she could quote the less well-written parts of the letters she had not received. He took this as a sign of her nervous disposition.

She thought she was very lonely. She had four children, one from a previous marriage. She had married at eighteen. She was born in Vallen, outside Lövånger, where she had married and where she had been widowed. Elmblad had found her there one day in the summer of 1896. He had somehow got it over to her that there was also a world outside Vallen, which was true, but she always took that as a special little insult to her native heath.

Her first husband had died of pneumonia, which he had developed when the prayer-house in Ersmark had burnt down. He had been a potential candidate for the church, a studious man and a serious Christian. Everyone assumed he would become a minister in the end, but then the prayer-house had caught fire and he had been up all night passing buckets of water, caught a chill and died of pneumonia. No doubt he had been inadequately clad. In some ways, many people looked on him as a kind of martyr: it was all considered particularly tragic because he was a candidate for the church and had died in a prayer-house fire. During her period of mourning, many people told Dagmar she had nearly been a minister's wife.

The fire was on a Monday. By Saturday, he was dead. He had always had a weak chest.

Dagmar was twenty-one then, the boy two years old. When her husband died, she was suddenly afflicted with despondency and lost her faith. People who knew her assumed she had become rancorous and it had gone inwards. She should be glad it hadn't taken her wits. But as far as her faith and conduct were concerned, Dagmar appeared transformed: she remained tight-lipped and silent, speaking harshly of the faith. Them Elmblad had come; by then she was already rather neurotic, but he took no notice, thinking she would improve.

Dagmar liked thinking about the reasons for her nervousness. She held several totally contradictory theories, all of which she liked very much. One of them was that a maternal uncle of hers had put the mark of lunacy on her when she was with child. Her uncle's name was Anton, and he'd gone loony, mad, that is: they had tied him to the arm of the sofa, and he had sat there bawling, rolling his eyes and singing psalms. All the pregnant women in the village had been warned not to go there, but as Dagmar liked Uncle Anton, she had not been able to resist it. He had stared straight into her heart, which had pierced her like a ray of fire, and she had started sobbing.

That was surely when her melancholy had started.

Elmblad told her all that was nonsense. They were constantly quarrelling about it, Elmblad always arguing back forcefully that what she said was superstition and typical of the decadent morality of the strange place in which she had been brought up. She always flared up at that, and shouted at him until he considered it as well to go out to the privy and stay there until she had calmed down. But she seldom did so. He kept wishing she would pull herself together and get a hold on herself, but he was constantly disappointed.

She was also constantly disappointed.

They had lived in a great many places because his work forced him to travel almost all over the country. It was a wretched life. In comparison with Social Democrat party workers, gypsies were lucky. They were at least their own masters. Because Elmblad himself appreciated the importance of good organization and method in his work for the Party, but failed at it in his private life, this became something of a torture to his whole family. They rented places wherever they could. Or rather, Elmblad tried to

155

arrange for a place for his family to live, then installed his wife and four children, leaving barely enough money, then disappeared on his search for the Swedish working-classes.

Dagmar hated the life, and found it hard to keep quiet about her feelings. Her nervous state fluctuated as they moved from place to place. When they lived in *Lycksele*, her melancholy was not so severe. Then they moved to *Västervik*, where it increased. Then it got slowly worse in *Falköping*, *Morgongåva* and *Månkarbo*, only to improve somewhat when they moved to *Bofors*. In *Hallsberg*, she was perfectly calm. 'You've started getting a hold on yourself,' Elmblad said to her encouragingly. 'You're doing fine.' That was where she had her fourth child, after which they moved to *Heffners*, where she became melancholy again. Worst of all was her depression during the day, when she would sit on her bed like Job on the ashes, crying for hours.

She was never free of it. It sat like a sandbag in her heart.

Sometimes she read Elmblad's letters to try to understand her husband and to get her depression to go away. He always wrote about the same things, about cancelled meetings, or about four people who had come to a meeting, of whom two were very positive, or about policemen who had threatened him with prosecution, about places where they had told him to go to hell, and about one or two successes, when he had managed to form worker councils which would be sure to collapse within a few months; this was the constant implication throughout all his melancholy and violent letters.

She knew the letters almost off by heart. When she had read them, her melancholy retreated slightly. She secretly suspected that her husband was not at all suited to be a Party worker. He was too hot-tempered, and at the same time kindly, strong and frightened. The more she got to know him, the more she lost her respect for him, and the more attached she became to him. She demonstrated this by constantly scolding him. She had no other way of showing her love; Elmblad understood this and was never offended.

When he was at home, she cried over something for at least two hours a day, mostly over life being so loveless and filled with tears, often accusing him of choosing the work because he couldn't stand living with her. That was not actually true, he told her, as he had started working for the Party before he had met her. Then she started crying over him always contradicting her and never respecting her views. Put together, all this might indicate that she was stupid, or nasty, or mean, but that wasn't true, either; on the contrary, and Elmblad knew it. He considered himself lucky to have met her. She was difficult, but he controlled himself and understood her. She had simply not bothered to sort out the pieces of herself that didn't match. Most people he met had sorted out what was illogical and what didn't match: they had then sat polishing and shining the remaining pieces so the rough edges would not hurt. But Dagmar hadn't done that.

Living with a person like that was hard work and meant a lot of sighing out in the privy, but nevertheless, things were better that way.

He had always dreamt of being able to live with people who did not polish away their humanity, who were quite openly wretched, and that was how he saw her, and he bore his cross. But it was not so good with the children.

The children may not have seen it in the same way.

He thought he understood, although she always maintained he understood nothing. Elmblad's wife looked upon herself as a person whose dignity had been stolen from her. They had stolen her human dignity, taking it away piece by piece. They cut pieces out of her and reduced her. First of all her husband (a candidate for the church) had died quite unnecessarily. That took away a piece. She had given birth to four children, and for each child, her humanity and tolerance and dignity were reduced. The second child she had had with Elmblad was an imbecile. He was squint-eyed, could still not speak, constantly dribbled, had a large chin, and she knew what he would look like when he was adult. The imbecile child had reduced her, too. Her husband reduced her by not being there. She learnt his letters off by heart, then burnt them. Her loneliness was considerable but she could see no way out.

She had once tried to hang herself, but had failed. That was in *Morgongåva*. Then she had considered taking a lover, a temporary husband, anything, an act she made reality in *Månkarbo*. She could hardly remember his name. He had flopped on top of her for a while, then fallen asleep, and when he had left in the morning, he had shaken her hand and thanked her. It would have been better if he'd slapped her face. But taking a temporary lover had not improved the state of her nerves.

She had finally begun to suspect that all the exaggerated talk about socialism was the reason for her melancholy.

157

Elmblad had found her as a twenty-one-year-old widow living on the Västerbotten coast, and he had got her with child three times. What he liked most about her was her aggressiveness, though it saddened him that it was only turned in on herself, making her nervous. Or else it was turned on to him in the form of endless nagging. But she possessed aggressiveness, and he liked that. He liked it for the same reason he hated the cowardly working masses who did not know what was best for them, and gave in. So things collapsed. He often thought most of his life had collapsed. It had collapsed over him, but it had not finished him. It was just that it hurt so hellishly. That was normal.

3

GIVEN TIME, the pain decreased. Elmblad's situation was also such that he was aware of his wife's unfaithfulness. He at once interpreted it as a sign of nerves and decided not to be offended. Nevertheless, he found to his surprise he was hurt.

It must have happened when they were living in *Månkarbo* or *Morgongåva*. He was inclined to guess the former. Fortunately, his wife did not know he knew about it; that would simply have made her sad and upset, which he did not wish her to be. So he hadn't wanted to refer to the subject. One ought not to dig into such things. Nevertheless, he had witnessed the event.

Witnessed the event.

He decided he would keep that to himself forever. He buried it, like a grain of sand, deep down in the chamber of his heart: it was painful and at the same time strangely tempting. What he had seen had burnt its way in, like a branding-iron on animal flesh, stinking of degradation and lust at the same time. But not indifference. Occasionally he thought life, torment and degradation were one and the same thing; that was good, that was life, things that were close to each other and gave strength. Or confusion.

He was very uncertain about all this. But in a muddled but obvious way it was all linked with his feeling that he was a bad Party worker, working for the cowardly and uninteresting working-classes.

Or also.

Anyhow. This is what had happened. He had seen a bicycle leaning against the wall. At first he had been worried, because he didn't recognize the bicycle. Or, to start from the beginning, he had been canvassing in *Skultuna* and in *Timbro* and had been away from home for four weeks, and when he arrived home early one morning, he had seen the bicycle and had been worried. It was early morning and summer. With no difficulty at all, he had seen them through the window, like a picture. Straight through the fly-spotted window-pane in the outhouse they had rented, he had seen the extremely clear picture of his wife in bed and the man beside her.

They were asleep. She had had her hand round his member, as if wishing to protect it, and she was being very careful with something warm and soft and defenceless: she seemed to be holding a little frog in her hand; the frog was not afraid, and was asleep. She, too, was asleep, openly and defencelessly secure like a child. He had stood there by the window that early summer morning, the deafening chorus of birds all round him. The sun would soon be up. And he had seen them sleeping.

At first he thought all kinds of things. But then the noise of the birds had grown so loud and shrill, he could no longer bear it, so he decided to move a little. He had gone for a little walk by himself. He thought about all kinds of things, but mostly about her. He kept thinking he had failed in his responsibilities to her. A whole series of thoughts ran through his head, and then gradually, the crazy wildly singing birds of *Månkarbo* or *Morgongåva* (later, he was fairly certain it was the former) had quietened. He had been surprised to find himself sitting right in the middle of the forest. So that he was, nearly, almost, unable to find his way home. Later on.

The frog had been very secure, sleeping, she secure, too, in her sleep. Elmblad would have loved to give her that security, but realized it was difficult, and he was pleased she had found it in some way.

He supposed the other man had been able to give it to her.

Although it was so light and the birds so noisy, Elmblad had fallen asleep. He had woken at midday, on the ground, slap in the middle of the forest, in some bewilderment. He walked home. The bicycle had gone. His wife had cried a lot that afternoon, and then roughly accused him of not writing to her, although he had been away for four weeks. Then he had said: 'I wrote to you.' Then she

159

had cried all the more and said he didn't trust her. So things were much as usual.

But he liked her all the same. The screaming of the birds had been unpleasant, he had almost got lost in the forest, and it had hurt a great deal, but then he had pulled himself together. Now he had everything quite under control.

The tour of Norrland arranged for Elmblad by Party headquarters came as a great shock to both Elmblad and his family.

On the morning he left, they had breakfast together. They had *bryta*, which she had learnt to make in her parents' home in Vallen and then brought with her to her marriage. *Bryta* was standard. They sat round the kitchen table, Dagmar and Elmblad and the four children, now fifteen, nine, six (the imbecile) and two years old. None of them said much, except Dagmar. At first she had brought up all the things she usually brought up, i.e. the possibility of him changing jobs, or how little they appreciated him at headquarters in Stockholm, and that they did not have to tolerate this, then in conclusion a little about the lack of appreciation out in the field. He realized she meant no ill, but was simply miserable. Then she talked for a while about the time they had lived in Lycksele, where he had had honest work as a gravedigger, and although there was not much to reply to, Elmblad did not exactly offer much in a way of reply. Then there had been a long silence, only the imbecile snuffling in his slightly troubled forsaken way, like a sad little pig, and then it was time for Elmblad to leave.

Dagmar started weeping loudly and despairingly, repeating over and over again, '*Take me with you. Take me with you!*' and then, '*I don't want to stay here and I'm so lonely!*'; then several of the children had joined in and it proved impossible to make them stop. All of them, all six, had sat round the kitchen table, Dagmar and the children (the imbecile, too) weeping. For a moment, Elmblad lost his temper (banging his fork down on the table), but the weeping continued (the imbecile, too, creeping over to Elmblad and hiding his ugly little face in Elmbald's lap, hiccoughing like a sad abandoned little piglet) and the little imbecile crying had almost been the worst, because he was so helpless you couldn't tell him, so suddenly Elmblad felt like joining them.

Nevertheless, he told his wife he *had* to leave.

He asked her whether she realized he was leaving for all their sakes.

160

She said no. Then he said he *had* to go up to that bloody, foul, strike-breaking hole in Västerbotten and he couldn't change that. She said no no no no. The children cried. The little imbecile snivelled and wet Elmblad's trousers with his dribble. It was total chaos. He was glad no one was looking. Anyone witnessing all this would certainly have wondered what sort of dreadful family he had.

Then she suddenly said perfectly calmly: 'Take me away, or I'll do away with myself.' 'You wouldn't do that,' said Elmblad. 'Yes, I would,' she said. 'I will. I'll do away with myself and all the children.' They all sat staring at her, and the children stopped crying. It was quite silent for a long time. They had heard all this several times before, but never so determined as this time, which was why they were quiet. Elmblad did not know what to say to the children. But he thought: *maybe they can look after themselves.* Doing away with four children can't be that easy. Maybe they'll stick together if things look stormy. The older ones.

He liked his children very much.

While it was silent, all kinds of things went through his head. It was tricky. It's tricky, he thought. He always thought that when he was about to crack up. It's a bit tricky.

Then Elmblad quite simply took Dagmar on to his lap. She was tall, and quite heavy, and suddenly he remembered with painful clarity the little frog sleeping so securely in her hand; but that didn't matter; no, it vanished. He took her on to his lap and sang a song. The children stopped snivelling, because they wanted to hear what he was singing, and he stroked her cheek and sang and sang, and in the end her sobs subsided into a resigned silence. He sang quite a happy little song for her, and at last he managed to get them all more or less calmed down.

In this way, their breakfast at last came to an end, that, too, and so Elmblad the agitator could start out on his long journey to the dark lands.

2

GROWING GARDEN

1

HE WENT ON BOARD in Gefle.

He slept in the hold as usual. Elmblad had long since learnt what things were like and what he could do. He could crawl under a tarpaulin, then wait for the sea and the waves. When they came, he would be sick. That was how all his journeys to the north started, beginning with him feeling sick and ending with him feeling sick. In between there were other similar torments.

His view of Norrlanders, for instance.

This evening, the sea was very calm, the sun heavy, then dusk fell and he sat on deck for a long time, looking round, turned to stone like Lot's wife, his gaze fixed obstinately on the vanishing coastline. He wished he were somewhere where he did not have to disintegrate, where his heart did not always feel like a sandbag. He wished a rope had been thrown to the coastline to keep it there, and when darkness had fallen, he had sat on for a long time in the biting cold evening breeze, trying to see right through the darkness. When he finally descended to the hold (still no waves, still no nausea), they were level with Söderhamn.

He had a very peculiar dream that night.

He dreamt he had been caught. They had exposed him. His bluff had been called. Now his trial had come. How all this had happened was never made quite clear in his dream, but he had been imprisoned, the other criminals with him.

The others were Janne Persson, Blixt, Gustav Johansson, Hallberg and all the other Party workers. There were about ten of them, but it seemed to him that he was kept slightly apart from the others, his crime the worst. In his dream, he also thought this just. No one was manacled. They all walked voluntarily to the court. Then the dream became peculiar and abandoned logic, and they were suddenly on the rock. The rock was square and black and in

162

the middle of the sea, like a gigantic cube, seven kilometres long and seven kilometres wide and seven kilometres high, black as ebony, and right in the middle of the rock a small frog was sleeping. They sat in a circle and held hands to keep up their courage. Elmblad, Blixt, Hallberg and the others. Then a bird came flying in from the darkness, a bird with a gentle sorrowful face, a small bird-like pig-face, and it sat down in amongst them and snivelled and twittered a brief song, then said with a childishly idiotic whimper that now they must realize how meaningless everything was. The bird sharpened its soft little beak against the gigantic rock and said that his soft little snout would wear out the rock before Swedes became socialists. Why torment yourselves so?

Elmblad nodded and said that was right, and he was prepared to take his punishment.

The rock was then immediately transformed, becoming golden and dissolving into a beautiful island in the middle of the sea, and a voice from heaven came to them and stirred up the sea and made the waves so high that it was as menacing and breathtaking and tense and exciting as on the Day of Judgement. But then the judge appeared, Branting himself, the Party leader. Now they were at the People's House in Enånge. As usual, there were five people in the audience and Branting was holding Dagmar and the little imbecile by the hand. The little imbecile had grown a head taller than all the others; he was round like a marzipan loaf, his lower jaw protruding, and constantly grinning. Dagmar was holding a torn letter in her hand, saying: 'You never write. Never never never, because you don't care about me.' Then Branting read out the judgement. All the other agitators had gone now and the wind was blowing hard and he was cold as Branting read out the sentence. He had been aggressive, Branting explained, and he hated the people and the working classes, and was contemptuous of the workers' movement, and he had neglected his family and found it hard to pee and he had talked rubbish about the farmers and made the situation out to be hopeless and wished the little imbecile dead. But his worst sin was considering everything hopeless. In the present situation, no one should paint the prospects so black. Apathy was a deadly sin, like negativism. He was a pessimist. He did not keep his finances in order. He did not write to his wife. He was a coward, and dishonest.

That was the judgement.

163

In his dream, the trial was over very quickly and not at all surprisingly. He found himself on the march. All the agitators were on the train. They were to go by train down into the grave, a gigantic grave he himself had dug, very rapidly with the same skill he had shown in Lycksele. It was a gigantic grave, apparently overgrown. It was like going by train into a slowly growing garden; no, a jungle. The plants moved, but at the same time were quite dead, as if a lethal downpour had struck the world, and now the dead plants were growing all the faster. A downpour of death, it was. After death, the plants came to life, the creeping plants covering everything, no life visible, and he found himself in the overgrown grave of life, his confusion ticking like a clock in the growing garden. He was imprisoned by death. He knew it was his own fault and had offered no resistance. That was why he now found himself in the garden of death; yes, in the actual jungle itself. He heard the padding of large brown animals and suddenly it was quite dark and there were no stars and all was quiet.

Them Elmblad and Janne Persson and Blixt and Gustav Johansson and Hallberg all held hands. In his dream, he could feel their hands. They all started up a fairly jolly song to cheer each other up, now the time had come to confirm the final solution. Elmblad had been condemned, had erred, but the balance could be restored. The bird was sharpening its beak against the rock in the sea, and would go on doing so into eternity, never giving up, working away to annihilate indifference.

They held each other by the hand, and Elmblad and Janne Persson and Blixt and Gustav Johansson walked into the growing garden of death in quite a good mood, singing quite a cheerful little song to each other, and thus in their dream they prepared themselves for the final struggle.

When morning came, the dream was still there. He couldn't shake it off and neither could he understand it; he stood in the bows for a long time, gazing over towards the coast of Norrland. That was the second morning.

The coast was low and faint and he had seen it before. A wooden boat was gliding southwards, endlessly slowly, apparently raised above the surface of the water by the light and sailing in thin air. It was going to England, with a cargo of work, people's work, for which a few people would get a huge sum of money and those who had done the work would get little or none. But when

164

he came to say all this, that the boat was carrying not cargo but work, they wouldn't understand. The dream would not go away, so he was very calm, not yet upset or aggressive; no, he found himself in the middle of his own calm.

He was back in Westerbotten.

But he thought: if only I could escape from it all. If only I could take them all with me, the cowardly and the outcast and the cheats and the traitors and the heroes and the aggressive and the starving, take them on my back and fly away. Like a giant bird. Take them to a country no one knew. A blissful island. Not America. Not the Congo. No, an unknown country, like the Holy Land, but without the holiness. The giant bird would land there and Dagmar and the children and the little imbecile with his little running pig-nose would be there; he would put them all down and then they would all work together. There would be no complaints and no poverty there, and they would all be able to pee unhindered and would dare to be cowardly together. No one would steal the fruits of their labour, no one would weep, there would be no diseases or cowardice, and he would be able to pee without pain.

Slowly, the coast rose. He had seen it before. But he was sure something had to happen now, a change, a settlement, if he were to be capable of going on.

He went ashore in Ursviken, and no one recognized him.

2

THE BOY HAD WALKED all the way to Skellefteå to meet him.

The boy was nothing like he remembered. He was now almost six foot tall, quite slim but square-shouldered, with thick dark hair and pale watery blue eyes, and he looked old for his age. Elmblad remembered nothing of this from the previous occasion. The boy had shaken hands with him, looking him straight in the eye, smiling happily and cheerfully without the slightest trace of fear or hestitation, saying that his name was Nicanor Markström and asking: 'Dost tha remember me?'

Elmblad had regarded the questioner in silence. Then the boy had said: 'Ah remembers thee, Elmblad. Tha'd worms in tha's mouth.

165

'When tha wuz fishin' dun in Bure.'

Nothing else was said, but they had set off together, walking south.

They walked the fourteen kilometres from Skellefteå to Bureå. People usually took the steamer along the river, the boy had said, but it had already left. There was nothing else to do but walk. They walked south along the coast road, Elmblad in the lead. He liked walking ahead, his body moving with astonishing lightness, his fat heavy body gliding lithely along the verge, clearly a man used to walking long distances.

The last twenty-four hours had been cold. It was the end of September and the first thin autumn ice on the puddles crunched under their feet. The walking was easy. Elmblad had his lunch-tin in one hand, his case in the other. He felt light and happy.

He could hear the boy breathing behind him. Now and again, stray bits of information of a geographical nature came sailing over from the boy, as if somehow he wished to keep the conversation going, though the information never touched on questions of real interest to Elmblad.

In the end, he asked:

'What about the dispute? What happened up here in the great conflict? Is it over here as well?'

He received nothing but a faint humming in reply. Elmblad stopped and looked at the boy. Dark hair, pale watery eyes, not timid in the slightest.

'T'weren't up t'much,' the boy said calmly.

Elmblad always preferred autumn. The colours were more distinct. He could see the very clear yellows and reds and what had no colour, the clear air. Autumn was the time when people and colours were clearest, most like themselves.

He liked to think of himself as a very clear person.

They rested in Yttervik. They sat down on a stone and Elmblad wiped the sweat off his brow, smiling benignly. The boy smiled back. Small grey barns, the hay-drying racks not yet taken in. The boy commented on everything Elmblad could see with his own eyes, keeping silent about the rest for the time being. The people of Yttervik were known for sometimes leaving their drying racks out through the winter. Oh, yes? Yes. Uhuh. Then came an explanation that this was an instance of the peculiar characteristics of the people of Yttervik. Other people had sense. The people of

Hjoggböle, for instance. Oh, yes? Yes, they took their racks in for the winter. Oh, yes?

There was no one to be seen. Everything had suddenly become so still. So quiet. How desolate the countryside seemed. So few columns of smoke.

'I sometimes wonder,' Elmblad said straight out into the silence, 'whether this really is our country. Sometimes it seems like a foreign country. I sometimes wonder if we're not in the wildest of jungles.'

3

The great conflict?

But the fact was simply that it was over. Not much to talk about, though at the same time, that was what the problem was.

The boy was very taciturn and apparently inclined to tone down the whole affair, as if it were not worth mentioning, though he was taciturn in a fairly pressing way. Well, there was nothing much to say about the conflict. It was over.

'Question is,' he said after a rather long gap, straight at Elmblad's walking back, 'what'll us do now, an' what'll them what doesna get work do?'

Because the situation, Elmblad slowly began to realize, was that, as far as Bureå was concerned, the great strike was definitely over; it had been a minor matter hardly worth discussing, but certain problems had arisen, and that was not much fun for some of the workers.

That was the core of the message. The rest came out bit by bit.

The situation with the great strike and Bureå was that it had started quite well, but then there was not much worth mentioning.

It had started with Gustav Blixt, the Party worker stationed in Ursviken, coming over. He had heard rumours about the independent workers' association and what had happened to it, and he had tried to scrape up the remnants. He gathered some of the workers together at Karl Hedlund's place, and in the greatest secrecy they had formed a trade union, the beginnings of what later became Sawmill 238, but the union was unofficial and no one was to know about it. Then a few months later, the great strike had come and everything had gone well for the first week, participation in the strike as good as a hundred per cent. More than six hundred workers had gone on strike in Bureå. They had set up strike pickets and tried to co-operate with other sawmills along the river valley. They had also formed a strike committee which included Frans Eriksson, N. A. Eriksson and Aron Häggblom. Later on it had also included Konrad Lundström.

Well, from then on things had not gone so well, so the whole thing had kind of come to an end.

'Kind of?' said Elmblad irritably. 'Kind of come to an end? What the hell does that mean?'

It kind of hadn't worked, sort of. Of course. You could almost have reckoned on that happening.

A big strike in Westerbotten is a difficult matter. It could hardly be planned. It might work if it happened during hay-making, or the corn harvest or potato-picking. But in between those the strike-breakers would pour in from the villages, eager for work and full of energy, strong in their faith and willing to show the lazy how work should be done if you are not afraid to set about it and do your best.

So a big strike in August is a difficult matter.

Perhaps not really to be recommended.

As soon as two weeks later, the company management was able to announce in the *Skelleftebladet*, very factually but with an undertone of suppressed pride, that they were working in Bure practically to full capacity. Indeed, there were six hundred men formally on strike, but great numbers willing to work had put in time and energy to save the situation. From the management point of view, it was regarded as gratifying that so many willing workers had appeared, for the damaging effects on the community were then reduced and third-party damage excluded.

The damaging effects, on the whole, had been virtually nil.

Men had come from the villages, which could be reckoned on beforehand. They came from Holmsvattnet and Sjöbotten and East Fahlmark and Vallen (true, though that was a low estimate; south towards Lövånger there were people who would do anything for a few kronor, even walk twenty miles) and Burvik (no, wrong, not so many, because the people of Burvik were of a special kind) and Trollåsen and Istermyrliden and Sjön and East Hjoggböle and Forsen and West Hjoggböle (though the West

Hjoggböleans were slightly less committed Christians and had three kilometres further to walk, which reduced the number of those wanting to work) and so on. God alone knows whether there was a single village that did not contribute to saving the situation.

And in Bureå?

Nicanor told him that the situation had been such that when people had poured in from the villages, solidarity in Bureå had to some extent cracked here and there. That was probably what had happened. At first they had tried to stop the flood by gathering down by the Skerry road and yelling and shouting at the strike-breakers. But they had only laughed. There was nothing to be done about it. They came with their lunch-tins in their hands and the word of God in their mouths, the possibility of earning an extra krona or so in their eyes, and it was like watching a horde of grey rats pouring in, industrious and hard-working men of faith every single one of them. And those who were not true believers were like most Bureå people, niggardly and mean. So the strike in Bureå had collapsed almost before it had even begun.

That was Nicanor's view of the whole thing. That was all there was to say about the great strike. It could be regarded as closed.

They were almost there, dusk, sharp clean air.

'Did they all give up?' said Elmblad straight out into the air.

No, and that was the present problem. It had turned out that some were prepared to fight on more than others. They were Konrad Lundström and Karl Nyberg and Amandus Wikström and Per Nyberg (brother of Karl Nyberg) and Aron Häggblom and Frans Eriksson and several more. For them, it was as if they'd said what the hell. They'd decided. This had been recorded in the minutes taken at the first strike meeting. For there it was: 'Para. 8. The question arose whether the struggle should be continued or not. Unanimously, with a resounding aye, it was decided to continue the struggle and just as we left work together so should we also return to work together when the struggle is brought to an end by the Confederation.'

So there was that resolution.

But on 25 August, the Managing Director had issued a state-ment. Access to available labour had indeed seemed to be good, and it was hoped that work was secured and damaging effects on the community could be avoided. However, he said in his statement, he was dismayed by the stubbornness and bitterness shown by many workers, presumably influenced by their leaders. But the Managing Director now wished to state, 'to avoid any misunderstanding', as it said in the statement, that 'after the end of the dispute members of the association could not expect work to any great extent'. The same statement included a brief note mentioning that on one occasion they had been forced to call in the police to protect men willing to work, and furthermore, sabotage had occurred by someone opening a logging-boom one night and letting the timber float out to sea. This act of vandalism, however, had been discovered within a few hours and the timber had been saved.

One Monday morning in September, they started drawing up the first lists.

Men who had wilfully deserted their jobs were told to report at seven o'clock to Gren the Setter in the timber yard, where they had to stand in line and state whether they wished to work or not. They went up to a table erected in the area, and there they had to report. After the men had reported their willingness, they were examined by the company management. Justice was mostly tempered with mercy, and those who had been unwilling to work were allowed their jobs back, though naturally according to the new rates, which were somewhat lower. About fifty names were put on a special list which was to be examined especially thoroughly, and on this list were the fifteen men who, at this point, maintained they were still on strike.

Their future was undoubtedly black, but they had only themselves to blame.

The queue of workers up to Gren's table was long, and it was to go on being long for several more mornings. Sensitive decisions were being made. It was no fun standing in a queue, but at least it wasn't raining. As they stood there in the queue, the workers had many reasons for gratitude. It wasn't raining, they were in good health, they were not being sacked, and there were large numbers of them involved in this whole wretched business.

The final list of men who in future 'could not expect work to any great extent' consisted of about thirty names. In one way, the list was correct: it consisted largely of those men who had somehow been active in a union way during the dispute, those who were reluctant to work as responsibly as before. The list was compiled by the company and thoroughly considered. Konrad

170

Lundström was on it, and Karl Nyberg and Aron Häggblom and Amandus Wikström and Frans Eriksson and all the others. As was to be expected.

One of the younger boys, by the name Nicanor Markström, was also on the list. And so was Aron Lindström.

On this blacklist.

They gathered in Aron Häggblom's kitchen. That was where Nicanor took him and that was where Elmblad went that late September day after the battle had already been lost; that was where they took him. There they sat, ten or so working men who had not been willing either to put in an appearance or turn up at the Monday morning penance with Gren, so were now definitely nailed to the blacklist.

Elmblad went round and shook them all by the hand.

They looked at him with that bright friendly expression that told him quite clearly they knew he would help them. He saw they were relying on him. They sat there in Aron Häggblom's kitchen, waiting with that immense calm that could be so frightening, their hands lightly clasped, and they told him what had happened. They added nothing, nor did they leave anything out. That was also frightening: their lack of hatred. Yes, they had left something out: now and again an appreciative word about Manager Tiblad (or was it Fiblad) being a good and honourable man arose, although he was forced to, he was made to, he had to dismiss people and put people there. On the blacklist. Which in itself was wretched. But. Anyhow. Now they had come to the mutual conclusion that they had carried out the strike with solidarity (true) and had not given in (true) and so were out of work (also true). They had behaved just as they ought to have done. Their reputation for solidarity as workers had been a vital primary issue and they had taken the consequences, gone on strike and now . . .

They were relying on him. He was the spokesman of the Party. He came from Stockholm, but would now be showing them which way to go.

Elmblad knew what would happen. In all probability, he would say a great deal at great length that evening, telling them the *context* of their actions; yes, there would be a great deal of context; he would tell them of the background and how they had been forced into the conflict. So far, no problem; they would probably sit there nodding in confirmation. No problem. When they had waited sufficiently long after his address and nodded their trusting heads benignly for a while, yes, then someone would ask what they should do now, and how would those who had been blacklisted manage, and how to do it, and what suggestions did he have, he, who was, after all . . .

Then he would have nothing to suggest.

He spent that night in Aron Häggblom's kitchen on the kitchen sofa. Things had turned out as he had thought. Clear cold outside, white stars, no dreams. Winter very close.

3

THE BULL-HOLDER

1

SOMETIMES WHEN he was speaking, he did not listen to himself. He knew his speeches by heart, and the words just came. Deep down, he was terribly frightened someone would find out.

You're hollow, Elmblad, he would hear. You're nothing but a shell. I don't believe you, Elmblad. You don't even listen to what you yourself are saying.

That was what he was afraid of.

What he dreamt about was a life in which everyone disbelieved him, never trusting him with a ha'penny, or confiding in him, or having the slightest respect for him, and yet listening to his words and believing them, and acting.

You're a shit, Elmblad, they would say to him. But you're right. You're an untrustworthy, objectionable shit, but you're right.

That would give him a kind of freedom. Relief. Trust was perilous. It could be used for anything.

2

IN HIS FIRST LETTER back to his wife, he described the great progress he had already made in Västerbotten, allowing the letter to breathe optimism and invincible triumph, for otherwise his wife might be miserable. He told her he had started two new workers' councils, and that the people up here had changed their attitude now. The great strike had certainly not ended in victory, but it had nevertheless had stimulating effects.

And so on.

Not a word of truth, in short, but a nice encouraging letter in every way.

He endured it in Bureå for four days. Then he simply couldn't stay a moment longer. Down at the sawmill, the blacklists were in perfect order and all the union activists had been excluded with perfect precision. They had caught the union activist cattle in a perfect trap in which they had complete freedom not to work. Elmblad had taken a walk down to the Skerry to speak to someone at the Company, but he had not even been allowed in. No, not even thrown out. Some subordinate clerk or other had simply grinned and shaken his head and gently closed the door.

There was no point in complaining.

He stuck it out for four days. He roamed round the community, feeling like a small boat torn from its moorings and aimlessly drifting about in the late Västerbotten autumn. He felt totally meaningless. What was really the point of someone like him? What was he doing? What could he achieve?

Nothing.

It was all one huge sadistic joke. On the evening of the fourth day he decided, and the next morning he took his lunch-tin in his hand and walked the six long miles south to the village of Burvik, in the direction of Lövånger. Sunday meeting. He had telephoned and was to have help. He knew the sawmill there had been closed, but the workers were still there: the usual story. Some of the unemployed workers from Burvik had gone to look for work right up in Furugrund and Ytterfors, and found it. That was sensational, but miles and miles to walk.

When he arrived in Burvik, he first walked straight through the village, sensing the eyes watching him from the windows. That was a good sign, though what usually happened in these villages was that people stared but the doors were nevertheless kept closed.

He sat down on the churn-stand and waited.

How quiet the world had become.

All at once, it comes to an end, and grows quiet. Nothing peculiar about that. One has to die some time. First one dies outwardly, then inwardly. How long had he been dead? Perhaps it had happened imperceptibly, painlessly. Suddenly one was dead. One moved about as before, but one was dead.

A man came out of one of the farmyards. He walked up to

Elmblad and shook his hand, explaining that Elmblad could stay overnight at his place.

He said his name was Lundgren and that he was a bull-holder.

Lundgren of Burvik was about fifty, a calm, silent man, an only son, his father dead, his mother (he said very correctly, as if it were important to have it said before Elmblad came to spend the night) had had a stroke six months earlier and become different. That is, changed in her mind.

She had been very quiet before. Completely different.

Elmblad had gone with him. Lundgren of Burvik at once started making porridge. He was not particularly talkative, so the conversation was scant. In the afternoon, his mother came waddling in from the bedroom; she was very small, very bow-legged, and she smiled in a friendly way at her guest. She offered him coffee. She had been a very quiet woman before (Lundgren of Burvik had now repeated this twice, so it was clearly important information), but now she had had a stroke (also mentioned twice) and she was different (her guest was able to establish this himself). She might possibly have held her tongue in her previous life, but the stroke had now loosened it. The words poured out, incessantly, like a dark secret flood pouring out from the mountain of silence. She now talked at length and willingly to this guest from Stockholm, and Elmblad very rapidly capitulated. All he could do was to listen and nod in ingratiating agreement with the old lady.

There was no chance of interrupting her. Now and again Elmblad tried to start up hesitant little conversations with the son, but he realized the mother would show no mercy. She spoke in a loud, shrill voice, and with frenzied determination she enthusiastically told him the story of her life. At least, that was what he presumed: she spoke an almost incomprehensible dialect, smiling all the time a crazy abandoned smile that revealed a scanty but very personal row of teeth in which the teeth were quite lightheartedly pegged into each other. She spoke in shrieks, ecstatically, ploughing her way with her insane smile right through an endlessly long story, which as far as he could make out was immensely instructive and entertaining, but which her son listened to all through with a constantly gloomy and melancholy expression on his face.

The son made no attempt to stop her, and nor was he capable of doing so. Elmblad occasionally made a few distreet attempts to interject some tentative little questions to the son, but in vain. '*Do you know if there are any blacklegs down Lövånger way?*' he began discreetly, but no, the old woman's hooting voice immediately took over. She seemed to be deeply absorbed in an enormously stimulating and lengthy story all about her own life; and was enjoying it. '*An' then,*' she said decisively and penetratingly, thumping her clenched fists in confirmation on Elmblad's knee, '*an' then our Alfid, what were so dim up top, half-gone as us says, her'd stuffed hay in hers blouse so that her'd look plump, so them'd think her'd got big titties, an' tha knows, them was all goin' a'dancin' up at Bygdsiljum, an' our Alfid, her comed wi' me, an' tha see, a man comed and wantit t'dance wit' her, see, an' him were so randy him grab'd her by t'titties,*' and at this memory, the old woman seemed to be as good as overcome by nostalgic joy and started laughing so much that her peg teeth almost became jammed. Then, in the rising hysteria, she came to her senses and went on: '*but when him teks her by them titties t'hay starts sprayin' all over t'dance floor and us larfs an' larfs an' larfs . . .*'

Her son went on sitting there, silent and grave.

He had turned his worn, haggard face to the window and was gazing out of it. Thin snow had begun to fall; the first snow of the year, lying lightly and sparsely on the ground and trees. There were still some yellowish-red leaves left on the birches. The snow touched the dead leaves as lightly as the kiss of death: the short painful moment when the Westerbotten autumn was at its most beautiful and menacing. Tomorrow the leaves would be gone, or the snow, but the colours and death and the snow and the cold still hung together. Snow on the leaves. A short step between life and death.

The son was still staring expressionlessly out at the birches. Elmblad was trapped by the old woman. He was holding his coffee-cup on his knee, now and again taking small helpless sips from it, coffee with cream. He suddenly recalled someone telling him it was a custom in small Westerbotten villages that when really grand company came, like the pastor or some other toff, the mother of the household would take the coffee-cups secretly into the inner room, open her blouse and milk the coffee-cream straight from her breast. This was supposed to be some kind of mark of respect. Company was always given tittie-milk in their coffee. It was probably only pure slander, but he found himself anxiously examining the old woman's pendulous breasts.

176

No. They couldn't have produced the cream in his coffee. Those titties were long past it.

The old woman suddenly began to sing, and she now seemed to be intent on allowing the dark flood from the depths of her inner life to well up and pour out: the deepest wells rising. Elmblad understood very little, but enough. Her song was immensely obscene. She had now gone far into the great story of her life and come to the furthermost, most secret room: the barriers were down, forbidden dreams pouring forth, a joy and a delight to let them come. Her song was partly incomprehensible, but it was possible to make out certain words: he could identify *long john* and *prick* and so on at once, but the actual epic events of the song were more difficult to follow. Broadly speaking, it was about a randy pedlar who had spent the night in a shippon and confused the wife with a heifer. Or some such. As she sang it, her body rocked back and forth in a demure and pious manner, as if only temporarily she had forgotten to exchange the bland expression from the thousands of hymns she had sung earlier in her life. The song was endless and very vivid, culminating after innumerable verses in macabre and detailed descriptions of a cat shitting in the porridge while the husband amused himself with the wife and so on and so forth.

The old woman came to the end of the hymn and slapped Elmblad happily on the thigh. End. Smack. The kitchen clock was now ticking alone in the silence of the kitchen. Yes, indeed, she had at last fallen silent; the old girl had stopped, but was now gazing wide-eyed at Elmblad with what appeared to be wild and uncontrollable joy, apparently wanting it confirmed by her spectator that what she felt was right, confirmation that the darkness she had plucked up from the depths of her life was not really excrement, but that her insane semi-indistinct words had been darkly shimmering jewels of priceless value.

Her son made no comment, simply went on staring gloomily out of the window. Yellow birches. Snow. Snow-leaves. The clock measuring out the time with calm slow ticks, the kitchen now very quiet. Elmblad did not know what to say. Nor was he given any lead. The old woman nodded encouragingly at him as if hoping for an immediate answer. Yes, he would have to reply. Elmblad knew that.

'That was both amusing and interesting,' he said cautiously.

The smile on the old woman's face slowly faded. She stared at him solemnly, in dismay, and with increasing confusion, Elmblad saw that her son had stopped staring at yellow birches and snow and was now also looking at him with astonishment and disbelief. They were both staring at Elmblad as if he had said something immensely vulgar and disgusting.

'Dost him thinks so,' said the old woman in a cross voice, an abyss of reservation and chill beneath. 'Indeed!'

'Well, it was both amusing and . . .' Elmblad began again, but this time he was cut straight off.

'Ah heard tha say't,' she almost snapped. 'Ah ain't deaf!'

She stood up laboriously, and giving Elmblad one last annihilating look, she waddled limping across the floor and vanished into the bedroom, closing the door behind her with a bang.

'Her's angry,' the son explained. 'Her's angry at what tha said.'

He turned away and again looked out at the birches, silent again.

The wall-clock ticked. The door remained closed and the old woman did not come out. The son stared stubbornly and silently out of the window at the yellow birch in the snow. It was the moment of the snow-leaf and he did not once take his eyes off the tree.

Elmblad could find nothing to say. It was all inexplicable, completely and utterly inexplicable.

3

TEN PEOPLE came to the meeting in Burvik. At first Elmblad spoke for an hour on the Social Democrats and their attempts at organization, then he drank a cup of water, then concluded with his other speech, the one on Socialism and the Trade Union Movement. The latter went on for an hour and a half.

Afterwards there was open discussion.

When everyone had gone, Lundgren of Burvik came up to him with a piece of paper, or rather, what happened was that all the rest had left and Elmblad and Lundgren were walking along the road together for a while. Elmblad was thinking of going to Bureå that same evening. Then, rather formally, Lundgren cleared his throat, stopped like a horse lost in thought, then thrust his hand into his pocket and pulled out a piece of paper.

'Them all thought t'were a good an' proper speech, them did,' he said in a friendly way. 'Tha's no sloven. Ah hear'd them liked it.'

Elmblad looked at him in silence and waited.

'Here's t'names,' said Lundgren. 'Names of them what might join a workers' association.'

The piece of paper had been torn out of a notebook and was lined. There were six names on it, in pencil. At the bottom, the last name was *Erik Lundgren*, and in brackets after it, 'bull-holder'.

Elmblad looked questioningly at the paper; for a moment Lundgren appeared slightly embarrassed, shifting his feet uncertainly in the mud, but then he said modestly:

'Ya'see, ah jist thought ah sh'd jot dahn them what's bin given tasks afore. What's used t'it.'

He paused, and then went on:

'Ah's bin a bull-holder all o'ten years.'

Elmblad realized what this meant. Lundgren had been a bull-holder for ten years. They had confidence in him. Perhaps this was a future union official in front of him. Elmblad could do nothing but nod in confirmation, then shake Erik Lundgren by the hand.

Clearer that evening, cold. he was walking in faint moonlight.

They had confidence in Erik Lundgren. How do you become a bull-holder?

Elmblad would have felt better if he had had some self-respect. Or confidence in himself. But he hadn't.

Or. No.

Winter, closer and closer.

4

SAUL ON
BUR MOUNTAIN

1

THE BREAKDOWN CAME as a great surprise, to himself as well.

He was on his way back from a very successful meeting in Burvik. He was going to Bureå and it was late evening, October, very cold and clear. Then he was suddenly struck down with melancholy. He liked to think of his collapse as melancholy, because the word was beautiful and slightly alien, and could not really be considered in connection with his canvassing work in the service of the Swedish workers' movement.

Melancholy sounded rather like apathy, but more mysterious. He liked that.

He had said goodbye to Lundgren of Burvik and set off northwards towards Bureå. It happened when he was only three kilometres south of Bure, the melancholy appearing right there, paralysing him completely in the pale moonlight beneath the clear starry sky. The stars had never looked so clear as they did just there, never so mercilessly piercing and menacing.

He stopped and looked up at the stars, then felt the need to empty his bladder. He stood for a long time trying to, but failed, and everything seemed to him to have suddenly combined, the immense black space with its icy menacing stars, his hopelessness, Dagmar, the little imbecile, the bull-holder from Burvik and then this business of not being able to pee.

Gets you down, he thought. Undoubtedly.

Undoubtedly it got you down.

He put his dick back without having been able to go. Then he simply could not make himself walk on. Again and again, he stroked his moustache and adjusted his belt. He couldn't understand how he could have got so fat, the way he lived.

Undoubtedly, it got you down.

The road ran in a slight right-hand curve down the west side of the mountain and he could see the faint lights of Bureå village in front of him. Everything simply grew worse and worse, as if his skin were swelling and thickening until he was like an elephant with a sandbag instead of a heart. Then that immense space which he could not cope with, the stars so menacingly clear, hope so far away, himself so fat and unsuccessful. This was the world to which he was to bring the glad tidings of the victory of socialism, but what the hell was he himself? Cowardly and fat. He could hardly write coherent sentences. He didn't have Janne Persson's skill at writing, nor could he speak like Blixt. A wife like . . . well.

If he strove for a hundred years, he would never be appointed as a bull-holder. In Burvik.

Then he snivelled and wept for a brief while; he usually did that when things got too difficult; like masturbating, it relieved him round his heart and scrotum. But now nothing helped. He stood there snivelling and crying, yes, Elmblad the agitator was a comical and pitiful sight. His moustache grew wet and the stiffness in the points dissolved; he wiped it, but that didn't help. He wept a little more, but nothing helped. He could not move. The space was so immense, these people so inscrutable, his task so appallingly difficult, his opponent so invisible, his friends so few. Not even in the wildest Congo, he kept thinking, among the natives in the jungle, could loneliness be as great as beneath this starry vault in Westerbotten.

For a long time, he stood there in the faintly glowing darkness, completely dead, like a leaf, with the snow suddenly falling round it, the tree dead and everything a tomb, and yet something alive in the growing garden. But it was quite silent within him. Before, there had been more there, at least he thought so. But not now.

Half an hour later, he started walking, very slowly.

It was past midnight when he finally knocked on the Markströms' door in Oppstoppet.

Josefina Markström opened the door. She stared in astonishment at the strange plump figure. She had seen him before, but he looked different now. It was Elmblad. At first she didn't understand what he was mumbling about. But then he repeated it. He was pleading to be allowed to stay the night.

181

He said he wasn't feeling very well, something wrong with his heart; it felt like a sandbag.

She realized at once that he had caught a chill and was poorly, so she pulled him inside so that he would not catch his death. She woke Nicanor, who helped Elmblad off with his clothes. Nicanor saw that his long underpants were soiled in the crotch, but he said nothing. Elmblad was given a fur bedcover and a bed in the attic.

There he lay, staring up at the ceiling; that was how the whole thing started.

2

EVA-LIISA BROUGHT PORRIDGE in the morning, but he didn't want anything to eat. Later on in the day, they tried again, with sugar-water and *finka*. He drank the sugar-water, thanked them, and went on lying there.

He was quite quiet and apathetic, and it was impossible to get a sensible word out of the man. None of them could know that Elmblad had come to the conclusion he was already dead, that he was a leaf embedded in snow. So he just lay there.

On the fifth day, Josefina Markström finally went up to him. She pulled up a chair, sat down at the bedside, pulled the bedcover off his face (he usually lay like that) and started talking to him. That is, she first said a prayer, a brief matter-of-fact plea, then she asked him what the matter was.

He said: 'I'm sick.' She said: 'Tha isna. Tha isna sick. Ah kin see tha isna sick. Tha's quite well an' tha doesna want t'git oop. But is him, grown man that him is, t'be like them young'uns what roam t'roads draggin' theirs feet an' thinkin' nothin' of sleepin' well int'mornin' outa pure idleness? That's what people'll be like if them socialists git them's way. Work-shy.'

He turned in the bed and stared at her in indignation. 'I'm not lazy,' he said. 'I'm miserable.'

'When didst tha git like that, then?' she said sharply, her eyes on him. 'Didst tha git like that in Burvik?'

'No, on the way to Bure,' said Elmblad in a muffled voice from where he had now hidden again under the bedcover.

'Tell us how't happened,' she said in a sharper voice, her eyes now fixed intently on his. 'Jist you git goin' an' tell us how't happened.'

'It's nothing to do with anyone,' he muttered from down in the bedstraw.

'*Nothing t' do with anyone!*' Josefina started as if he had slapped her. She leant forward and shouted straight into his face: "*Tis my business and tha jist tell us this very minit else ah'll knock tha block off!*' For a few seconds there was a paralysed calm beneath the fur cover. Then Elmblad's body moved, the bundle under the cover apparently shuddering, the bedcover slipping a little further, revealing the fat neck, his flickering eyes at last daring to be still, and he looked at her, his mouth trembling slightly, his eyes blinking. Implacably, mercilessly, she kept her accusing face above him, making it impossible for him to evade her, and he said once again, tentatively, almost pleading: '*But . . . it's . . . nothing to do with anyone except . . .*'

'*Tell us!*' she broke in categorically. '*Git goin'!*'

Elmblad swallowed. He looked apologetically at her, then nodded resignedly; a warm smile immediately appeared on Josefina's face and, with a satisfied expression on her face, she settled down.

She was in no hurry. She allowed him to take his time. Finally he told Josefina Markström what had happened to him during that brief spell on Bur Mountain, that evening under the menacing stars, when death had already eaten itself into his heart.

She let him talk, listening attentively. When he had finished, she thought for a moment, then had her interpretation ready.

'Tha's been bin converted to Our Saviour Jesus Christ,' she declared boldly but very firmly.

She went on to explain the situation to Elmblad, who listened, his eyes growing rounder and rounder. One was not lost just because one was a heathen. On his way to Damascus, Saul had had a vision and had been transformed into Paul, as everyone knew. He had seen that vision, and the heathen had been converted. When Elmblad was suddenly afflicted with darkness on his way from Burvik to Bure and was struck down, God's finger had touched him. He had let his ray of mercy strike down Elmblad the agitator, revealing his sinfulness to him. If he would now just relax and stop being as refractory as a rampant stallion, fighting his sinfulness, then he would be granted mercy.

Thus was he converted.

Elmblad wriggled beneath the cover, occasionally making small unsuccessful attempts to interrupt Josefina's summary of the situation, but determinedly she carried on with her story to the very end. Elmblad was forced to lie still, blinking like a clubbed burbot, without objecting; yes, it really was so; through the mediation of Josefina, God had cracked him one on the head and he could feel it.

'Dost tha unnerstand?' said Josefina finally in a firm voice, looking challengingly at him. He nodded obediently. 'Yes.'

That was safest, indeed it was.

'That's *conversion*,' she explained. 'Na tha's on t'right road. That's the order o' mercy. First 'tis awakening up on Bure Mountain. Then God gives t'sinner a crack on t'head so him's waked up. Then conversion.'

Elmblad lay as quiet as a mouse in order not to make the situation any worse.

'Elmblad,' she said gravely. 'Dost tha knows what tha has t'do now? Dost tha knows?'

He looked at her in silence for a long time, then shook his head anxiously.

'Tha hasta confess thy sins, an' avow thy faith,' she said, in tones that left no room for contradiction. He was to confess before them all.

Elmblad found himself in an extremely difficult position, and he knew it. Despite the cold in the room, he could feel himself sweating under the cover, his long underpants sticking to his skin, suddenly wet through. In actual fact, the situation was so difficult he suddenly felt his melancholy being pushed aside. Yes, it had gone. He almost missed it. On second thoughts, he missed it very much, definitely preferring the most profound and bottomless melancholy to Josefina Markström's firmly framed future plans for him.

'Tha hasta avow thy faith afore us all,' she repeated. 'So them sees tha's converted.'

Elmblad felt the sweat running more and more clammily.

'How?' he said in a faint voice.

'Tha's t'tek communion,' she said calmly and firmly. ' 'Tis communion on Sunday.'

'Communion!' he cried, sitting up. 'Like hell I will!'

She placed her hand calmly and firmly on his chest and pressed him back against the pillow. At first she said nothing, not even rebuking him for swearing, but he could see from her eyes that she didn't like it, and although she was not going to comment on it, she was requesting him not to do so again.

He could see that very clearly.

' 'Tis communion day after t'morrer,' she said calmly. 'Us'll all go then. Our Nicanor, an' our Dad and me and t'boys.'

She ransacked her memory for a moment and then added:

'An' our Aron and our Eva-Liisa, probably, too.'

For a few confused moments, he was on the point of saying that he hadn't been confirmed, so had no right to attend communion, so unfortunately would not be able to, but then he sensed that this would not go down very well, and would also perhaps be a fundamental tactical error. In some inexplicable way, he found himself at a disadvantage, dependent on her now, and if he admitted he hadn't been confirmed, these inexplicable people would be sure to grab him, tie him up and put him in a confirmation class, turning him into a child and . . . no.

No. He said nothing to worsen the situation; all he could do was to let her have her own way. She was still staring at him challengingly, and he sensed she was waiting for something, a sign, a word, a small signal, or something.

Then to his own incredulous astonishment, he found himself nodding.

Not much, just an almost imperceptible movement of his head, but it was a nod, an affirmative nod. Josefina Markström nodded back in approval; the contract was complete, but she stayed sitting there like a prison warder as the sweat poured off his body. His melancholy had now been completely and utterly vanquished, and he was missing it very much. This was something much worse. Yes, this was tricky.

'I need to pee,' he said in a weak, apologetic voice.

She nodded cheerfully, patted the cover . . . of course, he deserved that. A heathen soul had been struck down and now found himself obediently trotting into the celestial stables; of course he should be allowed to pee. She got up, went out, came back with the bucket that had stood on the top of the stairs, put it in the corner, looked at him with a smile now eternally filled with goodwill, went across to the door and, standing in the doorway, said:

'Steer straight na, Elmblad. A man what kin steer a straight course through life, him kin steer straight into t'piss-bucket, too.'

Then she closed the door.

Elmblad crossed the creaking attic floor, thinking: she's said that many a time. She's said it to her boys, and before that her mother said it to all her boys, and that's how it's gone on down through the centuries. And now she's taken me into her family of children.

He stood there above the piss-bucket, endeavouring, on the whole without hope, the sweat drying on his skin and his underpants feeling colder and colder. As he stood there, he thought about what had been said, reflecting on it as it grew colder, and finally he thought: maybe it's not quite so insane after all. Of course he hadn't been converted. But his melancholy had gone, and maybe, after all, this was the road he had to take.

This corner of the country was a loony-bin, anyhow. Maybe he might try another tactic. A broad people's front, perhaps, and cheat the bastards. Maybe a little compromise was within reach here, a usable little compromise; well, maybe a big compromise. Maybe even a historical compromise. Well, he could but try. It meant nothing; better this than that all should be lost.

Then, like a sign, self-evidently and wholly naturally, it came. A thick, healthy, natural and utterly painless stream appeared from his astonished prick, pouring out, and he steered the stream skilfully and correctly straight into the middle of the bucket, and it seemed to him as if God or Marx or whoever it might be had given him a sign. Liberated, Elmblad stood in front of the bucket until his bladder was completely empty, then, like someone cured by a faith-healer, he took his bedcover out on to the landing. Then he dressed and went downstairs, where Josefina was waiting with coffee and a slice of bun-loaf, and where he sat for a long time wondering how he would cope with all this.

The crisis had lasted for five days. Now he would have to think. On Sunday was Holy Communion.

3

WHAT IS THERE to do on a Sunday morning? In Västerbotten there was an old saying which correctly answered the question of what to do on a Sunday morning: 'Us *washes and ates* blöta.'

That was exactly what they did at the Markströms' that Sunday morning. Josefina had already commandeered the sad remnants of Elmblad's underclothes the previous day, washed them and mended them, and on Sunday morning, they washed first, then gathered in the kitchen to eat *blöta*.

The entire Markström clan was there, plus Elmblad. Like a guardian bird, a cross between a broody hen and a hawk, Josefina hovered around. She had on her black dress and was droning dismally as she served out generous helpings of *blöta* to each and every one of them. When she was in a good mood and the situation was serious on a spiritual level (and it was that morning, for the whole family, including the converted Elmblad, were off to communion), she made a habit of happily droning a truly dismal litany on eternal corruption and sin or some such. In short, she was on great form, in complete control of her small congregation.

K. V. Markström himself, the head of the household, was looking clean and respectable, concentrating hard on his food, but obviously pleased to be allowed to sit in peace and quiet in a few hours' time, smiling encouragingly at some judgement-day preacher: a film of calm and concentration had already settled over his face and it was impossible to speak to him. The boys were equally taciturn. It was their habit not to say too much on Sunday mornings before communion, a lesson learnt from painful experience. If they said the wrong thing on the threshold of the sacred meal, so to speak, it might be misinterpreted and taken exception to. Then there would be misery and tears from Josefina, who considered jokes in connection with communion mortal sin. Not for anything did they wish to instigate any weeping on this peaceful morning; it was in itself customary to appear at the altar rail with eyes reddened from weeping, so most of the serious Christians in the area took whatever opportunity to weep that arose on a morning like this. But the boys had no wish to offend unnecessarily, so they ate in silence.

Aron was also there.

He had come clumping in in his felt boots as early as seven o'clock, but after being scolded by Josefina, had returned to the barracks, changed and come back again.

Naturally one was alone before God's countenance when one knelt up there, but what the congregation saw was one's footwear, and Josefina was practical, too. So no felt boots. Too early in the year, as well.

Some time had gone by since that remarkable night when Uncle Aron had sat on the steps of the privy in the moonlight, wetting himself and weeping. Nothing had ever been said about what had happened, at least not in the Markström household, but Aron had taken it badly. He had vanished up to Piteå for a few months, working somewhere along the coast and returning more silent than ever. No one knew what had happened up there. He told Nicanor he had joined an association which protected the freedom to work, and which would protect those willing to work from the assaults of the socialists. But when the strike had started in August at Bure mill, Aron had also gone on strike, and he was one of the last to go back. Many of them wondered about this in their heart of hearts, anyhow those whose memories went further than the length of their noses, and that was quite a few.

Aron had had problems.

Aron spent nearly all his evenings with the Markströms. He came late, sitting silently on the kitchen sofa, his cap between his knees, his hands clasped, gazing vacantly out into the room and saying nothing special to anyone. People said he never had much to say and that he was rather lonely. His workmates at the mill reckoned the only thing he did in his spare time was to sleep or have it off out in the privy, or at least that was what they said. But the latter was not true, not really. He sat on the Markströms' kitchen sofa saying nothing. Josefina was careful with Uncle Aron and thought nothing of sitting silently with him, mostly. When they had sat in silence for a few hours together and then eaten fried-up porridge, he was given a cup of coffee and a titbit, then he sat on for a while, then went back to the barracks. Life was certainly not always very cheerful for Uncle Aron, they realized that all right, but nevertheless he had gradually started going to prayer-meetings again, perhaps finding his way to God. Anyway, this Sunday morning he was there eating *blöta*, wearing his best trousers and his shop tie, and he had cleaned his teeth with the vegetable brush, so was looking quite respectable.

The thing about Uncle Aron was that he often looked at Eva-Liisa. They all noticed it. She didn't take much notice.

Eva-Liisa was back again.

She had been away for four weeks. There had been a head-on collision between her and Josefina. The explosion had been in August. Politics were to blame. Nicanor and Eva-Liisa had come home late one night at the beginning of the great conflict, and that had not gone down well, because Nicanor had dropped the shoes he had been carrying as he was closing the outside door. Eva-Liisa had slipped quietly upstairs, but Nicanor had been immediately interrogated. It had gone badly, because Nicanor was a notoriously bad liar. In the end he told Josefina that it was nothing to do with her where they had been, because it was *politics*.

This was such insolence she was struck almost speechless, and out of sheer astonishment she let him go.

But she had noticed he was wet through. The next day it was generally known that in the middle of the conflict, someone had undone the boom so that the timber had started drifting. It had floated out towards Bur Island, but had been stopped there. Josefina put two and two together and made it four.

She was disturbed.

Never, no never, had she thought any of her children would commit an actual crime, regardless of what it was called. She summoned them all to a prayer-meeting in the kitchen in the usual way, but neither Nicanor nor Eva-Liisa attended (incredible!) and neither did tears help. This was a severe blow to Josefina, the blow turning in on her, making her rather quiet for a couple of days, but then she suddenly exploded at Eva-Liisa, who had tempted Nicanor into his undoing. The *pianist-daughter*. There it was again! So Eva-Liisa was hastily dispatched to Josefina's sister in East Fahlmark, where she would learn what was what. The people of Aistbinom were renowned for knowing what was what.

She stayed there for four weeks and now she was back. What had happened had not been forgotten.

Eva-Liisa would soon be sixteen, and it was said of her that she had done well and was a bonny girl. Spelt out this meant she had an attractive face but was a trifle short and plump ('bonny'). Her Finn-Swedish accent had been toned down slightly and Västerbotten dialect had crept into her language, so the mixture sometimes sounded rather peculiar. She had worked as a servant girl to the Lundströms that autumn. They had a café with a function room on the first floor where funeral parties were held. That was where she spent most of her time. Funeral parties were festive high points during gloomy winters, and it was considered to be much sought-after work, so she ought to have been pleased. What happened was that the mourners plus neighbours and friends gathered together after the burial: no children were allowed and to start with they all sat there being dejected. The weight and depth of dejection varied, however, according to whether the dead person had been gathered to God or was a lost soul. They usually knew which kind of corpse they had. If it were of a good kind, if the deceased had been gathered to God, then the atmosphere was sorrowful but fervent, and psalms were sung in a bright tone of voice. Then it was a good party. But it was less good, for instance, when the person who had passed away was young and had not been one of God's children. Then funeral parties were terrible, and there was much weeping. Sometimes guests were not quite sure which was the case, so the atmosphere was uncertain. Then some close relative or acquaintance would start by making a discreet and thoughtful speech, indicating whether the deceased was on the way up or down, and it was a question of reading between the lines; rather like somewhat more academic rituals, where someone reads a paper and, at the formalities afterwards, the professor makes a speech stating that the examiners have met, and briefly indicating whether a doctorate has been awarded or not, semi-poetically, with discreet implications.

Anyway: Eva-Liisa saw to temporal matters at these funeral parties. She moved round in a black dress clinging to her now almost worldly and generous body, and the dejected male mourners often raised their sorrowful eyes and gazed at her. She was not unlovely to look at, this young girl, who five years ago had come from Karelia in Finland and had now become a woman. Strange dark bird-eyes.

They liked looking at her.

Otherwise purely temporal matters were quite easy to organize. Every mourner was given coffee and five or so small cakes to go with the coffee, and a large saffron pretzel. The pretzel had to be at least a foot long. Eva-Liisa first went round handing out a pretzel to each mourner and then she brought paper bags. Then, after coffee, they could put the cakes and the remains of the pretzel into the bag to take them home for the children. All children loved funeral pretzels, so most of the adults took only a little bite out of the pretzel and took the rest home.

Had it not been for the great grief involved, they would have liked to have had a funeral every week.

Nicanor, on the other hand, was out of work. This was a matter of shame, though no one said so. He would soon be fifteen, and there was plenty to him, but after the conflict he was on the list. He could be a labourer, of course, though he did not like the idea.

Josefina's opinion was that the whole wretched business had started the day he had written to Elmblad. Not least, the ending of the letter had been unfortunate. *Giving away his whole name* like that was dangerous. He was not careful enough. As long as Nicanor could remember, she had constantly talked about how important it was not to *give away* anything of yourself. Nicanor was her favourite son, and she was uneasy.

She had taken him into the harness room way back in their Hjoggböle days and spoken seriously to him about being *careful*.

In those days they shared the horse with a neighbour, and Josefina had been scared of horses since childhood, so used to take Nicanor with her when she had to get underneath the horse, though she never admitted to being afraid. Anyway, she always used to preach caution to him there. 'Nicanor, tha mustna boast. Tha mustna think thasel' something. That must be careful. Never put tha name to things. Tha must be careful of tha name. Be honest. Dunna write all tha name when tha writes t'anyone. It may cum back on thee. Many a man's cum a cropper 'cos o'that. Write "a friend" or "you know who" or invent a name, but watch out for thasel'.

She was completely manic about this. She had got it into her head that it was fatal to sign your name below a letter. Then you were caught. It was a sign of arrogance, too. And then the poor lad goes and writes to Elmblad and puts his whole name at the bottom of it.

Though it might also have been the hand of God.

Now that Elmblad had been converted.

They washed and then gathered in the kitchen in a protective circle round the socialist agitator, who for the first time in his life was now publicly to avow his faith and eat *blöta*. Very early in the morning. Warmth in the air again. Elmblad was quiet.

He reckoned he had good reason to keep quiet, and he was a trifle nervous. They had woken him at half-past five and he had done a thorough toilet, his suit was pressed, he had eaten *blöta*, joined in morning prayers, and at eight o'clock he was already sitting in the extremely well-cleaned trap with Josefina, Nicanor, two of the boys, Eva-Liisa and Aron. A neighbour from Bureå with roots and family in Holmsvattnet had borrowed the horse and trap and was doing the driving. He stood behind and had bad breath and talked a lot; it was hard to breathe when the wind was behind him.

'Elmblad,' said Josefina in a bright triumphant voice, in her thoughts already far beyond this first victorious step for Elmblad and looking into the future; perhaps he would go out and preach to the heathens? 'Tha's used to preaching. An' after tha conversion, 'tis possible. Here too.'

Elmblad said nothing. They were to drive to Skellefteå parish church. He had good reason to keep quiet.

The journey was to take almost three hours.

Until his dying day, Nicanor never forgot that journey.

It was one of the events he could describe in detail and most lucidly, one of the first stories I heard him tell, as well as the strangest. The strange thing was that Elmblad should have acted as he did; it simply didn't sound particularly believable. But it was damned well true. When Josefina came down from the attic and announced that Elmblad had been converted, at first Nicanor did not want to believe it, and he was indignant. Then he saw from Elmblad that it wasn't really true, that Elmblad was lying, and then he was truly indignant. For of course it was visible: small sly smiles, evasive answers, silences, all pointing to Elmblad trying to get himself out of a fix (but what fix?) and playing with false cards (card-games were sinful!) and trying to do something he should not have done.

Nicanor could not understand. In this fat, weeping, sweating man he recognized nothing at all of the remarkable man with worms in his mouth, the man who had been tied to a tree on Bure Heath the night of the moonlight hunt. He preferred the first Elmblad, quite definitely, to this one. The more he thought about what was happening, the less he liked it.

Definitely.

Suddenly Aron spoke.

'When our Gabriel Annerscha preached in Långviken,' he said, 'them didna have no prayer-house. So him gets up on t'shippon roof t'preach. But it wuz rainin', an' t'roof wuz mucky. An' then him slips as him were standing there preachin'. An', see, him falls slap dahn int' muckheap below. An' sits there in t'horseshit. An' them all larfed. But then him gits oop and then him climbs oop an'

192

then him says: that's what happens t'people when them's arrogant, them falls in t'muckheap.'

He was silent for a moment and then added:

'Though him didna stay sittin' in t'muckheap.'

That was the second time Uncle Aron had told that story and Nicanor realized he was trying to say something. Perhaps this time it was about not giving up.

In ten kilometres there is time to think a great deal. When Nicanor had finished thinking they had got to Trollåsen, and he leant back and poked the man with bad breath and family in Holmsvattnet and told him to stop the trap.

He got out and stood in the road. They all looked at him in surprise.

'Ah'm not comin',' he said.

Josefina looked at him as if paralysed, but she said nothing.

'One shouldna tek communion if one feels forced t'it,' he said.

The horse fidgeted uneasily, as it was cold and vapour was coming out of its nostrils. All was quite quiet.

'Ah've not forced none,' said Josefina quietly, as if to herself.

'Aye, tha has,' said Nicanor.

Icy silence.

'If one's not ready fer communion, and feels forced, then one shouldna go,' Nicanor repeated.

'Ah've not forced none,' she said again.

'Aye, tha has,' said Nicanor.

He looked straight at Elmblad, who looked away. Josefina seemed to wake up, as if she had dozed off and found herself in a bad dream she had not deserved and which made her furious. She turned to her husband and said angrily:

'Does ah force thee?'

'Nay,' he said obediently. Apparently embarrassed by the whole situation but not knowing what to do about it, he glared straight into the forest, trying to look unmoved. Mercilessly Josefina continued the interrogation, the boys' turn now; no, no, they echoed obediently. Then Elmblad.

'Well, dost tha think ah'm forcing thee t'Holy Communion?'

He looked at her, then looked away. She waited. She looked at Nicanor, but he also said nothing, every second making her heart sink even further, her face turning rigid, and once again she repeated the question:

'Has ah forced someone?'

Slowly, fumbling and cautious, Elmblad put his hand on the ledge of the trap, hesitating for a second, then he climbed laboriously down. A moment later, Eva-Liisa followed suit.

'That's t'be expected,' said Josefina, quite expressionlessly.

And then, to everyone's total amazement, Uncle Aron also got down from the trap.

Nothing remarkable, and yet this was the actual turning-point. This was the first story Nicanor told me, in October 1971. He often went back to this turning-point. Ultimately, I at last realized that something significant and decisive had happened that moment when he had decided to get out of the trap.

Twelve months later, we drove past the place in a car. It was half-way between Trollåsen and Grubbedal; a couple of small fields on the left, a steep wooded slope on the right, not a house in sight.

'Mother was upset, ah think,' he said.

She had sat quite silently in the trap for a long time, looking at them, as if she had still not yet taken in the whole extent of the catastrophe. Losing Eva-Liisa perhaps didn't matter all that much. In the case of Aron, it was inexplicable, but he'd always been inexplicable. He was an inexplicable man. Elmblad was presumably a snake. She had been mistaken about him, that was all.

But Nicanor, her beloved Nicanor, had started it all. He was the one who had stopped the trap and had no longer wanted to go with them.

Slowly, she buttoned up her cardigan. She was cold. She buttoned one button up after another, and when they came to an end, she couldn't think of anything else to do. She looked at Nicanor one last time, her face rigid with anguish, her whole being one single pleading last question, but she received no answer, and she did not know if he had understood the question. Then she nodded mutely at the driver with the terrible bad breath and he said nothing, but he understood and the trap jerked to a start.

Josefina Markström continued on her long journey to Holy Communion, lonelier now, for four people had taken a decision

194

she neither understood nor wished to comprehend. The last they saw of her was her rigid offended face, closed and silent, and then the trap jerked to a start and she did not look round.

Four people walked the ten kilometres back to Bureå. People looked out when they arrived.

4

THAT VERY SAME EVENING, Josefina and the others returned home.

They had not stayed overnight in Bonnstan in Skellefteå, as had been planned. Josefina was red-eyed, and they could imagine that she had wept a great deal. She wore her black dress on the Monday as well, and no one dared ask why.

Early Monday morning, Elmblad went into the kitchen and almost apologetically, told her that he was leaving that day. Josefina did not seem to grieve a great deal over this news, and she glanced at him with a look of unambiguous, open black hatred. But she said nothing.

What happened next was even worse. Elmblad paused briefly, then brought up a more controversial matter. The fact was, he and Nicanor had agreed that Nicanor should accompany him on a short canvassing trip inland.

As his assistant.

She stared at him, speechless and paralysed, then turned abruptly, went into the bedroom and closed the door.

She did not come out again until late that evening.

'It's hard to lose a child to the Devil,' she said straight out into the kitchen to them all. That was all she said. That same evening she boiled a batch of Piteå blood-bread, filled a backpack with it, put a quarter of a kilo of salted butter in on top and put the backpack out in the cold-porch. These were provisions. As they were about to leave in the morning, she produced the backpack and gave it to Nicanor. Elmblad tried to say goodbye and shake her hand, but she refused to look at him. But then she suddenly seemed to change her mind and turned to Elmblad.

'Dost tha like blood-bread?' she said.

Grateful that she wished to speak to him, he said:

'Yes, indeed. I like it very much.'

She looked at him briefly, then turned to Nicanor, and spoke as if Elmblad were not there at all:

'If tha sickens o' this'n here socialist,' she said harshly, 'then put a bit of blood-bread out on t'thin ice for him.'

She slammed the outside door with a bang. Then they could go. They walked inland, in the direction of Hjoggböle.

5

THE VILLAGE BLACKSMITH

IT WAS SAID that they were heading in the direction of Burträsk, and that is what happened. This was the darkest of the dark lands, the secretive and profoundly backward area around Burträsk. That was not libellous, they said in the villages nearer the coast, but the brutal truth, because they all knew that the people of Burträsk weren't really quite all there.

When they came to Sjön, Hjoggböle, the first of the four villages grouped round Hjoggböle marsh, they were given a night's lodging at the village blacksmith's.

His name was Per Valfrid Enquist, and he also lived off fox-hunting and tar-boiling. He was a gloomy, prematurely bald man, who often told stories. He was my paternal grandfather, though that's not really anything to do with it.

He let them sleep in the little room to the left of the smithy.

At the time, the road between Hjoggböle and Sjöbotten had not yet been made, so the men working at the sawmill had great difficulty getting there and back. Making the journey every day was impossible, so the men at the sawmill stayed during the week, most of them tilling their small fields all the same, seeing to the cows and working in the forest in winter. My father, six years old at the time when Nicanor and Elmblad passed by, did not start at the sawmill until the twenties, mostly as a stacker, his early working years having been spent largely in the smithy.

In our family mythology, Elmblad's visit was a most bizarre incident.

Grandfather was a friendly soul and at such a young age was not quite so addicted to religion to the same extreme extent as the rest of the family. However, his soul was saved in plenty of time before his deathbed, so he succeeded in turning the funeral rites into a bright, almost elated performance. I was there, too, and was pleased he had been gathered to higher things. Anyhow, Grand-

197

father had naturally taken pity on Elmblad the agitator and his henchman (he had known Nicanor as a pup before he had moved to Bureå), and had offered them thick heifer-milk and whortle-berry juice and asked them which way they were going.

He heard to his horror that they were heading for Burträsk and were going to talk about socialism. The Stockholmer, maybe, but Nicanor Markström! Grandfather was profoundly and seriously troubled, not least because he knew what Burträskers were like, and gently he started giving them a fearful description of the risks they were running. But Elmblad was not particularly interested and mostly asked about political consciousness in Sjön. Grand-father had calmed him by saying all was well there. They were all poor and honest and worked themselves to the bone, and he himself shot a fox now and again and belonged to the People's Party. No, the Liberals they were called in those days. The Liberals. Strangely enough, Elmblad had not looked very pleased at that and had mumbled gloomily that the Liberals were a plug in the arse of the workers' movement (extremely unfair!) and that the shit would come out more easily if they removed that plug. Grandfather had thought it amusing and interesting to hear a Stockholmer say that, but he had not changed his opinion. If my grandmother hadn't been such a good person with such a strong hold on the family morality, I'm sure P.V. would finally have offered Elmblad a tot.

Grandfather remembered that little metaphor on liberalism until his dying day. Elmblad had said the Liberals were a plug in the arse of the workers' movement. While the plug remained, you escaped seeing quite a lot of shit. But you couldn't go on like that for ever. The sooner the plug came out, the better.

It would have been better if Elmblad had argued with any real conviction. His was a view not particularly current in the Skellefte area, where certain Liberals acted as interpreters and spokesmen for the workers' movement, but it was always fun to have a little healthy anal humour. Elmblad was in a good mood when he saw his utterance strike home and as an encore he sang 'The Inter-nationale'. This was the first time in the history of the village that it had been sung, and also the last, I was about to write.

Anyhow, Elmblad and his young assistant were allowed to sleep in the little room off the smithy, and the next morning they went on. Grandfather accompanied them along the path through the forest to West Hjoggböle, down to the marsh. It had been quite warm for a few days and brittle shards of ice lay along the shores; Grandfather rowed them across the marsh. He had built the boat himself. So he took the agitator and the lad in his boat (if you take the Devil in your boat, you have to row him ashore) and set them down on the other side, not far from Lillhalsen.

They had sat in the boat eating cold blood-bread and butter. They had had the blood-bread in a rucksack. Elmblad had eaten heartily. They had offered Grandfather some, but he had refused politely, and when to his dismay they did not insist, it was left at that.

No mould on the blood-bread. He put them ashore near Lillhalsen and rowed back. Fresh blood-bread and butter was actually the best thing in the world, he thought.

A month later there was a parish meeting in East Hjoggböle, and as far as Grandfather was concerned, this was the epilogue to the little affair. Someone had clearly informed the pastor, who asked what the two friends had said and done, and Grandfather probably told him everything, with the possible exception of Liberalism being a plug in the arse of the workers' movement. After his account, he was given a friendly but serious warning to be careful in future and to think before offering anyone a night's lodging.

It was said in the village that something had been requested of Grandfather. Perhaps it was simply an admonition. So long afterwards, this totally pointless family incident is apt to grow in my mind and become slightly more remarkable for each year that goes by. An admonition from the minister of the church for giving a man a night's lodging.

But Per Valfrid Enquist reflected on what he had heard and seen and hid it deep down in his heart, occasionally producing the story of how the two agitators slept in the little room next to the smithy and how he had rowed them across the marsh, but hadn't been given any blood-bread.

And that he had warned them about what was to come.

For then they all heard about what had happened over Burträsk way.

But Burträskers never really were all there.

They went ashore near Lillhalsen and walked due west along the stream. After a kilometre, they came up on to the Buträsk road.

They set off due south-west. And then Nicanor Markström and his mentor in the struggle of the working classes were indeed inside enemy territory.

6

THE RAM LAMB

1

FAR INSIDE in the darkness, the pain was at first very small, a tiny soft glowing point which then grew slowly and made the darkness less dark, then sank again, then rose, back and forth, and then came the sounds, faint bleating sounds, rustling like that of dry grass, obscure bodies moving, almost softly woolly, the pain still in the middle of his head, in the middle of his mouth, now very sharp, clear, real.

He rolled over, his mouth open, groaning. It hurt. His mouth hurt.

He tried to persuade himself it was a nightmare, but it hurt too much for that; it was absolutely real. He was lying in some kind of outhouse, figures moving about him in the darkness. He stretched out his hand; soft, was it wool? That bleating sound, sheep, a sheep-pen. He rolled over, the pain in his mouth still equally inexorable. A lighter darkness diagonally up there. Window. Filthy. Suddenly hysterical and frightened, the sheep started circling round and he tried to get up, feeling a body close to him with his hand. Fumbling. He knew at once who it was.

Elmblad. Was he dead?

At once he remembered what had happened, up to a certain point.

The sheep were bleating frantically now, apparently huddling together in a desperate little bunch in the corner of the pen. He could see better now. His mouth was still burning with un-diminished ferocity. He wiped his hand across his mouth and felt a dried sticky layer of something that must be blood. Elmblad shifted with a whimper; yes, he was alive, the bleating of the sheep fading, the contours clearer now, but the pain still burning in his mouth with a clear persistent flame.

There was a smell of shippon. He had bled.

From far away came the sound of a door slamming. Someone seemed to be coming, steps outside, a door opening, a light. The man who came in had a paraffin lamp in his hand. The sheep were standing quite still now, their eyes fixed on the source of light.

Nicanor saw at a glance where he was.

It was a sheep-pen, about three metres square, with straw on the floor. Elmblad was lying with his head almost in the middle of the sheep-pen, one leg bent up towards the boarded wall, lying on his stomach with his face turned away, one hand moving aimlessly round and round, as if searching for something he had lost. There were four sheep in the pen. Four sheep, two people.

'How's it then?' a man's voice said from behind the lamp. The man was almost invisible. The only result was that the sheep became agitated again and started bleating and circling round.

Nicanor looked down at his hands. A lot of blood. Dried. Filth, too, so perhaps he had had them in sheep shit. Lumps on the cloth of his sleeve. And the pain still unchanged, burning in his mouth. He moved his hand cautiously towards his lips, running it over them. It wasn't there. His lips were whole. They didn't hurt.

He suddenly began to sob.

'Here th'are,' said a man's voice in an almost friendly tone. 'Ate this na.'

Out of the darkness came a body, an arm, a head. The arm had a hand and the hand was holding something out. A can of milk. Brittle thin crispbread. He put it down by Elmblad.

The sheep were still again.

' 'Tis a bad business, that it 'tis,' said the man in a friendly voice. ' 'Tis a bad business.'

Nicanor simply wept. It was all so terribly humiliating and he didn't want anyone to be friendly and he didn't want anything to eat and his mouth hurt terribly inside and he kept remembering more and more and didn't want to remember and he didn't want anyone to see him and he wished he was dead and that the man with the paraffin lamp would disappear and leave him to the darkness.

'What's tha name?' said the man with the lamp.

Nicanor tried with some success to suppress his sobs, his breathing becoming calmer and once again he tried, and then again:

'Nicchh . . .' he began. 'Nihh . . . Masch . . .'

202

The man with the lamp waited, very calmly, the sheep bleating quietly. Nicanor's mouth was burning. Then he tried once again to say his name.

2

THEY HAD GONE ASHORE at Lillhalsen, then set off in a south-westerly direction towards Burträsk, taking it fairly easily, walking past Sidbergsliden and Renfors, eating blood-bread and butter in the middle of the day, and then in the afternoon they had come to Lappvattnet, which was quite a substantial village beautifully situated up on the ridge on the other side of the lake. There they were given permission to stay the night in an empty summer building. They slept there for the night, and that same night, winter came.

Winter came at eleven o'clock in the night, quite unexpectedly, as if the snowstorm had lain in wait somewhere in the Gulf of Bothnia and had then become furiously angry, refusing to wait any longer, assaulting the coast late one night when they least expected it and had been unable to defend themselves against it. Nicanor woke in the middle of the night and heard the storm, then fell asleep again under his sheepskin: but in the morning when all the peasants of Lappvattnet went out to the shippon to milk the cows, the farmyards were white seas of drifts and the well-vanes were white on one side and the snow kept on drifting. It was not cold, but it was windy and snowing heavily. It went on all that day, and the next night, as well as the following morning, but not until midday the following day did it suddenly turn quite quiet and calm, the temperature falling, the coastlands of Västerbotten all at once entering into winter.

They saw it would take all day to plough through that three foot of isolation. The horses could not manage the packed frozen snow and gave up, frothing warmly at the mouth. Three whole feet of snow in two days, and that at the beginning of December. It was going to be a hard winter getting the timber in from the forest, they all saw that.

Elmblad decided to take an administrative day off, as they had to anyhow. They still had a lot of blood-bread left. In Lappvatt-net, Elmblad spent a whole day writing out his reports, as well as a specially drafted missive to the Party leaders, together with pleas for more funds.

He filled page after page with his forceful, uneven, almost illegible handwriting. 'After the excellently attended meeting in *Burvik*, I went to *Bure* sawmill village, at which two meetings were held. Support was good, the atmosphere, too, and at any moment now it will be possible to . . .', at intervals closing his eyes, frowning frenziedly, trying to see in front of him just how things *should* be.

Nicanor was reading his discourse over Elmblad's shoulder with some surprise. He had seen the reality of it all and did not really recognize the poetically utopian description in the report. Nicanor sat down at the table and silently observed Elmblad for a long time. After ten more minutes of groans, pencil-chewing and eye-closing, he evidently became irritated by Nicanor's steady gaze and put down his pencil.

'What are you staring at?' he said crossly.

' 'Tain't true,' said Nicanor calmly, but with a strong critical undertone Elmblad had never heard before.

'What isn't true?'

'Tha's lying,' said Nicanor. 'Tha didna have no meetings in Bure, and nobody bin there.'

Elmblad examined his pencil for a long time before answering.

'You don't understand this business,' he said finally. 'You have to encourage them. If I write about it as it is, then no money comes from Stockholm, then they'll . . .'

He sat in silence for a while to see if his argument had sunk in. It hadn't.

'I used to write about it as it is,' he went on. 'They didn't like it.'

Still the same hostile silence.

'Tha didna tell t'truth, anyroad,' said Nicanor.

He was called Nicanor after his maternal grandfather. It was a family name. The family came from Vallen, Robertsfors and Västra Hjoggböle, and someone in nearly every generation had been called Nicanor. Some of the family on his mother's side came from Lövånger direction. No one from Burträsk had been connected with the family for hundreds of years. It was not customary to marry from there. At most from Renbergsvatten, but no further.

His stomach was troubling him.

When he had been in the trap on the way to Skellefte church and had decided that when he got down from it, he would turn back, it had felt right, but difficult. He no longer wanted to go. He was adult. He had taken the decision himself, but then he had seen Josefina's expression and had turned quite cold inside. He had broken her heart, and he knew exactly why. She had lost what she loved most, for ever. When the celestial trumpets sounded one day, their separation would be eternal, she would be united with the blessed, and her beloved Nicanor would fry in the Devil's pan like any rogue from the lock-up, and they would never be allowed to be together in the celestial church. This insight had come to her so suddenly she had not been able to arrange her features in time. Her faced had crumpled, nakedly filling with anxiety, her chin trembling, and all control gone.

That was almost the worst thing of all. Mother had been unable to control herself, though later she certainly had, and had wept the obligatory tear. After the trap had rolled away, that is.

He had made a decision, regretting it almost immediately, and he thought: I'll be made to atone for this for ever and ever.

He had felt an icy lump in his stomach, and although he had been trying to dispose of the lump for three days now, it was still there. Every time he looked at Elmblad, something inside him said: did I do right?

It was very annoying. He was not sure whether he was on the right side, whether the sacrifice had been worth the pain. What kind of ally had he acquired? This Elmblad was perhaps a good man, in spite of being a Stockholmer. But there was something peculiar.

About people who lied.

Elmblad had held no meetings in the Bure area.

Elmblad asked again:

'What are you thinking about, Nicanor?'

3

THE PAIN IN HIS MOUTH was very great, swelling, and he could not say his name. The man with the lamp leant over and Nicanor could see his face clearly as he stretched out his hand and opened Nicanor's mouth. The light flickered and then was still. The man mumbled something inaudible, then closed Nicanor's mouth again.

Elmblad rolled over on to his back and tried to sit up. The man with the lamp said:

' 'Tis a bad business, that it 'tis.'

They had arrived in Burträsk on the eighteenth of December, 1909, on a sparkling cold winter's day. In the afternoon, Nicanor had gone round putting up the small yellow posters. He was feeling rather out of sorts. This was quite a large community, and yet it seemed very quiet, the drifts already shovelled away, very neatly. He reckoned a good deal of watching was going on.

Crunching underfoot.

He was sure they were watching from behind the curtains.

There was something frightening about the whole situation. The posters he had put up had the same wording he remembered so well from his first meeting with Elmblad, the same poster he had put up in Bure timber yard the day before Elmblad had been tied to a pine tree in the moonlight. The same posters. Only the name of the place had changed, as if time had stood still. Now, six years later, he was doing exactly the same things as then. Elmblad would make exactly the same speech. The situation would be exactly the same. Nothing would have changed.

As he was putting a poster up on the Good Templars' notice-board next to the church, he saw three men standing only fifty metres away. They were not talking to each other.

Crunching underfoot. The crunching underfoot seemed to him to echo for miles and miles. He was sure they were watching. He could feel it in his back.

Meeting at seven o'clock.

Twenty people.

They were sitting in the Good Templars' Hall, right at the back, huddled together on the three benches at the rear. Elmblad started by trying to get them to move further forward, but nothing happened except a slight mumbling; no one wanted to move. Nicanor had sat far to one side, right up at the front. He did not like the parish. The three men who had been watching him by the notice-board were there, then two small boys, and about ten or so men in their sixties. Five half-grown youths. Twenty altogether. Not bad.

206

Not good, either.

Before the meeting, Nicanor had warned Elmblad not to go on too long. The people of Burträsk had to be treated with moderation. To Nicanor, the twenty people there did not seem a very representative selection of the people of Bürtrask, but by this stage, Elmblad was familiar with the terrible stories about them and didn't care. Thanks to innumerable witnesses, he already knew that Burträskers had piercing eyes, walked with a horrible dogged swinging gait, like the great apes in the primary school reader, grim in appearance and speaking a strange dialect which honest folk of Bure parish could hardly understand. They said 'thee' instead of 'tha', a foolish bleating sound, and were silently hostile to honest visitors from other parishes.

Elmblad walked up the aisle and started the meeting.

It was cold in the hall, but a stove was burning bravely at the very back. 'I realize,' Elmblad began, 'that you're sitting back there not because you're afraid of me or of the cause of socialism, but because it's warmer by the stove.'

No one laughed.

'Well, comrades,' Elmblad tried again to get the meeting going. 'If you won't come up to me, then I'll just have to come down to you.' He fired a warm smile at them; it sailed through the air, bounced off their serious, iron-hard faces and fell to the ground as dead as a butterfly in a snowstorm.

He wondered in the depths of his heart whether they even understood what he was saying to them. He said so to them.

He was amusing and entertaining, but there was no movement. No response. It was all very unpleasant. He suddenly thought how nice it would be to be at home listening to Dagmar crying and telling him he didn't care about her, and scolding him for not writing letters, the little imbecile happily grubbing around on his lap and dribbling from his friendly little mouth. That would indeed be better.

He launched into his speech.

It was his usual speech about the Social Democrats and their party organization, and labour experience and the necessity for socialism, and the ruthlessness of the employers. He stared at his twenty listeners. They all had completely serious faces, all of them, iron faces with iron jaws. Now and again the jaws rotated, like cows chewing the cud, as they shifted their plugs of snuff from right to left.

I mustn't think like this, ran through his head. They are comrades, workers. They are the people I'm working for. Together we'll build up the organization.

As he was speaking, he was slowly and imperceptibly moving down the central aisle. It was miserable standing all alone far away on the rostrum, so he edged his way slowly down the central aisle like a shepherd cautiously approaching his flock in order not to frighten them off.

It took several minutes, but finally he was standing right by them.

Then one of them, an older man, perhaps seventy, with a heavy, lined, cadaverous face, slightly like a horse (he would always remember it) pointed his hand and said in a high, whining, hostile voice that left no margin for protest:

'Stash'n thasel' o'there!'

'What?' said Elmblad in confusion.

'*Stash'n thasel' o'there!*' repeated the man with the obstinacy of an idiot, pointing inexorably at the rostrum.

Elmblad turned round and looked uncertainly at Nicanor. But the boy seemed not to have heard the exchange, and was sitting with his back to them all, right up on the front bench.

'Can you translate, Nicanor?'

Nicanor reluctantly turned round and said:

'He says tha's t'stand there. *Stash*'n thasel' there.'

Some of the men nodded in agreement. There was not a trace of life in any of the faces. What did this 'stash' really mean?

It sounded like a command. It was one, too. Presumably. Twenty silent Burträsk men were regarding the agitator without expression. His bowels contracted with unease.

He turned, went back up to the rostrum and looked out at his distant audience.

'Do you want me to stand here?' he cried in an exaggeratedly loud voice. 'Can you hear me?'

A subdued, disapproving mumble rose from the audience. Three men got up, apparently disturbed by something. The door slammed behind them as they left. A cloud of vapour poured into the porch, then another door slammed.

'Don't you want me to stand here, then?' he cried after them. 'I'll stand where you like. What *do* you want?'

Two more men got to their feet and left. Elmblad waited for them to push their way along the benches and the door slammed

208

again. First three, then two. Fifteen remaining, the meeting had not even begun yet. It might be said that the meeting had not exactly started in a fortunate manner.

He pulled himself together. He cleared his throat.

'Comrades,' he began.

Another man left.

4

HE HAD FELT IT all day. He could feel it in his backbone. He had tried to tell Elmblad something was wrong, that something was going to happen, but no, fat stupid Elmblad just carried on. He could feel it so clearly in his backbone that it almost ached. He felt he wanted to walk backwards all the time to ensure his back was not exposed, but then he would have had to turn round, anyhow. It was all right during the actual meeting (Elmblad had chosen the shorter of his speeches, the one that dealt with Social Democracy and took an hour and a half) and when it was over there were five men left. Nicanor had felt almost comforted that there were no more. There was a thick layer of ice on the threshold out in the porch. He and Elmblad had gone across the yard to the privy after the meeting.

There was no light in there.

First Nicanor had routinely felt the privy seat with his hand to find it the same as usual; they had peed all over the place and there was a thick ridge of ice round the hole. He heard Elmblad grunting beside him and wanted to crap himself, but he didn't want to sit down.

Nay, ah'll not sit on Burträsk piss, not never, he thought. Tha niver knows what it might be.

At that moment, he heard sounds outside, footsteps in the darkness, a great many footsteps. He turned quite cold.

Hell, he thought.

Hell, hell, hell. Dear Lord, help us now, for them's here. And now them's goin' ter do us.

A sharp bang on the door, scattered laughter, then another heavy bang on the door. Then silence. He heard Elmblad quickly stuffing his dick inside his trousers and start buttoning up. Aye, thought Nicanor, better get thasel' buttoned, 'cos the Burträskers is out there an' them's going to do us.

They seemed to be ramming a log against the door, and yet no one tried to get in. Were they barricading the door? So they'd be forced to stay there all night?

'Them's going ter do us,' he said quietly to Elmblad.

They seemed to be working hard out there in the darkness. Scratching noises, the sound of wood against wood, short laughs. There seemed to be lot of them, five or six men or so, though perhaps it was the menacing darkness doubling everything. Nicanor stood quite still, Elmblad shifting uneasily beside him like a fat frightened bear.

He went across and tried the door. Nicanor tried to stop him, but it was pointless anyway. The door was blocked.

'Let us out!' cried Elmblad in quite a hard voice, but not very convincingly.

No reply, only scattered laughter.

'We'll freeze to death!' shouted Elmblad, worried now. 'For Christ's sake, you must let us out.'

No reply. Silence.

Nicanor sat down on the seat, feeling the piss-ridge beneath him, but not caring. Means sittin' on Burträsk piss all night, he thought. S'pose I'll fruz to death then. Termorrer us'll be fruz to Burträsk piss and dead, an' them'll have ter scrape us off, and that'll tek us straight ter hell. Dear Lord, then ah'll has to sizzle in the Devil's frying-pan like a piece o' pork cracklin'. Ah'll singe and burn for ever an' ever. Why'd ah git out of that trap?

At that moment there was a great crash. Elmblad had driven his elbow through the little privy window above the door. Pieces of glass showered down; there was a moment of astonished and confused silence. Then came an oath, then steps crunching in the snow, voices more and more agitated.

'Him's broke t'winder,' said a reproachful voice just by the door. 'Him's gone in t'head.'

Another crack. Wood against wood. The outside expedition force was on its way inside, and suddenly the two people imprisoned realized it might be preferable to be allowed to stay there for the night. Then the door opened. Nicanor saw the white snow, then the silhouettes pushing their way in. Then they were off.

Afterwards Nicanor always thought: of course we shouldn't have resisted. It was pointless. Then it wouldn't have happened. But in the darkness, everything was so confused, dark shadows suddenly appearing and hurling themselves on to them. Nicanor fell backwards, bounced up again, hitting out wildly in panic, and to judge from the noise inside the cramped privy, panic and rage were equally prevalent in them all.

'Bash them's heads in!' yelled a voice just beside him, and for a second Nicanor went rigid with surprise. Did they say that sort of thing in Burträsk? It was almost like being at home. But the next moment he received a violent slanting blow across his throat that took his breath away, and he sank to the ground.

They were dragged out by their legs.

5

VERY SHARP LIGHT.

They had put Elmblad on a sofa. He had been bleeding from one nostril and snot he had not bothered to wipe away was running from the other. He was looking wretched, staring straight ahead of him like an idiot.

Five men. Nicanor recognized three of them at once, the three who had stood watching him while he had been putting up the poster, not speaking to each other. He had sensed even than that something was up. Now he *knew*.

Strangely enough, he was not afraid. They had hurled him to the floor in a corner, and there he sat. At first they had spent a lot of time addressing Elmblad only. But Elmblad had simply been miserable, occasionally swearing, occasionally snivelling, occasionally asking to be allowed to leave.

It was not amusing listening to Elmblad, nor had the interrogation produced anything of value. The questions were peculiar, almost impossible to understand. Anyhow, Elmblad had not understood them.

Then they started taking an interest in Nicanor.

'What's tha name then?' said a crooked-shouldered creature, bending over Nicanor so that his face was smothered with the foul smell of his rancid breath. 'What's tha name, an' who is tha an' who clipped tha hair?' It sounded like some magic ritual. Nicanor tried to hold his breath. Dear Lord Jesus, if only I was still in the trap now, or somewhere else; it'd be better to be in the privy sittin' on frozen Burträsk piss, everything would be better, and the man leant even closer to Nicanor and repeated, '*What's tha name an' who is tha an' who clipped tha?*'

Nicanor could see the face very close to, and that was when it started, in a confused raging panic he had no control over. Without even thinking, he cleared his throat and spat straight into the man's face, a great gob that slid down the man's nose and mouth and one cheek. For a moment there was total silence in the room, an astounded, almost admiring silence that became increasingly outraged.

The man wiped his face clumsily with his sleeve.

'Spits, does tha?' he said in tones of near amazement and injury.

'Spits, does him?' echoed one of the other men.

'But . . .'

'Spits, does tha?' the man repeated, in a louder voice this time, trying to get the mess off his sleeve.

They all stared at Nicanor, and for the first time, though far too late, Nicanor saw them not as Burträsk men, but as ordinary workers. There was nothing secretive about them, nothing threatening, nothing Burträsk-like, nothing at all. Five workers from Burträsk parish, and then Elmblad and him, in the same room, caught up in something that seemed to be turning into a mortal struggle.

He heard Elmblad start laughing, the wrong laughter, at the wrong moment, wrong, wrong, wrong. Then all hell broke loose.

It kept returning in his dreams much later, year after year, though extenuated by then and not so painful; in the dream it was still terrible nevertheless, and at the same time humiliating, and he was never able to tell anyone exactly that happened. But they had dragged him into an upright position and shouted indignantly straight into his face (Elmblad's laughter must have been silenced long before) and he had struggled and thrashed about in panic, and they had shouted at him, and he had tried to get free, but someone had got a grip on him and Nicanor had brought his knee up hard into the other man's groin.

A bellow. Now things had turned serious.

The man kneed in the groin doubled up in white concentrated pain, his eyes still fixed in rage on Nicanor's face, the other men

212

shouting indignantly. Elmblad had got up and moved across the floor, but was suddenly struck by a fierce blow and sat down heavily on his backside in the middle of the floor. Two men were holding Nicanor from behind.

The man he had kneed rose laboriously, still groaning, but he could speak.

'Got them lamb-pincers with tha?' he said to one of the others. 'This ram-lamb needs a'clippin'.'

Nicanor stiffened.

'Git them pincers out, Artur,' the man hissed again.

Nicanor suddenly started bawling, surprising himself as well. He was horribly frightened. He knew what they were talking about. He had seen what they did with the lambs. The ram-lamb. It was so easy to nip away the scrotum, and he'd seen the pincers. And once, the last time he ever wanted to see it, he had seen the lamb's eyes just as they had cut, its eyes and tongue slowly protruding further and further out, trying to touch something far far away with the very tip of its tongue. Never, never, never did he want to see that again.

He tried kicking himself free, but the men were holding on to him very hard now.

'Uhuh,' said the man. 'Tha's nowt sich a bigmouth now, eh?'

Nicanor screamed wildly, uncontrollably. At the back of his mind lay the thought that someone might hear him, come to his rescue, someone would break down the door and save him: he bellowed wildly and uncontrollably, Elmblad sitting on the floor with his legs wide apart, gazing at Nicanor with blank empty stupid terrified eyes, as if pleading with him to explain, or at least stop that terrible screaming.

'Shurrup!' yelled one of the men holding him. 'Shurrup! Stop tha row!'

But Nicanor did not stop, and a sudden panic seemed to spread through the room, the unrestrained hysterical screaming apparently never-ending, just swelling and swelling and rising. Someone tried to close Nicanor's mouth, but it wouldn't. He screamed and twisted like a calf, stamping his feet and shrieking, and for a moment the men looked irresolutely at each other as if they had instigated a course of events impossible to control, and from which they wished to distance themselves. The man who had been kneed in the groin had calmed down, though he was still enraged, but nothing could be said while this uncontrollable yelling youth kept on.

Exactly what happened next, he would never know. But a hand was thrust into his mouth and grabbed his tongue, reducing his bellows to groans; the hand held on to the tongue, someone held his head, and with the tip of his tongue out, outside his teeth, the faces very close to him, he would remember that hand, his bellows now quite inarticulate and almost subdued, they tied up his jaws, the pain that came, the faces very close now, that ill-smelling breath in his face, the slightly rancid smell of stale herrings, eyes very close, they burrowed in his mouth to silence him, and then came the blow.

Someone hit him hard, straight on the jaw. His tongue was out and his teeth sliced neatly and firmly into the end of his tongue. They sank in about an inch from the tip, virtually severing it.

They let him go at once. He sat down heavily on the floor, falling back on one elbow and fumbling cautiously with his hand against his mouth. The tip of his tongue was hanging loose, a lump of flesh held on by nothing but a thin thread of flesh, the blood spurting calmly and evenly, and he could not close his mouth.

'Christ Jesus,' someone said very quietly.

It was quite still in the room.

'Him's tongue's off,' said someone else.

Nicanor was sobbing like an animal. He tried to touch the hanging lump of flesh, but it hurt so terribly that he could not. Obscurely, he could see figures moving in front of him. Someone leant over him, a pair of eyes were there, right in front of him, a voice.

'Him's tongue's off! 'Tis off!'

Then one of the men came forward, lifted up Nicanor's head and looked anxiously for a moment at his now bloodied jaw, then, fumbling for his knife in his belt, he took hold of the dangling tip of the tongue and swiftly and neatly sliced through the little shred still holding the tongue. It did not hurt, no more than before. The man got up and looked at the little piece of flesh in his hand for a moment with a troubled expression. The boy was still sitting in the floor, staring in despair up at the man, moaning still, but more and more gutturally and deeply.

The whole of his front was bloody now. He was not a pleasant sight. Otherwise it was quiet in the room, the boy sitting there staring at them, moaning like an animal. Not an amusing sight.

The silence in the room revealed that not one of them thought it the slightest bit amusing.

'Tha'll nowt be much of a man fer words,' said the man, throwing the tongue into a corner. 'But tha can be a good man fer that.'

The boy's gaze was still firmly fixed on them, a stubborn look in his eyes, as if he did not know what had happened, or that he was pleading for it to be undone: his eyes begged and begged that it hadn't happened, but it had.

'That wi' them pincers were nowt but a joke,' said one of the men apologetically. 'If tha hadna rowed so much, t'wouldn't've happened t'tha tongue. Tha wuz unlucky.'

'T's some spunk in t'lad,' said another man, the one who had been kneed in the groin, now recovered. He put in a plug of snuff.

'Gi t'lad a tot,' he added, his voice almost friendly.

'He doesn't drink,' came suddenly from Elmblad, still on the floor.

'Time's come then. Or him'll not stop bleedin'.'

Someone went out of the door and was gone for a moment. Nicanor was lying on the floor, on his side. His eyes closed. He did not want them to see him. He wished it was dark. Then he heard the door opening, low voices, someone coming over to him. Holding his head.

Like the ram-lamb, he thought.

Then he felt someone trying to pour liquid between his lips; unresisting, he opened his mouth. It burnt horribly. He groaned, but swallowed. It was like a spear of fire. He went on swallowing, the spear of fire growing warmer and spreading, growing and growing and filling him, and he swallowed and swallowed and the voices grew softer and more friendly and warmer, and carefully he opened his eyes to what he had never wanted to see.

6

THE WIRES WERE STRETCHED to the house. The house was a sounding-box and he was in the middle of the box. The other end of the wire was far away in the stars and the celestial harp was thundering on and on. In his dream, the song of the celestial harp was deafening and frightening, not soft, muted and dignified as he remembered from winter nights in Hjoggböle, but piercing, thinner and more menacingly sharp. Then the song grew so sharp and penetrating that it hurt, going right through his head, and there was no one who could help him. Far inside the darkness, the pain was a soft glowing point that grew and swelled, the song of the celestial harp veering away, and finally nothing was left but the pain, sharp, clear and very real.

He rolled over, hearing sounds from sheep.

A man came with a lamp.

The sheep were bleating quietly, no longer in a panic. The man sat down beside Nicanor, his face almost invisible, a silhouette against the light, but his voice calm and friendly; in the middle of all the misery, it was good that he gave of his time. But the lamp. Nicanor wanted no one to see him, that nothing, absolutely nothing should break up the darkness, and he would curl up like a calf inside a cow, in total darkness; it would be warm and soft and dark and the cow would be like a sheepskin inside and no one would see him.

And nothing would have happened and the dream would continue.

' 'Tis a bad business, that it 'tis,' said the man again.

Nicanor also remembered something else very clearly; he had vomited. On to his clothes.

That must have been the liquor. When he tried to say his name, it had not worked. It hadn't worked at all. Elmblad had sat up and was staring vacantly at Nicanor, quite silently, only the lamb and sheep moving, anxiously bleating in one corner, and then Elmblad had said: 'Nicanor!', then fallen silent, as there was nothing else to be said.

'Best phone for help,' said the man bluntly.

Early morning, the light growing a lighter and lighter grey through the dirty window. It smelt. The agitators' trip into inner Westerbotten had been temporarily interrupted.

They each held him by an arm and walked across the yard. Grey over the water, so the other side of Burträsk was invisible. No colours. It was sleeting. The countryside was very flat, colourless, the wind driving the cold into them, right inside them, deep down. The well-vane. Snow shovelled off the road. The marsh that was Burträsk, white and then grey where the contours vanished.

They each held him by an arm; the blood down his front had dried now, but he still found walking difficult. He walked slowly, supported by the two men, his mouth slightly open. He had stopped groaning, but was breathing heavily, hoarsely, like an animal. He thought it good that it was possible to get used to it hurting; it wouldn't get worse, nothing could be worse than it was now.

Tha'll not be much of a man fer words, the man had said. Well, maybe that was so. Nor much of a man for socialism, either. Maybe that was so, too. But no doubt there were other things. Everything's better than death. And he wasn't dead.

He was shaking all over, breathing through his open mouth, thinking: I'm not dead. I'm alive. I'm alive. Alive, alive, alive.

Skelleftebladet, the local paper, ran a report on the event three days later. The report was very brief. A squabble had arisen in Burträsk when some workers gathered to discuss matters with Elmblad, the sawmill agitator. He had shot off his mouth and they had wanted to chastise him. There had been a fracas, and during the fight a sixteen-year-old youth had lost the tip of his tongue. The youth had been generally assisting the agitator, but had been taught a lesson.

The report was written in a jocular style. No names, except Elmblad's.

For the time being he was left lying on the sofa in the kitchen. They telephoned for help. But all the time he thought about death being worse. I'm alive. Alive. Alive.

Sixteen degrees below zero. Grey cold. Winter had finally arrived.

7

THE TIMBER-SLED

1

JOSEFINA MARKSTRÖM received a message that same evening to say that she should go to the Lundströms', as someone wanted her on the telephone. The voice on the line was distant and there was a lot of crackling, but what the voice had to say was easy enough to grasp. Josefina listened without saying a word. When the voice had transmitted the message, there was a moment of silence and expectation, and then the voice started crying, 'Hello! Hello! Is anyone there?' and Josefina answered curtly: '*Aye, that there is.*'

The boy had had some kind of accident. But it was nothing fatal.

On her way home to Oppstoppet she walked very quickly and did not cry. When she got back, she at once started gutting the herrings, but stopped after a minute or so and sat down and wept. Then she stopped that. She at once decided to go and fetch the boy herself.

She had always hoped he would go into the church. That was a great deal to hope for, almost arrogance, but in the depths of her heart she tucked away the dream that one of hers would one day rise above them, break free, not stay. It would be Nicanor. He had always been different.

The men were felling in Gummark. She would have to do it herself. She borrowed a horse and a timber-sled, rolled up two sheepskins, put them on the back trailer of the sled and left. It was already dusk by the time she was ready. Then the moon came out and it was easy for her to find the way.

This was the land of her childhood. Why should she not find her way? There was nothing that could frighten her and everything was familiar.

So she was travelling through countryside she knew, the familiar route, through Sjöbotten and Sjön and Forsen and West Hjoggböle, then inland towards Burträsk, and the familiar landscape, though no snow this time, and clear moonlight.

The horse, Josefina and moonlight.

I know no more, except the route. History is always like that. We have to fill it out. Otherwise everything becomes completely incomprehensible. It was all grinding round in her head, round and round, what had happened to Nicanor; and at some point, just *there*, she had tried to persuade herself that the worst and most satanic things in life also have a purpose. Inside herself there was more than just icy cold and hopelessness.

The sum total of her life was not just nothing; the meaning of life was not only on the other side of death, and it was worth resisting. Though resistance comes in many forms.

The last time I met Nicanor, in the autumn of 1972, he had asked a question which at first I hadn't even understood. Since then, I have understood what the question was, and it is the answer I am trying to stitch together.

When it came to himself he gave me little help; perhaps he didn't think he was interesting. Josefina was another matter. I never met her for the simple reason that she died in April 1911, in Porto Lucena in southern Brazil. But I have seen photographs of her, always something of course, though not very interesting. Nicanor described her, but in everything he said about her it was clear she was a loser. Her resistance must also have taken different forms.

The countryside where she grew up is still there: always something. That evening in the winter of 1909, in pale moonlight and cold, that evening as she sat on the front sled behind a plodding, sadly farting horse, it must have looked more or less as it does today.

One can always try out the working hypothesis that the landscape leaves certain signs behind it, secret signals, as aids to interpretation. I had grown up in the same landscape; I was about to say the same village, but perhaps that's not really true. A village is not the same half a century later, and a village can have many faces.

Forty years ago might be forty light-years. Then the song of the celestial harp becomes the faint echo from a long since extinguished star, or a vague and indistinct lure-call through the ice. That's what history is like. We have to fill it out. Actually, that's what history is.

Forty years after Josefina's night journey through Sjön and Hjogg-böle to Burträsk, forty light-years later, the conflicts had put on their Sunday best and behaved in a well-brought-up manner, the rebellion was over and it was almost impossible to see where it had gone. Or rather, both the conflict and the resistance had taken on different forms.

The same landscape, different forms.

Josefina Markström, née Lindström, was born in West Hjogg-böle. From a socio-religious point of view, the village was very interesting in the forties, clearly divided into a worldly part and a spiritual part. Josefina, born in 1870, grew up in what would be the worldly part (I presume it was different then) and I (sixty years later) in the spiritual part. The worldly part became famous for its first-class football, the spiritual part for its weighty piety. How I wished it was the other way round. It was in the spiritual part, the one which on Judgement Day would be taken up and placed among the sheep next to the Lord Jesus, and from there would regard with gloomy satisfaction the lost sporting fools among the goats, thus receiving final compensation for the pleasures denied them in the world – that was where I grew up. Religiosity there was profound, serious and honest, with no pleasures of a worldly nature (although, on second thoughts, I have forty-two cousins), no sport, teetotalism firmly established, and there was a Blue Ribbon Society with a junior club for children. If there were no preacher available on a Sunday, a true believer neighbour with a powerfully soporific voice would read for hours from Rosenius. It was just like *The People of Hemsö* but more boring, and more frequent, and never, never were two pages turned over at once.

But this was not where Josefina Markström had grown up. That was three kilometres away, to the west of the marsh, the part of Hjoggböle famed in the forties all over northern Norrland for its football team.

The team was called the Comets and played matches *on Sundays*. Its days of glory were the years after the second world war, and they were extremely hard to beat on home ground. This was partly due to the pitch, or the home field, which was only seventy metres long, very narrow, and had a barn as a changing-room at one end (this was before what was called the 'Norrland Window' in football had been opened, and there was no call to make a fuss of visiting teams); the surface of the pitch was an enigma and therefore interesting. This was due to efficient natural planning, and to controlled cultivation, with rationally placed hummocks and wisely laid sunken covered drains, constantly forcing foolish visiting teams into making outrageous mistakes. The team was full of characters: a strong honest centre-half who was good with his head, a swift, wily, dark-haired wing who was extremely bandy-legged, and a couple of brothers as the two backs: they were iron-hard, amazingly slow, but could kick hard. The team had tremendously loyal fans at home, who were also very noisy and enthusiastic in a linguistically interesting manner which always made visiting players uncertain. They shouted orders and advice, as well as instructions of a clearly didactic nature, always in dialect. If the defence gave way, the cry *Hold t'wingman!* soared excitedly into the skies. Certain tactical advice presumed good local knowledge. *Pars't northuds!* meant that you should send a pass to the north, so it was important to know the points of the compass.

All this would be quaint if there had not been certain other aspects to the picture: I'll come to them soon. After the second world war, the Comets were the first team in northern Sweden to bring in the idea of training camps. This happened sometime around 1950 and was carried out with such inexorable logic and under such tight discipline that it aroused an enormous amount of attention. They had come out top of the Fifth Division of the Central Northern League the year before, were promoted, and now it was spring and the end of the season. The team was hard up, but a training camp was decided on. A training camp should be apart, totally solitary, isolated from all temptations; they all knew that. So they decided to put it in the middle of the village.

At a mass-meeting in Frederiksson's Café it was decided that the venue should be the People's Hall, right in the centre of the village.

That was in March. The whole team, including the captain and reserves, appeared one Sunday. A crowd had assembled, mostly children. The players brought bolsters and quilts and marched up the wooden steps, the children standing outside in astonished but respectfully staring clumps. Then the door was closed, and after that no unauthorized person was allowed in. No fiancées, no wives, no children. No one knew for sure what was going on in the camp, but children who climbed up to the windows and managed to see in between the slits in the curtains reported that they had seen shadows moving. These were the sports idols of the district, and they had shut themselves inside a secret sports hall, into which no relatives were allowed.

Twice a day, the team came out, running through the snow every morning (they ran through the village in a silent group) and playing snow-football every afternoon before dusk. The children clung round the windows all the time, trying to scrape the ice off with their nails. They mostly saw shadows. One day there was a snowstorm and it was maintained they had cancelled afternoon outdoor training and instead had played a match between the organ and the platform. But no one was sure; there was something secretive going on in this 'training camp', as the local paper called it. Something mysterious and tempting. A new epoch had perhaps arrived in the village.

A local paper, however, was allowed to record the training camp pictorially. In the photograph, serious men from the coast-lands of Västerbotten can be seen spread out on the floor of the main hall. No card-games are visible. Far away, almost swallowed up in the dusk, a player can be seen half-lying with his hand raised slightly as if in greeting from the hinterlands of the forties.

The horse, Josefina and moonlight. No one knows any more, apart from the journey. History is always like that. We have to fill it out.

The second half of this remarkable story is about the defeat of the Comets. Their days of glory had made new demands on them; they all realized that. Thus the training camp, carried out with ascetic and consistent logic. The new epoch also made demands on the pitch. The old seventy-metre field, with its cunning hum-mocks that had mercilessly stripped visiting goalkeepers bare so many times (I admit it is a bad image, but it *feels* true), became unacceptable in the long run. So an application was made to the council for a grant for a new pitch. A neighbour of mine, a smallholder living in the spiritual part of the village and an ardent true believer, was seized with holy fury on hearing about this. He decided to instigate a planned rebellion against the Antichrists. Whatever the cost, he was not afraid. Ever since the training camp affair, he had harboured the deep-rooted conviction that this was

222

all the work of the Devil. Fanaticism had gone too far: isolating fifteen young men in the middle of the village for a week, forbidding them to speak to their relatives, and then them just sweatin' around an' kickin' a football. He himself was a taciturn but sympathetic man in his fifties, who had ten daughters, of whom I was partly in love with at least two (I sang 'Calm Rests the Sea' with the altos in the junior club). This man of faith proposed in the village council that all the football pitches in the parish should be ploughed up and sown with oats. There were, he said in his proposal, more useful things to do than playing football.

The conflict had now been driven up to the surface. The proposal aroused tremendous fury in the worldly part of the village and open warfare was declared. An inconceivably large sum of money was collected up in a very short time and a parcel of forest land bought next to my true believer neighbour, so near to him that every thud would be heard, and there the new pitch was cleared and laid down.

He could stuff those oats of his up his arse, they thought.

They could not have found a worse place. The work of levelling and clearing was enormously laborious, the money did not cover turfing and the gravelly ground was never really inviting: gone were the old field's cunningly placed hummocks, gone were the cleverly sunken drains, gone was the *personal*, in the best meaning of the word, touch about the fine old field. What's more, most important of all, the pitch was not in West Hjoggböle, but in the highly spiritual Sjön. It was not easy to play good football surrounded by such a weight of religion and it was a long way to bicycle for practices. The whole point, the diabolical cunning of placing the pitch alongside the oat-grower's farm faded as the years went by and finally became almost non-existent. In the end the original dispute was forgotten. Football languished and the Comets slowly sank through the league like the sun through sea mist.

God had taken his just revenge at last.

The man in the photograph in the local paper who is waving from the interior of the People's Hall, and the oat-grower. There should be something between them. It is there. It should have been retrievable.

It reminds me a little of the way in which Uncle Aron died.

Late evening, moonlight, and Josefina Markström passing through the village.

Forty years, what is that? Of course her world was also mine. People like her created the conditions. But I just didn't see it. She did not see the end of the story, nor the Comets, nor the oat-grower, nor Frederiksson's Café, nor me.

The person in whom hope is destroyed comes to hate the destroyer. Is that true? It should be, perhaps.

She turned off to the left at Forsen.

I am gradually beginning to see her.

Ever since that March day in 1973 when Nicanor died, when I still thought I was going to write a book about him and his life, the strange thing is that he has slowly, almost imperceptibly receded from me, and all the others round him have taken small, modest, imperceptible, Västerbotten steps forward, until I see only them and not him. That was precisely what he wanted. He seemed to have pictured the story as something being performed *outside* him, in the others: a truly humble and Lutheran attitude. As if it were only possible to understand the major direction of movement in us all if you turned your eyes away from the centre and looked at the unnoticeable, embarrassed, discreet, hidden and reluctant changes of movement in *the others*, the ones who pretended not to change direction, and yet clearly did so. Then you could extract the story and, like an unimaginative book-keeper, carefully register all these pious, affectionate, rather incomplete, powerless and outcast people who turn forgivingly to their oppressors and indignantly deny they are victims.

Of course they felt anger. Of course they possessed tremendous strength. Of course this could be seen.

But how?

Very cold, and moonlight.

She let the horse walk, winding the reins round the chain-pole. There was, after all, only one way. On the telephone she had learnt what had happened: the voice had been distant and the line crackling, but she had understood. I hope she wasn't feeling full of Christian love and forgiveness. I hope she was thinking she would soon start feeling anger. And if she did, what was the point of it all?

Or: what's t'point? What kin I do?

2

Nicanor was still lying on the kitchen sofa when she arrived. He was asleep. He had his mouth open, as if not daring to close it because of the pain, his open mouth giving him a childish, terribly young look, and in his sleep his eyelids were still twitching, in small cautious spasms, as if he were frightened and dared not wake. Or . . .

She had almost forgotten he was still a child. It was so recent, really. His eyelids twitching; perhaps he was dreaming.

She sat down carefully on a chair and looked at him. Nicanor was not alone in the kitchen; the others were sitting round the kitchen table. But she took no notice of them. The man who had come with the lantern was there, and Elmblad, but why should she bother with them? The boy had his mouth open, and she started thinking as she knew she had to think; silently to herself she went through the verses according to the Gospel of St Matthew about if thy right eye offend thee, pluck it out and cast it from thee: for it is profitable for thee that one of thy members should perish, and not that thy whole body should be cast into hell. And if thy right hand offend thee, cut it off, and cast it from thee: for it is profitable for thee that one of thy members should perish, and not that thy whole body should be cast into hell. And she thought through every one of the verses, but it wasn't right. Then she thought of them all over again, but it still wasn't right. So she thought that God was just and no great damage had been done after all, but what use was that?

All she could feel was anger, and she thought, quite without love or forgiveness, that this was unjust. He was only a lad still. And now he'd had his tongue cut off and maybe would no longer be able to speak. Who had decided on this punishment? And why?

It was not just.

She took out the blue handkerchief and carefully wiped his forehead. He at once opened his eyes and looked at her, immediately awake. She stroked his forehead, and his hair, again and again, as if he were a horse, and she said nothing, but went on stroking him for a long time, and he closed his lips and she wiped his face and mouth and neck, Nicanor looking up at her all the time, but he could say nothing, for he was ashamed. He did not know why.

Very quiet in that kitchen. She sat for a long time wiping him clean, as if wishing to turn him back into a child again, and in the end all the blood on his face was gone and he looked almost his usual self. Apart from his eyes. His eyes looked *different*; something had happened to them since the journey to Burträsk. They were slightly darker, a little . . . different.

'Ah'm teken t'boy home,' she said out into the room.

She went round and shook hands with them all, thanking those who had helped the boy. She was just as usual, almost. When she came to Elmblad, she seemed to hesitate for a moment: she looked at him, seeing the injury above his eye, the swollen upper lip and the watery bloodshot eyes, seeing him gazing out into the kitchen, embarrassed or frightened (impossible to decide which) and avoiding her eyes.

Then she held out her hand and several seconds went by before he noticed it. Then he noticed.

The palm of his hand was moist. She herself was quite dry.

'Ah'm goin',' she said.

Let us read the Klemensnäs letter once again.

> *The Manager.*
> *Mr. O. V. Wahlberg.*
> *Skellefteå.*
> *As the new sawing instructions have to some extent increased the square-sawing over and above the old instructions, and our earnings have thereby been reduced proportionally in comparison with those of the previous year, we respectfully request whether a levelling could not be made to anticipate this reduction? We would be very grateful for any accommodation in this case in ways that you yourself may decide upon.*
>
> *At the same time we testify to our gratitude for the extremely humane treatment we have received as always on your part, signed with true esteem.*
> *Klemensnäs, May 1894.*

At first you see only the humility, the deep-rooted caution, the creeping tone, then you slowly start distinguishing the rest. It takes time to recognize the resistance. But it is there. It is there all the time, embedded as if in ice, taking different routes, not appearing to be resistance.

But the important thing is that the coast is rising.

*

She rolled him up in a sheepskin, and he curled up beside her. She herself sat with her legs propped on the front bar, her arm round him. Two o'clock in the morning, still moonlight.

3

BUT WHEN DESPAIR IS PROFOUND it is also quite still. It does not preen itself, nor is it magnified.

It grinds slowly round and round, and never goes away.

When they got to *Lappvattnet*, the moon had gone, the snow suddenly darker. When they passed *Lappvattnet*, her despair was also still, very calm, grinding round and round inside her. She had always believed the righteous would one day receive their just reward, that injustice would always be compensated for, and that finally an eternal judge would add up the columns of figures and set up a final balance in which the sum totals for the poor and the exploited and the wretched, hitherto so small and miserable, would be *just*. For deep down inside her she had believed death would place a plus sign after the final figure, and for the wretched there would be a very large sum, perhaps a three-figure sum, as when her husband had been away felling in Glomers and had come home with a three-figure sum in his account book and everything had suddenly seemed different. When they reached *Renbergsvattnet*, the grinding despair was still there, a somewhat colder tone over the snow now, so she calmed the horse with his nose-bag. Nicanor mumbled something from the depths of the sheepskin and she leant over him, very close: his eyes were closed but he was not asleep. Perhaps he wanted water? She took up a fistful of snow and gave it to him; cautiously he moved his lips against the snow, and it started to melt. His eyes were still closed. She went round the horse's head and mechanically checked the chain fastenings, despair still grinding on and on in her head, refusing to go away. For if there were no final automatic balance, if death did not add up to that great three-figure sum, then the situation was that the righteous who had worked and toiled and struggled and not taken to the roads or been like gypsies and such like, then *injustice* had been done to them. Then there was no plus sign called Death who would add up, and so there was no balance.

It ground on and on.

She had seen his mouth and what she had seen she thought terrible. A raw swollen stump, worse than she could have imagined. He was so young. He was only a child. If only they'd taken another.

He was only a lad.

In *West Hjoggböle*, she did not turn right. The horse hesitated for a few moments and she clicked her tongue impatiently at him, jerking irritably on the left rein. The boy was to go to the hospital.

In the photographs, she is very tall and grave, almost menacing. She is to be found in two photographs. In both she is standing up. In both she has her hand on her husband's shoulder; he is sitting on a chair and it looks as if she is holding him firmly with a fatherly grip.

She was like a father to us, Nicanor said once.

The great strike? No one has any special memory as far as Josefina Markström is concerned. She no doubt disapproved, of course. She believed everyone should pull his weight. Yes, her one critical comment on the company management: 'tain't right. What wasn't right? Reducing the wages by twenty-five per cent. Then the employer was not pulling his weight. But one soweth, and another reapeth, she added mysteriously.

That was from the Gospel according to St John.

Critical? Yes, it was critical. She was thought to believe that those who did not pull their weight should be resisted. One should not accept them. One should do something about them.

During the great strike, she had ordered the whole family out to pick berries. How many hundreds of pounds of berries they had picked they did not know. But it was hard work. If any one of them stole a brief pause to rest on a tree-stump, they soon had Josefina on to them. Nicanor was to remember the great strike as one of the hardest times he had ever had. An aching back all the time. Constant rushing about. Josefina was determined to show that at least there were no lazybones among the Markströms.

Resistance takes many forms.

She stopped the horse in *Långviken*. There she allowed him to eat, and she wiped him down thoroughly with dry hay, going over every single bit of him, until he was quite dry.

It was important not to drive the horse to death.

She talked to Nicanor all through the last hours. She spoke calmly, without excitement and without the slightest undertone of anger. What she said was of less importance. Nicanor thought it was all rather disconnected, but it was nice to hear her voice. She told him little bits out of her life. How she had been at her uncle's and cut marsh grass. How the Lindströms of Västeröl had once made bilberry wine, maturing it for six months, then all the Lindström children had been allowed to taste it, and had behaved as if they were suffering from St Vitus's Dance. About how a light had shone from the top of the flagpole the night before her father's father had died.

He lay there with his eyes closed all the time. She had put his head on her lap. He was breathing against her leather jerkin, his eyes closed, listening. Towards morning her talking changed. She fell silent for long spells, but what she said was more connected.

Without even looking at him she said that it was probably like being hit. Like clubbing burbot in the winter. He knew that. You were hit, but nothing was hopeless. Sometimes it seemed as if you were going to die. But when you'd had a crack on the skull, there were always ways out, after all.

She wanted that said to him. She fell silent, as if expecting an answer. But he just went on breathing against her leather jerkin, his eyes closed.

Nothing is hopeless, he heard her saying again. Like a whisper, to the horse in front.

At dawn, small pricks of light from Skellefteå appeared to the north. They would soon be there. It had been a long night on the sled. From *Bureå*, she had driven all the way across *Sjöbotten* and *Hjoggböle* and *Lappvattnet* to *Burträsk*, and there she had turned, and fetched the boy, and then driven him to the hospital in Skellefteå, where they had treated him, sewn up his tongue and let him rest. Two centimetres of his tongue had gone. He vomited now and again. She stayed in town for two days, then drove Nicanor home. When she got back, everything was as before, though something had happened which was perhaps even more terrible, but that she just had to divine. However, she was told that Uncle Aron, who had first been blacklisted and then two days later restored to favour and then had had to leave again, had now been thrown out of the barracks as well. He had come to the Markströms that same day, pulling a sledge, and there he had been given a bed in the attic. And then something had happened.

That was it. But not until the month of March 1910 did Josefina Markström find out what had happened.

For the last stretch before Skellefteå, she sat with her arm even more firmly round Nicanor, talking loudly all the time, as if she had lost her wits. But she hadn't. The lights of Skellefteå pricked holes in the darkness, at its darkest now just before dawn, the horse walking. Three days to Christmas. She talked and talked, though Nicanor closed his eyes and pretended to be asleep.

For, she whispered into his face as the horse walked slowly down the mountain towards Skellefte town on this icy December morning, there is a difference between the people who are allowed to ride in the front of the sled, and the poor wretches who have to sit in the back. Because those who may ride in the front have the chance to steer and keep a look-out. But those in the back, them jist has t'foller.

So there's a difference. But innumerable cries rise from those in the back to be allowed to crawl forward and take the reins, and one day it'll be crowded up there in the front, and alarm and great anguish will arise.

That is how it is for those who ride in the front.

8

THE SACK OF STONES

1

ANNA-LENA WIKSTRÖM was the one to come shuffling in in her stupidly large boots, shrieking in her shrill, triumphant voice, gleefully excited: 'Them's finded our Aron! Them's finded our Aron!' And Josefina gave her a slice of bun-loaf and a bit of sugar and told her to be off.

He had floated up, after two months. The leather straps on his backpack had rotted away and he had sailed up to the surface like a swollen, stinking, white balloon. That was the end of all the speculation about Uncle Aron.

In fact, it had really started during the conflict.

They had started calling him Judas at the barracks. *'There's that'n Judas with him's droopin' lip,'* they started saying as he came shambling along with his humble crooked gait on his way from the timber yard to the solitariness of the barracks. For Aron had a rather protruding, almost ostentatiously drooping lower lip, and when they started commenting on it, it became a saying. *'There's our Judas wit' droopin' lips an' him's lost t'butter him got from t'manager.'* They had not forgotten what had happened during the minor conflict preceding the major one. They remembered even more clearly the three great lumps of butter they had found, overgrown with healthy sprouting mould, wrapped in that warm coat of eczema-like grey fur that made the lumps of butter look like three small sleeping lambs. Our Judas had sold his workmates to the company, and lost the butter. It was a fantastically comical story, and no wonder Aron's lower lip hung like a mourning flag on a windless day.

But when the great strike had begun and one August day in 1909 everything had been quiet down at Skäret, then this Aron with his drooping lip and squint eyes and crooked shoulder had been no use whatsoever to the Company, for nothing is more useless than a Judas after his betrayal; when betrayal has taken place, there is no way of erasing it. He had gone on strike with all the others. And yet he had heard that *hast tha lost t'butter, Judas?* during the quiet days, and the cheerful shouts had etched their way right into him. It was said later on about Aron that everyone had noticed he had gone peculiar, though while he was going peculiar, no one said anything.

He started sleeping badly, waking in the middle of the night and twisting and turning, everything grinding round in his head. Aron was perhaps not what you might call much of a thinker. But he was not stupid. He could not rid himself of the obstinate thought that an *injustice* had been done to him, that they had judged him wrongly, that he was no Judas, and that what he had done had been necessary. So he went to Piteå in May 1909 and joined a strike-breaking team and then he came back, and just as he had returned, the great conflict started.

He was one of those who held out far longer than the rest.

Though that did not really count, because for a man who has committed treachery, nothing can erase the treachery, nothing, least of all within himself. So he went on stubbornly waking up at one o'clock in the morning and staring at the ceiling, listening to the snores of his workmates. He couldn't get away from it.

In the summer of 1909, Uncle Aron was given a butter-tub.

The tub was made of juniper wood and had a strong, fresh, acrid smell, like that of a very dry sunny heath with juniper bushes smelling strongly of freedom and summer. I know the smell, as my grandfather made a similar tub for me, and the light sweet scent is still there, a faint lure-call from the coastlands, timber and freedom. He had burnt PVE on the bottom of it with a branding-iron.

That was the kind of butter-tub Aron had been given, though not made by PVE. The butter-tub was a donation.

What happened was that one Saturday evening, two weeks before the big conflict, a small delegation came into Aron's room in the barracks. The delegation mumbled secretively, then one of them said: '*Uhuh, so tha's here, is't tha?*' and Aron had nodded, as he could hardly deny the fact. Another man had then asked in a friendly way: '*Us almost thought tha'd be in t'shithouse havin' it off?*' and there was not much to say to that. But the delegation thought the question amusing and quiet laughter broke out, almost turning into open amusement when the same joker added: '*Us heard tha wuz engaged t'Miss Höger?*' But Aron had just stared down at the floor with his obstinately squinting eye and quietly clasped his hands in his lap, as if in prayer, and when no one could find any more funny remarks, they came out with what they had come for.

It was like this. Several workers had felt sorry for our Aron having to have his butter wrapped in paper and hidden down in the cellar. And the manager would be unhappy if he got to know his butter was getting spoilt. So they had decided to donate a butter-tub to our Aron.

As a token of gratitude.

The man holding the butter-tub took a step forward and held it out. It was quite small, and would hold at the most two kilos of butter. But it was well made. Aron, his feet bare, sat on the bed, staring rigidly and in bewilderment at the butter-tub, unable to find anything to say.

'Next time them gives tha butter at t'office,' the leader of the delegation said maliciously, smiling broadly, 'tha'll has a good tub t'put't in.'

Then Aron had actually accepted the butter-tub. He had held out his hand, taken the tub, turned it over, as if expecting to find some message stuck on the bottom, turned it back and stared at it. The members of the delegation were looking expectantly at him, waiting for a reaction.

Uncle Aron had received a gift. Slowly, as if wandering out of a dream, he had woken up.

'A butter-tub,' he said tonelessly, looking questioningly from one man to the next. 'Am ah to ha' a butter-tub?'

They all nodded encouragingly.

'For t'time's comin' when tha'll git more butter from t'manager, ain't it?' said one member of the delegation modestly.

'There'll be more disputes, for sure,' added another.

'An' them knows where them has our Judas,' said a third, concluding the detailed analysis.

Carefully, Uncle Aron put the tub down on the bed. For a moment he looked irresolutely from one man to the next, as if he were frightened or wished to apologize or wanted to ask for something else, but he didn't know what. Then he got up and quite simply thanked them, one after another. Uncle Aron had actually thanked them. First he shook the hand of the man who

233

had handed it to him and said, 'Thankin' thee.' Then the next. And the next. And the next.

He shook them firmly by the hand and said thank you, but he did not once look them in the eye. The room became completely silent, and as there was nothing to add, the delegation left.

That was how Uncle Aron received the butter-tub.

2

ARON WAS ONE OF THE LAST to go back to work after the conflict.

He was next but last in the queue that morning when Gren the Setter drew up the final registration of cattle led astray by the unions and now brought to heel and good order. Aron went up to the table and reported that now the conflict was over, he was willing to return to work. And that early September morning the sun was still just below the horizon of the Bay of Bothnia and vapour coming briskly out of every mouth, the leaves of the trees flaming like freshly dug carrots, and everything would have been fine for Uncle Aron if he hadn't been quite so anxious.

In the end, there were only two men left.

One was Uncle Aron. The other was Albin Renström from Yttervik. Albin Renström was known for his none too great enthusiasm for work. He was rather lazy and considered a bit weak in the head, and in Yttervik he was the natural butt found in every village; without a butt, Västerbotten villages were not really complete. He stuffed huge wads of snuff under his lip, making it look as if he had a hen's egg there. Famous is the occasion when a gang of small boys started teasing him, and for about the five hundredth time asked him how he had it with the 'fiancée' he always maintained he had in Risliden. Did she really exist? 'Aye, that her does,' he insisted stubbornly. He was there having it every month. Sometimes twice a month. A hell of a long way to go but what doesn't a man do to get it? But, the boys persisted, what do you do, Albin, when you're going to kiss your fiancée? With all that snuff in your mouth?

He had reflected for a moment, then, with a bright, almost discerning smile spreading over his face, he had said:

'Ah fends her off!'

He was not a proper sawmill worker. He took jobs now and

again, mostly staying in Yttervik, working as a labourer. He was actually not very much loved by those around him. He was always farting and it was said of him that he was bad for the soil because earthworms died to the depth of several feet when he let off. So when on that early September morning Gren turned his gaze on the last two men in the queue, it shouldn't have been difficult to decide that Aron, the faithful traitor, the butter-lover, the plank-bearer and the man with the reliable squint, should promptly be included in the gathering of trustworthy men to be favoured with employment by Bure Company. Anyway, before Albin Renström from Yttervik.

'Mmm, so 'tis thee, then, Aron,' said Gren slowly and thought-fully, nodding with deliberation. 'So, 'tis thee?'

'Aye,' said Uncle Aron, looking slightly embarrassed.

'Tha's here, then?' said the saw-setter, a slight critical nuance in his voice.

Abashed, Aron said nothing, not knowing what to say.

'Aye, 'tis like this,' Gren went on, looking down at the papers. 'Hmmm.'

'Aye,' echoed Uncle Aron faintly.

'So, tha's here, then?'

Nothing much more was said. Albin Renström had stood shuffling his feet and staring up in the sky, now and again letting out a little fart, as was his habit when he was uncertain and didn't know what to do. Aron had stared in the other direction, down at his feet, and Gren had leafed through his papers over and over again, making little notes and occasionally looking up and saying his suspicious little 'Hmm'. Then he had asked Aron why he had been unwilling to work during the dispute, when he had not shown such tendencies before.

Aron had nothing to offer or say.

Nothing.

Finally Gren had slowly, thoughtfully and very precisely written down a name on the list. And he had looked up and said to the obstinately shuffling man from Yttervik: '*Hmm, Renström, tha kin start work then,*' and then he had written another name down on another list and looked up at Uncle Aron, and in his *Swedish* voice and in *Swedish* so that Aron would really understand that it was not Gren the Setter speaking now, but the powers that be: '*Hmm, the situation is such that not everyone can expect work.*' Then Gren had paused and poked in his ear with his finger. Albin

Renström had looked with interest at Uncle Aron. Then Gren had added: '*The most reluctant to work cannot expect work to any great extent.*'

Aron waited. He appeared to be thinking this was just some kind of preliminary, and that in the end Gren would brighten and grin and tell Uncle Aron that of course he had been of great service to the Company and *first and foremost* he would be considered.

But nothing happened.

Uncle Aron was put down on the list on which the untrustworthy people were registered. For those are the rules of treachery; it cannot be erased, you get no thanks, mould grows on the butter, anxiety in your heart, and Aron backed away, spun round and trudged off, his shoulders crooked, his arms hanging. He started walking slowly, then more and more quickly.

That is what happened when Uncle Aron was blacklisted. It was simple. Only a name written down, and t'butter-Judas had now sold his birthright, been a traitor, and lost his reward, and it got around an' t'tell t'truth, 'twere a sorry sight.

But comical most of all.

A week later, Elmblad had come to Bureå.

Uncle Aron hardly knew how it had come about.

First he was an honest worker enjoying everyone's respect, and yes, he did have a squint and a crooked back, and no, he didn't have much luck with women, but all the same, not a man to be laughed at. And then suddenly, like spinning a coin, his honour had been erased. It didn't exist any more. The problem was that he didn't understand how it had happened. He seemed to have been borne along into the whole *situation*. He had just gone on doing what he had learnt to do, gone on as before and then the people who had accompanied him on the journey had gone in another direction and he was left alone.

He felt a little peculiar, suddenly becoming a traitor, when he had thought he was carrying on as usual. He found it hard to get used to.

A long time later, everyone who had known him said they had seen him going peculiar, and it showed in our Aron, and they'd always suspected it. But no one had *realized* he was so lonely down there in his stomach, and not even Our Saviour Jesus Christ could save our butter-Judas.

He applied for work at the sawmill again three weeks later, and was given it. They said they were short of men and by chance there was work for him. If he behaved. Then he was back with the others in the timber yard and it was early winter, but the sawing soon came to an end, and then one morning he was told he needn't come.

Only the permanent workers need report.

He still slept very badly at nights. He worried about how it had all happened. Sometimes he would stretch out his hand and pull the butter-tub to him in the darkness: sweet, tempting and secretive, out of the interior of the empty butter-tub rose the scent of juniper, liberation, possibilities, a lure-call that vaguely reminded him of the days when he thought everything was possible and life would also have some use for our Aron Lindström. He often lay there for a long time in the darkness, surrounded by the sounds of the barracks, letting that smell rise and fill him.

Uncle Aron was on his way into a dream. The dream was about being free of shame, of not being tormented, of not having to be ashamed. Of doing something *properly*. In the darkness of the night, a secretive whispering call rose from the strange, fresh, sweet interior of the butter-tub. His eyes closed and his hands cupped round the tub's smoothly polished wood, Uncle Aron began to pay more and more attention to what the scent was trying to say.

This was that traitors also had a blessed chance to *start again*. Or to regain respect. He lay there in the empty darkness, letting himself be filled with a sweet fresh scent, the scent that rose from Uncle Aron's butter-tub.

3

AFTERWARDS, several people said that it would never have happened if Josefina had been at home.

That was not true, however. What happened happened. No one can blame anyone else.

They came to Aron and told him there was no more work for the time being. And there would be no question of any more. That was roughly what they said. In some confusion he had tried to find out when the subject might come up again, and then they had said things would probably work out.

Did things work out?

At first he could find out nothing, but then the manager had let him into the room, and at first was too busy to say anything, but then had informed him in a sharp voice that it was not worth his while expecting work in future. If a worker was reluctant to work when he was really needed, then he might as well not work at other times, too.

That was it straight. And Uncle Aron was requested to move out of the barracks at once, as beds were in bloody short supply.

With that, the matter was closed.

He packed his sweater, trousers, four pairs of underpants, other underclothes (unwashed), his psalm-book, the butter-tub, his jar of hooks, two pairs of felt boots, a pair of leather boots, leather gloves, woollen mittens, the wall-clock he had had from his Uncle August when he'd died, two spoons, a knife, three forks, five bootlaces, his reindeer-skin bedcover, the blue wool shirt Josefina had given him, then placed everything on the sledge, put on his leather cap, grabbed the rope and left.

He would never return to the barracks.

In fact he had nowhere to go. His last chance was to stay with the Markströms. He didn't really want to do that, but he went there all the same. He arrived at about four in the afternoon, and Eva-Liisa was alone at home. He pulled the sledge into the porch, swept out the snow he had brought in with him, took off his gloves and leather cap, left the heap of possessions on the sledge, sat down in the kitchen and stared straight down at the floor. Eva-Liisa realized he was upset about something, so she put on the coffee. While it was heating, she told him what Josefina had said before she had taken the horse to fetch Nicanor. The story was incomplete, but its outer contours were clear.

The Burträskers had cut off our Nicanor's tongue.

He sat there in the middle of the sofa in the kitchen for a long time, staring straight down at nothing as it grew dark and the evening wind rose, squealing and whining in the chimney. Eva-Liisa looked at him closely, but said nothing, because she could see something was wrong with him. Father and the boys were away felling in Glomers, and Josefina had telephoned from Skellefteå to say she would be staying until she had heard what

238

they were going to do to Nicanor. Uncle Aron had gone peculiar and was sitting staring straight down at the floor and the wind was blowing, and the day after tomorrow would be Christmas. It was not a cheerful thought.

Eva-Liisa had somehow always liked him. She might not like a lot about the Markström family: their closeness, their arrogance. No, not arrogance, but *hardness*, perhaps. They were like a closed fortress, a handful of impoverished but stone-hard people who had entrenched themselves behind fortress-like walls. It was impossible to get in. Aron was the only one who was different. He was not nearly so *good* as the others; he was a semi-bad person, ugly to look at, squint-eyed and with a lower lip that trembled dismally whenever he was agitated, and he was neither especially pious nor especially successful, but when he spoke his voice was kind. He had never scolded her, but looked up kindly and thanked her when she served him coffee. Perhaps he hadn't always done the *right* thing, but there were so many people who did the right thing, it was nice to find someone different. Once Eva-Liisa had told him quite sharply that he shouldn't put snuff under both his top and lower lip, because then the brown juice just dribbled out of the corners of his mouth. He had glanced up at her with a look like that of an injured elk, and had never again put in a double layer when she was present.

She somehow liked him. She had started liking him the day after Josefina had held prayers in the kitchen for her. That night Nicanor had given her a lump off the sugar-loaf. The day after, Uncle Aron had brought her a penny twist.

It was just as Nicanor had said. She liked Nicanor very much, too. But with Aron it was different. He was the kind of bad person everyone laughed at. That wasn't fair. When Uncle Aron stubbornly refused to budge from the kitchen sofa all that long afternoon and just stared down at the floor, monotonously repeating that he'd been thrown out of the barracks and wouldn't she let him sit there in the warmth for a while, a tiny little while, until the warmth came back again, and he just went on sitting and saying nothing, then she became uneasy about Uncle Aron.

That was the day after Josefina's long journey to Burträsk. Everything happened at once. Perhaps there was some connection.

Or perhaps they had only saved it all up. Postponed it. That was also possible.

239

She woke to hear him crying.

At first the sounds were so small, they hardly reached across the attic floor, and she lay still in the dark, listening, thinking it was probably mice. The attic ceiling was lined and it was possible to sleep up there all the year round. Eva-Liisa was sleeping as usual in the cubbyhole, and Aron had been given Nicanor's bed. He had sat staring at the floor all evening, his hands clasped, reluctant to leave the kitchen sofa. Then it was time to go to bed and she ordered him upstairs. He disappeared upstairs without even looking at her, and without unpacking the sledge in the porch. Half an hour later, Eva-Liisa had gone to bed and there was no sound, so she had fallen asleep. Then the sounds had come right through her sleep, and suddenly she was wide awake and listening carefully.

No. Not mice.

There was something wrong with Uncle Aron. He had gone peculiar.

She sat up in bed.

The sound was perfectly clear. It was quite unmistakable. It was horrible, coming from a middle-aged, slightly squint-eyed man with a crooked shoulder said to be our Judas, and he had obviously lost control and started crying and moaning, or trying to hide his despair by pulling the covers over his head. She turned quite cold.

The attic was a black ocean and moans were coming out of the dark. Then breathing, a moment of strained silence, as if someone were trying to hold his breath so as not to reveal himself. Then a cough, or something of the kind, a subdued explosion. Then silence again, then a sound impossible to interpret.

She got up, her feet bare on the wooden floor.

She had never been afraid of the dark at Västerbotten. In Karelia, she had always been afraid of the dark; she remembered that, the darkness there denser and more secretive and full of uncertainty. But not here. Here the darkness was always slightly transparent, thin, like skimmed milk. But Uncle Aron lying there crying to himself and going peculiar, that frightened her. She walked with small groping steps across the attic floor. When she was close to his bed, she heard him turn over, trying to control himself.

'Uncle Aron,' she whispered out into the darkness.

No reply.

240

'Uncle Aron,' she whispered again. 'Ist tha poorly?'

She stood still, waiting. The silence was deathly, then came a long hoarse breath, then silence again. Uncle Aron's holding his breath, she thought.

He doesn't want me to hear.

She was just about to turn and go back, when she saw in the darkness a white surface which must have been a face. He had turned towards her and was looking at her. He was lying on his back, his legs drawn up to one side, his face turned to her.

' 'Tis all right,' he said in a guttural voice.

'Ist tha all right?' she repeated mechanically, without really knowing what she was saying.

No reply.

'Tha's not cryin', is tha, Uncle Aron?' she said after a while.

Then she sat down on the edge of the bed and put her hand out towards his face. He started at first, as if expecting a blow. It looked peculiar, almost comical. What had he got to be afraid of? She stroked his cheek. It was as she had thought. His cheeks were wet, just as she had thought.

Uncle Aron had lost control. He had gone peculiar.

She lay down beside him and stroked his forehead as if he were ill and had a high temperature. But she said nothing. He seemed embarrassed or afraid at first, but then he lay quite still and cried a little without being ashamed. Oddly enough, Eva-Liisa was no longer frightened, because he was so childish and because the darkness had now exposed all secrets. The ugly squint-eyed uncle, with his bad teeth and smell of snuff and notoriously dirty underpants which Josefina always scolded him about, had revealed that he really had been weeping and been miserable and lost control. She kept stroking him and was suddenly pleased no one else was at home.

She wasn't sure the others could have helped Uncle Aron, now that he had gone peculiar and miserable.

But she would manage. She knew that.

Uncle Aron said almost nothing all this time. He lay still and she kept her hand on his forehead. Only once did words come from him, and as soon as he opened his mouth, she smelt the familiar mixture of snuff and yellowing teeth: the worst she had to submit to.

'Ah thinks ah've made t'fool o'meself',' he said. 'Them made t'fool of me.'

'Oh, no,' she said consolingly.

'Them all made t'fool of me.'

She waited, but nothing else came. She thought he sounded rather silly, what he'd said, but she didn't say so. She suddenly felt he was a child, and obscurely and yet quite forcefully, she realized they had hurt him very badly and something within him was so out of balance his small foolish sobs had been necessary.

'Don' tha be sad, Uncle Aron,' she said in her soft singing Finn-Swedish. 'Tha's sure t'git work somewhere.'

She felt him roughly shaking his head.

'Nay, that ah won't,' he said.

'It'll work out,' she said.

Then he lifted his hand and put it against her cheek, and she felt him turning his head and looking at her.

He had the ugliest hand she knew, but at that moment, as he touched her, she felt a kind of peace.

She had thought he would never dare. She lay quite still, looking up at the ceiling, thinking about Uncle Aron daring to touch her cheek. Something terrible must have happened inside him, something that had almost broken him. She had seen him looking at her sometimes, but that meant nothing, because Uncle Aron was an old bachelor, ugly and crooked all over. Of course, she felt sorry for him. He'd never been married, and since everything that had happened during the strike he had become more and more solitary. Poor thing, she thought. He was no butter-Judas, as they shouted after him. He was just too kind. He hadn't the gumption to shout back.

He stroked her gently across the cheek and she thought: it's all right if he does that. The hand was rough and heavy, like sandpaper. It was tinglingly quiet in the attic, no telephone wires attached to the house, and in fact she missed the strange singing sound she remembered from Hjoggböle, the sound Nicanor called the celestial harp: it had been frightening and beautiful and sorrowful and crazy, just like everything else up in Västerbotten. You could freeze to death in the warmth of the kitchen if you weren't careful. You could go quite stiff inside, desolate and crazy and lonely, as if turned to ice.

And then you would sit in the icy rooms and do puzzles with

242

bits of ice and you could never cry, like in the story book about the Ice Queen. Sometimes she prayed to God it wouldn't happen to her.

It was completely and utterly silent. At that moment, he put his hand over Eva-Liisa's breast and held on hard, and he did not take it away.

She went rigid, as if an iron spike had been driven through her body.

She turned quite cold.

He held on to her breast as if it had been cold blood-bread. At first she tried to pretend that he had done it by mistake, but that didn't work, because he held on stubbornly and hard; she held her breath and it was so silent that the house tingled. Of course, one or other of the boys had touched her now and again, in passing, but all the same, she was not used to it. It hurt. Suddenly it was no longer poor Uncle Aron lying beside her like a child, crying and miserable. It was like an animal breathing heavily and agitatedly, it had hands and she could not see the face. The other hand moved, too, and he pulled up her shift. He touched her stomach. She tried to twist away, but suddenly she was trapped by his hands, and they were all over her, he panting heavily and the stink from his breath very close. He seemed to be sobbing. Yes, he was crying and he stank. She couldn't really understand what he was trying to say.

She suddenly felt herself becoming terribly frightened.

He pressed his loins against her left hip, jerkily and mechanically, jabbing with hard jerky insensitive thrusts against her hip, as if he thought there was an opening there, and that was how it should happen, still squeezing her breast as he groaned out words that sounded like . . . *Eva-Liisa, tha's like . . . 'tis like . . . kin ah put it in in a moment . . . tha's so fine . . . tha . . . kin I . . .* and he went on jerking and thrusting mechanically and mutely against her hip, repeating, *kin ah put it in . . . tha's nice . . . be nice . . .* and she kept saying very loudly, *uncle uncle uncle* and then loudly, *let me go let me go,* and he panted the stink into her ear *be nice, be nice, kin ah put it in, kin I put it in.*

He was now panting heavily and she thought of screaming, but the house was empty. She caught the heavy scent of snuff hanging above her face as he tried to press his mouth against hers, holding her head firmly, at first unable to get at her lips, but then succeeding. He pressed his big wet lip against her, and all she could feel was saliva being pressed out, as if he could no longer keep the saliva in his mouth and it had simply run out over her. He prized her open and thrust his arm between her legs, twisting and prizing, and she could feel his member protruding from his thick pants, stiff and wildly hacking at her stomach, and all the time he kept mumbling mechanically and desperately *be nice, be nice, kin ah put it in, kin ah put it in, be nice*. She almost vomited and hit out wildly at his body, but couldn't reach, as he had locked her arms and was fumbling with his wet weeping stinking mouth all over her face, mumbling *be nice be nice* and thrusting and thrusting with his loins and what in his mumbling moaning pleas he kept calling 'it'.

Suddenly she gave up.

She lay quite still, her arms soft, her body will-less. He flopped on to her and finally into her, sobbing, almost shrieking, and was at once far up inside her. She lay quite still and felt Uncle Aron's member ripping her and driving deep inside her. He took four or five powerful thrusts, then she felt his body contract in cramp. It hurt all the time. She lay quite still.

Afterwards she didn't know which was the worst.

Perhaps it was that she couldn't stop Uncle Aron crying, though it wasn't really crying, but mostly snivelling and moaning, like an unhappy pig lying beside her, unable to pull himself together, grunting and snivelling, unable to speak.

Eva-Liisa was still lying on her back. She did not want to move. Uncle Aron had curled up close to her.

The whole room was saying nothing now, the attic icy cold and quiet, and all she had to listen to was the sound of Uncle Aron. She lay thinking she would never be able to sleep up there in the attic again. It would be too awful. And there'd be trouble for her and for Uncle Aron, maybe real trouble. He sounded very peculiar.

He fell silent after a while. Then he stretched out his hand again and tried to touch her face, very cautiously, as if to apologize or convince himself she was there and alive, but she neither moved nor said anything, and he took his hand away again. He made a few attempts to speak to her, but she just said, 'Yes, yes,' faintly, and then, 't'hurts a bit,' and when he again tried to touch her cheek and said, 'Tha must forgive me, she just turned her head away, not much, but enough.

244

Then they lay there for a long time, very still. Uncle Aron's sobs soon ceased, the sweat dried and it turned cold. Eva-Liisa could feel it running, and she was sticky all down her legs. She was cold. She didn't want to pull the cover over her. She didn't want to move.

When dawn came, she went back to her bed, very cold now, the attic like a sea of ice. She was shivering. Aron had fallen asleep, curled up in one corner, his mouth open. She didn't really want to look at him. Perhaps somewhere the song from the telephone wires was thundering very loudly, like a roaring choir of celestial voices, but she was enclosed in a thin membrane of ice and no sounds penetrated.

It's winter now, she thought. And Nicanor. And Uncle Aron with no work. And then this happens. What shall I do?

4

SHE DECIDED on the sixteenth of March. She asked to speak to Josefina.

They went into the bedroom and stayed there for a long time.

When they came out, it was clear they had both been crying, but Josefina said nothing. She went about in silence for two days, and no one dared look her in the eye. On the third day, she took the psalm-book, the Bible and their copy of the works of Rosenius, and went up, late in the evening, to Uncle Aron. He was lying on his back, staring at the ceiling.

She sat down on the edge of the bed and looked at him.

'You know why I've come,' she said finally.

It sounded formal and strange, because she was speaking high-Swedish, and he looked at her.

'Our Eva-Liisa's with child,' she said very quietly.

She saw he had heard.

'She's told me,' she went on. 'Is it true?'

A short while went by. Then he nodded.

'Dear Lord Jesus,' she said in the same low, flat, expressionless voice. 'May our Lord Jesus preserve each and every one of them what seduces one of these our smallest ones. So that a millstone shall not be lain on his neck and he must be sunk into the depths of the sea.'

He sat up and put his feet down on the wooden floor. He was bare-footed. She saw his long pants had holes in the knees, and for a moment felt a pang of conscience that she was not better at looking after the only brother she had and whom she also liked very much. She really did. She had always liked Aron and had always scolded him for being what he was. She could not fathom out for herself what he was like, but she liked him very much all the same and was always scolding him. The two things went together. There was something wrong with him which she disliked very much and which made her love him dearly, though love was perhaps not the word she would have used. Perhaps it was because he had a squint. Perhaps it was those ugly hands or his crooked back.

She should have mended his underpants.

'What'll ah do?' he said straight out into the room.

She put her arm carefully round his shoulders and felt him shaking. Perhaps it was the cold. He had asked a question and she didn't know the answer, so she read a piece out of the Bible, opening it at random. It was the story of Jesus driving the moneylenders out of the temple, which said nothing to her, nor did it help, mute as it was, giving her no answer. So she sat for a long time beside her brother, her arm round his shoulders, with no answer and nothing to say.

He was still shaking. It must be the cold. She wished it was summer, then they could have gone out into the forest, then our Aron wouldn't have had to shake and the air would have been warm and she would have had an answer to every question.

In the end, he decided.

It was nine o'clock at night. He took his backpack and went down to the potato cellar with the paraffin lamp in his hand, closing the hatch behind him. They saw him disappearing, but, not realizing what he was going to do, they left him alone. When he was down there, he placed the lamp on the floor and started searching. The cellar walls were sandy earth, *pinnmo*, the soil not frozen to that depth, and he knew what he had to look for. He dug methodically with his hands, and soon a stone appeared, as large as two loaves: he at once put it in his rucksack. Then he dug further, finding three more stones, one the size of a hen's egg, two oblong but narrow, like somewhat enlarged turds. The fifth stone was a foot long: when he got it out of the earth wall, he sat for a moment looking at it.

On its own, that one would have been heavy enough.

The rest was mostly earth. He dug on for a while, but found nothing. To make quite sure, however, he shovelled a few handfuls of sand into the rucksack and placed a score of potatoes on top. The potatoes had begun to sprout, so he removed the wormlike shoots, scraped off the earth, then put the potatoes one by one into the rucksack.

That would have to do.

He put on the backpack and climbed out of the cellar. They looked at him as he walked through the kitchen; but no one realized what he was doing. On the porch steps, he stopped for a moment and drew a deep breath: his heart was thumping, and for a moment he considered going back in again to say something, just some little remark on the weather or something, because he hadn't really looked at them in the kitchen and suddenly he couldn't remember what they looked like, but then he realized that would be pointless, and went on out into the shed.

The iron spike was standing in its usual place.

Then Uncle Aron started out on his long journey.

He walked due east, between Björkgrundet and Yxgrundet. Halfway between them, it had to be. He knew that.

That was the right place.

It took half an hour to walk there, and he had time to think a good deal on the way. It was windy but very cold, the darkness quite dense, no stars, but the snow was brilliant. The backpack and iron spike were heavy to carry and he sweated a lot, but that didn't matter, for he was totally alone within himself and no loneliness is so terrible and merciless as when a lost soul goes on his last march to damnation in that landscape called Västerbotten. When he arrived, he was perspiring heavily. He thrust the spike into the snow and took off the backpack. There was a massively thick layer of ice as well as a layer of drift-snow on top. He kicked away the snow in a circle about two feet wide, picked up the spike and started.

Half an hour later, he had a hole about as wide as the length of his forearm and almost as deep, but there was no sign of water. Quarter of an hour later, the first water started seeping up.

Soon after that, the spike went right through.

He had been careful all the time, hacking diagonally at the sides and grasping the spike firmly, but all the same he couldn't hold it. The spike went through with great force and he was unable to stop it – the spike went straight down and vanished.

He stood staring at it heavily, out of breath. The spike had gone. Altogether, it had taken an hour.

He made an attempt to kick his way through with his shoe, but that didn't work. Then he took out his knife, removed his gloves and thrust his hand down into the slushy snow, hacking away furiously round the hole in the middle, but only small chips of ice came off and after five minutes his hand was quite numb. He sat back whimpering for a while, but that was no use.

Even if he went on all night the hole would not be large enough.

There was only one way.

He put on his backpack and gloves and turned back.

It was almost midnight when Aron Lindström knocked on the door of Egon Lundström's house. Some time went by before anyone woke. Lundström's youngest boy was the one who got himself up and opened the door. Outside was Aron. He had his backpack on and his nose and one cheek were quite white; he had ice up to the knee on one leg and he was looking peculiar. He asked to borrow an iron spike. As the Lundströms' youngest boy did not really understand what it was all about and was only half awake, and reckoning it was nothing to ask anyone else about, he simply nodded and told Aron where the spike was. Aron turned abruptly and went to fetch it. As it was cold, Lundström's youngest boy quickly closed the door to keep the cold out and went back to bed; he told them the next morning.

Aron took Lundström's spike and went back the same way, down to the sea and due east between Björkgrundet and Yxgrundet. The snow was still very white, the darkness icy cold, and he searched for a long time, but in the end gave up, as the snow was drifting, obliterating all tracks, and he could not find the hole.

He stopped, thrust the spike into the snow, took off his rucksack and started making another hole.

He was very tired by then. He fell back once or twice, over to one side, then scrambled back to his feet again. For a spell he felt inclined simply to sit down and let it happen, but as he had decided what should happen, and he was going to do it properly,

248

he went on. All feeling in one leg had long since gone, but that didn't matter. He wouldn't be using it any more, and as long as it supported him so that spiking was possible, that was enough. Then the water came and then he worked carefully, hacking out the hole at the sides for a foot or so and leaving the bottom of the hole for the moment. Then he took off his gloves to get a better grip, hacking cautiously through the last layer of ice, making the hole good and round, brushing away the slush and water. A good clean hole.

He thrust the spike into the snow and got his breath back. Now it was ready. Now he could go into eternal damnation.

He could see a somewhat lighter darkness to the east, as if dawn were hiding behind a grey mass of snow just below the horizon. The snow was drifting hard from the east, shining, but the grey dark of night obliterated every detail. No light in the west, but he could see the mainland as a darker stripe than the almost dark. The wind rustled faintly. He tugged at the straps of his backpack, took off his cap and put it down on the snow beside the hole, his gloves beside it, then he drew a few deep breaths. The water in the hole was black, heaving up and down with a tinkling sound, up and down. Barely perceptible, a slowly rising and falling water-eye. Now he was to go down. He had always been afraid of water, of drowning. Of being suffocated. The black icy water heaved slowly up and down, breathing. He had to sink deep down there, and be suffocated. That was what had to happen.

He looked down into the black waterhole and stepped straight down into the darkness.

There was a smacking sound, and he found himself caught round the waist. His hips had gone through, but the backpack was too big. He was stuck.

He waited for a moment without moving, until the rustle of the drifting snow drowned the sound of his breathing. Then he kicked out irresolutely with his legs, trying to force himself lower down into the hole, that that didn't work. The rucksack was definitely in the way. So he thrashed the top half of his body wildly back and forth, groaning loudly, but that was no use, either.

He couldn't get down.

Now, for the first time, he felt how cold the water was. At first his clothes had kept it at bay, but now the water was coming right through. He could feel nothing in his right leg, which was still numb and frozen, but otherwise an icy hand seemed to be slowly squeezing his legs and pelvis. He realized he hadn't much longer now, so in panic he jerked back and forth, scrabbling with his hands in the snow without finding a hold, tearing and clawing at it. He came up a little, his backside easing over the edge of the ice, then the rest.

He rolled round, got up, fell, and at last was standing.

His breathing was now very loud, as if he were bellowing quietly. He had to get down there. He must have the stone-backpack on him. For a moment he thought about what would happen if he just tore the backpack off and slid down into the waterhole, but he knew at once that was wrong, that it had to be done properly, as it *had to be done*. That was terribly important. He swung his head irresolutely, like an animal, walking round in a little circle: yes, the spike was still there. He bent down, fell, but got hold of it, grabbing at it with both bare hands. They were almost completely without feeling by now, and he grasped the spike as tightly as he could, feeling his hands freezing to it. Then he set about it.

He had to hack away a space for the rucksack, too.

The next time he stepped straight down into the black well, it was nearly right. He went down a little further, but the backpack still got wedged. This time he hung there longer, snivelling like a pig, clumsily and confusedly patting at the snow around him with his hands. The snow turned red. For a moment he considered giving up, but suddenly he was up on the ice again, the spike lying close to his face. He saw that his palms were bleeding and, quite close to his face, he saw the handle of the spike, pieces of skin stuck to the iron; not just skin, but small lumps of flesh as well.

He realized he would never again spike at the ice and now the need to hurry was great.

He had to take the sack of stones down with him.

Still lying there, he tore desperately at the leather straps with his left hand. The rucksack slipped; he slithered round and ripped it off. It would have to be the potatoes. The potatoes would have to be sacrificed; the stones were sure to be heavy enough. His hands were quite numb now, two bloodstained lumps which refused to obey him. He tore with his teeth at the string round the top of the rucksack, and suddenly it opened.

He managed to get out nearly all the potatoes, mostly with his mouth, like a dog.

When he had at last got the backpack on again, some time had gone by. There was a great deal of red round the black hole now. He could no longer stand on his feet, but the rucksack was at last as it should be, thinner now, but sufficiently heavy to drag him down the right way to eternal damnation.

Now, at last. With his very last strength.

He could only drag himself along on his knees. There was no more time for rituals, or looks for possible light from Bure country, or prayers, or second thoughts: for he realized that only minutes remained before he would lose consciousness and fall asleep up there on the ice, so he mustn't give up. He had to drag himself over to the hole as quickly as he could. Both legs were numb now, his hands, too, but he could push himself along with them.

It worked. The black icy water was still breathing down there, waiting for him.

Just before he made the last move he grew frightened his feet would get caught on the edge of the ice; he had to go in with both knees at once, and then sink as upright as possible. He pushed off with his bleeding stumps of hands and slid down knees first.

He sank downwards, the edge of the backpack catching for a few seconds, then jerking free. He slid into the ice-hole and the water closed over his head. The sack of stones dragged him down, his eyes wide open against the darkness, his mouth open, the air ejected outwards in a triumphant roar, and at last Uncle Aron sank down into the prodigious black hole that was the deepest darkness of the sea.

The wind died down towards morning, and grey mist rolled over Bure country from the east, drifts covering some of the red, and the spike also invisible now, only the potatoes protruding like small bewildered spots. Two groups of skiers made their way out on to the ice that afternoon, apparently looking for something. One group disappeared to the north in towards the mouth of Oxviken, the other went outwards, then up towards Yxgrundet.

The latter group found the tracks. Then it was simple. They reached the hole only half an hour before dusk.

The potatoes were still visible, but the hole had frozen over. They found the spike a little later. They opened up the hole again, but there was nothing to be seen, and they had no equipment to search with. They discussed what had happened for a long time, measuring the hole and covering the bloodstains with new snow.

There were eighteen potatoes in all: they hesitated for a while over what to do with them, but in the end they were picked up and taken back.

The spike was Egon Lundström's and had to be returned.

It was dark when they got back. The eldest of the skiers went to Josefina Markström and told her what he had to tell. He handed over the potatoes, eighteen of them, in an old sack. Josefina said nothing at all, apparently totally confused. When he had left, she started boiling the eighteen potatoes in a big pan, but it was clear from her behaviour that she was confused and did not really know what she was doing. When the potatoes were cooked, she seemed to wake up, and she threw the cooked potatoes into the rubbish bucket and carried them out. That was the first and only time they had ever seen her allow food to be wasted.

5

ANNA-LENA WIKSTRÖM brought the news that they had found Uncle Aron, and no one liked her. People maintained there was something wrong with all them Wikströms. The Wikströms, for instance, had a habit of using privy sticks several times. There was no paper, so they used split sticks to wipe themselves in the privy. That was quite usual. But while ordinary normal people threw the stick down the first time it had been used, the Wikströms used to put the privy stick back and use it again. If you went there, you might find nothing but used sticks in the box.

That was just an example. So it was with a twofold sense of distaste and grief that Josefina pressed a slice of bun-loaf and a bit of sugar on her and asked her to go. Or rather, she told Nicanor to tell her. She herself went over to the wall-clock, opened it, took out the key, wound up the clock, stopped the pendulum, put the key back and closed the door, the strictly ritualistic and precise little piece of symbolism announcing that it was confirmed and definite that Uncle Aron's heart had stopped beating and he was now one of the dear departed.

When Nicanor went down to the boom, the body had already been hauled out, the corpse-watchers standing in a circle round Uncle Aron, holding their noses and mumbling in distress. He could have hit them. He suddenly felt tremendously strongly that

Uncle Aron needed *defending*: that this pig-like, swollen, balloon-like corpse in all its stinking decay was so helpless, so in need of protection, and that there was still time and the means to *take responsibility* for Uncle Aron. The torn, blueish-white hands were like a sledge-hammer blow in Nicanor's stomach: he stared at them, remembering.

Uncle Aron had decided. And he had carried out his resolve with insanely purposeful logic far beyond Nicanor's understanding. If only this tremendously purposeful determination had been used for something like . . . something like . . .

But the circumstances were not like that.

Suddenly it seemed that a line, a sentence, from a story he had once read fell into a recess of his mind and took root, growing and refusing to go away: he stared at Uncle Aron's hands and swollen body and he whispered very quietly, so that no one should hear, but so that he himself could be assured that it was the only thing that could be said with any certainty: *There's always something better than death.*

He seemed to be able to breathe once again.

He turned and ran, and there was no hesitation in his movements.

Eva-Liisa first. She must not see. Not this, not as things were now. She must not. So that was why he ran along the Skerry road and managed to catch her and stop her as she came shuffling down in her green coat, her swelling stomach ahead of her.

He caught hold of her and she cried out, reluctant to be held, wanting to see, and so they fell. And they got up again. Then she tore herself free, but he caught her again and said in an almost completely intelligible voice, '*No*,' and then less clearly, '*Tha mustna*,' and that was almost enough. Though he would have preferred to walk quite calmly with her down to the boom, show her Uncle Aron, then let her cry a little and say to her: 'Eva-Liisa, *there's always something better than death*.'

But that wouldn't do now. Instead they walked home together. After they had been walking for a while, she said to him: 'They've cut you to pieces. This is what's happened to me. Uncle Aron is dead. People who want to work aren't allowed to. I don't want to stay here any longer.'

Nicanor held her hand. They walked home. That was what happened when Uncle Aron was found.

EPILOGUE

1910

POINTS OF DEPARTURE

'LISTEN, REDCOMB,' said the donkey. 'You shriek yourself hoarse
for the people who want to wring your neck. Come away with us
instead, and we'll be the musicians of Bremen. There's always
something better than death.'

Elmblad's letter. From Burträsk, he had journeyed to Kiiruna. He
had come to the end of the road and he knew it. From Kiiruna, he
wrote to Nicanor, telling him about the end of the road and the
roads beyond that end. Many people, he wrote, had come up to
the Norbotten mines after the Norberg strike. They were unemployed and blacklisted, and they seemed to see their last opportunity in Kiiruna and had taken it. Then the general strike had
come. After the conflict, hundreds of men were again blacklisted,
tucked away in their wretched earth-caves and their cabins made
of sleepers and dynamite boxes, their families with them: they
found themselves at a terminal and suddenly they were told they
must go on. Where do you go when you've got to the end of the
road? You go on.

Elmblad enclosed two newspaper cuttings in his letter to Nicanor, a correspondent's reports from Brazil, reprinted in the
Kiiruna newspaper *Northern Lights*. Elmblad had underlined two
passages in pencil. 'In all the opposition to our emigration policy,
however, one truth emerges, and that is that we have nothing to
lose but our lives. But as the majority of us have been in Kiiruna
for several years, and that time has convinced us that the greatest
aspirations of the companies consist in squeezing all life and
ability to work out of the workers as quickly as possible and then
getting rid of them − so we consider we have nothing to lose.
Should we succeed, then we will not only have saved ourselves,
but also those of our comrades who considered that under any

circumstances their lives were of little value, so long as they remained in Kiiruna.' '. . . often think that if the people on the employers' blacklists tried to come here, and some tens of thousands apart from them, both those favoured by the employers as well as co-operators, then the employers would have to make the best of it. It would be amusing if several hundred blacklegs had to be recruited to the Kiiruna mountain.'

At the end of the letter, Elmblad asks a question. He also mentions his wife by name for the first time: Dagmar.

Aron's funeral. All through the ceremony, Josefina maintained the same rigid, injured expression which simultaneously indicated grief as well as rage: wet snow was falling and the Pastor spoke in a high suffering voice of the dreadful fate of self-destruction and the grief self-destruction brought to relatives: she clenched her teeth and closed in on herself, and Nicanor was suddenly afraid she might go and hit the bastard smack in the face. But naturally Josefina Markström would never do such a thing. One of the very last bitter slushy snowfalls of the winter came that afternoon; the Pastor closed the psalm-book with a snap and at last it was over. Only members of the family were present. They all knew people were looking as they walked home. The whole family had put in an appearance for Uncle Aron's funeral.

Thesleff. The letter came on 25 April, 1910, and Eva-Liisa read it aloud to them all. They were sitting in the kitchen. It was the most peculiar letter they had ever read, such peculiar words. Colonia Finlandesa. Buenos Aires. Tango. That afternoon, Eva-Liisa and Josefina went for a long walk across Bure Heath: the roads were already partially bare. They came back after dusk had fallen. That evening, they decided.

'Listen, redcomb,' said the donkey. 'You shriek yourself hoarse for the people who want to wring your neck. Come away with us instead. There's always something better than death.'

The railway station at Bastuträsk. Josefina wanted to open the window, to see what it smelt like for the very last time, but the window was stuck.

Signal.

Stig Dagerman · *A Burnt Child*

Stig Dagerman · *The Games of Night*

Stig Dagerman · *German Autumn*

Grazia Deledda · *After the Divorce*

Grazia Deledda · *Cosima*

Grazia Deledda · *Elias Portolu*

Heimito von Doderer · *The Demons*

Marcellus Emants · *A Posthumous Confession*

Péter Esterházy · *Helping Verbs of the Heart*

Ennio Flaiano · *A Time to Kill*

Peter Paul Fuchs (ed.) · *The Music Theatre of Walter Felsenstein*

Carlo Emilio Gadda · *That Awful Mess on Via Merulana*

Andrea Giovene · *Sansevero*

Remy de Gourmont · *The Natural Philosophy of Love*

Julien Green · *Avarice House*

Julien Green · *Each Man in His Darkness*

Julien Green · *Midnight*

Julien Green · *Moira*

Martin A. Hansen · *The Liar*

Eugene Ionesco · *Fragments of a Journal*

Gustav Janouch · *Conversations with Kafka*

Ismaïl Kadaré · *The General of the Dead Army*

Pierre Klossowski · *Sade My Neighbour*